PRAISE FOR THE *NEW* BESTSELLING REAPER CLUB SERIES

"Raw emotion and riveting characters, I fell in love from page one!"
—Katy Evans, *New York Times* bestselling author

"Sex that blisters the imagination, resulting in a thrill ride as raw as it is well written." —*Publishers Weekly*

"Joanna Wylde has a great voice in this genre." —*USA Today*

"Hooked me so hard that I could not put it down."
—A Bookish Escape

"If you like . . . [a] grittier romance, definitely check this one out."
—Smexy Books

"I loved this book. It's raw, gritty, and incredibly sexy . . . Very real and very dangerous, and I couldn't stop reading. The sexual tension is off the charts . . . Prepare to get seriously hot under the collar. Sexy, dark, realistic, and yet romantic." —SeattlePI.com

"This was just the fix I was looking for." —The Book Vixen

"*Smokin'* hot! . . . I continue to recommend this series as a real peek into a different kind of life." —RedHotBooks.com

"The perfect balance of badass alpha hero, feisty kickass heroine, supernova-hot erotic sex scenes, real genuine emotions, and love and brotherhood." —SinfullySexyBooks.com

"Raw and intensely erotic." —The Book Pushers

Berkley titles by Joanna Wylde

Reapers Motorcycle Club

REAPER'S LEGACY
DEVIL'S GAME
REAPER'S STAND
REAPER'S FALL

Silver Valley

SILVER BASTARD

REAPER'S FALL

JOANNA WYLDE

WITHDRAWN

BERKLEY BOOKS, NEW YORK

BERKLEY

An imprint of Penguin Random House LLC
375 Hudson Street, New York, New York 10014

Copyright © 2015 by Joanna Wylde.
Penguin supports copyright. Copyright fuels creativity, encourages diverse voices,
promotes free speech, and creates a vibrant culture. Thank you for buying an authorized
edition of this book and for complying with copyright laws by not reproducing, scanning,
or distributing any part of it in any form without permission. You are supporting writers
and allowing Penguin to continue to publish books for every reader.

BERKLEY® and the "B" design are registered trademarks of Penguin Random House LLC.
For more information, visit penguin.com.

Library of Congress Cataloging-in-Publication Data

Wylde, Joanna.
Reaper's fall / Joanna Wylde.—Berkley Trade paperback edition.
pages ; cm.—(Reapers motorcycle club ; 4)
ISBN 978-0-425-28064-5
I. Title.
PS3623.Y544R42 2015
813'.6—dc23
2015025747

PUBLISHING HISTORY
Berkley trade paperback edition / November 2015

PRINTED IN THE UNITED STATES OF AMERICA

10 9 8 7 6 5 4 3 2 1

Cover art by Tony Mauro.
Cover design by George Long.
Interior text design by Kristin del Rosario.

This is a work of fiction. Names, characters, places, and incidents either are the product
of the author's imagination or are used fictitiously, and any resemblance to actual persons,
living or dead, business establishments, events, or locales is entirely coincidental.

Penguin
Random
House

For Dawn Dawn and Colleen.
Every writer needs a nurse and a lawyer in her corner,
and I got the two most badass ones available.
Thank you.

ACKNOWLEDGMENTS

Thank you very much to everyone at Berkley who made this book possible, especially Cindy Hwang. Thanks also to Jessica Brock, the Goddess of Publicity who not only works hard to sell my books, but also gives my online readers' group fabulous, shiny stickers. They like the stickers. A lot. (I'm also a huge fan of the stickers, but I'm far too cool and fabulous to ever publicly admit that.)

I owe much to Amy Tannenbaum, my incredible agent who I'm fairly certain is secretly a superhero. Someday I'm going to catch her riding a unicorn while wielding a rainbow sword against all who oppose me. (Okay, probably not, but she's really good about returning my emails and never makes fun of me even when I'm crazy.) Amy, you kick ass. I'm pretty sure you're already aware of this fact, but it never hurts to repeat it.

My writing friends keep me sane(ish) and I couldn't do it without you. Thanks to Rebecca Zanetti, Cara Carnes, Kim Jones, Renee Carlino, Katy Evans, and the ever dreadful Kylie Scott. I love all of you except for Kylie, whom I tolerate.

Every day, I'm supported by amazing friends online, including the Sweetbutts, the Junkies (dino-power!), Hang Le, Kandace, Danielle, Lori, the other Lori, Milasy, and Lisa. "Thanks" seems fairly inadequate for all that you've given me.

Special thanks to Matt "Boo" Hintz, who taught me all about paint, boards, matte medium, the art world, and Willie G. I'm still fangirling a little that you were willing to talk to me.

Finally, thanks to my long-suffering husband and kids, who still love me despite my writing career. I'm not sure how you put up with me, but it's much appreciated.

AUTHOR'S NOTE

Thank you so much for giving my book a chance. As with the previous books in my series, this one has been read by a woman who has lived the MC life for accuracy, although I never let reality get in the way of telling the story I want to tell. For that reason, it's worth noting a few realities that I've deliberately chosen to ignore while writing it.

In this book, the words "jail" and "prison" are used interchangeably by several characters. In real life, they're two very different places, but for the sake of word variety I've opted to ignore that.

Rodeo is a complicated sport that I've described in a very simplistic way for the sake of brevity. Please know that I made a deliberate choice to streamline my description of events.

Finally, I'd like to make it clear that any officials or law enforcement personnel portrayed in my books as corrupt are not there because I believe they're corrupt in real life. My stories would be very boring if there was never any conflict, which means someone has to be the antagonist. Because of the nature of the stories, that antagonist is often connected with law enforcement. Please know that in my own life, I have the utmost respect for the law enforcement officers who risk their lives daily to protect the people of Coeur d'Alene. Thank you so much for your service.

PROLOGUE

"Fuckin' hell," Horse said, looking out across the crowded club-house. I paused, beer halfway to my mouth, turning to follow his gaze. "Painter, brother, you gotta stay calm—"

That's when I saw her.

Melanie Tucker.

No.

This wasn't happening. Maybe I was hallucinating, because I couldn't imagine a reality where she'd actually be this goddamn stupid. I dropped my beer bottle, glass shattering as I stalked across the room. Everything narrowed, my vision fading to red.

"Hold on, son," Picnic growled. I respected the hell out of him, loved him like a father . . . but there wasn't a damned thing the Reapers MC president could've said to slow me down in that instant. That's because the mother of my child stood in the clubhouse doorway, eyes wide and scared. She knew she'd fucked up.

Standing next to her was a man. A biker. Hangaround? He'd wrapped his arm around her like she belonged to him.

Yeah. He put his hands on *my* Melanie.

Except she wasn't mine and hadn't been in a long time. Her

choice, so fuck her very much. But that freedom she'd wanted so badly came with one rule and she'd just broken the shit out of it. *No bikers.* Yet here she was with this cockwad asshole, some douche who thought putting on leathers gave him the right to exist.

In an MC clubhouse, no less.

This was a problem. A big fuckin' problem. That terror on her face was totally justified, because she was about to witness a goddamn murder. And no, that wasn't just a figure of speech. In ten seconds I had every intention of ripping the dick off his body, feeding it to him at knifepoint, and then jerking it back out his ass before repeating the process.

A hand wrapped around my arm, silently warning me—my president, trying to calm me down. I shrugged it off, tuning out whatever the hell Pic was trying to communicate as I lunged forward, catching the little prick by the front of his shirt. I jerked him savagely into the center of the room. A rushing sound filled my ears and in the distance I heard Mel scream. Then my fist connected with his face, sweet pain tearing through my knuckles as time slowed.

I love fighting.

Not just winning, but the rush of energy, the sweetness of the pain, and the incredible focus that hits when your entire existence narrows to one moment of terrible purpose. It's primal and beautiful, and it'd never felt better than it did in the instant Melanie's new boyfriend went down.

I followed him, pounding his face into hamburger and savoring the fountain of blood exploding from his nose. Fuckin' cathartic as hell—his life was *over.* More screaming cut through the fog of violence.

Damn straight, she should be screaming. She should be fucking *afraid.*

"You asshole!"

I smiled, because from Mel it sounded sweet as hell. She'd called me an asshole ten thousand different ways over the years, ranging from enraged hatred to whispered insults between kisses. It worked for me, too. I *was* a total asshole, but for once she'd just have to suck it up and deal with the consequences.

She'd broken the fucking rules by bringing him here.

No bikers.

Simple, right? One condition I'd given her. No. Fucking. Bikers. All she had to do was keep her ass out of my world, because so long as I didn't have to *see* her sucking someone else's cock, I could pretend it wasn't happening.

Not a complicated concept.

Arms came around me, strong arms dragging me off my victim before I could finish killing him. Then I heard Puck's voice in my ear.

Puck.

My best friend. Puck, who'd taken my back for a year and a half in prison. I'd trusted him with my life inside, and I trusted him now. I should be listening, but I really, really wanted to end this cockwad's life.

I shrugged Puck off, determined to finish it.

"He's not worth it, bro," Puck gritted out. Melanie was still making noise. Between us, her pussy of a date moaned and cried, whimpering about how he didn't want to die. *Yeah, you better beg for your life, bitch.* "You kill him here, you'll never see your kid again. Whatever shit goes down with you and Mel, you gotta think of Izzy."

Fuck. I took deep breaths, forcing myself to calm as I stood over the man, staring between him and Melanie.

Had to focus.

The image of my beautiful, fuzzy-haired blonde baby girl flashed through my mind. Izzy. I'd do it for Izzy. I ran a hand through my hair, holding back the fire raging through me.

"Get him out of here," I finally managed to growl out. Nobody moved as the man rolled to one side, whining like the little cunt he was. Fucking pussy hadn't even managed to get in a hit. A distant part of me noted he wore leather with Harley Davidson patches, but no MC colors. Who did he think he was, coming to the Silver Bastards clubhouse? This wasn't a game. "Get him out of here before I kill him!"

"Fuck," Horse muttered, stepping forward to grab the douche by the armpits. A path cleared as he started dragging the man toward the door. Melanie shouted at me again, and I turned on her, stalking forward. This was it—I'd had enough of her shit. She wanted to play games? Perfect, because I loved to play, and she knew damned well I liked to play rough.

Melanie was about to get one hell of a reality check.

Picnic stepped in front of her, arms crossed as he stared me down.

"Not happening, son."

"It's none of your business," I snarled. I was right, too—so what if his old lady loved the little bitch? He'd been standing between me and Melanie for way the fuck too long, and this little scene tonight wasn't club business. Melanie was *mine* to deal with. There wasn't a man in the room who had the right to say otherwise, including my president.

"She's the one who came here," I reminded him.

"I didn't even know where we were going!" Melanie yelled from behind him. "It was just a date, you asshole!"

Red filled my vision again. My jaw clenched, and I smelled the blood on my hands. "He's a fucking biker. You broke the rules, Mel. Get over here."

"Not happening," Pic said, his face grim. "I am *not* dealing with this tonight. Painter, get your ass home. Melanie, you're with me."

The air around us cooled. The brothers—Silver Bastards and Reapers both—had been watching all along, but now there was a new, quiet intensity in the air. This had just gone from a confrontation between me and a woman to a confrontation between two full members, and we didn't usually air that shit outside the chapel. Pic might be the president, but like I said, this wasn't club business.

He needed to step back. Now.

Suddenly Mel shoved him out of the way, although how she did it I had no idea—she weighed maybe a dime and a quarter soaking wet, the little witch.

"What I do is none of your goddamned business!" she shouted.

I caught Pic's eye and he shrugged, knowing he was beat. "Fuck it. I'm done with both of you."

About time. I gave Mel a slow smile, savoring the moment she realized what'd just happened. We might be in another club's house, but the Silver Bastards were brothers to the Reapers. Pic had spoken because Mel was tight with his old lady, but he'd been overstepping. If she'd kept her mouth fucking shut, she might've walked out of here. Now? Not so much.

"I'll give you a ride home, Mel," I said with soft menace, enjoying the sudden shock in her face. "We can talk when we get there. Privacy, you know?"

She glanced around, eyes wide. She knew half the men here tonight, but they could be strangers for all the good that'd do her now. Ruger. Gage. Horse. Puck. They all stared back at her, eyes cold. Not one of them would lift a finger to protect her—not from me.

"Fuck . . ." she whispered. *Yeah, enjoy your reality check, baby.*

"Maybe we'll do that, too," I said, thinking about that hot, sweet pussy of hers. Hadn't felt that for years now, but I still dreamed about it every goddamned night.

I reached for her, jerking her into my arms as she screamed. Nobody moved. Seconds later I had her over my shoulder, hauling her out into the night. Her hands pounded my back, which was adorable because she didn't stand a chance.

Little Melanie was all grown up.

I'd spent five years dancing to her tune, but that shit was over. In my mind, she'd lost her freedom the instant she threw her leg over another man's bike.

Now all I had to do was fuck some sense into her.

CHAPTER ONE

FIVE YEARS EARLIER
SOUTHERN CALIFORNIA, STATE CORRECTIONAL FACILITY

Dear Levi,

You know, someday you should really tell me how you got started with your artwork. It seems like I share everything with you, but you never tell me anything real about yourself. It's kind of weird. I keep thinking that I should stop writing to you, because it's not like we even really know each other. (I still don't quite understand why you let me borrow your car all this time, but I really appreciate it—I make sure the oil is changed and stuff.) Then something will happen and I find myself wanting to tell you about it, so I write again.

Anyway, you don't have to write back if you don't want to. I know you think I'm just some kid, but I'm twenty years old now and I've lived through my own shit.

Okay, so I had to stop writing for a while. Jessica stopped by—we're getting a house together this semester. (Um, just so you know, she told me. About you and her, I mean. She said it didn't mean anything, but I can't help but wonder if you still

*think about her like that.) She's doing really well, by the way.
We just finished summer session, and she got a 3.00 GPA,
which kind of kicked ass. I'm super proud of her, because she
has learning disabilities, so it's not like that was easy. I have
good news, too—they told me today that I'm getting a full
tuition/books scholarship, which means I can use the rest of my
financial aid to live on. I won't have to work this year, so I'm
loading up on the credits. If everything goes right, I'll transfer
to the University of Idaho in January, a whole semester early!*

*So . . . something happened that I wanted to tell you about.
I met a guy. He's cute, and we have the same birthday—isn't
that funny? We went to this party at a house downtown and
they were singing "Happy Birthday" to him and then Jessica
started singing "Happy Birthday" to me and things sort of
grew from there. We've been on a couple dates now, and he
just asked me if it could be exclusive.*

What do you think about that?

*I mean, do you think that a guy should be asking that after
such a short time? I know, I should probably talk to Loni
about it, but she totally worries all the time, and . . .
anyway . . . I just wanted to know your opinion.*

Should I start dating him for real? Any reason I shouldn't?

Melanie

*PS—thanks for the drawing you sent—it almost feels like I've
been there. Every time I see one of your sketches it blows me
away. I can't imagine being able to create something like that.*

I folded the letter carefully, looking out across the yard. The air
was warm—perfect, really—and I thought about Idaho, where you
couldn't sit outside like this for most of the year.

The only good thing about prison was I hadn't frozen my ass off
last winter. People back home saved all year to try and find some
sun during the cold months, but I'd gotten my snowbird "vacation"

for free. In the distance, Puck wandered toward me, his path apparently aimless. I knew better. He had shit to distribute, and it was my job to watch his back and make sure nobody noticed anything while he made his rounds.

That's when Prince Fester of the Fuckwits ran up to me, grinning.

"You get a new letter from Melanie?" he asked, eyes bright. I shrugged my shoulders, trying to ignore him. This idiot was me and Puck's cellmate, and I gave serious thought to shanking his ass at least twice a day.

"She send any pictures?" he asked, licking his lips. I fought back a snarl.

"Shut your fuckin' mouth. I catch you touching her picture again, I'll kill you. That's not a joke, Fester. Puck and I already planned out exactly how we're gonna do it."

His smile faded, his feelings obviously hurt. *Jesus help me, just one little slice . . . that's all I want. Just one swipe of the knife to take out his tongue.* "You don't mean that."

I didn't answer, because the man had the brain of an eight-year-old. A vicious, dangerous eight-year-old who'd been committing armed robbery half his life, but trust me—he was seriously lacking in the IQ area. Puck was always telling me to be patient with him, and I tried. Seriously. I tried fuckin' hard, but sometimes it took everything I had not to cut his tongue out for real.

"So, I had this idea," he said, leaning up against the wall next to me.

"Shut the fuck up and go away."

He frowned. I ignored him until he shuffled off like a kicked puppy, keeping my eyes on Puck as he drifted toward a cluster of skinheads. Always thought that was funny. They called him a mongrel behind his back, but when he had product they were happy to forgive Mr. Redhouse for his many sins against the Aryan race. I'd have laughed if I wasn't so busy making sure nobody murdered him.

Just two more weeks.

Two more weeks in this shithole, then I'd be headed home to Coeur d'Alene. Back to my bike and my club. My brothers.

Melanie.

Pretty Melanie, driving around in my car because I'd felt guilty about leaving her alone without transportation that last night . . . Christ, thought I'd be loaning it to her for a couple days, and now she'd had it for a year. Ridiculous, but who was I kidding? I liked the idea of her in my car—of her thinking of me every day. Of her *owing* me.

Not like I needed the damned thing in prison.

I reached down, feeling the letter in my pocket, wondering what the hell I should tell her about the asshole trying to get into her pants. Wanted to say she should blow him off—he wasn't good enough for her. She was too young, too soft, and too pretty for some twenty-year-old cocksucker looking to get his rocks off. He didn't care about her, either—he just wanted to get laid. They all did. Maybe he'd grow out of it someday, although I had five years on him and I hadn't yet.

I had no right to an opinion, though. She hardly knew me. We'd spent maybe eight hours together total, and trust me when I say there weren't any happy endings. I'd given her a ride home, watched a movie with her. Taken her to dinner to get her out of the club's way—it wasn't even a particularly nice dinner, not like she deserved. She was nothing to me.

Fucking hell.

Puck glanced in my direction, offering a jerk of his chin. Deal was done. I pushed off the wall, wandering slowly toward him. Fester tried to follow me, but I shut him down with a dirty look. Just another day, exactly like every other I'd spent in here the last thirteen months.

Except it wasn't.

Today I'd learned some prick was sniffing around Mellie, and there wasn't a goddamn thing I could do about it. For all I knew he was fucking her right now, balls deep, telling her how much he loved her.

Jesus.

She'd probably fall for it, too.

Mel,

You know, I write these fuckin' letters to you, but they're fake. I ask about your friends and your school and whether you're meeting people. It's bullshit, Mel.

Here's my reality.

Yesterday I stabbed someone before he could stab me. Puck and I sold some shit to a bunch of white supremacists and we turned around and sold the same damned thing to some Mexicans. We had pudding with our dinner for dessert.

Then I jacked off three times thinking about you.

Those are the highlights. Like a fairy tale, right?

Remembering you keeps me going, which makes no fucking sense at all. I hardly touched you. I still think about what you smelled like when you sat next to me on the couch, though. You were just this little thing and you shivered under my arm. I know you were scared of the movie and I could've picked something else, but I wanted the excuse to hold you.

That's when I started thinking seriously about us fucking.

I had this vision of shoving you into the cushions face-first, then ripping down your jeans and pushing so deep you'd feel it in the back of your throat. That's the kind of guy I am, Mel, and that's why you should stay the fuck away from me.

You give me the chance, I'll pin you down and keep pumping no matter how hard you try to get away. I dream about it every night, I jerk off to it, and today I gave serious thought to killing a man because he has the same fantasies about you as me. That first night, I promised London I wouldn't touch you, but my cock had already been hard for hours. Good thing she showed up when she did—saved your ass. How's that for luck?

When I took you to dinner, I was going to be good. Tried to be good. I know you didn't understand why I asked you out or what it meant. They needed you out of the way, Mel. That was my job—to keep you busy. And I promised London I wouldn't pull shit on you but she'd been lying to us all along and I kept wondering if that meant my promise didn't count anymore.

Pretty damned sure it hasn't counted for a while now.

You were talking and smiling and blushing. My dick was so stiff it nearly snapped in half when I tried to stand up. Took everything I had not to throw you on my bike and ride off with you . . . I want to tie you up and come in your ass and shove my cock down your throat until you choke. I want your hair in little-girl pigtails so I can hold on tight while I fuck your face. I want you to cry and scream and give me everything. I want to fucking OWN you. How's that for reality, Mel? You still want my advice about boys?

I'm coming home soon. You should run away while you still can, Mel. I'll make you dirty, so dirty you'll never be clean again. I'll make you pay me back the hard way. You think you're all grown up, but you're not. There's so much I could teach you . . . do to you. Jesus, if you only knew, you'd never write to me again.

You should move to Alaska.

Change your name.

Good luck, though, because I'll find you and take you and—

Fucking hell.

I dropped my pencil, wondering why I'd thought this was a good idea. I wasn't going to send it, of course. I'd send her some friendly little note and tell her she should be dating and having fun. But some part of me thought writing my real thoughts out might fix my obsession. Instead my dick was like a rock. Again.

Still.

Always.

I started shredding the paper into thin strips, because no fuckin' way I wanted Fester to read it. He always scrabbled through our garbage like a rat. Puck didn't need to see it, either. He was my brother—best brother I could have, and he'd proven it a thousand ways since they locked us up—but damn if he needed to know how pussy-whipped I'd gotten.

Right . . . Who was I kidding?

Puck was probably laughing his ass off about it right now.

I grabbed another piece of paper, thinking I should write her a real letter. Congratulate her on her grades and then tell her she should find a decent boyfriend. The words wouldn't come, though. Too busy thinking about her lips, I guess. They were round and pouty. Created by God expressly to suck cock. *My* cock. Right on cue, it went from hard to painful, a pillar of concrete in my pants, desperate for some action.

"I drew you a picture," Fester said, offering me a goofy grin from his bunk. He held up a piece of paper covered in bright orange and red crayon. The red was blood seeping out of stick-figure bodies he'd drawn. I had no fuckin' idea what the orange spirals were supposed to be. Maybe the voices in his head?

He liked to talk about his art with me, like we had something in common. Sometimes I could almost see where he was coming from. Scary fuckin' thought.

"Leave my brother alone," Puck told Fester, his voice hard. He was already down for the night, reading some history book. World War II snipers—he loved that shit. "Lights out soon anyway. Put away your crayons and go to bed, cocksucker."

Fester giggled, and I stood painfully. My bunk was only three steps away, but each one hurt worse than the last. Felt like my dick might split wide open, there was so much blood trapped in there. I collapsed onto my back, waiting for the lights to go out.

That's when I'd jerk off.

Again.

We all would.

Fester better not get jizz on my pictures of Mel. I really *would* kill him. The lights went off with a thudding noise, like something out of a movie. Never understood that—didn't seem like flipping a switch should be so loud.

Downright ominous.

Seconds later my hands were on my pants, shoving them down

as I lifted my hips. My dick sprang free and I wondered for the thousandth time how I'd be able to keep my hands off her when I got home.

Fester grunted in the darkness as I grabbed my meat.

Christ.

Two more weeks.

If I had any decency at all, I'd leave her alone. Yeah. I could do it. I'd probably imagined how beautiful she was anyway. Men built all kinds of crazy fantasies on the inside—always fell to shit when they got out again. Mel was just another bitch, one with too much baggage. I didn't really want her. Sure as hell didn't need her.

Right. Who the fuck was I kidding?

CHAPTER TWO

ONE MONTH LATER
COEUR D'ALENE
MELANIE

"So he never even called you?" Kit asked, eyes wide. "I mean, I get that guys can be confusing, but to loan you his car for a fucking *year*, write you tons of letters from prison, and then have you drop his keys off with my dad so he doesn't have to see you? That's bizarre."

"I don't want to talk about it," I muttered, shooting a death glare across the table at Jessica, the rat. My soon-to-be former best friend seemed deeply unconcerned by the fact that she'd betrayed me.

Wench.

"I don't blame you," Em announced, reaching for the wine bottle. "I don't like talking about Painter, either. He fucked with my head for way too long. I had the biggest crush on him when he was a prospect."

"You *let* him mess with you," Kit said, shoving her glass in front of Em's for a refill. Em smacked at her hand, and suddenly the sisters were wrestling over the bottle like kindergartners with a cookie.

I glanced over at Jessica, wondering how our Friday afternoon had turned into a random drunkfest with two women I barely knew, because Kit and Emmy Hayes were a trip. Jess gave me a "don't look at me" kind of shrug before draining her own glass of wine. I reached for some crackers off the little round cheese/meat platter thing Em had been carrying when she'd shown up at our house out of nowhere. (Kit had been in charge of booze.)

"Ha!" Em gloated, holding up the bottle triumphantly. "Suck it, Kit. Back to business—we have to figure out the perfect thing for London's bachelorette party. So far we've got a night out dancing and surprise strippers."

"I don't think Reese is going to like her having strippers," I mumbled, spraying crumbs because I'd forgotten about the cracker I'd just popped into my mouth. *Ick*. I grabbed my water glass, chugging. Liquid fire poured down my throat. I choked and then Jess was thumping my back while they all stared at me. Slowly I caught my breath, knowing my face must be beet red.

"That was straight vodka," I gasped, staring down into the green plastic tumbler. I'd grabbed Kit's cup instead of mine—obviously she wasn't a water drinker.

"I know," Kit said, nodding her head earnestly. "It's more efficient that way."

"So you're chasing your vodka with wine?" Em asked.

"No, I'm chasing my wine with vodka," Kit explained. "Saves time. Talking about Dad getting married again is creepy—the booze helps."

I sat back in my chair, looking between the two sisters, pondering the situation. Jessica and I had just moved in here a week ago. Our new apartment was actually one side of an older, two-story house downtown. The place was falling apart, and sooner or later someone would tear it down and build something new and spectacular. Until then, it'd been divided into four apartments—two down in the basement and two splitting the house in half, town house–style.

I loved it.

We had a giant porch out front, and there was a door off the kitchen leading into a shady yard surrounded by trees. We'd found an old wooden wire spool by the Dumpster to use as a picnic table. That's where we were now—clustered around it, sitting in old camp chairs. Handy, seeing as we didn't have a table for the dining room yet. Maybe we'd bring this one inside when it got cold . . . Like our new home itself, we considered the table a total score. London—Jessica's aunt, who'd raised her and taken me in, too—and her old man, Reese Hayes, insisted the place was a shithole.

Technically, they were probably right.

The house was a hundred years old at least, with peeling paint and a slant to the porch roof unsettling enough that I'd made a conscious decision not to think about it—especially since my bedroom (an old sleeping porch that'd been enclosed) perched on top of the rickety structure. The hot water worked only half the time, and it turned super cold if someone ran a faucet anywhere in the house during your shower. The walls were thin, so thin that they could hardly hold the tacks we used to put up posters, and the fridge made a creepy wheezing noise that sounded like the cold breath of a murderer in the night. (Not that I'd ever heard the cold breath of a murderer in the night, but I had a vivid imagination.)

It was still ours, though.

Our first *real* home as adults.

We had great neighbors for the most part, too. The other half of the house held three guys who went to North Idaho College, just like us. They were loud and rude, but so far they'd been willing to share the grill they kept on the porch, and they'd killed a snake for the girl who lived in one of the basement apartments. The second downstairs apartment held a guy who seemed a little sketchier than the rest of us. Jessica thought he might be a drug dealer. I hated to judge, but we'd been here a full week now and I'd never seen anyone have so much company coming and going late at night—there were cars pulling up for quick stops until two or three every morning.

We'd decided not to tell Reese—he'd probably kill the guy . . . well, unless he was on the Reapers MC payroll or something. Reese was the motorcycle club's president, and I'd never fully pinned down what it was he did for a living.

Sometimes it's best not to know.

Kit and Em were his daughters, and apparently now they were our new best friends. Jess had mentioned that they'd be in town—

the Reapers were having some sort of big party for Labor Day, and people rode in from Washington, Oregon, Idaho, and Montana for the festivities. They'd even invited us, as London's . . . what the hell were we, anyway?

Jessica was London's niece, so that made her family. I'd been Jessica's friend for years and London had half raised me, so I guess I was part of her family in some way, too.

There just wasn't a quick and easy name for a configuration like ours, although that didn't make it any less substantial. This really hit home when Loni asked me to be one of her bridesmaids. Now that she'd hooked up with the president of the Reapers motor-cycle club, I was realizing that meant the whole club was somehow part of our larger world. I supposed under other circumstances, I might've even considered going out to the party. I couldn't, though—Jess hated the clubhouse and she flat out refused to visit. Something bad had happened to her out there last year. I wasn't entirely sure about the details, and I didn't care, either. If she didn't want to go, then I didn't want to, either. We'd just stay home and get a leg up on our homework while they all partied. Or at least, that'd been the plan before Kit and Em and their booze showed up out of nowhere to talk bachelorette-party plans.

"Okay, we're completely off track here," Jessica said. I blinked at her, feeling the world around me spin just a little. That last big swallow had hit me hard. "Does London even *want* a bachelorette party? I just can't see her enjoying it."

"Every woman wants a bachelorette party," Kit announced. "And we're gonna do this right. I'll admit—I wasn't on board with them together at first. I still get creeped out thinking she's sleeping with Dad night after night . . ."

"Better her than the random girls he used to drag home," Em said, wrinkling her nose. "Half of them were younger than me. One time he even fucked a girl dressed like a carrot. London's a big step up."

Jess and I looked at each other. *Carrot?*

Ask her about the carrot! I mouthed silently at Jess.

No fucking way, she mouthed back, eyes wide.

"Okay, so I can see two ways to do this," Kit declared. "We can either do whatever it takes to make London happy or we can do whatever it takes to make Dad's head explode, which would make *me* happy. So I vote for exploding his head."

"The key is to plan something she'll like that *still* makes his head explode," I declared, falling into the spirit of things. "We should get her some strippers and then text him pictures of them grinding on her."

"Could we use The Line?" Jessica asked, intrigued. The Line was a strip club the Reapers owned. I'd driven by it but never been inside.

"It's a thought," Kit said. "They won't want to close it and lose money, but maybe we can get some sort of special ladies' night event set up. I know they've done them before. That way they still make their money, we can have a party for London, and Dad's head will explode. Everyone wins."

I stood slowly, swaying.

"I need to pee," I announced gravely, drunker than I'd realized. Should've eaten more crackers . . . except the last one I'd had tried to kill me. *Sneaky little bastards.*

"Do you need help?" Jess asked, and I started laughing at her joke, because of course I didn't need help. What did she think I was, a preschooler? Nobody else laughed, though, and I realized she was serious. That was even funnier, so I started giggling even harder. So hard I fell down, setting all of them off, too.

"You *sure* you don't need help?" Kit asked. I shook my head, which made me dizzy again.

"No, I think I can handle it."

It took a lot longer to finish than I expected, mostly because I'd accidentally locked the bathroom door on the way in and then I couldn't figure out how to unlock it.

I really needed to stop drinking out of Kit's cup.

"So all he did was look at her and say 'hey,'" Jess was telling them when I got back. Shit. She was talking about Painter again, possibly my least favorite subject on earth.

He'd been home from jail for two weeks now. I'd expected him to call me. Instead I'd gotten a text from Reese telling me to drop the car and the keys off at his house, then nothing. Not that I thought Painter owed me anything—of course he didn't—but I'd wanted to at least thank him. (Okay, that's not true—I wanted to jump him because I had a huge crush, but I also had some dignity. I would've settled for a quick "thanks" and maybe baking him some cookies.)

"Let's talk about something else," I declared.

"No, I want to hear this," Kit said, slurring her words slightly. "You distracted me earlier, but now that we've got the whole stripper thing figured out, we can focus."

I sighed, wondering if I could just strangle Jessica. No, probably not. She wasn't very big, but she was wiry and unnaturally strong. It wouldn't end well for me. Might as well give in to the inevitable and tell them.

"So, I met Painter last year," I started, frowning. I really didn't want to talk about this. "You know what? I'm hungry. Let's order a pizza."

"We'll let you eat once you tell the whole story," Kit said, scenting blood. "Spill it. I want to hear everything."

This sucked. I didn't even know Reese Hayes's daughters very well—we'd only met a couple times before today, at holidays. I'd already felt like an intruder in Reese's home, and with his kids there it'd been worse. On Christmas last year I'd left right after dinner for my dorm, making up some bullshit story about volunteering somewhere just to get away.

"So I met Painter last year," I started again. "Only a couple of times, really. Then he went to prison and I started writing him letters."

"I told her that was a bad idea," Jessica said piously. "He's not a nice guy, despite the whole loaning you a car thing."

"That's true," Em chimed in. "Not nice at all."

"Do you want to hear the story or not?" I asked, refilling my wineglass. Thinking about Painter was stealing my buzz. Couldn't have that.

"Tell the story," Kit said, narrowing her eyes.

"So when he took off for California he left me his car—it was just supposed to be for a couple days. Then he got arrested, he told Reese I could keep using it. I wrote to thank him, and I guess it just went from there," I said. "Painter's letters were so sweet, even though I only met him a couple times before they locked him up. He didn't even treat me like a girl, not really. But he was so . . . protective. I felt stupid writing to him to begin with, but when he kept writing back I felt special. Then one day—right before they let him out—I got this letter from him saying it was weird I didn't have a boyfriend, and that maybe I should be dating more. I felt like I'd gotten kicked in the stomach. I think I'd managed to fool myself about how big my crush on him was."

"I tried to warn her," Jessica said mournfully. "She didn't listen."

"They never do," Kit replied, her voice full of sad wisdom. "I swear, if people would just follow my instructions they'd all be a hell of a lot happier."

I glanced at Em, who rolled her eyes.

"Might as well spill the rest," Jess ordered. I sighed.

"Okay, so after that I never heard from him again—he didn't call when he got back to town. Nothing. Then we moved in here last weekend and Reese showed up with some of the club guys to help us . . ."

The words trailed off as I remembered. It'd been so humiliating. Reese and Loni had pulled up with this big truck, and right behind them was Painter, riding his motorcycle, along with a couple other bikers, younger guys not much older than me. I watched— mesmerized—as he carefully backed his Harley into place then swung one broad leg over his seat, looking up to catch my eye.

He was more beautiful than I remembered.

Bigger, too. I guess he'd spent some of that time in jail lifting weights. His hair had grown out some. When I'd first met him, it'd been short and spiky and bleached so blond it hurt. It still wasn't long, but it wasn't bleached bright white anymore and it was shaggy. Natural. His cheekbones were sharp, his features chiseled and harder than I remembered, and there was something scary in his pale blue eyes.

He wasn't looking at me—he was looking *through* me. Up to

that point I'd held out hope that he was just busy or something. How stupid was that?

"All he said was 'hey,'" I told the girls. "Like I was a stranger, and it was obvious he didn't want to talk. Just nodded his head when I thanked him and walked away. He helped move our shit, but I swear, he was friendlier to Jessica than he was to me."

That part particularly hurt, because I knew their secret. Jessica and Painter had slept together. Or fooled around. Whatever. She'd never given me all the details, but I knew her lips had been in contact with his dick at one point, back before she pulled her shit together and settled down.

"Mellie, that didn't mean anything," my best friend said softly. "You know he's not interested in me."

"In *you*?" Kit asked, her voice sharp. "I thought the issue was between him and Melanie?"

My mouth snapped shut, because it wasn't my story to tell.

"I used to be wilder," Jess said, taking a deep breath. "Last year I got drunk and went out to the Armory for a party. I fucked around with Painter and another guy named Banks. Then London showed up and dragged me out and a lot of other shit happened."

"Wow," Em said, eyes wide. "He must not like you very much, Jessica. He never sleeps with the girls he actually likes."

I gaped as Kit leaned over and smacked her head.

"That's a shitty thing to say," she snapped. My chest felt tight— Jess had enough on her plate, she didn't need to hear stuff like that.

"Hey, it's not my fault he has a Madonna-whore complex," Em protested.

"Shut the fuck up!" Kit hissed. "Jesus, Em, what the fuck is wrong with you?"

"It's okay," Jess said, flapping her hand at them. "I'm so sorry, but just the thought of the whole thing is so ridiculous. Believe me—I could give two shits if Painter likes me or not. It's just . . . he doesn't fuck girls he likes? What the hell is wrong with him?"

"How much time do you have?" Em asked seriously. "It could take a while to break it all down."

I held up a hand.

"Do I get a vote?"

"No," Kit said. "Em, give her the short and dirty."

"I spent more than a year chasing after Painter," Em said. "He was into me—everyone said he was. But the club always came first, and it's like he expected me to be some kind of perfect, precious angel while he fucked around with his club whores. Finally I got sick of it and ran off with Hunter."

"Seriously?" I asked. She blushed.

"Okay, it's a little more complicated than that," she admitted. "But there was definitely something between us, yet he never got off his ass and did anything about it. The guy has issues."

"Painter's problem is he likes the idea of a relationship but he's too fucking chicken to follow through," Kit said, giggling.

"No, Painter's problem is that he's complicated," Jess said, her voice more serious. "I'd say he was a total asshole, but he helped save my life last summer. He wound up in jail because of it. It doesn't change the real truth, though—Painter is a great guy to have around if your life's in danger and you need someone to rescue you. But other than that? He's not one of the good ones, Mel. You shouldn't talk to him, because he's dangerous. They all are."

Kit and Em had grown quiet—now the awkward had changed direction.

"You do realize you're talking about my dad and Em's old man, too?" Kit asked softly. Jess met her gaze head-on.

"I think I know what I'm talking about," she replied, her voice hard. "Melanie should stay the hell away from him."

"Someday you'll have to tell me that whole story," I finally said, my voice soft. Jess offered a sad smile.

"The club saved me," she said again. "They can do good things, Mel. Just don't let that trick you into thinking their world is a good place, because it isn't. Bad things happen there."

Silence fell over the group as we contemplated her words.

"We should drink more," Kit announced suddenly. "And where's the music? How can you plan a bachelorette party without music?"

"Good call," Jess said, clearly relieved to change the subject. "I'll go put something on." She stood up, walking across the half grass, half dirt of our backyard toward the kitchen porch. Em and Kit looked at her.

"She okay?" Em asked.

"She's always okay. Jess has a lot going on, but she pulls through. She's tough."

"Fucking hell," Kit burst out.

"What?"

"We're out of booze," she announced, mournfully turning the wine bottle upside down. Her vodka cup was empty, too. "Now what are we going to do?"

"We'll go get more," Em said. "Except I'm way too buzzed to drive . . . Fuck, now what are we going to do?"

"This is a problem," Kit replied. "A big problem."

"We could stop drinking," I pointed out. Both sisters stared at me blankly. "Okay, we could walk down to Peterson's and buy some more. It's only about six blocks."

"I like this one," Kit said seriously. "She's a thinker."

"Yup. We should keep her," Em said. "So who's coming with? I want some chips. And maybe some of that squirty cheese shit that comes in a bottle."

Kit curled her lip. "That's disgusting. You'll die from eating that."

"You'll die from eating cock," Em sneered back at her.

"You're just jealous because I've got some variety in my life," Kit said, unconcerned. She glanced at me. "Are you a virgin? Em was a virgin when she got together with Hunter. She doesn't even realize that there's other dicks out there. For all we know, he's got a four-inch stick. Never settle, Mel."

I giggled.

"I'll keep that in mind."

"We might need some of this," Kit said, lifting a long, hard tube of summer sausage out of the deli cooler, hefting it thoughtfully. The thing had to be a foot and a half long, and it was a good three inches thick.

"Not my place to judge," Em replied carelessly. "But that doesn't look very sanitary to me. I think you should just buy a dildo."

I gasped, glancing around to see if anyone had heard us. We were standing in the meat aisle. Peterson's didn't sell hard liquor, but we'd loaded up on wine, along with some fresh fruit to make sangria. Why we needed sangria I wasn't entirely sure, but Kit had been insistent. She kept rolling a lime thoughtfully between her fingers and muttering about scurvy.

Clearly, the Hayes sisters were batshit crazy.

"Let's just grab some chips and go," I said, starting to worry about how much the bill might be. I'd gotten enough financial aid that I didn't have to work this semester, but only if I pinched my pennies tightly. "If you really want tubed meats, I'm sure you can find some guy to share his for free down at the Ironhorse."

Jess gaped at me.

"Melanie, did you actually just say that?"

"What?" I asked. "You seem to think I'm some sort of quivering virgin. I'm not—I'm just more worried about school and my future than getting laid. Doesn't mean I'm a prude."

"Of course she's not a prude," Kit declared, throwing her arm over my shoulder proudly. "And tonight we'll show Painter just what he's missing out on, because he's a whiny little pussy. A bunch of Hunter's brothers from Portland are in town—I'll introduce you around. You'll have a great time. Painter can sit and spin if he won't step up."

"We're not going to the party," I told her. Kit shook her head slowly.

"No, you're definitely going," she said. "Someone has to put him in his place."

Jessica and I looked at each other, eyes wide. She shook her head at me, mouthing, *Don't do it!*

"I've really got a lot of studying to do . . ."

"You're coming to the party," Kit repeated, her eyes going hard.

"Don't worry—we won't leave you hanging. But this shit needs to end. I'm not letting another girl get hung up on that cockwad for years just because he's got his thumb up his ass. Dealing with Em's situation was bad enough. The girl was useless. Totally useless."

"I'm standing right here," Em pointed out.

"I'm aware," Kit replied, her tone suddenly sweet. "You know how much I love you, sis. Now hand me my sausage."

Two hours later I still wasn't sure how I'd wound up staring at myself in the mirror, trying to figure out what to wear. I didn't want to go to the party, yet here I was, primping and preening, feeling almost sick to my stomach every time I imagined meeting Levi "Painter" Brooks on his home turf.

Jessica wandered into my bedroom, frowning.

"I still can't believe you're going," she said. "They'll eat you alive out at the Armory. You have no idea what those parties are like."

"Kit and Em promised they'd keep an eye on me," I reminded her. "And this is a family party—not some crazed fuckfest like you went to."

"Don't let them fool you," Jess said darkly. "Bad shit happens at the Reapers clubhouse. Doesn't matter if they saved my ass or not, the Reapers are dangerous and I'd be a lot happier if you'd just stay home and work on homework with me."

I turned to look at her, marveling yet again at how much my best friend had changed over the past year. Back in high school she'd been obsessed with her looks, with partying, and with boys. Now it was a Friday night and she was leaning against my doorframe wearing ragged, cutoff sweats and a stained tank top, hair up in a messy bun. Not one of those cute, sexy messy buns, either. This one looked like a hairy mutant growth on her head.

Turning back, I studied my reflection in the mirror.

"Well I'm going anyway," I told her, reaching over to grab my jelly glass of sangria. "So do your duty as a friend and help me get ready. Does this make me look fat?"

Jessica licked the Fudgsicle she held thoughtfully.

"No, but it makes you look about forty. And not a hot forty—sort of like a homeless woman going on a job interview, I think."

I stared at her. "I can't decide how to take that."

"Take it as a sign that you should wear something else," she said, shaking her head. "Now, don't interpret this as my blessing to go to that party tonight, because I'm still one hundred percent against it. But seriously, Mel. You're beautiful. All that dark chocolate hair and permanent tan of yours? Fuck, if I had that to work with I'd be . . . Well, I wouldn't be sitting here watching you get ready to go out when I'm going to be stuck at home studying all night. I see no reason to disguise all that pretty as a bag lady."

"First up, those are some big words from a woman whose hair is so messy it's got white-girl dreads," I replied, frowning. "And second, you're the one who's refusing to go out, remember? I *want* you to come with me."

"Whatever. Change your clothes."

Rolling my eyes, I studied my reflection. She was right. Totally right. These were job interview clothes, not party clothes. "I've got no idea what to wear—can I borrow something?"

Jessica pondered, walking slowly around me, eyes sharp and critical.

"I can help," she said. "But I require complete obedience, grasshopper."

"Never min—"

"Silence!" she snapped, holding up a hand, palm facing me. "Don't distract me. I've got an image . . . We need something very special. Something to make him regret blowing you off—just don't be a fucking idiot and go crawling back to him."

"I was never with him in the first place."

"All the more reason to do this right," she said. "If you're going out there, you're going to look hot. *Really* hot. He'll blow his wad when he sees you, I swear. Then you can make him grovel and come back home."

Ewww.

"I don't want him blowing his wad."

She cocked her head at me, smirking.

"Now who's living in denial?"

I sighed, because the bitch was right.

Jessica worked fast, and fifteen minutes later I found myself looking in the mirror again, but this time I'd definitely left job interview territory behind. I looked good, I had to admit. Jess had me in a black push-up bra and a loose, off-the-shoulder black summer top with silver bangles around my wrists and big hoop earrings. She'd paired it with a short plaid skirt, sort of a cross between a kilt and one of those little skirts girls wear at Catholic schools. She'd finished it off with combat boots.

"You can use those to kick Painter in the nuts if he says something stupid," she said, smirking at me.

"But shouldn't I be wearing something more . . . I don't know. *More*. Heels or something?"

"Trust me, you don't need the fuck-me pumps. You have fuck-me lips and a fantastic rack. Not only that, *Painter*"—she sneered as she said his name—"is an idiot, so I can almost guarantee he'll need a nut punch and you don't want to break a nail or something. Any shoe with a real heel would get stuck in the grass anyway, and flats are simply *not* an option. That leaves us with wedges or sandals, and those would totally ruin the feel of the outfit. This is what you need to wear."

I studied my reflection again. It wasn't me at all, but I had to admit, the clothes totally worked with my dark hair and smoky eyes. Half sexy skater girl, half . . . hell if I knew. Something not Melanie, something almost reckless.

"I guess so. It just feels weird."

Jessica came to stand next to me, wrapping her arm around my shoulders.

"When you helped me write my first English lit paper, I listened to you," she said, her voice serious. "I listened because you understand that stuff better than I do. It's what you're good at. Here's the thing—I may have taken a temporary vow of celibacy, but I know guys and sex. This works on you. You're gorgeous. I wish you could see yourself the way I do."

I blinked rapidly, unexpectedly emotional. Then Jess leaned forward and whispered in my ear, "If you were a hooker, I'd pay full price for you, baby. And you know I don't pay full price for anything."

I pulled back and she burst out laughing.

"You're crazy, you know that?"

"Yeah," she replied. "I'm the crazy one, you're the one who's good at school and shit. So tonight we'll switch it up. You go out and have fun—just stick close to London, okay? I'll stay home and do my homework. That should fuck with all their heads."

"Head fuckery is a noble goal," Kit declared, stepping into the room to join us. "London's gonna be here soon—she's our ride. She's doing a Costco run for more ice and chips—you can never have too much of those. Nice work on the outfit, Mel."

"It was all Jessica."

"Figures. Now let's go. We're out of sangria again and Em's looking thirsty. God only knows what she'll do once she realizes I drank it all while she was talking to lover boy on the phone. That bitch is violent when she's sober. We need more to drink—safety first, you know?"

"This is Mel," Kit announced proudly, pushing me toward a tall guy with dark hair pulled back in a man bun. (Those always confuse me—they really shouldn't be sexy yet on some guys they just *work*.) He wore a denim Devil's Jacks MC cut, and I would've been interested in studying the patches if he weren't completely bare chested underneath it . . . and what a chest. Damn.

I know it's shallow, but if you asked me to pick his face out of a police lineup I would've drawn a blank. Those pecs? I think they were burned on my soul.

"Mel's connected to London, my dad's old lady," Kit continued. "She's nice, so try not to break her."

"Hey, Mel," he said, his voice smooth with just a hint of humor. "I'm Taz. Over from Portland."

"Taz is in the same chapter as Hunter, Em's old man," Kit informed me. "He's a great guy, aren't you, Taz?"

"Fuckin' prince," he agreed. "You want a drink, Mel?"

I nodded, mesmerized. Taz was very, very pretty. No, "pretty" was the wrong word. Hot. Yeah, that was better. Taz was *hot*—like, on the alphabet of hotness I'd give him an "H" for Hemsworth. I wanted to lick him, to see if he tasted as good as he smelled, although that may have been the sangria talking . . . His eyes were green and sparkling, his lips were quirked in this adorable half smile, and when he put his hand against the small of my back, guiding me gently toward the kegs, I nearly fainted.

Fuck Painter—he had his chance.

In all fairness, I'm not usually that shallow . . . but I'd been at the party for nearly two hours now, and while I'd seen Mr. Brooks in the distance, he hadn't even bothered acknowledging me with a friendly wave, let alone talked to me. He'd glared for a minute, then stomped off toward Reese without a second look.

At least London had been happy to see me, although I could tell she was disappointed Jess wasn't here. I knew she'd been banned from the Armory for a while last summer after she'd gotten herself in trouble at one of their parties. But she'd really pulled her shit together since then. Reese had even started inviting her to some of the club's family events last winter.

So far as I knew, she'd never been back out here, and I'd only been out once, helping London with some groceries. Today, Loni had warned me to stay outside in the courtyard with the main group and to let her know when I wanted to go home so she could arrange a ride. Then she'd given me a hug and a kiss before setting me free to run around with Kit.

Em had already ditched us by then, glued to her old man, Hunter.

"She's dick-whipped," Kit had confided. "Pathetic. If I ever fall for some guy like that, please shoot me. My dad has lots of guns—you can borrow one if you need to."

We'd spent the next two hours wandering around together. Kit had grown up playing at the Armory and she gave me the full scoop on everyone we saw. She seemed to agree with London about staying outside with the main crowd in the courtyard, rather than exploring the big, three-story building behind us. It looked sort of like a castle to me—apparently they'd bought it from the National Guard.

Surprisingly, the party really was family-friendly.

Mostly.

There was loud music and plenty of booze, but there were also kids running around laughing and screaming, stealing cookies and drinking endless lemonade.

It wasn't all sunshine and light, though. There were lots of big, scary-looking guys surrounded by women wearing a lot less clothing than I was used to seeing. Something told me the whole family-friendly vibe would end once the sun went down. At least Jess made the right call on the boots—the few women I'd seen wearing slutty heels were having a really hard time getting around, given the mixture of cracked concrete, gravel, and grass that blanketed the area.

My boots made me feel strong and tall and capable.

That's why—when Taz poured me a drink and smiled big at me—I didn't even notice Painter watching us. I also didn't notice him after the second drink, which was really more like my . . . well, I'd sort of lost track at the house, to be honest. (Let's just say I was feeling festive.) That's also why I completely forgot what London told me about staying in the courtyard. To be fair, I'd pretty much forgotten about everything by then—I'd been drunk before, but never quite like this.

It was fun. No wonder Jessica used to do it so much.

"You want to go for a walk?" Taz asked me after we'd been talking for what felt like forever and no time at all. I looked around, realizing that the sun had started to set. There were a lot fewer kids running around. Someone had lit a bonfire, and the music was louder.

"Sure," I said, feeling adventurous. Maybe he'd kiss me. That would show Levi Fucking Painter Brooks a thing, now, wouldn't it? Just because he wasn't interested in me didn't mean I wasn't sexy and fun.

Taz caught my hand, leading me back along the big cement-block wall surrounding the courtyard toward a gate in the back. It was open, but a guy wearing a prospect's cut stood guard, watching everyone who came and went. I didn't recognize him, but when he saw me, his eyes widened. Then he whipped out his phone and started texting.

"This is really pretty," I said, looking over the wide meadow we found on the other side of the wall. Beyond it the ground rose in a steep slope covered with trees, but back here it was just like a park. Gorgeous. There were quite a few tents and even another bonfire.

"We're camped over there," Taz said, nodding toward the far end of the meadow. "Let me show you."

I frowned as his words penetrated my brain fog. My sense of self-preservation kicked in, pointing out quietly but insistently that going off with a strange guy in the dark at a biker party might not be the brightest of moves.

Shit. I really *was* turning into Jessica.

"Mel, get over here."

I knew that voice. Turning slowly, I saw Painter standing behind us, arms crossed in front of him.

He didn't look happy.

In retrospect, my mistake had been letting Kit into the house that afternoon. Truly, from that moment forward the whole day had been fucked, a runaway train careening down the track into a dark void of . . . well, mostly one very angry biker.

Why Painter was pissed, I had no clue.

Wasn't like he'd spoken to me even once during the damned party. I'd been there for hours, yet the only times I'd seen him he'd been talking up slutty girls wearing painted-on jeans and stamp-sized bikini tops.

Not that I cared. Not at all. He could screw around with who-ever he wanted, because . . . Double shit. His gaze met mine, burning through me, and I swear—the world started spinning. I forgot all about Taz as I fell into Painter's eyes, mesmerized. Then I realized what I was doing and forced myself to look down, which wasn't much better. I swear, the man was made entirely of muscles—delicious muscles that I could see all too clearly because he only wore a short-sleeved T-shirt under his leather Reapers cut. Faded blue jeans covered his legs, clinging to his thighs in a way that made my own clench. Worn black boots covered his feet. Together it was too much. Throughout the party, I'd tried to convince myself that he wasn't as strong—or sexy—as the man I fantasized about every night. Nobody could be.

Except he *totally* was.

Painter's gaze flicked between me and Taz, calculating and cool as he swaggered our direction, because apparently it wasn't enough to look so sexy that my heart nearly exploded. Nope. He had to *walk* sexy, too. *Breathe* sexy.

I remembered every second I'd spent with him last year, every touch, every time I'd wrapped myself around his big, strong body while his Harley throbbed beneath us. He'd given me three rides. Less than thirty minutes total . . . And that one kiss—enough to mark me forever.

I wanted more in a big way.

"Painter," Taz said, startling me. I'd forgotten he was there.

"Taz. Should probably let that one go. She's protected."

"She yours?" Taz asked, sounding surprised. "Guess she didn't get the message. Not like I dragged her out here."

"She's a kid. Drop it."

"Hey, I'm not a kid," I protested, indignant. "I'll be twenty-one in four months."

Taz gave a low laugh. "You heard her. Fuck off, Brooks."

Painter stepped toward me, his expression colder than I'd ever seen it. "Mel, get your ass back to the party."

I stilled, unsure what I should do. I really did want to go back to the party . . . but I didn't want Painter to win, either.

Shit.

Now I found myself trapped between him and Taz, and because I'm a freaking idiot I wanted to forget Taz and jump on Painter, right there in the middle of the yard. Just wrap my legs around his waist and grind on him like a whore. One very, *very* happy whore.

Where is your self-respect?

CHAPTER THREE

PAINTER

Mel was staring at me like a spooked rabbit.

She didn't belong here and she knew it, the little sneak. She *had* to know—she'd been avoiding the Armory the whole time I was in jail. She'd written me all about it, among a thousand other things. You'd think a guy like me would get bored hearing about her life. There'd been a few club-whore types who'd written me, too—letters full of sex and promises and pictures that should've crowded Mel right out of my mind. Never stopped thinking about her, though. Not once. She'd become my anchor. Then she'd stopped writing after I told her to go find herself a boyfriend. Once I got home, I made a conscious decision to be a dick about the car, too. I had to be.

It was the right thing to do.

I'd made it a whole week back in Coeur d'Alene without hunting her down, holding out against temptation. Then Pic had mentioned the girls needed help moving last Saturday and it was all over. I'd kept my hands off her that day—didn't do more than say hello—but it'd been torture. She was more beautiful than I remembered. Had filled out, going from pretty to gorgeous, all smooth, rich, tanned skin, dark hair, and long legs designed specifically by God to wrap around my waist.

When she leaned over in front of me to grab a cardboard box I'd nearly popped out of the front of my pants.

My fuckwad of a president had been laughing his ass off at me, while London went into full mother hen mode. I'd promised her once that I'd leave Mel alone—a promise that no longer stood in my opinion, given how she'd lied to the club and tricked us. One thing was for sure, though. No fucking way I'd gone through a full year of blue balls so Taz could swoop in and steal the prize.

"London's looking for you, Melanie," I lied blandly. "She told you not to come out here, remember? There's a reason for that. It's not safe."

"Perfectly safe with me around, babe," Taz said, eyes dancing. I didn't think he was seriously interested in her, but he was definitely getting off on annoying me. Fucker. He was one of Hunter's brothers, and they'd never liked me. Em might be Hunter's old lady now, but at one point she'd been mine for the taking. He hated me for that.

I'd hated him, too—he'd stolen her away from me. Looking at Mel, though . . . Fuck, what had I ever seen in Em?

"I probably should get back to the party," she said slowly. *Yeah. No shit.*

"Fantastic," I said, catching her arm and pulling her toward me. Taz laughed behind us as I dragged her off, not toward the gate in the back of the wall but around the side of the courtyard wall, into the darkness. She stumbled along beside me for a few, then tugged on my arm as we rounded the back corner.

Nobody could see us here.

"Hey," she said. I ignored her, my blood pressure too high already. I could smell her in the darkness. Actually *smell* her. She wasn't wearing heavy perfume or anything, but she smelled like oranges and spice and nice . . . What the fuck was wrong with me?

"Hey," she said again, jerking on my arm hard this time. I stopped, turning on her abruptly. She took a step back, hitting the wall. "This isn't the way back to the party."

"You're not going back to the party."

She cocked her head, and I saw the confusion in her alcohol-glazed eyes as she wrinkled her nose at me. All cute, like a rabbit.

"You look like a bunny."

"You look like an ax murderer," she said, frowning. "And I thought London was looking for me. Aren't we going the wrong way?"

"I lied. I do that a lot," I told her, staring at her lips. I reached out, catching her chin in my hand, running my thumb across her lips. Our eyes locked, and I don't know if her pulse started to rise but mine sure as fuck did. What the hell had I been thinking, writing to this girl? She was so pretty and perfect and had this amazing, magical life just waiting for her and all I could think about was dragging her down into the dirt and shoving my cock into every hole she had.

She'd scream while I did it, too, the same sweet screams that played in my head every night while I jacked off.

I hated myself.

"Why did you lie?" she asked, her voice a whisper.

"To get you away from Taz. It's not safe with him."

Mel's forehead creased in confusion, her brain moving so slowly I could practically see the wheels turning behind her eyes. She might be smart as fuck most of the time, but she'd transitioned to drunker than fuck tonight. Kit. Kit and Em. They'd done this to her.

I leaned in closer, catching her scent. For an instant I swayed, so tempted . . .

"They told me all about you," she whispered.

"Who?"

"The other girls. Kit, Em. Jessica. I know how you operate," she continued. One of her hands rose, touching my chest. Fire burst through me, because if I'd wanted her before I was desperate for her now. She was so soft, so sweet . . . so perfect.

Then her words sank in.

"What did you just say?"

"They told me all about you," she said, eyes dropping to stare at my lips. "They told me you have a Madonna-whore complex."

I froze.

"A *what*?"

"A Madonna-whore complex," she repeated, her voice earnest. "You like to screw dirty girls and you put clean girls on pedestals, where they can stay perfect and pure. That's pretty messed up, Painter. There's no such thing as Madonnas and whores. We're all just people."

The words stunned me. What the hell was she talking about? Just because I didn't want her dragged down in the drama and bullshit of this life didn't mean I had some sort of fucking complex. And who the hell were the Hayes sisters to have an opinion? I couldn't tell what pissed me off more—the fact that they'd talked to Mel about me or that they hadn't done a better job of scaring her off.

She wasn't supposed to be here.

"Kit and Em are crazy, and that friend of yours—Jessica? She's like a car crash. You don't belong here, Mel."

"And where do I belong?"

"With some nice kid who'll treat you like a queen and work his ass off to give you everything perfect for the rest of your life." The words were practically a growl.

Her eyes widened.

"What if I don't want perfect?"

"Too fucking bad, because that's what you're getting."

"Excuse me?" she said, her voice hardening. I saw a flash of anger in her eyes—good. Maybe it would clear her head enough to pull it out of her ass.

"I'm taking you home and you aren't coming back out here again. And you can stay the fuck away from Em and Kit. Hell, you should stay away from Jessica, too. Why are you two sharing a place, anyway?"

"What do you want from me?" she asked softly, her lips moving against my thumb, which had somehow started sliding back and forth without my permission. I took a deep breath, looking into her face. Christ, but she was beautiful. Dusky skin, thick, dark brown eyelashes and all that hair I wanted to wrap around my hands while I skull-fucked her.

If she'd cut it off while I was in prison, not sure I could've handled it . . .

"I want you to leave and never come back," I said. She flinched, and for an instant I thought she might turn and run. Then her tongue flicked out and licked my thumb. Hot. It was hot and wet, and when she caught it with her teeth and then sucked it into her mouth my head started throbbing. Okay, more than my head. I could actually feel my pulse in my cock, which was rock hard and pushing against the front of my jeans.

Mel's eyes held mine as she sucked me deep, swirling her tongue as her fingers dug into my chest. Those lips of hers . . . they were soft and puffy and looked fucking fantastic wrapped around my thumb, but they'd look a whole hell of a lot better wrapped around something else. Then she caught at my wrist with her other hand, pulling me slowly out of her mouth, even as her tongue flicked out for one last playful taunt.

"Painter, I want you to listen to me very carefully," she said, holding my gaze as her face hardened. Damned if I didn't love the way my name sounded on her lips. "I thought you were my friend, but you ditched me. You treated me like I was an annoying pest when I tried to thank you for loaning me your car. You acted like all those letters between us meant nothing. That hurt me, Painter. Hurt me a lot. Maybe I'll regret telling you this once I'm sober, but right now it feels good to say the words, so listen up."

My eyes widened—who the hell was this girl? Mel didn't have a backbone, not like this. But apparently she did, because she wasn't done talking yet.

"So far as I'm concerned, you have no right to tell me what to do," she said, the words careful and deliberate as she reached out to poke me in the chest. "*Ever.* I was having a great time until you interrupted me, and I'm going to leave you now and go back to having a great time without you. If you don't like that, you can shove it right up your ass."

MELANIE

I'd lost my mind.

Only possible explanation for what'd just come out of my mouth. Wait—there was another one. I'd been possessed by a demon. I blinked slowly, thankful for the wall behind me because I'm not sure I could've stayed upright without it.

This is what drunk feels like, I realized. I thought I'd been drunk before, but I'd only been tipsy or something, because tonight was totally different. Take this whole situation with Painter. I knew he was a big, scary guy. I knew telling him off—alone, in the dark— was a bad idea.

I just didn't care.

Talk about liberating . . . Painter's face darkened, and I giggled. Couldn't help myself, it was just too funny. Mr. Big Bad Biker Man didn't know what the hell to say because I was right and he was wrong and—

"You have no idea what you're fucking with," he growled. He reached out, burying a hand in my hair and twisting it tight, tilting my head up toward him. Leaning into me, his eyes searched my face as his jaw clenched. "You think this is a game, Mel? Not even Em and Kit would be stupid enough to take off into the night with some guy they don't know."

"You mean like Jessica took off with you?" I asked, feeling bold. "You're such a hypocrite."

"All the more reason to stay away from me. You need to go home and stay there."

"Do you even *hear* the words coming out of your mouth?" I demanded, frustrated because he was full of shit and I'd just been sucking on his thumb and . . . Em had been right—Painter *did* have a complex. I had no interest in getting stuck on top of some stupid pedestal, though. I wanted to lick him all over, not sit on an inspirational platform of womanly virtue. "Now let me go and we'll call it good. I'll go back to the party and have fun. You can go fuck some whore if you're horny or say a few prayers to the Virgin Mary if you're feeling guilty about something. Just leave me alone."

His fingers tightened in my hair, his other arm reaching out to jerk me forcefully into his body. Then I was plastered against him, our faces inches apart. Yikes. Somehow he was bigger up close . . .

"You should listen to me," he said, the words low and more intense than I'd ever heard from him. "You realize Taz could do anything to you out here? He's not part of this club and you're nobody's property. There's no protection for you if you don't use some fucking common sense."

"Taz seemed really nice," I whispered, surrounded by his heat and strength and the realization that there was absolutely nobody who knew where I was right now. Okay. Painter might've been onto something—going out into the dark with Taz had been stupid, because I knew Taz even less than I knew Painter, and I had a feeling that hanging in the dark with my prison pen pal wasn't going to end well. Suddenly his hand caught my ass, lifting me up and slamming me back against the wall. My arms clutched his shoulders and my legs wrapped around his waist.

Holy. Shit.

Bad idea or not, I don't think I'd ever been more turned on in my life. How many times had I dreamed about something like this? Painter's mouth dropped down to my ear, catching it in his teeth just tight enough to hurt. I felt the hardness between his legs grinding into me as need exploded through my body. He smelled so good . . . My hips twisted, desperate for more. Painter groaned.

"Fuck me," he muttered, almost to himself. "You realize what I could do to you out here? Christ, Mel. There's nobody to hear if you scream. I can strip you down and fuck your brains out whether you want me to or not."

I couldn't breathe for a minute—*he could strip me down and fuck my brains out*. Something clenched, deep inside. (My vagina. It was my vagina doing the clenching.)

"What if I don't want to scream?"

He groaned again, pulling his head back to look at me. Then he licked his lips and I wanted to kiss him so bad I thought it might kill me.

So fucking do it already.

I didn't give myself a chance to think it through—I just grabbed his head and smashed my mouth into his. He froze for an instant and then I felt his hand twist tight in my hair, tilting my head to the side as he took control of the kiss.

Now's the part where I tell you that a choir of angels descended from the heavens, while unicorns frolicked and I spontaneously orgasmed against the wall of the Armory courtyard. That's how it always reads in books, but what can I say? There weren't any unicorns. Pretty damned sure I heard the angels singing, though, and I was definitely working my way toward an orgasm. Painter's hips were grinding into mine and my nipples were hard as rocks, his chest crushing me as his tongue took over my world.

Then he shifted, his dick finding exactly the right spot. I wanted him inside me *so bad*, but this was amazing, too, because I felt every muscle in my body twisting tight. My fingers spasmed in his hair and my hips bucked and then his hand squeezed my ass hard and I fell over the edge.

Damn. *DAMN.*

Not sure, but I think I caught a glimpse of a unicorn. Could've just been the alcohol. Slowly I came back to myself. Painter was still kissing me, softer now although I knew he hadn't come. Nope, that cock of his was still hard and ready for more. Then he pulled back and lowered me to the ground, breathing heavily. I swayed as I reached down between us, finding the denim-covered bulge between his legs and squeezing it.

"No," he said, teeth gritted. "We need to get you home."

His body didn't agree, though, because his hips were pushing back against my hand, begging for more. I squeezed again, running my hand firmly up and down his considerable length, wondering what he'd taste like.

I decided to find out and dropped to my knees.

That seemed to set him off, because he grabbed my arms, jerking me up and shoving me away in one rough motion. I stumbled back and tripped over a tree root, weaving for an instant before falling on my ass into a clump of grass.

"You ever hear the phrase 'No means no'?" he snarled, looking down at me with something as close to fear as I'd ever seen on his face. "Pretty sure I read that on a poster somewhere. I don't want you like this, Mel."

The fall hadn't been enough to knock the wind out of me, but that one sentence sure as hell did. Shit. I'd attacked him and gotten off on it. He didn't want me to do it and I'd done it anyway. There was a name for people who pull shit like that.

That wasn't a protest you felt grinding against you, girl. That was a cock and it wanted inside in a bad way.

No. That didn't matter, because whatever his body might say, his brain wasn't on board. I'd been dropping down to give him a blow job and he didn't even want it.

Fucking pathetic.

"I'm sorry," I whispered, feeling like I might throw up. God, why did I drink so much? It turned me into an idiot. Painter reached down, offering me his hand.

"C'mon, let's go," he said, his voice still strained. "Didn't mean to knock you down. Christ, what a cluster."

"S'okay," I mumbled, wondering if I could just slink off somewhere. Sit and wallow in my own pathetic juices for a while before calling London and begging for a ride home. "I'm really sorry I kissed you."

"I gotta get you out of here. Jesus. You need to stay the fuck away from me, Mel. I can't handle this shit. Next time just come at me with a gun—it'll be fuckin' easier for both of us."

What followed was an exercise in humiliation, blended with ghastly, drunken spins and topped off with utter exhilaration. Why? Because he decided to give me a ride home on his motorcycle. I'd forgotten how big and intimidating his black and gold Harley was. I mean, I'd seen it parked on the street last weekend during the move and knew it wasn't some little dirt bike . . . but it still seemed bigger up close—somehow more real. Scary.

Sexy.

Why did it have to be sexy?

Painter threw his leg over the bike and sat down, gesturing for me to join him. I climbed up, sliding down into his butt as I tried to tuck my skirt in somehow. He caught my hands, wrapping them tight around his waist. Holy hell.

I spread my hands out, feeling the hard flex of his stomach muscles under his shirt as I rested my head against his back. His Reapers colors were flush against my face, and I smelled the leather of his vest.

How was it possible to be so embarrassed and turned on at the same time?

Then Painter gunned the Harley to life between my legs, and let me just state this for the record—anyone who tries to tell you that a motorcycle isn't a phallic machine has obviously never been on one. Before the kiss, I'd have given anything to ride with him on his bike. Unfortunately tonight had fallen to shit and back—all I wanted was to crawl into my bed and pull the covers over my head.

If I got very, *very* lucky, maybe this whole thing would turn out to be a crazy nightmare.

The ride passed in a blur. One second we were pulling out of the Armory and the next we'd stopped in front of my house. I was off the bike and headed up the walk in an instant, praying that Jessica had left a Fudgsicle for me because I needed one. Purely medicinal.

"Mel," he called from behind me.

"Thanks for the ride," I answered, refusing to look at him or slow down.

"Mel!" he said, raising his voice in command. Reluctantly I stopped and turned to look back at him, almost falling on my ass again. I didn't like being drunk, I decided. Nothing was working right and it'd stopped being fun.

"What?"

"You need to text London and Kit," he said, his voice almost kind. "Let them know you're okay. Tell them I brought you home."

"Oh," I said, feeling sheepish because it hadn't even occurred to me. (Definitely no more getting super drunk—I just wasn't very good at it.) I pulled out my phone and saw several missed texts. Crap. The first was from London, about forty-five minutes ago.

> LONDON: Have fun but be careful, Mel. Taz is cute . . . he's also a player.

Then fifteen minutes later.

> LONDON: I didn't see where you went—you okay?

And finally . . .

> LONDON: I'm worried about you, Mel. Please text and let me know you're all right.

Ugh. I had to be the worst not-quite-daughter ever. Right after that was a message from Kit.

> KIT: Londons freaking out and someone said you went off with Taz be careful xx

Crap crap *crap* . . .

> ME: Sorry I got tired and decided to come home. Caught a ride with painter and its all good. See you later and thanks for the invite

I looked back toward the street, where Painter was still sitting on his bike, watching me. I gave him a perky little finger wave— *why did you do that? You look like a total dork for doing that! Ugh*—then walked up to the door, pulling out my key. I stood there, considering, then turned and walked back across the lawn to him before I could chicken out because we still had unfinished business.

Painter cocked his head, questioning.

"Thank you very much for letting me borrow your car while you were in prison," I said carefully, holding his gaze. "It was really nice of you and it helped me a lot."

"You're welcome," he replied, some strange emotion stealing across his face. Nodding, I turned and walked back up to the door, pulling out my key again. I heard the bike roar to life behind me as I stepped inside.

Jessica had been right about one thing. Going out to the Armory had been a big mistake.

CHAPTER FOUR

I found Jess on the couch, working on her laptop and eating a red licorice whip. Her hair was still in the disturbing amoeba-growth-shaped bun and she'd balanced a can of Red Bull on the faded couch arm next to her. Music played in the background, her usual mix of upbeat dance and boy bands. As much as I loved Jess, her playlists made me want to gouge my ears out of my head.

When she saw me, her eyes got wide and she pointed accusingly.

"You got laid, you little whore!"

"Excuse me?" I asked, totally confused. *God, I must be even drunker than I thought.*

"You. Got. Laid," she repeated, stabbing her finger in my direction for emphasis. "All your lipstick's worn off. You met some guy and sucked his dick, didn't you? Did he go down on you, too? I'm assuming he got you off—there's that sparkle in your eyes . . ."

"No, I didn't suck anyone's dick. I mean, we—"

Then I stopped, swallowing. Wait, what? Why were we having this conversation? More important, did I want to tell her what'd happened with Painter? I blinked slowly, trying to figure out what to say when Jess burst out laughing.

"Mellie, you're too easy," she said, rolling her eyes. "I know you didn't get laid—but can you blame me for giving you shit? You always blush so hard. It's really funny because you'd never hook up at a party. You're always the good girl."

I scowled, then dropped down next to her on the couch. I couldn't decide whether to be offended she thought I couldn't get any action or thankful that she didn't suspect anything. Reaching down, I tried to loosen my boots. This proved harder than it should be, because my fingers weren't working quite right.

"Just because I'm good at school doesn't mean I can't hook up," I reminded her. "It's not like I'm a virgin."

"You've slept with three guys, correct?" she asked, arching a brow. I nodded, wincing as I thought about that last one . . . none of them had been great, but John had actually hurt me. Terrible, *terrible* aim that boy had.

"And when was the last time you got laid?" she continued.

"It's been a while," I admitted.

"Since you met Painter."

I shrugged, refusing to dignify her questions with a reply. That would only encourage the wench.

"That's a dead end and you know it," she said, flapping her hand in dismissal. "I need you to get off your ass and grab some action—since I swore off sex, I'm counting on *you*, Mel. You're my everything."

She stared at me with adoring, mocking puppy dog eyes.

Flipping her off, I flopped back into the couch cushions, propping my feet up on the coffee table we'd scrounged at the St. Vinnie's thrift shop. It was battered and hideous, but it was solid enough to hold a pizza and a six-pack, which was all that mattered (at least according to Jess).

"You're not as smart as you think," I mumbled. "It's not like that."

"I'm surprised Loni didn't come in to say hi when she dropped you off," she said, flopping back next to me. "She usually does."

"I didn't ride home with Loni," I hedged, still feeling raw and embarrassed about what'd happened. I didn't like lying to Jessica, but I wasn't ready to go there. Not yet. Especially since I knew she'd been to a party out at the Armory—*not* a family party—and she'd gotten further with Painter than I had.

Guess I was good enough when he was bored in jail and wanted letters. Now? Not so much. I looked over at Jess, wondering exactly what'd happened between them. She'd said that they'd "fucked around," but what did that really mean? She said not to worry about it, that it wasn't important . . . But Jessica was gorgeous. Stunning. And while she might be younger than me, she was decades older in terms of experience. No wonder Painter wasn't interested in yours truly.

I wasn't his type.

"So who gave you a ride?" she asked, frowning. "Em and Kit were drunk. Was it Hunter? Or did they send you with a prospect?"

I thought about lying . . . making up a name or something. Jess tended to have a short attention span, so she'd probably forget all about it unless I was stupid enough to tell her—

"Omigod, you got a ride home with Painter!" she accused suddenly. "I can see the guilt written all over your face. How the hell did that happen?"

Shit.

"Yes," I admitted slowly. Might as well tell her the whole ugly story. "He's not interested in me—just ignored me, like he did the day we moved. But then I met another guy and . . ."

"What?" she demanded. I closed my eyes, trying to think and then opened them again because the room was spinning like crazy. For an instant I thought I might puke. Thankfully it passed.

"So he dragged me off and told me I didn't belong there," I admitted. "We were arguing about it and he was all up in my face, and then he was holding my hair so I kissed him."

Jess scowled.

"He's not a good guy," she said. "I mean, he's done some good things, I'll give him that. But these bikers are dangerous, Mel. I've told you all along—you have to stay away from him."

This wasn't the first time we'd had this talk—she'd been furious when she first learned we'd been writing to each other. Suddenly a dreadful thought occurred to me. I'd had it before, but I'd never asked her about it because it seemed wrong.

I wasn't feeling so inhibited tonight, though.

"So, I have to know . . ." I started, wondering how to say it. *Gee, Jessica, do you still want to have sex with my weird, nonfriend prison pen pal?* Hmm. That didn't sound right. What exactly *was* the most tactful way to ask your BFF if she hoped to bone the guy you're secretly in love with but who has no interest in you because he sees you as a helpless child?

This hadn't been covered in my English lit class.

"What?" she asked, shutting her laptop and leaning it against the side of the couch. "Let me guess—you're trying really hard to figure out a nice way to ask me if I'm still lusting after Painter, because that's the kind of girl I am? Always chasing guys?"

I coughed, feeling like a complete bitch for even thinking about it. But that was the problem—it'd been eating at me for a while, which was so not fair on so many levels, because Jess had changed her ways. Mostly. (It was the "mostly" part that caused the concern.)

"Maybe. I noticed he pulled you aside to talk to you for a few minutes during the move . . ."

"I can't decide if that's funny or insulting as hell."

"Funny?" I asked weakly. Jessica leaned her head on my shoulder and sighed.

"One, I've taken a temporary vow of celibacy."

"Yes, but you've never said for how long and even you have to admit you're impulsive as hell," I pointed out, figuring I might as well play it out now that we'd started the discussion. "For all I knew, the vow ended earlier today."

"Good point," she said, rolling her head to grin at me. Oh, thank God. She wasn't too pissed. But she hadn't answered my question yet, either. "No worries. I'd never touch Painter, Mel, assuming he was even interested—and he isn't. He doesn't give two shits about me. Not only that, you're way more important to me than some asshole biker. And I'm really working on the whole impulse control thing. I know I've got a long way to go, but it's actually going pretty well. Admit it—there's been at least a twenty-five percent reduction in drama."

I laughed, feeling almost giddy with relief. "Give yourself some credit—I'd say thirty. You'd be at forty if it wasn't for the Tire Iron Incident."

Jessica sighed.

"Yeah. That wasn't my finest moment. Although you want to know a secret?" she asked, pulling back to offer me a wicked grin.

"What?"

"I know I told Reese and Loni that I was sorry, but I'd totally do it again. The asshole deserved it in a big way. I swear, I practically came when I finally broke through the windshield on that dickwad's car. I'll take vengeance over sex any day."

She waggled her eyebrows at me again, and I gave her a fake stern look, channeling Reese.

"This isn't a fuckin' joke, Jess," I said, mimicking his tone and words exactly. "Your ass would be in jail right now if that little fuck wasn't so scared of the Reapers. Next time I'll let them haul you away, too."

"I'm sorry, Reese," she replied, lowering her head and biting her lip. "I guess I just lost control. I'll have to talk to my counselor about it . . ."

That was enough to set us both off laughing, which really wasn't very nice because Reese was a good guy—not only was he batshit crazy about Loni, he treated both me and Jess like his own daughters.

"I have a secret for you, too," I admitted as our giggles finally died down.

"What's that?"

"Loni totally thought he had it coming, too. I overheard her telling Reese that if you hadn't taken out the windshield, she would've. He got *pissed,* too."

"Really?" Jess asked, obviously surprised. "Holy shit."

"Yeah, he said that if she needs windows broken, she should talk to him. He'll send a prospect to do it for her, because he doesn't want her getting cut. Then they started kissing again and I snuck off before all the PDA made me barf."

Her mouth dropped.

"He's a seriously good guy," she said quietly. I nodded, thankful that things felt right between us again.

"I'm sorry I asked you."

"I know."

She gave me a sad smile, and there were secrets in her eyes I still wondered about. There was a connection there, between what'd happened to her and Painter going to jail. I'd written to him, asking what he wanted me to do with his car. He'd told me to hold on to it, and sent a funny cartoon sketch of himself studying a tray of prison food, looking confused and disgusted.

Tilting my head up, I stared at the ceiling, contemplating the situation. Were we ever really friends at all?

"Jess, I know everyone says the Reapers do some seriously fucked-up shit," I said softly. "Do you think the rumors are true? I mean, if Reese is such a good guy . . ."

Jessica sighed heavily.

"The rumors are true, Mel," she said, her voice bleak. "Whatever shit you think they're doing, it's worse. Way worse. Trust me on that one."

I blinked rapidly, wondering why the hell my eyes were suddenly watering, because I'd been through way too much in my life to cry over a boy.

No, not a boy. Painter Brooks was definitely a man. Jess reached for the remote, turning on the TV we'd gotten as a housewarming present from Loni, along with three big bags of groceries. Some stupid reality show came on, and after a few minutes I remembered that I needed a Fudgsicle so I went into the kitchen to hunt one down.

Shitty to be me, because Jess had already eaten the last one. I grabbed a Greek yogurt instead, then settled in to watch a bunch of spoiled rich women arguing over whose life was the hardest.

Ha. Maybe I should fix one of them up with my dad—now *that* would be reality TV.

CHAPTER FIVE

PAINTER

I didn't bother driving back out to the party.

Taz needed his ass kicked and I had the feeling I wouldn't be able to stop myself if I saw his fucking face. That wouldn't be good—the Devil's Jacks might be our allies at this point, but the history between the two clubs wasn't pretty. Pic still "joked" about killing Hunter, his daughter's old man, all the time. Last thing he needed was me throwing gas on the fire.

So here I was, alone on a Friday night, balls blue as a Smurf's butt despite the fact that I'd gotten sucked off earlier, before Mel showed up. Now that I'd seen her—felt her against me—I couldn't deny reality. She was different. Special. Just touching her felt better than fucking anyone else, and I didn't want to settle. Felt like the real thing.

But sooner or later this little infatuation would pass.

I knew that about myself. I'd thought Em was the woman for me. Then I'd held off too long and lost her. Thought my world was ending. It didn't. I felt not one damned thing when I looked at her these days, despite the fact that I'd been 100 percent convinced I'd never get over her.

Whatever I felt for Mel would pass, too.

I pulled the bike into the alley behind my new place, an old carriage house that had an apartment up above and a garage down below. The rental was only about four blocks from Mel's house, something that was a total coincidence. The fact that I'd decided to look for something downtown right after we moved her didn't mean a thing—pure coincidence.

I opened the door and walked inside, turning on the work lights in the garage. They were strung along the ceiling on hooks, plugged into each other in one long chain. Walking upstairs, I grabbed a beer, then started back down because I was way too worked up to sleep.

Instead I walked over to the oak veneered plywood I'd been prepping, testing the surface to see how the matte medium was coming along. Dry. I'd been working on it for close to a week. Now it was finally ready, which meant I could start my first real painting since I'd gotten out. Between work—both legitimate in the body shop and side stuff for the club—and finding somewhere to live, I'd been too busy.

Tonight it was exactly what I needed.

I took off my club colors, grabbing my rolling mechanic's stool and tugging it toward the workbench. My paints were waiting, along with the brushes I'd bought to replace the ones I'd lost when they locked me up. A couple of the old ladies had gone to my old apartment and boxed shit up after the arrest, but they hadn't known how to pack the brushes. These ones weren't nearly as good, but they were the best I could swing for now and I didn't want to wait any longer.

An hour later I took a break, finishing off my beer as I studied the outline of the Reapers symbol I'd started. They'd asked me to do a sort of mural for the chapel. Originally I'd planned to paint it on the wall, but Pic suggested I do it on a board so they could move it around. It was a solid idea—a board like this could last for decades.

Damn, but it felt good to be painting again.

So maybe I didn't get to have Mel—at least I still had this. I was good at it, too. I'd done some custom design work for guys even inside. Now that I was out again, I'd already talked to a couple of them about hand-painting their bikes. One was a weekend warrior who had too much money and didn't mind me holding on to his bike for a couple weeks while I did the art.

Guess some of us live to ride more than others.

Not that I cared either way, so long as they brought cash.

Cranking up the music, I leaned toward the board again. Looked good. Real good. Maybe I'd take my brother Bolt's suggestion and set up a website for my work. See if I could drum up some more business. It occurred to me that a guy with his own business—a commercial artist—might be the kind of guy a girl like Mel could settle down with. Christ, but I needed to stop thinking about her.

Wasn't gonna happen.

Time to get over it.

Justin Bieber was singing in my bedroom.

The fuck?

Blinking, I stared at the ceiling, trying to wake up. Maybe figure out who I needed to kill to make the unholy wailing end. After an eternity, the noise died and I rolled over, pulling the pillow over my head, trying to figure out what crime I'd committed to deserve that nightmare.

That's when it started again.

Fucking hell, it was my phone. I reached for it, a random picture of Puck's middle finger flashing across the screen . . . And yeah, I recognized the finger because I'd seen it pointed at me at least ten times a day for more than a year. Sort of his morning salute back in prison . . . I frowned, answering.

"Like your new ringtone?" my best friend asked.

"Eat shit and die, fuckwad," I managed to growl, but the insult wasn't my best work—brain was still foggy.

"Someone didn't get laid last night," he replied, and I could practically smell him gloating. Dick. "Saw you took off with Mel and didn't come back. Disappointed in you, bro."

I hung the phone up, dropping it next to me on the bed. Damn, I felt like hell. Staying up all night painting can be worse than drinking, at least in terms of hangover. I'd finally passed out around six that morning—according to the clock it was only nine now. Used to be I'd pop something to wake me up, but I'd stayed clean through prison and I planned to keep it that way, so no joy for me.

Justin started howling again. I grabbed the phone, resigned.

"How the fuck did you break into my phone?" I demanded.

"Guessed the password, dumbass," Puck said. "Know you too well—you can't hide shit from me. Got a reason for calling, though, so don't fucking hang up on me like a butt-hurt teen girl this time, 'kay?"

"You got thirty seconds."

"We're having the meet in an hour—all three clubs," he told me, his voice growing serious.

"Thought that was this afternoon."

"They changed it. Something came up. Guess Boonie needs to head out early, so we're talking at ten."

"Fucking great," I said, rubbing my eyes. Shit, I was tired. "I'll see you then."

Hanging up, I dropped the phone back on the bed, staring at the ceiling. The water stains overlapped each other in circular patterns and I had a feeling things might get damp in here once the weather turned. Not that I gave a shit—the garage below made a perfect studio, and that's all I cared about.

The Biebs burst out singing again, polluting my airspace. I should really kill Puck, I decided. Community service.

"What now?" I asked, answering.

"Just thought you'd like to hear the song again."

"I hate you."

"I know."

Once I was awake, the ride out to the Armory wasn't so bad—fresh air felt good. This was the first big club gathering since I'd gotten out. They'd thrown me a party when I got home, of course, but we'd kept it small. Seemed safer that way, given the drama with Puck down south.

Today we had representatives from the Devil's Jacks, the Reapers, and the Silver Bastards. Between our clubs we could claim most of Idaho, Montana, Oregon, and Washington. I wasn't aware of any urgent business, but I'd been out of the loop for a while now.

The Armory was crawling with people, although how the hell they were all up so early after the party last night, I had no fuckin' idea. I backed my bike into line and walked toward the main door. Standing outside was a group of Silver Bastards, including Puck. He looked ridiculously healthy and well rested. So far as I knew he hadn't partied at all last night—guy was still fucked in the head over what'd gone down with that girl in Cali.

Couldn't blame him for that . . . ugly shit.

These last couple weeks since we'd gotten home, I'd missed him, especially at night. Kinda messed up, but it'd been just me and him for the past year. We'd kept each other safe, standing guard, watching each other's backs. Surviving. That kind of brotherhood doesn't just end once your time is served.

"How goes it?" I asked, walking up to him.

"Nonstop thrills and excitement," he replied, his voice dry. "Got a new driver's license yesterday. Had to wait forever and the bitch next to me wouldn't shut up. Still the most exciting thing that's happened to me since we got home, so maybe we need to explore our options."

"Callup's a great little town to settle down in," I told him, smirking. "You'll get used to hitting the sack at seven every night, I swear. Of course, you could just go back to Montana. Love havin' you around and all that shit, but if you're not happy there, why stay?"

He shrugged. "Feels like I have unfinished business."

"Yeah, but that business is jailbait, so you might as well get over it. Unless it's true love, of course," I said, taunting him. "True love is worth any sacrifice, right? Up to and including your balls?"

"Fuck off," he said, punching my shoulder. I punched him back, but it didn't go any further. Much as I loved sparring with him, now wasn't the time.

"Good to see you again," said Boonie, the Silver Bastards' president. "Puck's been tellin' us everything you did for him inside."

"Went both ways," I admitted. "Woulda been a lot worse in there without him. Just glad we both came through alive."

"Well, we appreciated it."

"He's a good brother."

I glanced over to see BB lumbering toward us. The big prospect should've been a full member by now, but he'd dropped out for a while when his mom was dying. Cancer.

"Prez says it's time to go in," he told us. "They're ready to start. Up in the game room."

We all shuffled inside, passing through the main room, which served as a lounge, bar, and general hangout space. It filled the front half of the bottom floor, with a kitchen in the rear on the left, offices in the center, and a workshop that mirrored the main room on the backside.

The place wasn't in half-bad shape, considering how big the party had been. There were empties tucked here and there, and a bra that'd gotten caught on the light hanging over the pool table. I saw a few girls wandering around, cleaning shit up. Didn't recognize any of them, which wasn't a huge surprise. I still wasn't fully integrated back into the life of the club, and none of them gave off old-lady vibes. Then I spotted the one who'd blown me last night. She offered a little wave. I gave her a nod but didn't make eye contact—no reason to encourage her.

The game room was upstairs on the second level, off to the right. By the time we got upstairs, most of the brothers were already waiting. Puck and I found a spot toward the back, leaning against the wall to watch. He'd only had his full patch for three weeks now, and I knew he planned to keep a low profile. So did I.

Picnic surveyed the room, flanked by other chapter presidents who'd come for the weekend, including Deke, Hunter, and Boonie.

"Thanks to everyone who came. Over the past couple years we've had a lot of conflict. Shit's gone down, brothers have served time"—he nodded respectfully toward me and Puck—"and we've lost some along the way. It's good to have some time just for socializing. But we can't waste this chance to talk business, either. Deke and Hunter are gonna update us on the cartel situation, and then we've got some new business. Deke?"

The president of the Portland Reapers' chapter stepped forward, crossing his arms as he looked across the room.

"The Jacks have been holding strong in the south," he said. "We've caught a few cartel runners in the Portland area, but so far as I know they aren't making it up into Washington anymore. La Grande's stood firm, covering the central corridor. Much as I hate to admit it, the Jacks have been solid. Not a hell of a lot to report. Hunter, you got anything to add?"

Em's old man stepped forward. I studied him thoughtfully, trying to decide if I hated him any less these days. I'd gotten over Em a while ago—hadn't thought about her much at all on the inside. You'd think that would smooth the way with me and Hunter, but it didn't—I'd still happily cut his throat, just on general principle. Arrogant asshole.

He stared right at me, eyes hard.

"Gotta thank those who served time for us all," he said, offering me a small, mocking salute. *Cocksucker.* "We all know the cartel will recover and come after us again at some point, but for now they're mostly staying south of the Oregon state line. Northern Cali's a little harder—we're not in control, but they aren't, either. At some point we'll probably have to make a tough decision about whether we want to keep fighting for the territory. That's for the club to decide, and right now we're holding off making any solid plans. Our allies down south are being infiltrated. Not sure we can trust them long-term."

Puck and I shared a look—we'd seen plenty of that in prison. Our "allies" were useless.

"Painter, you want to share what you told me about your time inside?" Pic asked, apparently reading my mind. I nodded, pausing to consider before I spoke.

"Well, you all know we had allied club brothers with us," I said. "A few Longnecks, Bay Brotherhood, and one guy with the Nighthawk Raiders. Longnecks are shit, sorry to say. Couldn't trust 'em inside, and now that I've visited one of their chapters I'd say that runs true for the whole fuckin' club. The Brotherhood seemed solid but they're having a rough time holding their own. The Nighthawks guy was interesting . . ."

Puck and I shared a quick glance as I paused, trying to think of the best way to explain Pipes, our jailhouse contact.

"Puck, you want to jump in here?" I asked.

"Sure," he said. "Pipes was on his own and we bonded up pretty fast, given the history between our clubs. He was in for a weapons charge, too. But here's the interesting part—we all know they've been bringing in product through the Canadian border for a while, right? Well get this . . . According to Pipes, their pipeline's choking out on the Canada side."

Picnic and Boonie weren't surprised by this, but Hunter obviously was. Interesting—Pic hadn't briefed him ahead of time. Guess the Hayes family wasn't one big happy. Not a huge surprise—I had all kinds of reasons for disliking the guy, but they were nothing compared to Pic's. So far as I could tell, Christ himself wouldn't be good enough for Reese Hayes's daughters, at least not in his eyes.

Rance, the president of the Reapers' chapter in Bellingham, stepped up. He already knew what Puck and I had to say, of course. We'd told Pic and Boonie all about it, and I knew Reese had been in touch with Rance afterward, seeing as his chapter was the closest to Hallies Falls, where the Nighthawks were located. Now I was curious to hear his take on the situation.

"We've heard rumors," he said. "I've suspected something was up for a while now. They've been short on their payments, product has gone missing, that kind of thing. They blamed it on some local cops gone bad—cost of doing business—but it never rang true. Now we've got a better idea of what's going on. Tell 'em the rest, Painter."

"So, there's a new player up in British Columbia," I continued. "They call themselves a club, but Pipes says they're just a bunch of tweakers who bought themselves bikes and threw on some patches—not a real brotherhood at all. Kinda like that shit that went down in Quebec, you know? Now they're fighting with the

Nighthawk Raiders for control of the cross-border traffic. He's worried the whole club will go down, lose their patches entirely."

"Why didn't they come to us themselves?" Hunter asked, frowning. "Seems like the kind of thing you'd want to discuss direct, but we haven't heard jack shit from them."

"Pipes thinks their president—Marsh—has thrown in with the BC guys," I explained. "Not only is he bringing in new brothers who are loyal to him, he's cutting the older brothers out of the loop. They haven't been voting on shit, and no officer elections, either. Pipes says he tried to call Marsh out. Got his ass kicked and then they sacrificed him on a run. He isn't talking to the cops, but he's reaching out to us for help. Desperate for it. Knows that if the club falls, he'll lose his protection inside."

"Bad situation," Boonie murmured. "Thoughts, anyone?"

"We should go check it out," said Bolt, the Coeur d'Alene vice president. The man was Picnic's age, and they'd been friends their whole lives. If it wasn't for Bolt I wouldn't even be here—I'd met him when I was nineteen years old, fresh in my first prison term and scared shitless. He'd taken pity on me, teaching me how to stay alive and covering my ass when I needed it. I'd had a bike before I went in, but I'd never known shit about MC culture. By the time I'd gotten out two years later, I was ready for the Reapers. Bolt had pulled some strings and the next thing I knew, I was staying at the Armory, doing odd jobs, and earning my way into the club.

Best damned thing that ever happened to me, no fuckin' question.

"I'll go," Gage announced, stepping up quietly. I wasn't surprised—until last year, Gage had been our sergeant at arms, and he never backed down from anything. He'd been running The Line for the past two years and I knew he was restless. "Go in quiet, get a feel for how things are going. Maybe just a couple of us?"

"Thoughts?" Pic asked, looking to the other presidents.

"Seems solid to me," Boonie said. "No need to tip them off—if it's nothing, they'll never know we questioned them, and if we have to take action, I don't want them tipped off ahead of time."

Rance nodded. "You got anyone in mind to take with you,

Gage? They know most of the Bellingham brothers, so we can't be much use to you."

Gage looked to me, eyes speculative. "How about you, Painter? You've heard about the situation firsthand, and you've been out of circulation for a while. Less likely they'll recognize you. I know you're on parole, but I think we've got that covered."

"Sure," I said, mentally rearranging my week. I had shifts at the body shop, but seeing as Pic was the boss, that wasn't an issue.

"Great, let's talk after we finish here," he replied.

"Moving on, let's discuss the situation near Whitefish," Pic said. I only listened to him with one ear, thinking through every conversation I'd ever had with Pipes in prison, wondering if I'd missed anything along the way.

"You want help?" Puck asked, his voice a whisper. "Know you're going in quiet, but it never hurts to have backup."

I liked the idea—felt natural to have Puck at my back. "Let me talk to Gage. See what he thinks."

An hour later we'd finished all our business. There wasn't a ton—this weekend was more of a social event than anything else. I caught Gage's eye on the way out, and he waved me over.

"Puck's offered to come with us," I told him. "We're tight, and it probably wouldn't hurt to have someone from the Bastards along for the ride."

Gage frowned.

"I'd rather not. I know he's a good kid, but if we bring in a second club that complicates things. We take one of the Bastards with us, then the Jacks will want one of theirs along and suddenly there's ten of us hitting town. Right now it's contained in our territory and I'd like to keep it that way."

"Fair enough," I said, seeing his logic, even if I didn't like it. Puck was a good man to have at your back. Of course, so was Gage. He'd been sergeant at arms for a reason—the man was a brick. Solid, dangerous, utterly loyal to the club. "So when do you want to go?"

"I'm thinking we head out soon," he said. "Already talked to Pic about putting someone else in place at The Line. It could take a while and I don't want to leave them hanging. Now I'm trying to think of something that'll let me set up shop there for a while, but also give me an excuse to take off whenever I need to . . . I don't like going undercover but it's for the best right now."

"I hear you. So you think it'll take a while?"

"No idea," he replied. "You flexible? I won't need you there all the time, but I'll want you backing me at least part of the time."

"Sure, I can make it work," I said, figuring I'd bring along a few sketch pads or something. I'd gone more than a year without doing any serious art—no reason to get worked up about it now. "What if we say you're a trucker? Lets you come and go, distances you from club life while still giving you an excuse to ride a bike when you're in town. Not only that, Pic's got his hands on Pace Howard's big rig right now—he let him park it behind the shop while he's deployed, promised he'd keep it up and running. Maybe we can use that."

Gage nodded thoughtfully.

"Not a bad idea," he said. "I'll talk to Pic, see what he has to say about it. How are you holding up? Two weeks out now, right?"

"Good," I said, realizing it was true. Aside from the Melanie situation, I was happy with things overall. "Parole officer—I'm with Torres, he's on the payroll—seems to know his place. Not supposed to be heading out of state, but he'll cover for me."

"All right, then," he said. "I'll talk to Pic. Let me know if there's any complications on your end, and we'll plan to leave tomorrow or Monday."

I nodded, then headed down the stairs toward the main floor of the Armory. There were more people up and about now. I could smell breakfast coming from the kitchen and figured they'd be doing the usual—cooking inside, serving food out in the courtyard.

Might as well get myself something to eat.

Outside I grabbed a plate and then loaded up on eggs, ham, and hash browns. I'd just sat down at a table with Ruger, Horse, and Duck when Kit Hayes—Em's evil sister, and I don't use those words lightly—plopped down next to me.

"We're going to the fair tonight," she announced. "A bunch of us want to see the rodeo and maybe eat some of those little donuts that they throw in the bags with powdered sugar. Sophie and Marie want to go, but your ladies won't if you guys don't. What do you think?"

"Note how she pretends our opinion matters," Duck muttered, leaning toward me. I had to smile. The older man was in his sixties, and while he was always shown respect, he tended to stick close to the clubhouse most of the time.

"Don't look at me," I told him. "She's here to recruit Horse and Ruger."

Kit glared at me.

"Don't spoil it," she said, arching a brow. "We want everyone to come with us, but I know for a fact that Marie won't go if Horse doesn't, and the same for Sophie and Ruger. They feel like there's work to do out here at the Armory."

"There *is* work to do out here," Horse said, his voice dry. "We've guests camped out back. They'll need dinner."

"Which they can buy at the fair," Kit said, her smile growing grim and fixed. "Not only that, there's plenty of other women who aren't going. And it's not like the rodeo goes that late. You can all come back here and party when it's over . . . and it's not like sitting around drinking in this courtyard is anything special. You guys do that all the time. The rodeo only comes once a year."

Ruger sighed. "It'll be easier to give in now."

"Pussy," I said, although the man never really had a chance. Nobody could stand up to the Hayes girls when they set their minds on something, and apparently their minds were set on going to the fair.

"Oh, and Painter?" Kit asked, and I swear to fuck she fluttered her eyelashes at me. "We're bringing Melanie with us, so if you want to stay here that'd be just great. I'm sure she doesn't want you around."

That little bitch. Now I *had* to go.

I took a bite of my eggs, pretending to ignore her. She laughed, then skipped off across the courtyard, presumably looking for fresh victims.

"I'm real glad that girl moved to Vancouver," Duck said, sighing. "I love her like my own, but damned if she doesn't stir shit wherever she goes. I assume you'll all be out at the fair tonight?"

I stared down at my food, pretending to be fascinated by the pattern of ketchup across the hash browns.

Duck laughed.

MELANIE

"Pleeeeese . . ." Kit whined, kneeling on the ground in front of me. She'd caught me and Jess out in the front yard—*note to self: never go outside or even unlock the door again when the Hayes girls are in town*—and dramatically demanded that we go to the rodeo with her, because "Those cowboys aren't gonna pinch their own butts."

While I'm sure this was true, I still wasn't planning to go with her—I had a paper to work on, and I'd already made a fool out of myself the night before. Avoiding the Reapers was high on my list of priorities, yet here Kit was, on her knees in all her Bettie Page–inspired glory.

Parked behind her on the street were no less than five Devil's Jacks riders led by Hunter, Em's old man.

No pressure at all, right?

Out of the corner of my eye, I saw Taz climb off his bike and start walking toward me. Gaw. I felt my cheeks heating up as the memories of last night flooded me.

Alcohol. Alcohol was the enemy here. Alcohol and the Hayes family.

Taz came up next to me, draping his arm over my shoulder.

"You sure you ladies don't want to come out with us?" he asked. "Fried food. Horseshit. What's not to love?"

Jess glanced at him, cocking an eyebrow.

"Not a fan of the rodeo?" she asked. Taz laughed.

"Motorcycles don't leave piles of crap everywhere they go. I think that sums up my feelings on the issue."

Jess grinned, startling me because she wasn't exactly a fan of bikers.

"I'm Jessica," she said. *Ruh-roh*. That was her cute "I'm available" voice. So much for the celibate streak.

"You're coming with us, right?" Kit asked hopefully, honing in on Jess. The girl could smell weakness.

"I think we could swing it, don't you, Mel?" Jess asked innocently. I narrowed my eyes at her.

"Sure," I replied my voice dry. "Can't wait."

Taz snorted, giving my shoulder a squeeze.

"Don't get so excited," he murmured in my ear. "You might strain something."

"Okay, go grab your stuff," Kit said, jumping up and beaming at us proudly. She was really taking this "new family" thing seriously now that they'd set a date for the wedding. After this weekend, I couldn't wait for it to be over. December couldn't come soon enough. "Everyone else is already out there."

"All right," Jess said brightly, grabbing my arm and jerking me away from Taz. "We'll be five minutes, tops."

"I thought you hated bikers," I reminded her once we were back inside. "And five minutes isn't very much time to get ready. Not to mention I have a paper due this week, you know."

"You can pump out a paper like that in half an hour," she said. "And you look great. Just throw on some lip gloss and grab your stuff. I've been rethinking my position on bikers . . ."

"Oh really? Since when?"

"Since I saw Taz—that guy is completely and totally fuckable. Now here's what I need to know—is there anything between you and him? I know you came home with Painter, but Taz was all over you outside. Usually I'd say that meant something, but those guys are so damned touchy-feely that it's hard to tell."

"I hung out with him for a while last night," I admitted. "But

I'm not looking for anything more—my head's messed up enough as it is, with Painter. I don't need another biker running around in there, too. He's all yours."

"Perfect," she said, licking her lips. "I've been a very good girl for a long time now. I think it's time to put myself back on the market."

Poor Taz.

The man was screwed. Literally. Somehow I had a feeling he wouldn't mind too much.

Exactly four minutes and fifty-nine seconds later, we were back outside. I wasn't looking my best, but I didn't look bad, either— cutoff shorts, cute tank top, and an old pair of cowboy boots my mom had left behind when she took off.

Not much of a legacy, but they'd be useful today.

"So who are we riding with?" Jess asked coyly when we came back out.

"I've got room," said a tall, lanky guy with dark hair and tattoos up and around his neck. I smiled at him, figuring I'd take him up on the offer, but Taz dropped his arm across my shoulders again.

"She's with me," he said. Em and Kit exchanged looks, and Jessica managed to hide her disappointment, running a hand up and along Mr. Tattoo's shoulder.

"I'd love to ride with you," she said, turning on the full charm. It was almost creepy, how quickly she dropped the good-girl facade. I'd forgotten how fast she worked.

Jess might be older and smarter, but she was still Jess.

It only took about five minutes to reach the fairgrounds, although it was enough time for me to establish that Taz had very nice abs. Volunteers on horseback had us park in a big, empty field back behind the horse barns. There were already at least thirty bikes there, guarded by prospects from the Reapers, the Silver Bastards, and the Devil's Jacks. Taz caught my hand as we walked toward the gate, casually possessive in a way that both thrilled and scared me. Ultimately he wasn't the guy I wanted, and I didn't want to lead him on . . . but what kind of woman doesn't enjoy a hot guy holding her hand in public? *Could you be more superficial?* Doubtful. Crap. I should probably end this before it turned into anything, I decided. I tugged on his hand.

"Can we talk for a minute?" I asked.

"Sure," he said, stepping to the side so the others could pass. Jess cocked a brow at me but I ignored her.

"What's up?" Taz asked. I looked up at him, taking in his nearly perfect features, that sexy hair still pulled back, and the way his eyes all but oozed sex. Had I lost my mind, turning this guy down?

Probably.

"Um . . . I guess there's no easy way to say this, but I was really drunk last night," I started. He gave me a gentle smile.

"Picked up on that."

I felt myself blushing—I should never drink like that again. I knew that compared to some people, it hadn't been very bad, but I hated feeling so out of control. My dad was always doing stupid shit when he was drunk.

I was better than that . . . at least, I *wanted* to be better than that. Right after I made it through this trip to the fair.

"So I'm not really looking for a relationship," I started. Taz's smiled grew wider.

"Works for me. I'm just trying to get laid," he said bluntly, and while you'd think his words would've been offensive, somehow—from him—it just felt like he was shooting straight with me. "And I already know I'm not getting anywhere with you. But your little roommate is hot for it, and it's driving her crazy that I'm with you. Painter'll probably be out here later, so you can piss him off by hanging on me. Right about the time he loses his shit and hauls you off, she'll be ready and willing to comfort me in my sorrow. It's win-win, really."

I gaped at him.

"I can't believe you just told me that," I said finally. "That's pretty shameless."

"Shame isn't really my thing," he said, radiating cocky confidence. "Just roll with it, babe. We'll have a good time, and then you'll go home with Painter while I nail your roomie."

I blinked.

"You realize I'm totally going to warn her about you," I finally managed to say. He smiled, pure sin on a stick. Or would that be sin with a stick? *Heh.*

"I'm counting on it," he said. "She likes trouble—I can tell. It'll turn her on, challenge her. The more you warn her, the easier it'll be."

I frowned, trying to decide how that made me feel.

"Let's go," he said. "I'm hungry, and Em says the BBQ out here is incredible. I'll even buy you dinner. Sound good?"

I nodded, still confused. I wasn't sure how to deal with this, but he was right about one thing . . . fair BBQ was the shit, and damned if I wasn't hungry.

CHAPTER SIX

PAINTER

The fair sucked.

Taz had shown up with Melanie at his side, and I'd spent the last two hours wandering the exhibit tents, watching them and festering, because he was doing everything he could to fuck with me.

Cockwad.

Whenever she turned away, he'd thrust his hips toward her or pretend to grab her ass. Flick his tongue. Squeeze his dick. Nothing but a damned pervert. Hunter was in on it, too, taunting me quietly whenever he had the chance. My own brothers were fucking useless. Horse just rolled his eyes, and when we finally headed into the BBQ tent for dinner, Ruger pointed out that if I didn't have the balls to claim her, I should let it go.

God help me, if these fuckers were supposed to be my backup, I'd do better on my own. The night was fucking endless. I could give two shits about rodeo—thought it was decent entertainment, but I wouldn't be out here if it wasn't for Melanie. I kept trying to catch her eye, but she wouldn't look at me. I knew she was aware, though, because she kept blushing. Probably embarrassed about last night.

Fair enough . . . But the longer I watched her with Taz, the harder it was to keep my distance.

She deserved a man who was perfect, and that fucker didn't qualify.

At least the food was good. There were a hundred different places to eat around the fairgrounds, but the BBQ had to be the best. If I needed proof I was fucked in the head, it came when I reached the line. There was a pretty little thing ahead of me who kept bumping into me "accidentally." I'd be all over that if I weren't completely focused on Mel, and the fact that Taz couldn't keep his fucking hands off her.

Ten minutes later I headed toward the long tables set up outside the tent carrying a plate of ribs, potato salad, and corn bread. I found a spot at one end, where Horse sat down next to me, flanked by Marie. Ruger and his old lady, Sophie, sat across from us, leaving plenty of room for the others farther down. Soon Kit, Em, and Hunter joined us, and then Taz and Melanie sat next to them. The girls started laughing and giggling together as Jessica joined them.

She seemed to have hooked up with Hunter's best friend, Skid. She might not be my favorite, but she deserved better than that fuckwad. *Better keep an eye on her.* Looking away, I caught Horse checking out Jess and Skid, too. Then he caught my gaze and we shared a wordless conversation—Jess was young. We'd both be looking out for her. Taz stood up.

"Anyone want a drink?" he asked, staring right at me. "The ladies look thirsty—thought maybe I'd buy a round."

Oh, that asshole. He was trying to get Mel drunk again.

"I'm fine with water," she insisted, and I bit back a smile. *Suck it, cockwad. She's onto you.*

Dinner lasted way too long. Between Kit's nonstop mouth and Taz's little digs, I wasn't entirely sure I'd make it through. Then everyone scattered to hit the bathrooms after we cleared our plates.

Taz stood next to me—whistling happily—while we took a piss, and that's when I decided I'd had enough of his shit. As we walked out, I nodded at him to follow me behind the nearest display tent for a private word. Too bad it was the Kootenai County Sheriff's booth—not an ideal spot to murder a man. Shitty to be me.

"What kind of game are you playing?" I asked him, forcing my tone to stay steady and relaxed.

"Having fun, Brooks? I'm likin' that Mel girl. She's got a real nice pussy." Taz cracked his knuckles thoughtfully. "Later—you know, when I'm fuckin' her while you're making sweet love to your hand? I'll be sure to take a few notes, let you know how it goes."

A year ago I would've taken him down, regardless of the fact that only a canvas wall separated us from six cops. Prison had taught me self-control, though. Puck and I had been almost completely alone down in Cali—we couldn't afford luxuries like acting on our anger. Not if we wanted to live.

Now I used that hard-won self-control to hold my shit together.

"This ends now," I told him flatly, refusing to play his game. Taz raised a brow.

"This?"

"Don't be stupid, you know what I mean," I replied, tired of all the bullshit. "She's nothing to you, so when she comes back out, she's with me."

"How do you figure?"

I smiled slowly, reaching a hand down to touch the survival knife I always kept sheathed on my hip. "You touch her, I'll gut you here and now, in front of witnesses. You'll be dead and the peace between our clubs will end—all because you wouldn't drop a girl you don't give two shits about. That really how you want this to play out?"

His face sobered.

"You're bluffing. I know you're on probation—they'll send you back to jail, and we'd get you on the inside," he said slowly. I shrugged, almost hoping he'd call me on it. Not that I wanted to end my life rotting in a cell, but killing this fucker might be worth it.

"Maybe," I replied, offering him a sweet smile. "Guess there's really only one way for you to find out."

"You'd really start a war over this girl?"

I paused, considering. "Yup."

Taz shook his head slowly, holding up his hands in surrender. "Fuckin' have her. I'm after her roommate anyway. Just messin' with you, that's all."

I felt my shoulders relax, because I'd actually been ready to do it—I'd have killed him if he touched her again. *Jesus.*

"You should seek some professional help," Taz said, sounding almost concerned.

"Like a shrink?" I asked, biting back a laugh. "Yeah, I met one of those on the inside. We didn't get along all that well."

"I was thinkin' a good whore," he replied, smiling reluctantly. "You do get that a pussy's a pussy, right? Hot, wet, and tight's all that matters."

Fuck. Why'd he have to say that? Now I was thinking about her pussy, which I was 100 percent certain was primo in every way. My phone buzzed. I grabbed it, finding a text from Horse.

HORSE: All good? Everyones back by the food tables
ME: Be there in a sec

I looked at Taz again. "We good?"

He nodded.

"Sure, whatever," he said. "But seriously—you might want to go ahead and claim that girl. This kind of crazy can get dangerous, you pull it on the wrong guy. Only fair to let the rest of us know exactly where things stand ahead of time."

I frowned, because I wasn't ready to do that. I still wanted better for her. Someone nice, who'd work a steady job, maybe take her to Hawaii every other year. Wash her car on Saturday mornings. Unfortunately, every time I tried to picture that guy, he was dead at my feet.

Maybe I did have a complex.

By the time we reached the group, the rodeo was about to start. While I wasn't a huge fan, I couldn't deny there was something about seeing a guy go the full eight seconds on top of one of those big bulls. The rodeo queens weren't half bad in their tight jeans, either. I walked over toward Melanie, offering her a grim smile.

"Taz is busy," I told her, blatantly ignoring the fact that Taz was standing less than six feet from us, doing exactly jack shit. "You're with me the rest of the night."

She coughed, choking a little, and I gave her back a thump while the rest of the group watched, obviously enjoying our little drama.

"Don't you have your own lives to entertain you?" I asked, annoyed.

"Nope," Kit said, eyes wide. "Carry on."

Fucking devil girl.

Mel glared at her, flipping her off. Damn, that was sexy. Speakers crackled to life on a pole raised high above the fairgrounds.

"Folks, we'll be starting our rodeo in another fifteen minutes or so. That means now's the time to grab a drink or a snack and make your way to your seats."

Everyone turned toward the grandstands, thankfully losing interest in us. Taz was drifting toward Jessica, and I noted that Mel didn't seem particularly surprised by this development. Interesting. And if Taz hooked up with Jess, that was one less thing to worry about—Taz might be a dick, but he wasn't a fucking sociopath like Skid was.

We were too late to get really good seats, but there was still plenty of room toward the top of the covered bleachers. Ignoring her frowns, I deliberately herded Mel toward the end, then sat between her and the rest of the group, staring at her ass the entire time.

"I'm grabbing some beer," Horse announced. "Anyone?"

I nodded, lifting my hips enough to pull out my wallet, which I wore attached to a chain. I pulled out a couple bills and handed them over. Then Horse and Marie started back down the stairs toward the bar, along with Kit, who approached bringing booze to the masses with near religious zeal. That left a sizable gap between us and the rest of the group, which worked just fine for me.

"You know Taz is a player, right?" I told Mel, eyes on the arena where the rodeo queens and princesses rode around in circles, warming up their horses. She blushed, refusing to look at me. Yup, definitely still embarrassed about last night.

"It's really none of your business . . . but yes, I'm aware," she whispered. "I'll admit—I was drunk and stupid out at the Armory, but I'm sober now and normally I'm not a total idiot."

"I don't think you're an idiot," I said. "I just wanted to warn you."

"I think I got enough warning last night. I'm only here because Kit dragged me. She's evil."

My cock jumped at the memory of that "warning," and I took a deep breath, reminding myself that jumping a girl in public was probably a parole violation.

"Aren't you girls supposed to all be in this together?" I asked, pushing through the wave of lust. "And for the record, I think she's the devil incarnate. Been making my life a living hell for years, little witch."

Melanie gave a cute giggle, shooting me a shy look from under her eyelashes. "If that's the case, how did she get you out to the fair?"

I cleared my throat, not wanting to get into details. Damned if I'd admit anything.

"Doesn't matter," I said, looking back toward the arena. Where the fuck was Horse with the beer, anyway?

"Hey, I'm really sorry about last night," Mel said, so quietly I nearly missed it.

"What? No, don't worry about it," I told her, wishing I hadn't come down on her so hard. Fuck, and now I was thinking about coming and going down on her. I'd just been so damned horny and she'd been right there, on her knees in the grass like a thousand fantasies I'd beaten off to in the darkness . . . I'd had to do *something* to make it end, even if it meant hurting her.

"I was really drunk. I didn't mean to take advantage of you."

Fucking hell, I was a douche.

"You didn't take advantage of me," I said. "Let's just drop it. No harm, no foul."

"Okay," she whispered. Awkward silence fell between us again. I wanted to ask her about school, about how things were going with Jess and her living together . . . I also wanted to know if she'd kept dating that dickwad she'd written to me about—the one who wanted to get too serious too fast.

The same one I'd told her I thought she should give a shot, because I'm a fucking masochist.

"Beer," Horse said, handing me two aluminum bottles of Bud. "Enjoy."

He dropped down next to me, and I glanced over to see Marie snuggling into his side. Christ, but they were cute together. Made me want to vomit. I twisted off a cap and handed the bottle over to Mel. She looked at me, surprised.

"I was super drunk last night," she reminded me. "I thought you were pissed about that."

Oh, I'd been pissed, all right. Mostly pissed about Taz touching what belonged to me, except she didn't belong to me and she never would. I opened my own drink and sucked it down.

"Suit yourself," I said, shrugging. "I don't care either way."

Her face closed up and she looked away. *Stop being such a dick, dumbass.* I reached over, catching her hand. I'd meant to give her a reassuring little squeeze or some stupid shit. Somehow the touch of her skin short-circuited my brain, though. She felt warm and soft. I wanted to crawl inside her, and not in the way you think, you fucking pervert.

Okay, so maybe I wanted to do *that*, too.

"I'm sorry," I told her, the words soft. "I don't give a shit either way if you drink the beer, Mel, that's all I meant. I'm a jackass, but I'm not actively trying to make tonight bad for you."

She gave me a faint, almost trembling smile as her fingers wrapped around mine, giving a little squeeze, which I swear I felt all the way to my cock.

The loudspeakers crackled to life.

"Please stand for Coeur d'Alene's own Josina Bradley, who will be singing the national anthem," the announcer said as riders started pouring into the arena at full gallop, American flags streaming from staffs braced against their stirrups. All around us cowboy hats came off as the troupe of girls on horses—young rodeo queens and princesses—came to a halt in a long line in the center, pinwheeling toward the audience with as much precision as the club did when we rode in a pack.

The music started, and I held Melanie's hand—*friends hold hands, right?*—through the whole song, and then through the Canadian national anthem that followed. All around us people were cheering but we stayed quiet. I suppose I could tell you all about how hard it was not to pop a boner in front of everyone or all the different ways I was imagining fucking her. Right here, right now. Under the bleachers. In the bathroom.

In the sheriff's tent . . . *Nice.*

It was all true, of course. But that's not what stands out to me the most. More than anything, I remember standing next to her, holding her hand. Smelling her and knowing that she was safe and perfect and beautiful.

And for tonight, she was all mine.

MELANIE

It felt like a dream, just sitting next to Painter, holding his hand while we watched the rodeo. I was still embarrassed over what'd happened out at the Armory, of course. But his presence seemed to fulfill that strange craving I'd felt from the moment I'd met him—like an aching itch inside me was finally satisfied. (Well, not totally satisfied, but you know what I mean.)

On the far side of him, all the club people were laughing and talking and cheering. We were quiet. I don't know about him, but I was scared to say the wrong thing, to break this weird spell that had fallen over us . . . so I sat back to watch the roping and the barrel racing, savoring every second in his presence. Didn't hurt that the side of Painter's leg pressed against the side of mine, every inch of it hot and hard and so close I could've just reached out and dug my fingers in deep, if I'd had the nerve. Somehow I managed to hold off—I'd already humiliated myself once in the last twenty-four hours.

Still, when Painter wrapped his arm around me, I told myself that I might as well enjoy it, seeing as it'd gotten dark and was starting to get cold. (Okay, so it was at least eighty-five degrees and I was sweltering, but what's a woman to do under those kinds of circumstances?)

The rodeo was winding down when his fingers started moving across my shoulder. I could smell him all around me—male sweat, which was weirdly sexy. Leather from his cut. A hint of beer, although not too much. He'd only had a couple over the course of the night.

I wanted to lean over and sniff his neck like a creeper.

The Devil's Jacks and Reapers who'd come with us had gotten louder with time, although not so much that they were obnoxious. I'd seen the way people shied away from us, though. I understood why, too. I still remembered how I'd felt the first time I'd seen London with Reese—he'd looked like a monster to me. Then the monster had taken me in and given me a home, so I guess I couldn't exactly point fingers.

My head had fallen to Painter's shoulder, and I found myself drifting as he continued to rub my arm. Somehow along the way, my hand fell to his thigh despite my best intentions. I wasn't feeling him up, exactly, but I was definitely feeling him. Strong, thick muscles tensed beneath my touch. And I do mean tensed—he wasn't relaxed at all. Not even a little. Painter was all coiled strength and power just waiting to break free in a burst of violence or . . . something. Best not to think about that.

God, but I wanted him.

By the time the bull riding started, I'd fallen into a Painter-induced haze. I watched lazily as big Dodge Ram trucks pulled out into the arena to drop off the barrel for the rodeo clown.

"Ladies and gentlemen, now is the time you've all been waiting for—does anyone like bull riding?" asked the announcer.

The crowd went crazy, cheering as loud music poured through the speakers.

"We always save the best for last here at the North Idaho Rodeo, and tonight you'll see ten men brave the most dangerous eight seconds in all of sports. First up is James Lynch, all the way from Weezer, Idaho. This is his third year on the circuit, and he's looking to take home a prize tonight. Feel like giving him a little encouragement?"

All around us, people shouted again as the music got louder. I sat up a little straighter, watching as two men came out to stand on either side of a gate against the back fence, loose-limbed and ready for action. One of them looked almost familiar, although it was hard to tell from so far away. Seconds later the gate opened, and the bull exploded out. Lynch held on tight to the ropes, one hand held high in the air as the massive animal tried to buck him off. I found myself forgetting to breathe as eight of the longest seconds in history ticked slowly by, counting down on the big display board.

He'd almost made it when the bull twisted, and then he was flying through the air. One of the men who'd been flanking the gate darted in between the bull and the fallen rider, using his body to distract the beast. The other grabbed the cowboy, pulling him to his feet.

Holy shit.

Lynch ran for the fence, jumping up against the metal bars as men waiting on the other side pulled him over. Riders raced into the arena toward the bull, chasing it toward the far gate.

The whole thing had taken maybe twenty seconds, tops.

"Better luck next time, James," the announcer said. "Now let's take a moment to put our hands together for our bullfighters this evening, folks. You saw them in action just now—these athletes have a tough job out here, because it's up to them to protect our cowboys once they hit the dirt. They do it the hard way, too. Tonight is a special night for one of them . . . He's playing for his hometown crowd for the first time this weekend. Chase McKinney is a Coeur d'Alene boy, born and raised right here in this community. Chase, how does it feel to be here tonight?"

Around me people exploded in excitement as one of the bullfighters raised a hand, waving at the grandstands before giving a thumbs-up toward the announcer. No wonder he looked familiar—

he'd been a few years ahead of me in high school. Not that I really knew him, but I'd seen him around. Pretty sure he'd been a senior when I was a freshman . . . Past Painter, I saw both Em and Kit on their feet, hooting and shouting like crazed monkeys.

"Next up is Gordo Gallagher, an experienced bullrider down from Calgary, Alberta," continued the announcer as Chase moved back toward the gate. "He's looking for points and prize money, and it'd sure be nice if he could go home with both. Give him a warm North Idaho welcome!"

We all cheered again, and then I watched as one bullrider after the next tried to hold on for the full time period. Only about half of them made it, which meant the bullfighters were busy. Over and over, they jumped between the bulls and their riders, protecting the cowboys with their bodies. Why the hell would someone do that to themselves on purpose?

Craziness.

Of course, I was going a little crazy myself as Painter ran his fingers across my shoulders and down my arms, all the while pressing his leg against mine. By the final ride of the night, I'd fallen into a warm haze of desire that just wouldn't go away.

"Ladies and gentlemen, let's put our hands together for Cary Hull," said the announcer. "We've saved the best for last, as Cary was our top prize winner during last year's rodeo. From there he went on to become a circuit finalist. He's been patiently waiting all evening to show you what he's got."

Down in the arena, Hull had climbed up and over the chute, ready to drop onto the bull for his ride. Then the horn sounded and the pair burst out into the center of the arena.

At first I didn't realize anything was wrong—bulls are supposed to buck at a rodeo. But this one seemed wilder, crazier than any of the others. I mean, his eyes weren't literally glowing red—no ominous chanting—but that thing was scary. The cowboy was holding on for his life, flanked on either side by Chase and the other bullfighter, light on their feet as they tried to anticipate the beast's next move.

That's when things fell to shit.

Without warning, the bull bucked higher than I'd ever seen. So high it hardly seemed real. The rider's body flew free, turning through the air above him. That's when he should've launched off but he didn't. The bull bucked again, and this time the cowboy flopped along the side of him, which seemed to piss him off even more.

Up to that point, I'd assumed that Hull was holding on out of sheer stubborn badassery. Now I could see he was caught, flopping helplessly as the bull tried to kill him. The crowd fell silent as the monster bucked backward—higher this time—shying away from the fighters desperately flanking him. Chase ran along the side, trying to reach the rider while his partner distracted the animal.

It didn't work.

In an instant, the bull spun to charge Chase. As the beast lowered its head for a killing blow, Chase reached out and caught its horns, throwing himself up and over its back in a move I couldn't quite believe was humanly possible. He hit the animal hard—sideways across the ridge of its spine—somehow catching the rope holding the cowboy prisoner. We all watched, horrified, as the beast bucked again.

Hull broke free, bouncing as he hit the ground.

Enraged, the bull flew up and backward, twisting midair to land heavily on its side.

Right on top of Chase.

CHAPTER SEVEN

The bullfighter was dead.

He *had* to be dead—no human could possibly survive something like that.

We watched in horror and shock as the bull struggled to its feet, then turned on him, lying still in the dirt. In an instant, the other bullfighter darted between them, catching the beast's attention. The big head swiveled as the man took off across the arena, mere feet ahead of the deadly horns, leaping high as he hit the metal barrier. Hands reached out to catch him, jerking him up and over the side.

He'd distracted the monster, but only for an instant. Now it turned back toward Chase's limp body, snorting and stomping. The crowd grew silent, and directly below me a mother pulled a toddler into her lap, forcing his head into her chest so he wouldn't see. If by some miracle Chase had survived the first attack, there was no way he'd get through this one.

That's when the rodeo clown leapt into action.

For most of the evening, he'd been working the crowd with the announcer, joking and doing tricks between events, flirting with the girls and generally making a nuisance of himself. Now the clown was deadly serious despite his bright, floppy clothes and the paint covering his face. He sprinted at the bull, flapping and shouting, taunting it until it turned toward him.

Toward him, but away from Chase.

The bull charged, and now the clown was off again, leading the beast into the center of the arena. He reached the barrel and jumped into it seconds before the bull thundered into it with a bellow, sending the barrel rolling. Then riders tore by, chasing the bull away from the trapped clown. The bull tried to turn back, but no matter what direction he went, the cowboys were waiting.

I focused on Chase, lying on the ground, limp and still. Beyond him was Hull, rolling in obvious agony, but clearly very much alive. EMTs were running out onto the dirt now, as the riders formed a living wall between the animal and its victims. They herded the bull toward the far end of the arena, where a gate swung open, creating a safe path. It charged through and I hoped to hell they were ready for it back there—enough people had been injured already. Then an ambulance pulled in from the other side, and the announcer's voice came over the loudspeaker.

"Ladies and gentlemen, that was our final ride of the night. Normally we'd announce winners and hand out the prizes, but the North Idaho Rodeo officials have decided that under the circumstances, it's best to end the event at this time. I've been told that fair organizers will announce updates on Chase McKinney's condition as they're available. We'll be clearing the arena shortly. Until then, please keep all our rodeo athletes in your thoughts and prayers."

I watched silently as the EMTs worked over Chase. Hull was already strapped to a backboard and they were lifting him into an ambulance. Unlike the bullfighter, he was clearly alive and aware of what was going on around him. Painter shifted next to me, and I realized I'd burrowed against him, digging my fingernails into his thigh.

"Sorry," I whispered, loosening my grip. I gave his leg a little rub to make it feel better. His hand caught mine, stilling it—shit, I'd been all but massaging him just inches away from his dick. Classy.

"Do you think he'll live?" I asked Painter quietly. He squeezed me tighter.

"Dunno," he said. "Guess we'll have wait and see."

"Ladies and gentlemen, we'd ask that you leave now. Normally I'd say I hope you enjoyed the show, but instead I'll ask you again to keep Chase and his family in your prayers. God bless each and every one of you, and God bless the cowboys and cowgirls who came out tonight."

It took about forty-five minutes to make our way out of the grandstands and back to the bikes. The crowds were quiet for the most part. Em and Kit held each other's hands tight, whispering to each other as they checked their phones.

When we finally made our way out of the stands and into the main fairgrounds, Hunter came up to me and Painter, the two men staring each other down. For a minute I was worried, because there was obvious tension between them.

"You'll get her home?" Hunter finally asked Painter, nodding toward me. "She rode here with Taz, but I think he's giving Jessica a ride. Em and Kit want to go to the hospital—I guess there's going to be a candlelight vigil. Em says she didn't know him well, but he went to school with Kit and she's pretty upset."

"I've got her," Painter said, squeezing my hand. "You headed to the hospital, too?"

Hunter nodded tightly, glancing toward Kit with a frown. "Gonna be a long night, I think."

I shivered, thinking about Chase lying in the dust. I'd seen him around school, but couldn't remember ever talking to him.

"Yeah," Painter agreed. "Get going—I'll make sure Mel is okay. No worries, okay?"

Hunter nodded, eyes flicking across me as he turned back to Em and her sister. "Sure thing."

I watched him walk away, leaning in close to Painter.

"Do you want to go to the vigil, too?" he asked. I considered the question.

"No," I said finally. "It would feel fake. I didn't really know him . . . But I definitely want to get away from here. There's too many people here who didn't see the rodeo, and they're all having fun and going on rides. It doesn't feel right."

"Let's say good-bye, then."

He kept hold of my hand while we made the rounds of his club brothers and their old ladies, almost like we were a real couple. It should've felt awkward, but it didn't. Jess was clinging to Taz, whispering to him quietly. When I hugged her good-bye, she whispered in my ear, "Okay if I bring him to the house tonight?"

Wasn't sure how I felt about that—of course, she had every right to bring someone home. I just hoped she wasn't doing something stupid.

"You sure?" I whispered back. "I thought you were happy just keeping things simple."

"I don't want to be alone right now," she replied, squeezing me tight. Yeah, I could understand that. Too bad I didn't have anyone interested in going home with *me*.

I kept my arms wrapped tight around Painter as we rode back downtown. He smelled good and he felt good . . . safe, somehow. Under normal circumstances, I'd be all over him, but right now I was too busy picturing Chase's limp body in the dirt—would he live?

I'd never seen anyone die before.

We turned down my street and I braced myself to say good night. I had no idea where we stood or even whether I'd see Painter again. Had tonight changed things? Obviously he wasn't pretending we weren't friends anymore . . . but exactly what were we supposed to be?

Then I saw Taz's bike parked in front of the house. Of all nights for Jess to abandon her celibate streak, why now? I needed to talk to someone and she was unavailable . . . Painter rolled to a stop, and I'd started to swing my leg over the bike when he put a hand on my thigh.

"Taz gonna be there for a while?" he asked, his voice low and quiet.

"Yeah, Jess said she'd invited him to stay over," I replied, feeling uncomfortable. He frowned.

"Feel like a ride? I'm not ready to call it a night."

"That sounds really good," I whispered. Maybe I wasn't the only one who didn't want to be alone.

"Hold on," he said. "It's a beautiful night, despite what happened. We should try to make the best of it."

We headed south, down toward Moscow and then turned off at Plummer to ride around the south end of the lake. I had no idea how late it was when he slowed the bike and pulled into a gravel parking lot surrounded by trees. The big Harley's engine died, leaving us alone with the soft chirping of crickets and frogs.

"You wanna go down to the water?" he asked. "It's right through the trees."

"Sure."

I slipped off the bike, and we walked down a grassy slope to a long, sandy beach nestled among the trees. The moon shined bright, painting a trail of silver across the lake's gentle waves. Here and there, dark shapes broke the water. Took me a minute to figure out what they were—floating logs.

"You want to sit for a while, watch the stars?" Painter asked. I looked around, spotting a patch of grass sloping down toward the sand that seemed perfect.

"How about there?" I asked him. Silently we settled ourselves, close to each other without touching—I could feel him, though. Feel his heat and his presence and the unbreakable tension that ran between us all the time, whether we chose to acknowledge it or not. "I've never seen anything like that. I don't see how a person can live through a bull jumping on them."

He didn't answer for a minute. "People can live through a hell of a lot. Didn't look promising, though."

There wasn't much emotion in his voice, which threw me. My

mind was swimming, images from the rodeo running through my head over and over again. I'd assumed Painter was as upset as I was . . . that maybe he needed to talk, too.

"You aren't bothered by it?" I asked, my voice soft.

"I've seen a lot of shit, some of it not so good. I don't take it lightly and I don't enjoy seeing a man suffer, but you can't afford to get involved emotionally."

"You mean, in prison?"

"Yeah," he said after a minute. "In prison."

Neither of us spoke for a moment. I stared up at the stars, watching as a satellite blinked its way across the sky.

"And in the club," he added softly. "Bad shit happens there, too. Although so far nobody's started dropping bulls on their enemies."

The words caught me off guard, and a little giggle burst through. I bit my cheek, feeling awful. "I can't believe I laughed at that."

"It's okay—you have to laugh when things fall apart. Otherwise you'll go crazy. Better not to think about it too much, at least that's how I do it."

Rolling over, I leaned up on my elbow to stare at him.

"So you just turn off your brain when something bothers you?" I asked, studying his face in the moonlight. His features were softened by the shadows, leaving him handsome but less intimidating than usual. He met my gaze, giving away nothing. "That must be nice—wish I could do that. Sometimes I lie awake in bed for hours, wondering why my mom took off and left me."

"I keep my attention focused where it needs to be focused," he replied, reaching up to touch the side of my face. It took everything I had not to turn toward his hand, rub against him like a cat. I felt breathless, expectant . . . Hold on. Why was he touching me like this? It didn't make sense—he'd made it damned clear he didn't want anything more than friendship.

"You shouldn't be doing that," I whispered. "We're just friends, remember? You made that very clear last night."

"Friends can touch," he whispered back. The words hung between us, teasing me. I wanted to lean over and kiss him. Crawl on top of him and grind and writhe and hump and do things I was relatively sure qualified as molestation in the fine state of Idaho. "Stop looking at me like that."

"Like what?" I asked.

"Like you want to . . ."

He stopped talking, licking his lips as his eyes drifted to mine. He was going to kiss me. My eyes started to flutter closed. Then his phone chimed, breaking the spell.

Painter blinked—he'd been as lost in the moment as I was.

"I should check that," he said. "Might be an update on Chase."

Chase. How could I have forgotten about Chase? A man was dying, yet all I could think about was getting laid. A man I'd gone to school with. What was wrong with me?

I flopped back as Painter pulled out his phone, the screen obscenely bright in the darkness.

"Group text from Em," he said. "He's alive. There's about three hundred people at the vigil so far, and more showing up every minute. He's in surgery."

I shivered, trying to imagine what his family was going through. How awful would it be, sitting and waiting to hear if the man you cared about was dying? *How would you feel if it was Painter?* The thought chilled me, and I closed my eyes, willing it to disappear.

"You cold?" he asked. "Come here. I'll keep you warm."

I wasn't cold, and touching him was a very bad idea. Whatever this thing was between us, touching wouldn't help. But then I imagined the warmth of his body around mine. The strength of his arms, not to mention that broad chest. I wanted it. I wanted it *so bad*.

And he did make the offer . . .

"Thanks," I whispered, sliding toward him. Seconds later I was tucked against Painter's side, one arm under my head. My body had turned into his, and there wasn't an easy place to hold my arm. I shifted awkwardly, and then he was catching my hand and resting it on his chest, right next to his own.

Our fingers weren't touching, but they would be if I slid my pinkie over half an inch.

Painter's head tilted toward mine—was he smelling my hair? Oh

God, I think he was. This was going to kill me. My leg shifted rest-lessly, because I wanted to lay it over him and straddle his thigh. I forced it to be still instead. Now what? I needed to make some con-versation or something, because this was too weird and stressful.

"So are things good, now that you're back?" I asked. "How's the work situation? You'd mentioned that they were holding a job for you at the body shop."

"It's all good. I do the custom design there," he said. "You know, bikes and cars and shit like that. A lot of it's for guys in clubs, but we get RUBs in there, too—city types who play biker on the week-ends, looking to dress up their rides. Also a lot of rich fuckers who want hot rods. I've done some paintings of motorcycles and cars that are up on the walls—people seem to like 'em. Got two guys waiting for me to do portraits of theirs. Right now I'm workin' on something for the club, though. Sort of a happy-to-be-home-again present for the Armory."

"Do you ever get pissed off about what happened?" I asked.

"At who?"

"The club—I mean, I don't totally understand how you ended up getting arrested down in California, but obviously it had some-thing to do with the Reapers. Do you ever get pissed that you were put in that position?"

He didn't answer right away, and I wondered if I'd overstepped with my question. I'd just opened my mouth to apologize when he spoke again, answering.

"Yes and no," he said. "I hate the fact that something needed to be fixed and I took a hit for it. But I'm not pissed at my brothers. They did their part, I did mine. Shitty luck that I got caught, but that's just the game, you know? Could've been any of us."

I pondered his words.

"So you'd do it again?"

"Well, I'd be more careful about following the speed limit," he said, giving a low laugh. "Me and Puck only got caught because we were doing forty in a twenty-five zone. Cop pulled us over and then they found the guns. But other than that? Yeah, I'd do it again. It needed to happen, and your girl Jess wouldn't be alive today if we hadn't done it. You think the rest of her life was worth a year of mine?"

Holy shit.

"So you were down there to save her?" I asked. "I mean, I sort of suspected something, but she's never really explained what happened. Nobody will talk about it."

Painter sighed.

"I'm too comfortable around you," he admitted. "Feels safe, but I need to watch my fuckin' mouth. Already said too much. I regret getting caught, nothing more. It is what it is. Just hope I never have to go back."

"What do you mean, go back?" I asked, stiffening. "You don't go *back*—they let you out. You've done your time."

He gave a laugh, and I felt his arm rise, rubbing across my back to soothe me. "No worries, babe. I'm not planning on it. But I'm on parole, remember? That means they let me out early, on the understanding that I'll play nice and make good choices. They catch me so much as running a red light, my ass is in a cell again. That's all."

I pushed against his chest, raising up to see his face. I'd never considered that he might go back inside—just the thought made me feel almost panicky.

"You've got to watch yourself," I told him, dead serious. "Is the club making you do things that might land you in prison? You don't have to do what they say, Painter."

He grinned at me, rubbing my back as he shook his head.

"Nice to know you care," he said. "But they don't *make* me do anything, Mel. I'm a big boy—I can take care of myself. It's not like that."

"Like what?"

"I'm not some little pawn for them to play with. Anything I do is by my choice. I know there's clubs out there where men blindly follow orders and get sacrificed like chum. But the Reapers are my brothers—we stand up for each other, we vote on everything, and if I didn't want to be here, I wouldn't be. I'm a Reaper, too, you know. This is my world. I'm proud of this patch and I'd do anything to protect it."

His eyes bored into mine, cold and hard. Even the hand around my back tightened, like he was bracing for action.

"But you're careful, right?" I asked. Painter nodded.

"Yeah, of course I'm careful," he said. "But I'm also one of the younger full-patch members, and I don't have a family or anything. When there's shit that needs doing, I volunteer. All the brothers do, but some of us got less to lose than others."

I closed my eyes against the painful clenching deep inside of me, laying my head back down so I wouldn't have to look at him.

"You mean the guys with old ladies?" I asked, already knowing what the answer had to be.

"Old ladies, families . . . The guys with kids do their part, no question. But I'm not gonna stand back and watch while a brother with that kind of responsibility takes risks he doesn't need to. And a lot of the guys do work that's important—they'd never pussy out of anything, but we can't just replace them if something happens. Horse is a fuckin' genius with money, and Ruger can build anything. We need those skills. It's my job to protect the club, and part of that's protecting the brothers who keep the club alive."

"That's crazy," I said. "What about *your* life? Doesn't that matter?"

"The club is my life, Mel."

Gee, brainwashed much? His hand rubbed me soothingly as he spoke, which sucked because I wanted to hit him or yell at him or at the very least give him a stern lecture, although I don't know what it would be about. Maybe the top five reasons jail sucks?

But I guess he already knew that a lot better than I did.

Instead I settled into his form, forcing myself not to think about what he'd said—there were plenty of other things to focus on. The warm night air. The frogs. The way his hand felt, still rubbing up and down my back, soothing and distracting. Then his fingers caught on the bottom of my tank top, sliding it up just a couple inches until I felt his skin bare against mine. My stomach twisted.

"Why are you doing this?" I asked, feeling almost desperate.

"Doing what?"

"Touching me. You're sending some seriously mixed signals for a guy who's not interested."

He froze, the hand on his chest reaching to catch mine.

"I never said I wasn't interested," he replied, his voice quiet with a hint of strain. "I said you deserved better."

"God, you're so fucking frustrating," I said, pushing myself up to glare at him. "You ignored me when you got out, you made me come last night, and now you're sticking your hand up my shirt while you're telling me I deserve better. Have you ever considered seeing a shrink? Because I think you could use one."

He gave a low chuckle, his hand sliding my shirt back down across the small of my back.

"No, but earlier tonight someone else told me I should talk to a professional."

"Well maybe you should," I huffed, glaring at him. "Because you're playing games and that's not very nice."

"I've never pretended to be nice," he said, his voice hardening. "And I've never promised you anything, Mel. Remember that. Nobody made you come riding with me tonight—not like I held a gun to your head. What the fuck do you want from me?"

"The truth," I snapped. "Let's start with that. What the hell do *you* want from *me*?"

He gave a low, dark laugh.

"We're not going there."

"Oh yeah, we are," I informed him, poking his chest with a finger. "Because I'm done playing mind games with you—we're hashing this out, here and now. Otherwise you're taking me home. Or I can call someone and get a ride."

Painter's eyes narrowed, then his hand caught mine, holding it tight.

"You're not calling anyone—I'll take you home when I'm ready. And you think you want answers? How's this for a fucking answer. I want *this*."

He dragged my hand down his stomach toward the front of his

pants. My pulse rate rose. Then he was pushing my hand down across the length of his cock, which was hard and ready. His hips lifted under my touch and his fingers squeezed around mine, gripping himself tight.

Need wrenched through me.

"What I want is to fuck you," he said, his voice a harsh, intense whisper. "I want to fuck your pussy, I want to fuck your face, and I've given some serious thought to fucking your ass, too. I want to lock you up and play with you . . . Sometimes I think about owning you, and what I'd do if you tried to get away. Christ, you have no idea."

He pushed my palm down hard across the top of his erection, hips twisting under my touch. His other hand reached down to catch my butt, digging in deep. My leg went up and over him, which was perfect because it brought my clit into contact with his thigh.

God, why were we wearing so many clothes?

"Oh crap," I whispered, dropping my head against his shoulder as his fingers worked down between my ass cheeks, finding the crotch of my pants. Why hadn't I kept my mouth shut? Wait, fuck that. *Why the hell hadn't I worn a skirt?*

The whole time, he kept my fingers wrapped around his dick, jacking him slowly through the fabric while his fingers danced between my legs. His hands were big, strong, working me as the world started spinning. Then his hand slipped off mine, coming up to catch the back of my head, forcing me to meet his gaze.

"Here's the ugly truth, though," he whispered. "I'll want all of that—all of *you*—for about a week. Then I'll get busy or bored or whatever, and I'll stop calling you. That's how I am, Mel. I'm the guy who doesn't call and I don't even regret it, because I truly don't give a shit who I hurt. Except for some fucked-up reason, I care about you. If some guy treated you the way I dream about every night, I'd kill him. I'm not into suicide, so that means we can't go there. Got it?"

Our hands had stopped moving as he spoke, although his cock still pulsed under my hand. His fingers dug into my ass, holding me captive against his body even as I processed his words.

"You'd really do that to me?"

Painter's mouth tightened.

"Yeah, Mel. I'd really do that to you. We'd have a few great days, maybe a week. Then I'd get bored and dump you, because that's who I am. But you're the only female friend I've ever had and I actually give a fuck about you, so I don't want to hurt you like that. Is that such a terrible thing?"

My breath caught, torn between the rush of joy at hearing us called friends and utter, pissed-off disgust that he'd assume he had the power to break me. I opted to run with the angry disgust—far more empowering.

"You know what?" I said. "I get that we don't have a long-term romantic relationship ahead of us . . . but don't treat me like a child. I'm an adult and I can make my own decisions. If I get hurt, that's on me, not you. You don't have that kind of power, asshole."

Painter's eyes widened, and a slow smile crept across his mouth, utterly confusing me.

"God, you're amazing," he said, loosening his grip on my hair. "I need you, Mel. I need you way too much as a friend to risk it. I know I've done a truly shitty job trying to communicate with you about this, but if you had any idea how important you are to me . . . Christ, you're one of the few things that kept me sane inside. Thinking about you, getting your letters. We gotta find a way, babe. We can't do this."

"I hate men," I muttered, rolling off him and onto my back, glaring at the sky. How could one guy be so evil and so sweet at the same time? Because he *was* sweet. I swear, my heart was melting even while I wanted to strangle him.

I wasn't ready to forgive him, though. Not yet.

"And take your fucking arm out from under my head. Cuddling is for closers."

CHAPTER EIGHT

PAINTER

The ride back to town took forever, every minute torture because Mel was wrapped tight around my body, totally fuckable and completely off-limits.

Sometimes I wished I didn't know myself so well. It would be easy to lie, to pretend that she'd be different from the others. But she wouldn't be, and hating myself for who I was wouldn't change the endgame here. If I wanted her in my life longer than a few weeks, I couldn't fuck her. This was my reality.

By the time we reached town, I was still utterly resolved to keep my hands off her . . . but Taz was at her place, and I didn't trust that asshole for shit. That's why I took her back to my apartment instead . . . and you can shut right the fuck up about that.

I already know I'm a douche.

"Figured you wouldn't want to be alone tonight," I said, cutting the engine. Mel slowly unpeeled herself from my body, sliding off the bike. I waited for her to protest, maybe tear into me because I hadn't taken her home. Instead she surprised me with a tentative smile.

Guess she'd had enough thinking time on the ride back to get over her snit.

"Thanks. I wasn't looking forward to dealing with Jess and Taz crawling all over each other. I don't know about him, but she's a screamer."

The words fell between us like a brick, because I would know, wouldn't I? Except I didn't, because Jess's mouth had been full the entire time we'd . . . Oh *fuck*. This wasn't good.

"Look—"

"I know—"

I coughed as Mel gave a nervous laugh, looking anywhere but at me.

"Let's get it out there, once and for all," I said, deciding it was inevitable. I swung my leg off the Harley and started toward the garage's side door, reaching for my keys.

"Get what 'out there'?" she asked. I turned to look at her, raising a brow. It was hard to tell in the dim glow of the porch light, but I think she was embarrassed. Whatever. We had enough shit to figure out already, we didn't need London's niece coming between us, too.

"You know—me and Jess. I'll tell you what happened, because you're obviously wondering. Didn't she tell you the details?"

"Um, not really," she admitted, frowning. I opened the door, reaching for the cord next to it to turn on the lights. I found the switch and the room flooded from the six work lights I'd hung along the ceiling. "I know part of it, but I'm not sure that I want to know the rest. It's kind of—oh, wow . . ."

She stepped inside, looking around my studio space. Lining the walls were narrow workbenches, one side covered with motorcycle parts and the other with my art supplies. There was the mural I'd started for the Armory there, but I'd forgotten about another half-done painting I'd leaned against the wall. I'd been working on it when I got arrested. It wasn't in the greatest condition (the girls had done their best, but they hadn't known how to handle it), and I was trying to decide whether to toss it or not.

Now I watched as Mel walked over to study it, eyes wide. I came up behind her and she glanced back at me.

"You're good."

I laughed. "Don't sound so surprised. I do this shit for a living, you know."

She gave a rueful smile.

"Sorry. I guess I thought you painted flames on bikes and stuff like that, but this is real art. How did you learn how to do it?"

"I picked things up here and there," I said. "Although for the record, depending on the design, what you see on motorcycles is real art, too. Not just anyone can do that."

"Sorry," she said. "Didn't mean to insult anyone."

"No worries, I understand. Just wanted to clarify," I said, wondering what she'd look like naked and covered in paint. Pretty fuckin' good, probably. "So I took a bunch of art classes when I was in juvie. They were pretty basic, but the teachers always seemed to reach out to me—I learned a lot from them. Then I took some more classes when I got out. I mostly just sketched down in Cali. They didn't have art classes or anything."

"Well I really like them," she said, and I felt my pride swell. Okay, *something* was swollen—no need to get into specifics.

"Thanks," I told her, heading toward the stairs. "My place is up here. It's nothing fancy, but it's quiet."

I hadn't had the apartment long enough to get it truly dirty, thank fuck. Not that I worried too much about impressing anyone, but for some reason I didn't want her thinking I was a total pig.

"So, this is it," I said, flipping on the light. Mel looked around, and I wondered what she thought. It wasn't big—just a small living room and kitchenette under the eaves. There was a separate bedroom and bathroom behind us, too, but considering I'd been living in an eight-by-ten cell for the last year with two other guys, it felt like a palace to me. "The studio space below is what really sold me . . ."

"It's great," she said, turning back toward me with that shy smile that went straight to my cock. "I mean, it's a dump, but it's yours and I like it."

I burst out laughing and she joined me, wandering over to sit down on the couch.

"Nice," she said, running her hands across the faded, dirt-brown upholstery. "Vintage. I'm pretty sure I saw this at the Idaho Youth Ranch thrift shop last week."

"I will neither confirm nor deny that. You want something to drink? I have water and beer."

"How about a beer?" she said. I grabbed a couple cold ones and came back to sit next to her on the couch. It felt good to have her here. Good and weird and wrong, all at the same time.

"You want to watch a movie or something?" she asked, nodding toward the TV. I had a decent one, too. Giant-ass flat-screen—homecoming present from the club.

"Sure," I said, reaching for the remote. I didn't have cable, but Ruger had set up some kind of box thingie for me so I could stream stuff. "Whatcha in the mood for?"

"Not horror," she said quickly, and I laughed again, remembering that first evening I'd spent with her at Pic's house. She'd been so young and scared and vulnerable . . . I'd wanted to eat her up.

I still wanted to eat her.

"I can't believe that you and Puck were supposed to be watching over me, and then you put in a slasher movie. That's not how you make a girl feel safe."

"No horror," I agreed, although the thought of holding her for a couple hours while she was scared shitless appealed way more than it should. *Watch it, asshole.* "How about *Star Wars*?"

"You like *Star Wars*?"

I shrugged. "Everyone likes *Star Wars*. You know, I'm pretty damned sure Han Solo was a biker."

She giggled. "A space biker?"

"See, when you say it like that it sounds stupid."

"I wanted to be Princess Leia. She's badass," Mel said, taking a deep drink of her beer. I watched as her lips wrapped around the neck, her throat swallowing. That was a little too sexy for my comfort. She set the beer down on the coffee table with a clink, then let loose with the biggest burp I'd ever heard.

"Fucking hell," I said, stunned. "I didn't think girls could burp like that. Shit. Impressive, Mel. Very impressive."

She grinned.

"We're *friends*," she told me. "And friends don't need to worry about this stuff. Let me guess—you've never had a female friend before?"

"Not really," I admitted. "I think I'm a little scared."

Scared and turned on, which was unfortunate.

"You should be. I can do the whole alphabet."

Damn. I kinda wanted to see that.

"So, we watching that movie or not?" she asked.

"Um, watching it," I said, flipping through the search options to find *Star Wars*. I hit play, leaning back against the couch as words started scrolling across the screen. Mel was less than six inches from me. Close enough to reach over, shove my hands into her hair, and kiss the hell out of her.

Instead I just sat there, horny as hell, watching Luke Skywalker whine about power converters.

"Hey, you okay?" she asked.

"Fuckin' great."

MELANIE

The sunlight hurt my eyes.

I blinked, trying to remember where I was, because I definitely wasn't home in my room. The bed felt weird, and the water-stained ceiling above me wasn't familiar, either. I turned my head to find Painter sleeping next to me, his face just inches from mine, and it all came back.

He looked softer asleep.

I mean, he was still the same big bad biker, but there was nothing mocking or calculating on his face right now. Not only that, he looked young. He was older than me, but not by much, and right now he could almost pass for a high school student.

My eyes trailed down, and sadly I discovered he was still fully clothed. So was I, apparently, because my underwire was poking me something fierce. Also needed to pee in a major way. This was a problem, because if I moved, Painter would wake up and turn back into a scary biker on me.

I wanted to reach out and trace his face with my finger, feel the little bristles of his morning beard. But we were friend-zoned, and despite what we'd pretended last night, in the friend zone people don't touch like that.

His eyes opened.

"Hey," I said.

"Hey."

We stared at each other for a few seconds, staying quiet.

"You sleep okay?" he asked. "I carried you in here, figured you'd be uncomfortable on the couch. Then I crashed here, too, because that couch is shit. Hope you don't mind."

"No, it's all good," I said, willing myself to make the best of things. So maybe we weren't meant to be a couple. Didn't mean I'd stopped liking him as a person—he was still the same guy who'd sent me cartoons and jokes and pep talks when I was frustrated with one of my classes. "As a *friend*, I'd hate for you to have shitty sleep."

He grinned. "Appreciate the thought. You wanna go get some breakfast?"

I looked around, wondering what time it was. Where was my phone? Something chimed, and he reached over, picking his up off the floor—the bed was really just a mattress, I realized.

"I gotta go," he told me, frowning. "Something's come up."

"No worries," I said, thinking wistfully of breakfast. I'd decided one benefit of the friend zone was you could pig out all you want, and I was hungry for biscuits and gravy. All I had at home was cereal.

"I'll give you a ride home," he said, rolling off the bed.

"I can just walk," I told him. "It's only a few blocks."

He shook his head, offering me a hand up.

"I'll give you a ride," he insisted. "Just give me ten for a quick shower."

"All right—you want coffee or something? I can fix it while you're in there."

"No, I gotta get going."

• • •

It was a long ten minutes, mostly because I'd forgotten to pee before he started his shower. The apartment looked even smaller in the daylight, and the sound of running water filling it didn't help. One silver lining? Hard to feel horny while you're doing the pee-pee dance, even though I knew he was naked right on the other side of a narrow, flimsy door. Took all my energy not to have an accident in my pants.

I found my phone out next to the couch, so I grabbed it, looking for a distraction. It was nearly ten in the morning. Wow. Jess had texted me about an hour earlier.

> JESS: You alive? Looks like someone didnt come home last night. Painter? We should talk.

I sighed, then messaged her back.

> ME: I stayed at his place but not like you think. We're just friends. How was Taz?
> JESS: Useful. He fucked me hard and then fixed the sink because it was dripping and wouldn't stop. Now he's cooking me breakfast
> ME: Wow. Sounds like a keeper.
> JESS: Im not into keepers. I've decided from now on I'll just stay mentally celibate. That way I can get laid but still hold firm to my ideals. You coming home soon?
> ME: Yup, just a few
> JESS: Ha! You said your coming. I meant cumming. Shit, that would be funnier without autocorrect ducking it up.

"What are you smiling about?" Painter asked, stepping out of the bathroom. I would've answered him, but I'd temporarily lost the ability to breathe or form words. This was because he'd pulled on a pair of jeans, but no shirt. Throw in the fact that his hair was wet and tousled, and little drips of water were running down his pecs and across his abs?

Unfair. Deeply unfair.

I managed to collect myself, then scowled at him.

"Put on some clothes," I said, pointing toward his bedroom. "If we're going to be friends, you need to keep it decent."

He raised a brow.

"Guys leave off their shirts all the time," he pointed out reasonably. I crossed my arms, staring him down.

"The friend zone only works if you stay in it," I declared. "You're out of bounds. Put on a shirt, okay?"

He smirked at me, then swaggered into the bedroom, leaving the door open behind him.

Jerkface.

Later that afternoon, I still held out hope that our new friend zone status meant I might get taken out for dinner, given that we'd missed breakfast. Then my phone buzzed.

> **PAINTER:** Hey—I have to leave town for a week or so. Not sure how long. You can reach me by text if you want, or call if anything comes up.
>
> **MEL:** Since when do we text?
>
> **PAINTER:** Since I'm allowed to have written communication that hasn't been screened by a guard first. You know, to make sure you weren't sending me secret code messages about global domination or something in your letters
>
> **MEL:** You mean you didn't figure out the messages? But I thought they were so clear. First you get the guns, then you get the women . . .
>
> **PAINTER:** No wonder the revolution didn't pan out. Prob for the best. Knowing my luck I'd be first up against the wall.

Okay, so I wasn't getting dinner. But at least things weren't weird anymore. This friend zone thing wasn't all bad.

CHAPTER NINE

PAINTER

"So tell me more about this guy, Pipes," Gage asked, staring ahead at the highway. We'd been driving for nearly four hours, and I knew we had to be close to Hallies Falls by now. Damned good thing, too, because I was more than ready to be out of this fucking cage of a semi cab. When I suggested we set him up as a long-haul trucker, it'd seemed like a good idea. Gave him an excuse to come and go, a place in the back to sleep if he needed it, all good shit. I hadn't been thinking about how small that sleeping space was, or that I might get stuck in it, too.

Small spaces made me think of prison.

Of course, so did talking about Pipes.

"So, he was in our block with us," I said. "Probably about thirty years old, and with our club alliances, partnering with him seemed natural enough. He prospected when he was eighteen—Dad was a patch holder. Things started going downhill when their old president died about two years ago. Marsh was their VP at that point—he's the president now. Seems weird that we've never met him at a rally or anything."

"That's enough to raise red flags right there," Gage agreed.

"We're supposed to be allies, but they never come to any of our events. I knew Rance was on it, though, so I never gave it much thought. Always been a profitable partnership. In a weird way, I'm glad it came up—gave me an excuse to get away from The Line."

"What's up with that?" I asked, curious. Gage rubbed his chin thoughtfully, then answered.

"Guess I was bored," he said. "Been looking for a reason to step back for a while. As fun as it sounds to be surrounded by bare ass and tits all the time, those tits are attached to a lot of fuckin' drama. I'm burned out on it."

I gave a laugh, because you couldn't argue with that.

"I have a feeling that we'll be involved here for a while," he continued. "This situation will need watching, and I wanted a change of pace. Timing was good."

He slowed the truck as we reached the outskirts of town. Buildings started to appear alongside the road. Not much farther to the truck stop where we planned to set up shop for the night. The bikes were trailered behind us, along with some basic furniture and shit—just enough to set up an apartment or something. We'd debated that approach initially, because showing up in a semi underloaded with motorcycles would make us stand out. But standing out wasn't necessarily a bad thing. We needed to make contact with the club, hopefully sooner rather than later. Our cover story pegged Gage as a trucker looking for a new base of operations after an ugly divorce. I was his cousin, here to help him find a new place and get settled.

If we played it right, they'd hear about us hitting town but wouldn't give it a second thought. Just a couple of independents— no threat to the club.

Up ahead I saw the lights of the truck stop. It wasn't as big as I expected—more of a souped-up gas station than anything else, although I knew from their website that they had a convenience store with showers around the back. Gage slowed the big rig, pulling behind the building, where they had parking for the trucks. We rolled to a stop, then climbed out to look around.

"Not a whole lot here, is there?" I commented.

"Population is about three thousand," he replied. "Small, but not so small that they don't see the occasional stranger. Rance filled me in. He stops by every couple of weeks to check on Marsh."

I nodded—Rance was smart. We could trust his intel.

"Rance thinks the best way to get in is through Marsh's sister, Talia. Apparently she's always bringing home some new guy. She and Marsh are close, so he puts up with it. Even lets 'em in the clubhouse, which seems wrong somehow. Perfect way to get in as a hangaround, though. Collect some good information that way."

"No shit," I said. "You planning to fuck her, or is that on me?" Gage snorted.

"Get right to the point, don't you?"

"Saves time," I replied. My phone buzzed, and I looked down to see Melanie's name pop up with a text.

> MEL: Jess dragged Taz home again this afternoon. I'm going to
> strangle her—turns out he's a screamer, too . . .

I snorted, not thrilled by the fact that Taz was at her place, but at least she didn't sound interested in him.

"What's that?" Gage asked.

"Melanie," I replied. "Says Taz is loud during sex."

"Really . . . Do I want to know?"

I laughed. "Probably not. Taz hooked up with Jessica at the rodeo—wonder how Pic feels about that?"

"I think he's given up on controlling the girls in his life," Gage replied. "Why's Mel texting you? I thought you weren't gonna tap that."

"We're friends, I guess," I replied, uncomfortable with the word.

"If you're just friends, you mind if I hook up with her?"

I nearly took the bait, then I caught the shit-eating grin he was trying to hide.

"Fuck you. So what's the plan now?"

"We'll check things out," he said. "See if we can establish a presence, take it from there. That work for you?"

"Sure," I said, trying not to think how much time that'd mean away from Mel. "But I'd rather not fuck the sister if I don't have to."

Gage snorted. "You haven't seen her yet."

He grabbed his phone, swiping at it and then handing it over so I could see a picture. Damn—the girl was gorgeous. Long red hair, bright green eyes. Brilliant white smile. Oh, and it didn't hurt that her tits were huge and halfway popped out of the tiny little American-flag bikini she wore. Allegedly covering her legs were a faded pair of Daisy Dukes. The top button was even open.

Hell.

"Pulled that off Instagram," Gage said. "She likes posting pictures of herself. You still want to pass?"

I studied the photo again. She was hot, definitely. But the red wasn't doing it for me, not really. I preferred brunettes. Chocolate brown hair was the best, not to mention smooth skin tanned darker than this girl would ever get outside of a spray booth.

"Still pass," I said. "Unless you're not up for it? I know you're older than me, so if you need some of those little blue pills . . ."

"You're an asshole," he said, laughing as he pulled the truck over into one of the parking spots lining the old downtown. "Okay, here we go. Try not to fuck up too badly."

"Fuck up what? Existing? I thought we were just here to check it out."

"Just act normal."

I snorted, opening my door. We'd see if I could pull it off or not.

It didn't take us long to unload the bikes, and then we were headed down the old highway toward town, which had been bypassed by the freeway years ago. Felt weird to be riding around without my Reaper colors. Unnatural. The small downtown held two diners, clearly in competition with each other. At one end was Clare's, which seemed to have a coffee shop/hipster kind of vibe. On the other was the Hungry Chicken, which was all greasy spoon. We parked on the street between them.

"There," Gage said, nodding his head toward the chicken place. "We'll get better gossip there."

"And more food, too," I said, noting the sidewalk board advertising their big breakfast platter, served all day. Nice.

We gave the bikes one more check before starting down the street, and I wondered if Gage was as unsettled by the current state of his ride as I was. I'd stripped off the whips and anything that could identify me as a Reaper. Felt kinda like standing outside naked without them . . . I got why we needed to go undercover, but it felt wrong. I was used to wearing my colors proud, and fuck anyone who had a problem with that.

The restaurant door gave a welcoming chime as I pushed it open. It was only midafternoon, so there weren't a ton of people inside. Just a couple old guys sitting at the counter nursing their coffee and a table full of girls giggling and drinking milk shakes.

"You boys hungry?" a middle-aged woman asked, stepping around the counter to walk toward us. I forced myself not to react, but I swear to fuck she looked like a cartoon parody of a greasy spoon waitress. Big blonde hair, all up in some kind of beehive. Bright red lips and eye shadow so blue it could've been neon. Pair that with the pink uniform she wore and she was literally the least attractive human female I'd ever met in my life. I mean, not just unsexy, but actively creepy. I sort of wanted to take a picture of her, just to prove to myself later she was real.

"We've got our breakfast special," she said. "It's the breakfast platter. Three eggs, your choice of meat, hash browns, toast, and a bottomless cup of coffee. Best food in town."

"Sounds great," Gage said without blinking. She smiled at him, the expression transforming her face until it seemed less cartoonish.

"Seat yourselves," she said. "Not like we have a shortage of space."

I nodded toward a table near the window that'd give us a good view of the street while keeping us off to the side of the diner. Gage put his back to the wall, leaving me exposed—which I fucking hated—but he'd been the club's sergeant at arms for nearly a decade. Not a guy you want to piss off, if you catch my meaning.

I settled myself, looking out across the street. The buildings here were old—lots of character. The one directly opposite us was built from some kind of sandstone, and above the windows it read "Reimers Pharmacy" with the Rx symbol. The Reimers seemed to be long gone, though, because below was the girliest shopfront I'd ever seen. There was china, antiquey shit, and even some old-fashioned toys in the window front, along with some fancy little tables on legs that didn't seem quite strong enough to hold a man's weight. Kind of like an old-fashioned ice cream parlor.

Across the window, a sign read, "Tinker's Teahouse, Antiques & Fine Chocolates."

I nodded toward it.

"You see that?" I asked Gage. He glanced over at the store.

"Huh. That's different."

"You boys want the special?" our waitress asked, and I'm man enough to admit she scared the hell out of me. Not only was she suddenly damned close, she'd snuck up on us without making a sound. I stared at the neon eyeshadow, mesmerized.

Shit. Maybe she wasn't human.

"We'll have two specials," Gage said, offering her one of those smiles that made women's panties drop. "Could use that coffee now, too. Been a long day."

She offered him a sickly sweet smile, and I sighed, wishing I was back in Coeur d'Alene with Mel.

By the time the waitress finished taking our order—it took a while, given how chatty she was—a cherry red Mustang convertible had pulled up outside the restaurant. The car was a beauty, but it was the driver who really caught my attention when she stepped out into the street, all long dark hair and sunglasses. Deep red lipstick, pale skin . . . I couldn't peg her age from here, but based on those curves she wasn't a teenager.

Then she walked around to the back of the car and leaned over to open the trunk, clearly outlining the silhouette of a perfect ass wrapped beautifully in a skinny, knee-length skirt with a slit up the back.

"Fuckin' hell," Gage said, his voice soft. "Who is that?"

"That's Tinker Garrett," our waitress said, sneaking up behind us again. "She owns the little tea shop across the way."

There was something snide and nasty in her tone. Gage and I shared a glance.

"She doesn't look like she owns a tea shop," Gage said, leading her on. The waitress sniffed.

"She moved to Seattle after high school," she said. "Thought she was hot shit. Then her husband dumped her and she came crawling back to town. That shop of hers can't earn enough to stay open— not enough people pass through here. If you ask me, she's up to something."

Gage glanced at me, mouth twitching. I leaned toward the woman, asking a follow-up question in a tense whisper.

"What kind of *thing* do you think she's up to?" I asked, eyes wide. "Do you think it's . . . *nefarious*?"

Gage choked on a cough. Nice. Holding down that laughter was probably killing him.

"I have my suspicions," she sniffed. "She dresses like a whore, you know. And I heard she goes dancing sometimes down in Ellensburg. Likes to pick up college boys. What do they call that? Being a mountain lion? Shameful."

Gage turned away, shoulders shaking.

"Good to know," I said seriously. "We'll stay clear of her."

"You do that," the waitress replied, nodding sagely. "God knows what kind of stuff she's selling in that place. I'll bet those chocolates have drugs in them. Marijuana."

I glanced out the window again, watching Tinker Garrett's perfect ass twitching as she walked away.

Somehow she didn't strike me as a drug kingpin. Cougar? Now that I could see.

MELANIE

The week after Chase's accident was strange. He survived, but he had a long recovery ahead of him. Everyone in town seemed sort of gloomy and unhappy, although they'd really pulled together to support him, too. There'd even been a group of kids who set up a lemon-ade stand down the street from us as a fundraiser. Sometimes I got tired of living in Coeur d'Alene—it wasn't a big city and it wasn't exciting like Seattle or Portland, but when something like this happened, we all liked to help. Kit had even organized one of those online fundraiser things to help with his medical expenses.

Contributing to the gloom was the fact that I hadn't heard from Painter for several days. I'd sent him a couple text messages at first, but stopped after he didn't respond.

"You think he lost his phone?" I finally asked Jessica. It was Thursday night, and we'd built ourselves a study nest in the dining room. She'd found an old table on Tuesday, dragging it back home to show me, proud as a kid with her first buck.

Now it was so covered with books you'd never have guessed it hadn't been here for months.

"Yeah, I'm sure he lost his phone," she said, typing aggressively on her laptop. "He's *totally* been meaning to call—you know, because he has such a great history of staying in touch—but he's completely forgotten how to use text, email, social media, or any other kind of telecommunication."

"Shit, you don't have to be a bitch about it," I snapped, glaring at her. She sighed, sitting back in her chair.

"Sorry—Taz hasn't called me or anything, either. Guess I'm feeling hostile toward men. Bikers. Fuck all of 'em."

"Did he say he'd call you?" I asked.

She nodded. "Don't they all?"

On Friday I broke down and walked by Painter's apartment. No signs of life. I was feeling all sorry for myself, so after that I went down to the coffee shop to indulge in one of their brownies with all the thick, fudgy frosting. I was halfway through it (staring at my phone, willing him to message me) when I had my big revelation.

This was fucking ridiculous.

Here I was, a twenty-year-old woman with all the potential on earth, and I was sitting in a coffee shop stuffing my face because of a man. All I needed was to start singing "All By Myself" and buy a cat to complete the stereotype.

What the hell was wrong with me?

My life had sucked before I moved in with London, but she gave me a second chance. I'd busted ass, working constantly to build a life for myself. It wasn't perfect, but it was damned good—I had a full ride to college and all the potential on earth, yet here I sat, eating chocolate.

Fuck this.

I grabbed my phone, shooting a text off to Jessica.

ME: What are you doing right now?

JESS: Working on stuff for the carnival tomorrow. You still volunteering, right? Kit's still around and she said she'd help, but I'll need more than just her.

Oh shit. I'd totally forgotten in the midst of my Painter-induced haze. Oops.

ME: Of course I'm still volunteering—can't wait. What did you want me to do?

JESS: Face paint.

ME: Um, you remember how artistic I'm not?

JESS: I want you painting little duckies and ladybugs and lizards and stuff. You know, on the kids cheeks. How hard can it be?

ME: I suck at painting

JESS: I have a book you can use with directions. Super easy

ME: Can't I run the popcorn machine or something?

JESS: Chicken

ME: Yes I'm chicken. I can acknowledge that

JESS: Stop being such a giant pussy. I'll give you paint tonight and you can practice. Easy

I glared down at the phone, because it was just like her to stick me with something hard and uncomfortable that I didn't want to do. Hateful girl.

ME: Ok but you owe me
JESS: Put it on my tab ;)

Fucking winkie face, taunting me . . . I sighed and finished my brownie. I wouldn't let myself get all pathetic again, I'd already decided that. But I couldn't just walk away from a brownie midway through a sad eating binge. In all fairness, there wasn't even enough to wrap up and take home.

ME: If I get all fat we r blaming Painter
JESS: Your insane. I love you butthead.

And just like that, I was smiling again. Grabbing my phone and bag, I started walking down to the college. Class didn't start for another hour, but I could get some work done on my paper at the library if I hurried.

No more letting Painter get in my way. Life was too damned short.

It was eleven p.m. that same Friday night, and I was all alone (in the dark) getting my ass kicked by a ladybug.

Wasn't even a real ladybug.

I stared down at the little instruction booklet, trying to figure out how something so allegedly simple—painting a harmless insect in six easy steps—was completely beyond me. I'd been trying for forty-five minutes now, dabbing unattractive, runny gloops of red, black, and white over and over each other in an endless cycle of incompetence. Some looked like aliens and others looked like mutant trolls, but not one of them could possibly be mistaken for a ladybug.

Not even a ladybug that'd been squished. (And maybe run over a few times, just for good measure.)

Jess was going to give me so much shit over this, I just knew it, because the instructions were so fucking simple that any idiot should be able to follow them. Crap. I dropped the paintbrush, walking into the kitchen to grab a glass of water. In the distance I heard a faint knocking sound outside followed by a weird, serial killer–esque wheeze from the fridge. I spun around, convinced I was about to be murdered.

Nothing.

I tiptoed slowly back into the dining room, where the corpses of my botched ladybugs waited in accusing silence.

Then I heard the knock again, more clearly this time. Someone was at the door . . . Of course I was here by myself, because Jessica *would* be out visiting Taz when I needed her most, leaving me to be murdered. The same Taz who—after not calling all week— suddenly had urgent "shit to deal with" at the Armory. Shit so easy to deal with that it only took about an hour, giving him plenty of time to take Jess out for the night. Right. I didn't buy that for an instant, and I told her so. Obviously he was up to something. But she insisted that she was a big girl, and that she knew what she was doing.

I walked over to the door, wishing for the thousandth time that we had a peephole. Instead we had to peer through the window to see people outside, which Jess had helpfully pointed out gave them an easy target if they wanted to shoot us or bash us with a hockey stick. Bracing myself, I twitched the curtain to the side to see *him.*

Painter.

For an instant I got stupidly excited, then I remembered that I'd stopped liking him this past week. We might not be a couple, but we were good enough friends that I thought I deserved at least *some* acknowledgement or contact. Were his fingers broken, that he couldn't return a friendly text message?

"What's up?" I asked coldly, opening the door.

He stared at me, eyes tracing my face in silence long enough to be uncomfortable. A part of me wanted to babble nervously, fill the air, but I managed to shut it down—from now on, I set the rules.

"I'm sorry I haven't been in touch," he said.

"Seems to be a pattern with you," I pointed out, trying to act tough. "I know we're just friends, but you dropped off the face of the earth. What gives?"

He shrugged and then offered a smile so sweet and charming it almost got me. Almost. But not quite.

"My phone broke," he said. "I was off on club business, so I just picked up a burner to use. Didn't even have real texting, and I didn't have your number anyway."

Ah . . . See, he had a good explanation! The stupidest, most gullible part of my brain was totally ready to fall for his excuses. *No. No no no no.*

"Don't you have Picnic's number?" I asked reasonably. "He knows how to get in touch with me."

Painter's smile grew sheepish. "He wouldn't give it to me—said I'm a bad influence and I should stay away from you."

Well, I could certainly see that. Painter *was* a bad influence. Here he was at my door after nearly a week of radio silence, and in under a minute he was already eroding my sense of self-preservation.

"C'mon in," I said, giving in to the inevitable. "I still think you suck for blowing me off, but here's your chance to make up for it. I've got to figure out how to paint small animals on children by tomorrow."

"What?" he asked, staring blankly.

"Jessica's got a carnival thing going on at her work tomorrow morning," I explained. "She works with the kids at the community center—in the special needs program. She asked if I'd volunteer, and because I'm an idiot I agreed without making her tell me exactly what it was I'd volunteered to do. Now I have to paint faces and I have no idea how. If you really want to hang out, hang out and help me."

He followed me into the dining room, stopping next to the table to study my pathetic efforts.

"What the hell is that supposed to be—a squirrel fucking a dinosaur?"

I sighed, forcing myself to look at the paper. I sort of wanted to bitch him out, but to be honest it looked a lot more like a squirrel fucking a dinosaur than I wanted to admit.

"It's a ladybug."

Silence.

Ignoring him, I sat down in the chair, poking at the hateful paintbrush with one finger.

"That's terrible," he said.

"I know."

"No, it's really bad. Like, I don't know how a person can be this bad at painting something. Anything."

"Do you think they'll cry?" I asked, feeling a little sick—I think some secret part of me had hoped they weren't quite as dreadful as they seemed.

"Who, the ladybugs? They don't have any eyes, babe. They can't cry. Although it's safe to assume they're crying on the inside . . ."

I flipped him off, giving a reluctant laugh. "No, the children. How am I supposed to paint their faces if I can't even paint the damned paper?"

He sat down on the end of the table, kitty-corner from me.

"Well, it's not really that hard," he started to say, but I held up a hand.

"Look those ladybugs in the face when you say that," I suggested. "Do they look easy to you?"

His lip quirked and he shook his head. "I'm trying really hard not to make a sex joke about easy ladybugs."

"Don't," I said, fighting my own smile. "Besides, they're not anatomically correct. So, do you think you can help me? *Friends* help each other."

They also reply to texts, so people know they haven't been murdered or something.

"I'm sure I can help," he said, reaching out to run his finger down my nose. I forgot to breathe for an instant. "Let's start with the paint. Sit down and we'll go through it step by step."

Half an hour later I was doing better. I mean, it's not like painting faces was really that difficult, but for some reason I'd been getting the paints way too watery, so they kept running together.

"You're doing great," Painter said, watching me brush green across the paper. "That one definitely looks like a lizard."

I considered telling him it was supposed to be a flower, but decided to just add eyes instead. Still, I had a very nice sheet of rainbows, ladybugs, and clouds. I figured I'd do all right with the kids so long as I offered them only a few choices.

Glancing up, I smiled, because he was close to me and being around him always made me happy, even if it probably shouldn't.

"So, can you tell me where you were this past week?"

His face shuttered. "Why do you want to know?"

"Don't be so suspicious—I'm just making conversation," I said, deciding that I'd get crazy and try to paint a Pokémon next. Jess had warned me the kids were hard-core about them right now, and the little yellow one looked like it wouldn't be all that hard. Struck with sudden inspiration, I put my left hand palm-down on the table, outlining Pikachu on my skin instead of the paper.

"Wow, it's different like this," I said, glancing up at him. "Harder, because the skin moves more than the paper. So where have you been? Unless you can't tell me."

"I probably shouldn't get into it," he admitted, eyes fixed on my hand. I bit my lip, focusing on getting the little black points for the ears right. Nice. "Club business, that kind of thing. But just so you know, I'm going to be out of town a lot for the next few weeks, maybe longer. Not sure how things will play out."

Frowning, I dipped my brush in the red for the cheeks.

"Aren't you on parole?" I asked. "Can't you get in trouble for traveling around?"

He startled me, catching my chin and turning my face toward his.

"You know I'm not like those guys you meet down at school," he said with quiet intensity. "My life isn't like theirs. I don't want you to worry about me, Mel, because I'm being careful—but I'm never going to follow the rules, either."

I swallowed, mesmerized by his gaze.

"But you don't want to go back, do you?"

"Of course I don't," he said. "But I'm not going to let fear get in the way of what I need to do, either. If it makes you feel better, I'm not doing anything particularly crazy and I'm not on my own. We just need eyes on a situation. If anything serious goes down, they'll keep me out of it, because my brothers don't want me going back, either. FYI—you're getting paint everywhere."

I pulled back, looking down to see that I'd let my brush slide off my hand and across the sheet of little animals I'd worked so hard to produce.

"This sucks," I said, and I wasn't talking about the painting . . .

"It is what it is," he said, shrugging. "And I can't share it with you. Say the word and I'll walk out, leave you alone. I'm not trying to fuck with your head, Mel, but I can't change who I am, either."

I swallowed, deciding to ignore that particular reality for now.

"Can you show me how to make a flower?"

He nodded, pulling the brush out of my fingers slowly.

"First, you need to start with a clean surface," he said, catching my chin again, turning my cheek toward him. He dipped the brush into the green, raising it to my face. The paint was cool where it touched my skin, but it still burned deep inside.

"Long, smooth strokes will keep the color even," he continued, as the brush slid down my face, all the way down to my chin. I studied his expression, intent and purposeful as he started another line. His eyes were so blue, so clear and full of light. Intellectually, I knew he was one of the bad guys. I just couldn't reconcile that with the man sitting here next to me.

"Will you help me tomorrow?" I asked. He cocked a brow. "With the face painting, I mean. Do you want to come to the carnival with me? You're way better at this than I am."

A strange look crossed his face.

"I'm a felon, Mel," he said. "I don't think they'd want me there."

"A lot of people are felons," I said earnestly. "Spending time in prison doesn't mean you can't do any volunteering for the rest of your life. Well, aside from sex offenders, I guess, but that's not you. Why couldn't you volunteer? Aren't you friends with Bolt? It's his old lady—Maggs—who runs the program. He's helped out a bunch of times. The club even did a fundraiser for the program last year."

A thoughtful look crossed Painter's face.

"I met Bolt in prison, have I told you that?" he asked. I shook my head. "The first time I was inside. He helped me figure shit out, hooked me up with the club. Good brother."

"Well, your good brother is going to be there tomorrow, so I guess if he's okay, you're probably okay, too. And I know they can use the help—I mean, if they're desperate enough to have me painting, you know it has to be bad."

He gave a low laugh.

"Point taken. You win. Happy now?"

Yes. Yes I was.

"Thanks," I said, smiling widely. Then I lost the smile as he scowled at me.

"Don't move your face—I'm working."

"Yes, sir," I said, trying to relax. I didn't know what he was painting on me and I didn't care. Every stroke was like a finger running over my skin, sending chills through me while sparking a slow-burning need deep inside. He leaned in closer, eyes searching across my features, then darting back down toward the colors, utterly absorbed in his work.

This seemed a little unfair, because ten minutes later he'd covered most of my face (which I didn't have a problem with) and I'd seriously soaked my panties (big problem). So far as I could tell, Painter hadn't even noticed that I wasn't just another mural board.

"Lift your chin," he said, his voice soft. I lifted, shivering as the cool brush stroked down the length of my neck.

"What are you doing?"

"Expanding the picture," he said, sounding almost detached. "This is fun and I'm not ready to stop yet. In fact, why don't you unbutton your shirt and take it off? Gives me more room to work."

I pulled back, staring him down.

"That sounds like a pick-up line from a bad porno," I said, torn between laughter and frustration, because deep down inside I wanted nothing more than to strip down in front of him.

Well, actually what I wanted was *him* stripped in front of *me*, but you know what I mean.

"You wanted me to show you how to paint," he said, frowning. "I'm doing that. And you've got a bra on—trust me, I'd know if you didn't—so it's not like you'll be naked. And you should stop watching bad porn. The good stuff is harder to find, but it's worth it."

I opened my mouth to reply, then snapped it shut because no way in hell did I want to discuss the varying quality of porn across the spectrum. But he made a good point about the bra . . . I had no issues with wearing a bikini top down at the beach during the summer.

(And yes, I knew I was rationalizing—I was in heat, not stupid.)

I started unbuttoning my shirt, pretending his eyes weren't following my fingers like his life depended on it, because if I had to suffer, it seemed only fair that he should, too.

Painter's breath caught when I pulled my shirt apart, then slowly pushed it back and off my shoulders. I had a decent body—I knew that. It wasn't as great as Jessica's, but when I made the effort I could definitely hold my own. Even so, I wasn't used to the kind of appreciation I saw in his eyes.

The shirt dropped back down behind me, and I found myself sitting up straight. Thankfully, I'd put on a decent bra that morning. Black and lacy, dipping low between my breasts. It wasn't a sexy push-up, but it wasn't plain white cotton, either.

Painter reached out, running the brush down my neck and along my collarbone, sending shivers through me. When he did the other side, I felt the first goose bumps breaking out, all along my arms.

"Are you cold?" he asked, his voice a husky whisper.

"No."

His eyes burned through me, and I thought I saw the same aching need in his that had to be in mine.

"Okay."

Things sort of blurred together after that. He kept my head up, refusing to let me watch as he traced patterns across my chest and down along my stomach. Aside from the occasional finger on my chin, he never touched my skin once . . . Just that soft, cold brush passing across my flesh, over and over, deep and strong.

After what felt like hours, he had me turn away from him, straddling the chair so he could start on my back. By this point my entire body was humming with need, but also a strange sense of calm.

Like we'd transitioned into some separate reality, where there was only me, him, and the cool slide of the paint against my skin.

He started down my shoulder blade, pausing to slide my bra strap to the side. I heard a sound of frustration, then he was dabbing at my skin with a damp paper towel.

"Do you want me to take it off?" I asked, the words hardly more than a whisper.

CHAPTER TEN

PAINTER

I stared at Mel's back, wondering if I'd actually heard her right. Hell yeah, I wanted her to take it off.

For the painting, of course.

This was about art, not about being a perverted horndog who wanted to get laid. Not even a little bit.

"Yeah, that would be good," I said casually, reaching out with my left hand to unhook it before she could change her mind. Shit. Should've set the brush down and used two hands—no need to advertise how many times I'd done this. She didn't say anything, just sitting there quietly while I lowered each of the straps, reaching up to catch the front against her chest.

Her back lay open in front of me, the perfect canvas. It was lightly muscled, tapering in at her waist before flaring out to her hips. She wore jean shorts that were stretched out and loose, gaping ever so slightly at the small of her back, giving me a glimpse of black satin below. God, I hoped they matched the bra she'd taken off. That thing was fucking perfect—sexy, but also sort of sweet and almost virginal compared to what most of the women I knew wore. Not that Mel was a virgin . . . I'd done enough checking up to know she had some experience.

Shouldn't matter to me—I had zero intention of sleeping with her—but knowing she'd been with other guys was a relief, in a way. Less pressure not to fuck things up, which was a nonissue because we absolutely weren't going to do a damned thing together.

Fucking hell, this friend-zone thing sucked. For the first time I admitted to myself that maybe it wasn't going to work out.

Gee, what gave it away, asshole—the shirt coming off or you unhooking her bra?

I dipped the brush back in the paint, noting that I'd have to get up early and go buy more tomorrow morning. I'd run most of the way through the green and the red already, and had made good headway with the yellow and purple, too. I was painting flowers. Lots and lots of flowers, a tangled mass of them like something you'd see in the rainforest. Lush and sweet and ripe and deadly, just like Melanie. Vines to tie me up and hold me prisoner until I didn't even care anymore . . .

She lifted an arm, pulling her hair out of the way as I started up the back of her neck.

"Do you have one of those little thingies?" I asked.

"Thingies?"

"Thingies for your hair. I can put it up for you."

"Oh yeah. There should be one on the coffee table."

"Be right back."

I walked into the living room and found a purple elastic sitting right next to her phone, which had just lit up with a text.

I swear I didn't read it on purpose.

JESS: I just heard painters back in town and that he went over to our place looking for you. Don't let him in or I'll kill you dead with my bare hands. Xx

Frowning, I turned the phone off, then tossed it onto the couch. It might've fallen behind the cushions—hard to tell.

Mel could read the message later.

Yeah.

No need to worry her about something that probably wouldn't even be an issue.

MELANIE

This was stupid.

Really, really stupid.

I sat in the center of the dining room, dreading every stroke of the brush, because sooner or later I was going to snap and things wouldn't end well . . . But it felt so good, and it wasn't like we were doing anything bad. Just painting. And his work was truly beautiful—I'd snuck a peek while he was grabbing my hair elastic, stunned by the riotous explosion of vines and flowers he'd painted using my skin as a canvas.

It was amazing. Almost unreal. How something like *this* could be created by the same brushes responsible for the Ladybugs of Death and Dismemberment was almost impossible to comprehend. Raw talent, I guess.

That and technique.

I wondered if he had any idea how good he really was. Hell, whatever he was doing for the club, if he just sold those paintings of his to the right people he'd be able to make them more money that way. Except it probably wasn't about money. What did they have him doing, and how likely was it that he'd get himself thrown back in prison?

"Let me get your hair," he said, his soft voice sending shivers all through my body. I still held the cups of my bra against my chest, like somehow it held the power to protect me.

Assuming I *wanted* to be protected.

"Thanks," I whispered as his fingers started combing through the tangled mass. It took longer than it should have. I'd like to think he was as mesmerized as I was, because for all his insistence that we could only be friends, even I was smart enough to know that guys don't sit around on Friday nights painting flowers on their half-naked, platonic friends. His head lowered next to mine—was he smelling my hair?

"Almost finished," he whispered, warm air touching my ear.

Then my hair was up in a messy ponytail-slash-bun thing and he was lifting the brush, ready to start torturing me again.

PAINTER

I finished way too fast.

The original colors had run out, forcing me to mix my own. I think that made it better—toward the end, the greens were darker, projecting something shadowy and almost angry.

Frustration.

Fair enough, because that was exactly how I was feeling. I'd spent more than two hours painting Melanie's perfect body. Now my cock was like a fucking diamond, so hard it could cut glass. I want to push her down across the table and pound her until the paint smeared with our sweat . . .

Christ. My dick was going to explode.

"You can go look now," I said, standing up. She rose from her chair awkwardly, still holding the black silk in front of her tits, which made no fucking sense.

"There's a mirror up in Jessica's room," she said. She brushed past me, and I shuddered as her arm touched mine. I tended to get very focused while working, but just being near her was a class A mind fuck. She started up the stairs, then turned back to look at me, a puzzled frown on her face.

"Aren't you coming?"

Coming? No, not yet. Not until you wrap those lips around me.

"Um, sure," I managed to say. "Didn't realize you wanted me."

She stared at me, her expression so intense that I swear the air between us sizzled. Okay, it didn't sizzle at all, because that's fucking lame, but it did *something*. Felt like there was a tight string—no, a piano wire—stretching between us, quivering and pulsing with every beat of my heart.

Mel started up the stairs and I followed her, eyes glued to the gentle, feminine sway of her ass. Those legs weren't half bad either, and seeing my work all over her body made me feel something strange . . . I had no idea how to describe it, but I liked it. I liked it a *lot*. Felt like I owned her. Now if I could just tattoo my marks all over her permanently.

No, probably not a good idea to cover her face, even I had to admit that. But the thought of my work across her back, so I could look down on it while I wrapped my hands around her waist and fucked her ass?

That'd do.

"Here's the bathroom," she said, pointing to a door at the top of the stairs. "And here is Jessica's room. Mine's at the far end of the hall, over the porch."

I glanced down toward her door, the step up into her space. I wanted to see where she slept, but she pushed through to Jessica's room instead. The place was all clothes thrown in piles across the shaggy green carpet and posters half falling off the walls. I had an ugly feeling the plaster was so weak it couldn't hold them . . . The place felt about as solid as a wasp's nest.

"The mirror's on the back of the door," Mel said, closing it behind us. She stood still, studying her image, and I came to stand behind her. The lines of green twisted across her body, spattered with flowers that bloomed and faded in a pattern I wished I could keep forever.

No, I wanted to keep *her* forever.

God, I deserved to be shot, because I wanted to defile her. Defile her and then lock her up so no other man could even see her, let alone touch her.

"It's beautiful," she said softly, touching her face. I reached up, setting a hand on her shoulder. She covered it with her own, winding our fingers together. Her eyes burned through mine in the mirror, and that's when my world shifted.

I'd fallen in love with Melanie Tucker.

Not some little-boy, bullshit needy "love" like I'd felt for Emmy Hayes—this was nothing like that. This was deep, almost painful in its unholy intensity. It was like she'd sent tendrils burrowing deep inside, binding us together so tightly I'd die if I ever tried to pull them out.

I was truly, deeply, and utterly fucked, because I fucking *loved* this girl . . . and she wasn't for me.

"Hey," I whispered.

"Hey . . ." she whispered back.

"I think we should—"

Suddenly the door flew backward, knocking Mel right into me. My arms flew out to catch her as Taz lurched into the room, Jessica riding on his back.

He stilled, eyes crawling over Mel as I realized she'd lost the bra when she'd fallen.

"Nice artwork," he said, grinning broadly. "But I think you missed a couple spots."

I wrapped an arm across Mel's chest, doing my best to cover her up. She gave a shriek. Then she was breaking free, running out the door to her bedroom as Jessica launched herself at me, smacking at my face while Taz laughed his ass off.

"You aren't allowed to touch her," Jess shrieked. I raised a hand to protect my eyes, wondering how the hell I'd ever considered this girl sexy enough for a drunken one-night stand. Could you even call it that? It'd been a partial, and a shitty partial at that.

"Get your woman off me," I yelled at Taz, who laughed harder. Finally I managed to shake off the screaming banshee queen, shoving her toward Taz so I could go after Mel.

"I'll kill you!" Jessica yelled behind me. Fucking witch. First Kit, now her. I was surrounded by devil women. Mel's door was slammed shut, and I could hear her sobbing.

Fucking hell.

I'd broken her already, and I hadn't even gotten laid first.

MELANIE

I lay back on my bed, laughing so hard it actually hurt. God, the look on Jessica's face. The crazy hypocrisy and weirdness and the way I'd dropped my bra . . . it was all too much. And about time I freaked her out, too. She'd been freaking me out for years.

"Mel, are you okay?" Painter asked, knocking on my door. I gasped, trying to catch my breath to answer. It came out on a sob, and every time I tried to tell him I was fine, the words ate themselves and I would start laughing again.

Finally he pushed his way through the door, dropping down on the futon next to me to pull me into his arms. Then he rolled me on top, wrapping his body around mine.

"Hey, it's okay," he whispered, sounding all sweet and tender. I snorted, still incapable of catching my breath. "Mellie, it doesn't matter what he saw. You're okay."

I clutched at his leather cut, pushing my head up so I could see him.

"I'm fine," I gasped, although I was pretty sure there were tears running down my face, probably all mixed with paint. Attractive. His hands rubbed up and down my back, and my legs fell to either side of his hips. Oh hell. I could feel him there—exactly where I needed him—and he was longer and harder than any man had a right to be.

"I'm fine," I repeated, sniffing. "I was laughing, Painter, not crying. It was just so funny. The look on Jessica's face. You'd think she'd caught us screwing on her bed. And for the record, I've caught her having sex on my bed twice before, so she'd have no right to complain even if we had been . . ."

My voice trailed off as one of his hands dug into my ass, pulling me hard into his pelvis.

"You were laughing?" he asked very carefully.

"Yeah. It was funny. Didn't you think it was funny?"

A slow grin started to steal across his face, and then he shook his head. "Well, yeah. But girls don't usually laugh about shit like that."

I smiled, letting my face drop against his chest.

"I'm not most girls."

The leather of his club colors was rough against my nipples, and I thought about the look on Taz's face as he took me in. Appreciation, although not in a creepy way. Felt kind of good, actually. Now I had those unpainted sections he'd so helpfully pointed out pushed up against Painter's chest. Okay, I hadn't exactly forgotten . . . but suddenly I was more aware of how my breasts felt rubbing against the fabric and leather covering his body. Then Painter's hands found my ass, gripping it and giving a squeeze, sending thrills running through me.

"You know, Taz was right about one thing," he said softly.

"What's that?" I whispered, feeling the spell fall over us again.

"I really should've gotten the bra off you earlier—I'd have loved to paint these tits of yours."

That set me off laughing again.

"You're quite the smooth talker, aren't you?" I managed to gasp out. Painter shrugged, grinning at me.

"Never pretended to be," he said. I felt him rub up and along my back, and then his hand was in my hair, catching me and pulling me down hard for a kiss. I opened to him, savoring the feel of his tongue sliding along mine.

There'd been a slow fire building in me all night . . . every brushstroke had been sweet torture, and now that fire exploded. My hips shifted as I found myself grinding slowly against him. His big hand cupped me tighter as one knee rose, thrusting his thigh between mine.

Suddenly he broke free from the kiss, gasping and staring at me.

"You really wanna do this?" he asked, his words offering me an escape even as his hands held me prisoner. I smiled down at him.

"Don't you?"

He gave a short laugh, fingers tightening on my rear. His cock dug obscenely into my stomach.

"This could fuck up our friendship," he whispered.

"Our friendship's already fucked," I reminded him. "There's no good reason for us to be together, you know. We have nothing in common, different life paths . . . Nothing makes sense, yet it works. Why not enjoy it?"

He nodded slowly, then his mouth took mine again.

PAINTER

Fuck, but she tasted good. I tried to hold back and keep it sweet for her, but once she started grinding on me I sort of lost it. In an instant, I had her on her back and then I was sucking on her tits, one hand ripping open the fly on her shorts. I should've been gentle, but my fingers found her pussy like a magnet, thrusting deep inside without any warning.

Wet.

So wet. And hot. Christ, that was gonna feel amazing wrapped around my cock. Sucking her nipple in deep, I worked her, savoring every funny little noise and sigh she gave as my thumb brushed her clit.

"Oh my God," she whimpered, bucking her hips against my hand. "Fucking hell, Painter. That's really good."

I pulled back, giving her a little nip before staring down into her eyes. "You scare the crap out of me, Mel."

She gasped and I twisted my fingers until her back arched. My dick was thick and heavy, a painful prisoner in my jeans. It wanted inside that pretty cunt of hers in a bad way. I'd planned to get her off before fucking her, but at this rate I'd blow in my pants. Giving her one last, hard kiss I pulled away.

"Strip," I ordered her, ripping off my shirt. Then I was kicking off my boots and tearing off my jeans to fall back on her again, catching her thigh with one hand, pulling it up and around my waist. That brought her wet cunt into my cock, the tip sliding through her juices, our bodies in perfect alignment.

I slid back and forth across her pussy lips, savoring the touch of her bare skin. Somehow I had to get a condom on without losing contact. Breaking off the kiss, I closed my eyes for a second, taking deep breaths.

"Condom," I grunted.

"I have some," she told me, and I frowned. Why the hell should she need condoms? And what kind of fuckin' hypocrite was I, anyway? I carried condoms all the time.

"I'll grab one," I said. No way I'd use a rubber she'd bought for another man. Reaching for my jeans, I pulled out the wallet and got the condom, ripping open the package with my teeth.

"Let me," Mel said, reaching for it. I let her have it and then her hand was on my cock, covering it with a long, sexy stroke of her fingers. Then I was on her again, pushing the head into her opening.

Tight.

So fucking tight.

Tight and wet and hot for me in a way that no other woman had ever come close to matching . . . She gasped as I pushed deep, moving slowly but steadily until I bottomed out inside her. Her inner muscles tensed around me and my vision started to swim.

Then I pulled back and thrust again.

I'd had a thousand different fantasies of us together over the past year. In my mind, I'd fucked her every way a man can fuck a woman. Twice. I'd always known it would be good—how could fucking a woman like Mel *not* be good?—but no way could I have imagined this. Sure, her cunt was hot. And the way she squeezed my dick worked for me in a big way, don't get me wrong. The best part, though, was the way she looked at me, eyes all big and wide and full of surprised excitement because *we were just that good together.*

She'd been with other guys. I knew this. And I'd been with a shitload of other women . . . somehow this felt like the first time, though. Like I'd just been jerking off before.

Dropping my head, I kissed her as I pumped even deeper.

This couldn't last forever, but I wished to fuck it could.

MELANIE

I'd never experienced anything quite like sex with Painter. It seemed wrong somehow, the way that he stretched me to the point of pain with every thrust, like it shouldn't feel so good.

Yet somehow it worked—like our bodies were in tune with each other even though our lives were so mismatched. I'd never actually managed to come during traditional sex before, but I knew the instant he filled me that I'd be satisfied. Not only had he prepped me right (*God, had he ever!*), but somehow he'd tilted my hips so that every stroke brought his pelvic bone up against my clit.

By the time he started kissing me again, I was already close to the edge. The need and desire and craving that spiraled through my body were building, and I could feel it just ahead of me. A little more . . . All I needed was a *little more* and then all that energy could explode out of me, setting me free again.

I was already hovering on the edge of overload when he reached down, sliding a hand under my ass to roll us over again. Suddenly I was on top and in control, perfectly positioned to take exactly what I needed from him.

Finally.

I'd been waiting for this moment for more than a year . . . Leaning forward, I braced my hand against his shoulders, jerking my hips back and forth, riding him for all I was worth. His firm grip on my waist steadied me, allowing me to focus on one thing and one thing only—getting off.

Then it hit—my body tightened as all that twisted need unraveled at once, destroying me in the process.

"Fuck," he groaned as I spasmed around him. I felt his dick swelling inside me, pulsing as he flew over the edge, too. "Jesus, *fuck* . . . Mel."

Collapsing down over his body, I let him pull me into his arms. Nestling into his shoulder, I decided I wouldn't think about what this might mean in the grand scheme of things.

Better to just savor it while it lasted.

With that as my last thought, I fell asleep.

CHAPTER ELEVEN

I woke slowly, stretching out across my futon like a satisfied cat.

Sunshine filled the boothlike room, and shards of multicolored light sparkled against the wood-paneled walls from the prisms I'd hung in the window. They'd belonged to my mom, and when she'd taken off, she'd left them behind. I reached for my phone, catching a glimpse of the dried, flaking remains of the face paint.

Memory flooded back.

Painter.

I'd had sex with Painter. Really *good* sex. I looked to the pillow beside me, finding the imprint he'd left. No sign of him, though . . . Had he taken off? He'd warned me that he wasn't the type to commit, but had our friendship really fallen apart that easily?

No, I should give him the benefit of the doubt. For all I knew he was downstairs cooking me breakfast.

Standing slowly—*isn't that an interesting little ache between my legs?*—I found my bathrobe, then started toward the bathroom, trying not to think about how many times he must've fucked and run with other girls. Not like he made me any promises.

God, I was stupid.

I'd left my phone downstairs, so I wasn't even sure what time it was. Still early. Maybe he'd left me a message.

A quick stop in the bathroom later—*holy crap, I need a shower to get all that dried paint off*—and I was heading downstairs to find it.

My phone wasn't on the coffee table or in the dining room, which didn't bode well. I could hear noises in the kitchen, though, and even smelled bacon. I had a brief, intense fantasy it was Painter. I found Jessica and Taz instead. The Devil's Jack was leaning back against the counter drinking a cup of coffee, which he raised to me with a smirking salute.

"Good morning," he said. "Have fun last night?"

Too bad I didn't know him well enough to flip him off, because I wanted to in a big way. Jess turned from the stove, my favorite red spatula raised like a weapon in one hand while the other was braced on her hip, which she'd cocked belligerently.

"You look like shit," she said, eyes flicking over me. This wasn't news. I'd seen my reflection in the bathroom mirror—the paint had dried and flaked into a molting lizard pattern, so I couldn't really fault her for her words. "Why did you let him in? Didn't you get my text warning you? I can't believe you slept with him, are you totally fucking cra—"

"Hey, Jessica," Taz said, cutting her off. "Shut the fuck up. It's none of your business."

Jessica's mouth gaped open. Then her eyes were narrowing as she turned on him. "You're just my booty call, don't think you get a vote—"

Taz reached over and casually caught her behind the neck, jerking her into him for a kiss. Somehow he managed to give me a thumbs-up behind her back as I tried to bite back my laughter. Jess had been so subdued for a while after whatever the hell it was that'd happened to her down in California. I'd been happy to see her showing signs of life again, but this thing with me and Painter? Yeah. None of her business.

I wandered back out into the living room, looking around for my phone. Jessica's was next to the TV, and I grabbed it to call myself. (She'd been using the same pass code since she got her first phone—

I'd cracked it years ago.) The couch buzzed at me before I could even dial, though. Incoming text. The phone must've fallen down between the cushions.

I pulled it out to find a series of messages from Painter.

PAINTER: Mel—you're still asleep so I went to get breakfast. Back soon.
PAINTER: Dunno what you like so getting you a latte.
PAINTER: Back in five.

I smiled, feeling a tension I hadn't even fully acknowledged release in my chest—he hadn't pulled a runner on me. Not only that, he'd be here in less than five minutes . . . and I still looked like a *diseased lizard!*

Oh no. Not gonna happen.

"I'm taking a shower!" I yelled at the top of my lungs, hoping Jess wouldn't be too busy screwing Taz to let Painter inside. It was a risk I'd have to take, because no fucking way was I answering the door in full molt.

Our tub was one of the best features of the house—a big, old-fashioned claw-foot. An oval shower curtain rack hung down from the ceiling, and I always felt vaguely elegant and exotic in it. Well, at least I felt that way until I turned the water on . . . then things occasionally went ugly. Our hot water was unreliable in general, because we shared plumbing with everyone else in the house. That meant if anyone in the other apartments flushed a toilet, ran the sink, or even blinked too hard, icy cold water exploded over whoever was unfortunate enough to be in the shower when it happened. For once I was lucky—the water ran out hot and strong, liquefying the paint as it ran down my body in streams.

I'd gotten most of my arms and front clean and was trying to figure out how to do my back when a hand came in through the shower curtain. I gave a shriek as Painter stepped inside, covering my mouth with his to swallow the noise. The kiss was hard and hot and desperately hungry, taking me from zero to sixty in an instant.

Yeah, my high school boyfriends hadn't kissed like this.

Not even a little bit.

Great as it was, though, the kiss wasn't enough. I found myself running my hands up and down his side, then reaching around to cup his ass. It was sculpted and tight with muscle, tensing under my touch. This set his cock rubbing against my stomach, still slippery from the soap I'd used to scrub off the paint.

Painter broke free from the kiss.

"Holy fucking hell, you're gorgeous," he gasped, lifting me and wrapping my legs around his waist in one smooth movement. The contrast between our skin—him all pale and me dark from the sun—was striking. We'd make beautiful babies together.

Wait. Where had *that* come from?

Before I could explore that disturbing thought any further, his mouth took mine again. I was squirming all over him, and then his dick was pushing against my opening and I was sliding down over him.

It hurt more than before, which startled me.

It was a good hurt—more like a stretch—but I was definitely sore from the night before. Then his hips pulled back for another thrust, and it struck me just how strong he must be to hold me like this. I mean, who *does* that in real life?

Each stroke pushed him deeper. Kissing was too complicated now—I needed to focus everything on the sensations building between my legs. I bit into his shoulder instead, feeling and hearing him groan at the same time. Everything was moving so fast, but I was almost there. Close. Really damned close. All I needed was a little more—

Ice-cold water hit us with the force of a truck.

"*Motherfucker!*" Painter shouted, slipping. My legs were all tangled around his and then we were falling toward the tub and all I could think about was how hard that bitch Jessica would laugh at me for this. I closed my eyes, bracing for a hit that never came because Painter somehow managed to twist midair, protecting me. Then we crashed into the side of the tub together, in a tangle of body parts and very cold water.

"Are you okay?" I gasped, trying to push myself up. Painter blinked, looking a little stunned.

"Yeah, I think so," he said, raising an arm to the side of the tub. "You know, that was pretty fuckin' good until the cold water hit."

Jessica burst into the bathroom, lurching to a stop in front of the tub, Taz right behind her.

"Are you guys okay?"

"We were taking a shower," Painter said, his voice dry. "Now we're taking a bath."

"Nice rack," Taz chimed in.

"Pervert," I snapped, trying to pull the shower curtain in front of me. That's when the oval hoop that suspended it from the ceiling collapsed, sending curtain and metal bars down and around us in a giant clatter.

Then the water went from icy cold to burning hot and I screamed. I'm not entirely sure what happened after that, but I do know it involved Taz laughing, Painter wrapping a towel around me, and Jessica getting carried downstairs over Taz's shoulder.

PAINTER

Well, at least Taz enjoyed himself.

Fucker.

I followed Mel toward her bedroom after our bathroom cluster-fuck, her all wrapped up in a towel and me buck naked, clothing in hand. Despite the whole shower-collapsing-on-our-heads-while-the-water-tortured-us episode, I was still horny as hell and ready to go at it again.

So much for keeping things in the friend zone.

This might be a problem, because I had the feeling that Mel wasn't the friends-with-benefits type and I wasn't exactly the king of loving relationships . . . yet the thought of walking out of here and setting her free wasn't working for me. We probably needed to have a serious talk to resolve these issues, but I'd gotten a message an hour ago from Gage, saying he needed me up in Hallies Falls by the early afternoon. That left me about twenty, thirty minutes max before I had to kiss Mel good-bye with no idea when I'd be back.

So we had to talk fast.

Of course, I could just fuck her again instead.

Might be my last chance.

I processed all of this as we stepped up into her room. It felt like another world in here, our own place where reality couldn't touch us and things were perfect.

"Hey," she said, turning to me and smiling, playing with the edges of her towel where she'd tucked it in across her breasts. "So, we have to leave for the carnival in about forty-five minutes. Got any ideas how we might pass the time until then?"

So much for getting laid again, because I was about to piss her off even more than I'd realized. I'd forgotten that I'd promised to help her, although I'd remembered to stop off and get more face paint, thank fuck. I'd burned through an entire carnival's worth last night.

I sighed. Time to grab sack and do the talk.

"My plans have changed," I said, feeling like an asshole. This wasn't a new sensation for me, but the guilt that came with it was. Not that I ever went out of my way to be a dick—it just came naturally, you know? Melanie frowned, tightening her towel.

Definitely not getting laid. Fucking Gage.

"What's up?" she asked carefully. "I mean, I know you didn't make any promises about us, but I kind of thought—"

"No, this is about the club," I said. "You know how I've been traveling for the club? They just called and said I need to head back out. Like, I need to leave in half an hour, and I gotta go pack a bag and shit. So I can't do the carnival with you."

Mel cocked her head at me.

"Are you blowing me off?" she asked, her voice very serious. "Because I'd really prefer it if you had the decency to do it directly, rather than leading me on."

"No, I'm not blowing you off," I said, wishing I had words to explain how I felt about all this. "Look, I'm a jackass. I get that. But

I really have to go and I'm not even sure how long I'll be gone. I promise I'll stay in touch and text as much as I can. I'm hoping you'll wait to make any judgments about us and what happened until I get back. I know that Jess is probably just waiting to fill your head with shit about me, and I'm sure a lot of it will be true. But this is between you and me, nobody else."

She nodded slowly.

"I can do that," she said.

The relief I felt was enough to scare me—I'd never cared about anyone like this. Hell, what I'd felt for Em was nothing. Why had I been so obsessed with her?

"I wasn't in love with Em," I blurted out.

"What?"

Smooth, asshole. Real smooth. But I was all in now, so might as well run with it.

"They probably told you I'm an asshole who led Em on for a long time. I did that, and then I lost her. But you should know that I wasn't in love with her. I think I just liked the idea of marrying into the club. Pic's been like a dad to me—guess I just wanted it to be official."

"Okay . . ." she said slowly, obviously confused. Christ, I was botching the hell out of this.

"Look, I know I don't have any right to ask this, but I want you to stay away from other guys while I'm gone."

I saw a flash of something cross her face—satisfaction? Hard to tell. "And if I do? What about you?"

"Me?"

Mel rolled her eyes, crossing her arms over her chest. "Will you be dating anyone else?"

"I don't date," I said. From the look on her face, I wasn't helping my cause. "But I won't fuck anyone, if that's what you're asking."

I thought about Marsh's sister and our plan. Could I keep that promise? Did it even count, if I did it for the club?

"Okay," Mel said after a long pause, giving me a shy smile. I fell into her eyes for a moment, and then I was stepping forward and pulling her in for a kiss. Her arms wrapped around my neck as I pushed her down onto the futon. This was more awkward than you'd think, because she was wearing one of those big bath sheets wrapped around her at least three times. I kept trying to reach under it but I couldn't get through the damned layers—fuckin' thing was better than a chastity belt.

"This is like trying to bang a burrito," I said finally, frustrated. Mel burst out laughing, which didn't help because now she was wiggling around and I couldn't even find the edge of the damned thing.

"Let me up," she gasped. "It'll never work."

She was right. I let her go, lying back on the bed to watch as she stood. She turned away, peeking over her shoulder at me, which was simultaneously adorable and sexy as hell, a combination that usually doesn't go together. I mean, I think bunny rabbits are cute, but I don't want to fuck one. *What the hell's wrong with you? Mellie's stripping down and you're thinking about rabbits!*

They'd been right—I really did need professional help.

Mel had the towel completely open now, although she still held it loosely around her. She looked like a Harley pinup girl, all teasing curves and dripping water.

"You're the most beautiful thing I've ever seen," I managed to say, and I meant every word. "I have no idea how I'm lucky enough to be here with you right now, but please know you have my eternal appreciation."

Christ, did I just grow a pussy?

I gave a quick glance to check, because the shit coming out of my mouth sounded like a fucking Hallmark card. Nope, that was definitely my cock down there, and he was saluting Mel's towel-wrangling skills.

She gave that shy smile again, letting the towel fall slowly to the floor. I waited for her to turn around and come to me—I had plans for that cunt of hers, and while I was in a hurry, I was also fucked for time, too. Might as well take advantage of the moment.

Melanie didn't turn around, though. Nope. Instead she dropped slowly to her knees, still facing away. I pushed up on my elbows to find her stretching her back and thrusting her ass out toward me.

My brain short-circuited. Then she crawled slowly in a circle across the floor toward me. Like Catwoman, but totally naked and much, much hotter.

My knees were hanging off the side of the futon. She rose up, catching her tits and squeezing them together as she licked her lips.

I may have blacked out briefly.

If there was a God above, I was about to feel those boobs around my dick. Instead she leaned over and went after me with her mouth. I probably owed a lit candle in church or something, because I'd asked for a titty fuck and the man upstairs had raised me a blow job. The fervent *Jesus fucking Christ* I whispered probably didn't cut it.

Then I lost the ability to think, because her lips were wrapped tight around my cock.

MELANIE

Painter seemed bigger during the daytime.

Going down on him was an impulse that came out of nowhere, but I'd never felt sexier—or more powerful—than I did the instant I first wrapped my lips around his hard length. He let out a moan that was half begging, half worship as I flicked the underside of his cock in what I hoped was an expert move. Based on the noises, I was doing just fine for a beginner. The one and only time Jess had convinced me to smoke pot, she'd ended up giving me a blow job lesson using a banana in London's living room. She showed me how to lick a cock and suck it and even jack a guy off, but I got the munchies before we made it to deep-throating, so I'd eaten the banana.

Probably just as well, because that monster of Painter's wouldn't fit down my throat in a million years anyway.

I followed the flicking with a swirl of my tongue, running it around the ridge ringing his cockhead.

"Shit, Mel," he murmured, reaching down to gather my hair in his hand. Turning my head to the side, I licked up and down his length, exploring the ridges and bumps of him with my fingers and tongue. Then I started working my way back up again, looking up to meet his gaze as I opened my mouth wide, wrapping my lips around him.

Salt.

That was my first impression. He tasted salty, but not in a nasty way. Tightening my mouth, I started bobbing my head up and down, taking care not to graze him with my teeth. He was too big to go far, so I used one hand to grasp him firmly, pumping in time with my head.

"That's fuckin' unreal," he said, and the words were strained, as if it caused him physical pain to speak. I liked this, I decided. I liked the sense of control it gave me, because no matter how big and tough he was, in this instant Painter was all mine.

My nipples tightened at the thought, and the desire I'd felt for him in the tub came roaring back. I could touch myself, I realized. Give myself exactly what I wanted while I sucked him off. The thought felt dirty, which should've put me off. Instead it turned me on even more. Reaching down with my free hand, I found the spot between my legs so hungry to be touched.

Wow . . . Oh, wow.

That was really nice. There must've been something about tasting him that enhanced my own sensations, because touching myself had never felt like this before. Pausing, I pulled back to lick him like an ice cream cone. His entire body trembled. Then his hand tightened in my hair, pushing me back down over his length.

Something changed then.

Up to that point, I'd been in control. Now both of his hands cupped my head and I realized he could do just about anything to me and I wouldn't be able to stop him. It should've scared me. Instead my fingers worked faster, because I wanted him that much more.

"Mel, I want to come on your tits," he muttered, tugging back on my hair. It took an instant to sink in, and then I was pulling free. That's when he spotted my hand down between my legs. His eyes widened and he came with a gasp, come spurting out of his cock, spraying across my chest. Then he caught me under the armpits, dragging me up his body. An instant later his hand reached down between my legs from behind, plunging into my depths.

The world exploded.

I closed my eyes, sinking into the sensation as stars danced behind my eyelids. Holy crap. Who'da thunk blowing a guy could be *this good*?

"You're fuckin' gorgeous when you come, Mel," he said, his voice almost reverent as he ran his hands up and down my back. Sighing, I snuggled into his warmth, wishing he didn't have to leave. We lay there quietly, and I didn't know about him, but I figured so long as I didn't actually *see* how late it was, I could pretend time wasn't passing.

"Babe, I gotta go," he whispered after not nearly long enough. I rubbed my nose against his shoulder, then gave it a little nip. He laughed. "What was that for?"

"That's your punishment," I said, pretending to glare at him. "You ruined my shower, you know. I was getting all cleaned up for this hot guy who was coming over."

He laughed again. "Yeah, sorry about that. He's not gonna make it, though. I ran him over with my bike. I bought breakfast—didn't want it getting cold."

That made me giggle.

"This sucks, but I really do have to go," he said, kissing the top of my head. Giving him one last squeeze, I rolled to the side, watching as he sat up and pulled on his pants.

"Let me guess—you can't say where you're going?" I asked. Painter shook his head.

"Nope," he said. "And much as it sucks, it's time to head out. It's important."

"Okay," I said, feeling let down. He leaned down over me, giving me one last lingering kiss on the lips before running a finger down my nose.

"I'll stay in touch this time," he murmured. "Promise. If you don't hear from me, it's because I'm working and can't risk it."

"Let me guess . . . This isn't doing something for the Reapers like painting that mural for the Armory? You know, I bet you could make good money with your painting. Those portraits at your place were really good, even if they weren't finished."

"Yeah, because art is so fucking lucrative," he said, rolling his eyes. "It's fun, but the club has more important shit that needs doing. I'm gonna go now—take care, okay?"

Then he gave me a hard kiss and walked out of the room. Five minutes later Jess opened my door without knocking as I scrambled to cover myself with a blanket. At least Taz wasn't behind her this time . . .

"You and I *will* be having a talk later," she said, her face stern. "But right now I need you downstairs and ready for the carnival in ten minutes."

I scowled.

"When you're trying to recruit volunteers, it's a good idea to be nice. You know, the opposite of your normal self?"

She sighed and shook her head.

"I'm not being mean—I'm just worried about you. This is a dangerous game you're playing."

Oh, she was so out of line. *Sooo* out of line.

"Hypocrite, much? At least I know Painter's real name. You dragged Taz home and I'll bet you don't know his. Do you?"

Her eyes flicked away. *Ha! Suck it, bitch.*

"That's different," she replied after a long pause.

"How—*exactly*—is it different?"

"I don't care who I sleep with," she said, shrugging. "Maybe that makes me a slut, but I don't get emotionally involved when I fuck someone. It's just sex . . . but I don't think it's just sex for you and Painter, and that means you're going to be really hurt when he screws you over. And he *will* screw you over—he's like me, Mel. Slutty. He doesn't care who he hurts and he's got the track record to prove it. You deserve better than a guy who'll use you and then disappear."

Wow. That was dark.

"I think that's simultaneously the nicest and nastiest thing you've ever said to me," I admitted, frustrated. I reached for a

T-shirt, pulling it over my head before leaning toward my dresser for some fresh panties. (One of the joys of having a very small bedroom—you can always reach everything.) She sighed, dropping down next to me on the bed.

"Melanie, you're the best friend I've ever had," she said, catching and holding my gaze. "You're the one who never judges me or hates me for the stupid shit I've done—"

"Oh, I've hated you a few times."

She rolled her eyes, bumping into me with her shoulder. "You know what I mean. It's not a secret I've had issues. The counseling has helped, but you've stood by me through everything, even before I pulled my head out of my ass. You're always the smart one, the one making the good decisions. You keep me on track and tell me when I'm doing something stupid that'll hurt me. Now it's my turn. Painter and Taz are fun guys—they're sexy and exciting, and I'm sure Painter's really good in the sack. Taz sure as hell is. But don't think for one instant that I believe what he says or that I'm counting on him to be around when I need him."

"Hey, just because you had a bad experience with Painter doesn't mean he's incapable of doing good things," I snapped. "And what's with this 'I bet he's good in the sack' shit? I thought you slept with him last year, out at the Armory."

The thought of them together still ate at me. I'd always sworn I didn't want to know the details. Now I did. I totally did.

Jess looked away.

"It wasn't a bad experience because of him, not really. I was fucked up that night, drunk and stupid. We spent about half an hour together in a room upstairs, me and him and another guy, Banks. That's when London showed up to rescue me, along with Reese."

"But how did you go from drunk and stupid to screwing two guys?" I asked without thinking. Shit, how inappropriate was *that* question? "Sorry."

"We've covered the whole slut thing already," Jess said, looking embarrassed. "So, moving along—that sucked. I was humiliated and pissed and I probably blamed him for a while, which is ridiculous because the whole thing was my idea in the first place. Not only that, he saved my life down in California and spent a year in jail for his trouble, so if anything, I owe him even more than I owe you. But here's reality—he's not interested in being with anyone long-term and unless you've been kidnapped and reprogrammed by aliens in the last twenty-four hours, you're not looking to be a club whore. I just don't see what good can come from the two of you sleeping together."

"Maybe I just want to have fun," I told her, resentment building. "Have you considered that? I've busted ass for years, trying to hold my dad together and my life and school and everything else. Maybe it's my turn to have some fucking fun, so you should back off."

Jess stared at me, stunned.

"Mel . . ."

"No," I continued. I was on a roll. Maybe we should sort this shit out once and for all. "I love you and I appreciate the fact that you're worried about me. You did your duty as a friend. I'm awarding you a gold star and a cookie, but now it's time for you to walk out of here and let me make my own decisions."

Jess stood slowly, still looking unhappy. "All right, then. I'll leave you to it. But Mel?"

"Yeah?"

"When it all falls apart around you and you're scared shitless? I want you to remember one thing."

"What's that?" I asked, narrowing my eyes.

"Remember that I'll always be here for you, because I love you," she said quietly, her voice breaking. "Just like you've always been here for me."

"Shit, Jessica . . ." I said, eyes filling with tears. I stepped toward her as she stepped toward me and then we were hugging and I couldn't quite remember why I'd been so pissed. We stood like that—holding each other—for long seconds. Finally she broke the silence.

"Mel?"

"Yeah?"

"Don't think for one minute you're off the hook for face painting."

I pushed away, trying to glare at her but I started laughing instead, and then she started laughing and everything was okay.

Ten minutes later, I came racing down the stairs, my wet hair pulled into a loose bun on top of my head. I'd managed to clean up again, get dressed, brush my teeth, and even slapped on some lip gloss.

I hit the dining room, discovering the remains of our painting marathon the night before. Shit. I'd forgotten I needed to go buy paint. Jessica was going to kill me.

"Looking for these?" she asked, a shopping bag dangling from one hand.

"Face paints?" I asked hopefully. She nodded.

"Painter went out and bought them this morning."

"See, he's not that bad!"

She cocked a brow at me. "Seriously? He can buy you off with fifteen bucks of paint?"

"Don't be a bitch."

"But I do it so well," she said, a reluctant smile coming across her face. "It was thoughtful. I can admit that. He left a note, too."

"Let me see," I said. She dug out a piece of folded paper, handing it over.

"I'll save you some time. He said he's sorry he had to bail on volunteering, but that he didn't want to leave you hanging after he used up all the paint. He'll be in touch as soon as he can."

I opened the note, and sure enough—she'd quoted it almost perfectly. Suddenly I had an ugly thought.

"Jess?"

"Yeah?"

"You know how you've had the same phone code since high school, and I know that code?"

"Uh-huh."

"Do you know *my* phone code?"

She stared at me, raising a brow.

"Of course."

"I would never read your email or text messages. Just so you know."

"Glad to hear it."

"Jess?"

She blinked at me innocently. Like Bambi. "Yeah?"

"Is it even remotely possible that you don't read my messages?"

My best friend gave me a beautiful, loving smile.

"Anything's possible, Mellie. Now get your ass in gear—those kids get pissy if they have to wait too long for the carnival to start."

CHAPTER TWELVE

PAINTER

Five hours later I pulled up to the shithole of a hotel Gage and I had been staying in the past week, wondering how long I'd be stuck here . . . I was ready to be home again already. Mel had done a number on me, no question. Never gave a damn before where the club sent me or worried how long it would take.

When I turned into the gravel parking lot—yeah, the hotel was *that* classy—I saw the cherry red Mustang convertible we'd seen in town last weekend parked next to Gage's truck. Well, wasn't that just interesting . . . the scandalous Ms. Tinker Garrett was leaning back against it, laughing at something Gage had just said. He was standing just a little too close to her.

Dirty fucker.

I bit back a grin, pulling my bike up next to them.

"Hey there," I said. "Aren't you going to introduce me, Coop?"

"You got here earlier than I expected," he said, eyes narrowing just a little, although his voice was friendly enough. "This is Tinker—looks like I'll be renting from her. I need a place and she's got one, so it works out perfect. Tinker, this is Levi, a good friend of mine."

She turned toward me, smiling brightly. God, she really was a pinup girl. All shiny hair, innocent face, and a body that wouldn't quit. Up close I could see she was older than I'd realized—probably in her mid-thirties. Shooting Gage a speculative look, I had to bite back a smirk.

He had a thing for her, big-time.

Wasn't that just unfortunate as hell, given the fact that he'd spent the last week chasing Marsh's little sister, Talia. She had a bangin' body, but no softness. No, that girl was a first-class bitch. Wouldn't be a bit surprised if she had a pussy full of teeth. Sharp teeth.

Damned good thing I wouldn't be the one fuckin' her. Dodged a bullet there—Talia liked the older guys.

"Nice to meet you, Levi," Tinker said, giving me a look every bit as sweet as the one she'd given Gage. Oh, that'd piss him off. "Looking forward to you moving in, Cooper. I need to get going, though—I'm headed down to Ellensburg for the night. Later!"

We stepped back, watching as she climbed into her car, backing it carelessly out of the parking lot before tearing off in a spray of gravel.

"Damn, she handles that stick like a pro," I murmured.

"Eat shit, *Levi*," Gage said. "Play nice or I'll give you to Talia. She asked about you last night—guess one of her girls is into you."

"Yeah, not interested. I'd just as soon my dick not fall off. Never seen such a diseased-looking pack of bitches."

"Now, that's not very nice," he said, throwing an arm over my shoulder. "Especially since you're a bigger slut than all of them combined."

I fucking hated it when he was right.

"Was there a reason you made me drive all the way across the state?" I asked. "I was in the middle of something."

"Fucking some skank? We have skanks here, too. You'll get over it."

"Actually, I was with Melanie," I confessed. "I spent the night at her place."

Gage raised a brow.

"I thought she was your new princess," he said. "Since when do you touch those?"

"Since last night, apparently," I admitted. "She was good, Gage. Really good. I think this might be the real thing."

"Give it a week and you'll be over her. C'mon inside. I need to fill you in on some shit."

He was all business now, and I followed him into the room, wondering what'd happened.

"Beer?" he asked. I shook my head, flopping back on one of the sagging full-size beds, propping my hands behind my neck. Hadn't gotten much sleep last night—might as well relax while I could. From the look on Gage's face, we'd have a shit storm to deal with soon enough.

"We're going to a party out at the Nighthawks' clubhouse in a few hours," he said, sitting down across from me. "Talia was at the bar again last night. We danced for a while and I bought her a few drinks. Then her brother showed up with his crew and I finally got an introduction. We started talking and I fed him my line about being an independent rider. Bought a couple rounds and the next thing I know, I'm taking Talia to the party tonight. She wants you along for her girl."

"I'm not gonna fuck her," I told him without a second thought. *Huh.*

"Pussy-whipped?" he asked, his voice serious. "Club needs you on this, Painter. You think I wanna screw that bitch Talia? Fuck no, not with a sweet piece like Tinker around. We all gotta do our part, bro."

I shook my head, frowning.

"I'm serious about Mel."

"She doesn't need to know."

"How 'bout this—I'll take it one step at a time, see how it plays out."

Gage cocked his head. "You'll do what needs to be done?"

"Don't I always?"

"Always have before. There's more."

"What?"

"This morning I saw someone I recognized," he said, his tone grim. "Someone who will recognize me."

"That's no good. Passing through?"

"It's possible," he said. "He was by himself. Could be a coincidence."

"Who was it? Anyone I know?"

"Unlikely—this shit went down before your time. Few years back, we had a hangaround whose girlfriend worked at The Line. Turned out he was a snitch, and it's 'cause of him and that bitch of his that Bolt served time. She set him up—they were working with the Feds. The snitch pulled a runner. Called himself Hands, no idea what his real name is."

"You don't think it's a coincidence he turned up here?"

"I got a bad feeling about it," he admitted. "Can't think of a good reason for him to be in Hallies Falls. If he's still workin' with the cops, he may be targeting Marsh and his boys now. Much as I hate the fucker, last thing we need is LEO sniffing out the cross-border trade and shutting it down. Throw in the fact that he could blow my cover and we got a big problem."

No shit.

"You didn't just call me because of a party," I said flatly, forcing my body to stay relaxed. Gage shook his head, looking almost regretful.

"Hopin' it won't come to that, but we can't let him talk. Assuming he's even here—could be he was passing through. But if he's after Marsh, odds are good he'll be at the party tonight."

"Pic know?"

"He knows we have a complication," Gage replied. "Couldn't risk giving any details—when Bolt hears, he'll lose his shit, so I'd like to handle it before that happens. It's on you and me. I see him at the party, you'll have to find a way to get him out of there without raising suspicions. On the bright side, Rance is ready and waiting—we get Hands, we'll haul his ass to Bellingham for questioning. After they get as much info as they can, they'll take care of him for us."

"It's never simple, is it?"

"Never has been before, so no reason to expect it to start now," he said, shrugging. "I need to ask you something."

"What?"

"You sure you're up for something this heavy? I know you take a big risk every time you come over here, but they catch you with Hands, you'll go away for a long fuckin' time. Doesn't matter how much money we give Torres, he wouldn't be able to cover up something this serious."

"Then I won't get caught," I said. "Whoever does the job takes the same risk, and it's not like I have kids."

"Yeah, but it sounds like you've got something goin' on with Melanie."

"I didn't see Horse or Ruger turning soft when they met their old ladies."

"I don't see them in this hotel room, either."

"I'm here," I told him, my voice steady. "The club comes first— that's the way it is. We'll handle this situation, no worries."

"Gotcha, brother."

Talia's friend—a brown-haired girl named Sadie—was wrapped tight around me, squealing as we tore down the highway. Her fingernails were long and red like talons, and they were currently digging deep into my stomach. For reasons completely beyond me she seemed to think this was sexy.

Gage was ahead of us, leading the way to the Nighthawk Raiders' clubhouse, Talia on the back of his bike. The girls were already wasted when we'd pulled up to their place. Sadie had done her best to crawl inside my pants while Gage disappeared into the bathroom with Talia for a quickie. I could hear her screaming "Harder, Daddy!" through the door the whole time, so I guess it was good we sent Gage after her instead of me—according to Sadie, Talia thought "old guys" were hot.

I had every intention of sharing that little tidbit with all the brothers back home, too.

Now we'd reached the Nighthawk clubhouse, an old commercial

building on the northern edge of town. A chain-link fence lined with razor wire surrounded a large, open parking lot to one side of the building.

We parked our bikes on the street, away from the line of club bikes in front of the building. A couple of prospects were lurking around outside. They didn't particularly impress me. Neither did the club's motorcycles, for that matter. Most of them were dirty and a couple were flat-out rat bikes. Back home, our prospects would be all over that shit, shining up the chrome and making sure everything stayed clean.

No fuckin' pride.

Loud music poured out as we walked toward the large rolling gate into the fenced area. Talia dragged Gage along proudly, like a cat with a particularly juicy mouse. Sadie was giggling and hanging all over me. Much as I wanted to hate her, she didn't strike me as nasty like Talia—just young and fucking stupid. I could already see her in a few years, all played out and broken-down. Girls like her didn't last long in this life, not if they couldn't find themselves a good old man.

Talia headed straight for the prospects. "Is Marsh here?"

"He's out back."

"This is my friend Cooper," she said. "And his friend Levi. Keep an eye on their bikes. I find one scratch and you'll pay, got it?"

The fuck? I could hardly believe what I'd just heard . . . No fuckin' way she should be talking to a prospect like that—that was business for patch holders. Gage shot me a quick look, as if to say *Told you so.* The Nighthawk Raiders had really fallen to shit.

The prospect gave me an evil glare as he turned toward the gate, and I couldn't blame him. We were out of line.

The party wasn't much better. There was the usual mess of club whores, all fucked up on God knows what. A few old ladies here and there, some loud music. Kegs. The brothers were a bit of a mix—there were a couple who looked pretty solid to me, which matched what we'd heard from Pipes. Most of the others were high as shit.

No wonder they kept running short on product.

As we went to grab some beer, Talia started introducing us around. I noticed the Nighthawk brothers fell into two distinct groups. Those with newer, shinier cuts were falling all over themselves to suck up to her—at least to her face—while a slightly older group with more faded colors kept their distance. I caught a few of them staring me down, and the looks weren't friendly. The rumors about Marsh recruiting heavily had to be true, because no way this many new members had prospected in. I wondered how the hell things had gotten this far. Something was deeply, deeply fucked in this club.

We wandered over to the keg and pumped ourselves some beer, which Sadie sucked down like her life depended on it. After a while I started swapping cups with her, letting her drink my share, too. They had a couple of fire barrels set up around the back side of the building—also fenced in—and Talia herded us toward a big man standing in the center of a group.

He had long, dark blond hair pulled back in a ponytail, with a girl under one arm and a bottle of tequila in the other. His patches identified him as the president. Marsh.

Showtime.

Talia slipped up to him, and I noted how the other girl ducked away from Marsh, making room for his sister without being told. He wrapped his arm around Talia, giving her a squeeze.

"How's my baby girl tonight?" he asked, his voice strong and booming.

"Great," she said, popping up on her toes to kiss his cheek. He looked closer to Gage's age than mine, so she had to be a good ten, fifteen years younger than he was. Interesting. "You remember Cooper? We met him at the bar the other night—he's that independent rider I was telling you about. And that's his friend Levi."

Marsh looked us over, nodding toward Gage.

"Good to see you again," he said. "You find drinks?"

Gage raised his cup in salute. "Thanks for the invite. I'm new to the area, still finding my way around."

"You'd mentioned that. What's a long-haul trucker doing in Hallies Falls? Isn't this a little out of the way for you?"

Gage shrugged.

"Had to get away from my bitch of an ex," he lied smoothly. "The cunt's tryin' to take away my kids. She's got a new man down in Ellensburg—figure this is close enough to go see 'em but not so close I have to see her fat ass on a daily basis. You got any kids?"

"No, but I raised this one here," he said, smiling at Talia proudly. *Huh. That explained a lot.* "She's been my little shadow her whole damned life."

Talia giggled, kissing him again . . . just a little close to the mouth. I kept my face blank. Marsh looked toward me next.

"So what's your story?"

"Coop is my cousin," I told him. "Just got done serving time—tryin' to figure out my next step. He's been helping me out."

Marsh nodded his head thoughtfully, and I knew he'd taken the bait. Two independents with questionable backgrounds could be useful to him.

"You ride, too?"

I grinned—wouldn't have to lie about this part.

"Live to ride," I said. "Worst part about bein' inside was losin' my bike. Now I'm on the road every day. Feels like I can breathe again."

Marsh nodded.

"Enjoy yourselves—we throw a good party, and there's always room for independents around here, so long as they know their place."

"Appreciate the hospitality," Gage said. "We'll keep our eyes open, let you know if we see anything you should know about."

"Sounds good."

Marsh gave Talia one last squeeze, then turned away, clearly done with us. I shared a glance with Gage—that'd gone well.

"More beer," Sadie whined, but Talia wanted to do shots, pulling us in another direction. Marsh's sister might be hot as hell, but thank God that Gage had to deal with her. All issues with Mel aside, no fuckin' way I'd want to stick my dick in that cunt.

Teeth, I'm tellin' you.

Bitch would probably bite it right off.

• • •

Hours passed—felt like the party was endless.

We'd been drinking all night, although I'd been dumping mine quietly or pawning it off on Sadie, who was now so wasted I wasn't sure how I'd get her home again. She sure as shit wouldn't be able to stay on a bike. Talia thought this was hysterical—apparently Sadie did the same thing every weekend with a new guy (or two, or six) and sometimes she just crashed at the club, where anyone could have a go at her. Good friend that she was, Talia assured me that she always rolled Sadie onto her side before leaving her behind.

You know, so she wouldn't drown in her own vomit.

Generally I tried to stay pretty open-minded about people—not my place to judge—but Talia made it difficult. As for Sadie, I felt more sorry for her than anything else. I mean, she was an adult making her own decisions, but shit like that doesn't happen in a vacuum. Something had fucked her up along the way. Horrible human being that I am, I mostly just felt relieved it wasn't my job to rescue her.

We hadn't seen Hands yet—so far the best part of the night. Maybe his passing through town had been a random coincidence after all. Generally I didn't believe in those, but I guess anything's possible.

As it turned out, I was right.

There's no such thing as coincidence.

We were standing out by the barrels talking to some of the brothers—the newer ones, Marsh's puppets—when Gage reached up to scratch his nose. That was our sign. I followed the line of his gaze to see a stringy little guy, hardly taller than Sadie, talking to Marsh. His hair was shaved, with a tattoo of a swastika on the back of his head. Aryan. Fuckin' great, Gage hadn't mentioned that. Those guys were crazy as shit, with their bombs and their bunkers.

We had to take care of this fucker and do it in a way that wouldn't raise any questions. Gage was already turning away, making sure that Handsy-boy couldn't get a look at his face.

I needed a diversion.

Up to this point, I'd seen Sadie as annoying and pitiable, but she chose that moment to make herself useful.

"I'm gonna puke!" she wailed, turning toward Talia frantically. Her friend—also drunk off her ass by this point—started laughing and then Sadie exploded.

Literally.

I've never seen so much barf come out of one human being, and that includes the time six of the brothers got food poisoning from some bad macaroni salad. She was spraying everyone and every-thing, including Talia, who went from laughing to screaming in an instant, pointing and yelling like a fuckin' banshee.

Empathetic fuckers that they were, the Nighthawk guys lucky enough to be out of range seemed to find this hilarious, Marsh and Hands included. I edged toward them, keeping an eye on Handsy-boy as a prospect came running with a hose. He passed me and I took the opportunity to "trip" over the hose, crashing into the snitch as hard as I could. We hit the pavement together *hard*, and I'm not gonna lie—it hurt like a sonofabitch.

The fuckers around us laughed even harder.

"Jesus," I moaned, rolling to my side as I tried to catch my breath. Hands's face was right next to mine, mouth slack. I watched as someone reached down, checking the pulse at his neck.

"Out cold," a man said, sounding vaguely pleased by this news. I looked up to see one of the older brothers—part of the pre-Marsh crew, I guess, because he wasn't wearing a shiny new cut—kneeling next to us.

"Hey, I'm really sorry about that," I whined, trying to sound harmless and sincere at the same time. "I don't know what happened."

"Prospect tripped you," he said. "You okay?"

"Yeah, I'm fine," I said, although my side ached like a mother-fucker. If I'd cracked a rib, Gage was gonna owe me. "He gonna be okay?"

Hands chose that moment to groan, blinking slowly.

"What the fuck happened?" he asked, his voice a hoarse whis-per. Time to bring it home.

"I tripped over the hose and knocked you down," I told him, hoping I didn't sound too pleased with myself. "I'm really fuckin' sorry about that. Here, let me help you out."

Slowly I rose to my feet, reaching down to pull him up behind me. He swayed, obviously still a little stunned. *Damn, I got him good.*

"How's the head?" the Nighthawk brother asked. "You gonna be okay?"

Hands started to nod, then he winced. I exchanged a look with the older man, eyes flicking to his name patch. Cord. Huh.

"You think he needs the ER?" I asked.

"No ER," Hands said quickly. "I just gotta sit down for a while."

"I'm real sorry," I said again. "No hard feelings?"

Hands stared at me, and I could see he was having trouble tracking. I really needed to buy Sadie some flowers, because this couldn't have gone better if I'd scripted it. Sometimes the good guys actually win.

"Uh, no prob . . . *fuck* . . ."

"Let's get him home," Cord said. He turned to look around, spotting another prospect. "Get your ass over here!"

The kid hesitated, as if wondering whether he should listen to Cord. That confirmed it—there were definitely two factions, and this guy wasn't on Marsh's side. Good to know. The big man cracked his knuckles and spoke again. "Get your ass over here. You're not in the fuckin' club yet, cocksucker."

Interesting—how the hell had Marsh come into power with this guy around? Didn't add up.

"Take this loser home," Cord said, nodding toward Hands. "You can use the truck."

The prospect leaned over, grabbing Hands under the arms to drag him out.

"Want some help?" I asked. "Feel kinda responsible."

The prospect looked to Cord again, silently asking for permission this time. Better. It was already clear that we'd have to clean house at some point, but this particular brother gave me some hope that it wouldn't be a totally lost cause.

"What's your name?" Cord asked.

"Levi," I told him. "Just came by for the party with my cousin, Cooper. Talia—that girl over there—she invited us."

Cord nodded, looking faintly disgusted.

"I'm sure he could use the help with this piece of shit," he said. "Thanks."

And that was that. I helped the prospect carry Hands out to a battered old truck parked on the far side of the building. He was conscious but not particularly alert as we tossed him into the backseat. Perfect.

"Thanks for the help," the young prospect said, firing up the engine as I took the passenger seat. "He's small but he's heavy. I'm Cody, by the way."

"Good to meet you," I said. "Sorry about this."

"Not your fault. I'm pretty new, but stuff like this happens all the time. That girl always pukes, too. No idea why they keep letting her come around—we always have to clean up after her."

That's your fuckin' job, prospect. This guy would last about ten minutes at the Armory.

"Yeah, that's weird. So how long you been with the club?"

"Only a couple weeks," he admitted. "They're looking for new members, though, and it's always sounded kind of fun. I'm saving up for my bike right now."

It took a minute for his words to sink in.

"You don't have a bike?"

"Well, I've got a dirt bike, but nothing street legal. Marsh said it was okay, so long as I get one in the next month."

I had literally no place in my head to put this information. Fucking hell, the club wasn't just dysfunctional . . . it wasn't even a real club. No wonder Pipes had issues. He must be losing his mind, hearing about shit like this, powerless to do a damned thing to stop it. We passed through town and turned down a gravel road off the highway, stopping after half a mile at an isolated trailer. I bit back a pleased smile—couldn't have asked for a better setup. I'd head out here later tonight and take care of this fucker, easy.

Almost *too* easy. Was it some kind of trap?

"Here we go," Cody said. "Hands, you got a key?"

"S'unlocked," the man in the backseat managed to say. "No worries."

Cody gave me a concerned look.

"You think he's gonna die here, we leave him?" he asked. I shrugged.

"You got an order to take him home," I said. "That means we bring him home. He'll be fine, I'm sure."

"Okay."

Ten minutes later we had Hands laid out across his couch, and I'd even covered him in an old afghan I'd found tossed across the back of a chair. I'm thoughtful like that.

"Back to the party now?" Cody asked. I nodded.

"Yeah, gotta figure out how to get my date home. She's kind of fucked up."

"Who're you with?" he asked, eyes lighting up. I could've laughed, the poor kid looked so desperate.

"Sadie," I said shortly.

"Sadie the Sprayer?" he asked, wrinkling his nose. Fuck, not even the prospects wanted her.

"Yeah. Sadie the Sprayer," I admitted.

"Hope you like barf," the kid said, snorting. "She's hot, but watch out—that chick is disgusting."

Christ. No wonder she needed Talia to find her dates.

I wasn't able to shake Sadie until nearly three in the morning. The good news was I managed to get the Princess of Puke home without her falling along the way. She'd even sobered up a bit, probably because none of the booze managed to stay in her for long.

Fucking hell, but the club owed me for this one in a big way.

I got back to the hotel first, so I settled in to watch some TV and wait for Gage. He showed up around four a.m., looking rough.

"Have fun with Talia?" I taunted softly, sitting up to grab my boots. Still a lot of work ahead of us for the night—Hands was waiting.

"Fuck off."

"Did you know they call Sadie 'the Sprayer'?"

Gage shook his head, and he had the grace to look sheepish. "Only met her once before, and she wasn't that drunk. Sorry about that—I had no idea what you were in for."

I nodded, accepting his apology.

"What's the story with Hands?" he asked.

"Took him home with the prospect, so we know where he lives now. We can go over there and talk to him, then bag him up for Rance. Nice to have a witness that I left him safe and sound hours ago. Nothing to connect me when he disappears. You ready to go?"

Gage sighed, reaching for the mini-fridge. He pulled out a Red Bull, offering it to me silently. I shook my head, knowing the adrenaline would wake me up once we got to work on our victim. Hopefully he'd be alert enough to talk. Gage popped the can open and chugged it.

"Talia tire you out, old man?"

He flipped me off, then grabbed a backpack and pulled out a snub-nosed pistol.

"Let's go."

Ten minutes later we were driving toward Hands's trailer in a little SUV Gage produced out of nowhere. I wasn't sure how he got it and I sure as shit wasn't going to ask. I also didn't ask about the tarp, the duct tape, the two metal bats, or the pliers—I trusted he knew what he was doing and that he hadn't left a trail behind us.

Hopefully there wouldn't be any complications, but if there were, our cover was that I'd lost my phone and we'd come out to look for it. I'd mentioned it to Sadie, and she'd even helped me hunt for it as we left the party.

"Nice place," Gage said dryly as we pulled to a stop. No lights on inside, no signs of life at all.

"Fuck, I hope he's not dead or something," I said as we walked toward the door.

"Nah, he didn't hit that hard. You take point, I'll cover."

Hands didn't answer the door when I knocked, but I'd left it unlocked. Opening it slowly, I saw the fucker was still laid out on the couch, sleeping like a baby. A really ugly, Nazi baby.

I'd expected more of a challenge.

"Inside," I told Gage. He followed me in, keeping his gun close as he did a quick search of the trailer. I wasn't carrying these days—that'd be a one-way trip back to Cali if they found it. My parole officer might be on the club payroll but he wasn't a miracle worker.

Gage came back into the living room, then jerked his chin toward our target. *You ready?*

Yeah, I told him with a nod, taking up a position out of his line of fire, but close enough I could jump the fucker if he tried to pull something stupid.

"Wake up, asshole," Gage said. Hands didn't move. Shit, did he have brain damage or something? The fall *had* knocked him out . . . That'd suck. I mean, it wasn't like the guy had much of a future ahead of him or anything—not after what he'd done to Bolt—but we needed answers first.

"Hands—we're talkin' to you," I said, kicking the couch. The man stirred, frowning as he opened his eyes. I clocked the instant he saw the gun pointed at him, because his entire body jerked before going very still. Handsy-boy might've been sleeping before, but he was sure as shit awake now.

"Oh fuck," he said, staring at Gage. Guess that solved the question of whether he'd recognize him. *"Fuck!"*

In an instant, Hands launched himself across the room toward Gage, obviously aware he wouldn't be talking his way out of this one. I jumped for him, tackling him before he could get close. There was no real question who'd win, of course. I was a big guy, and the little rat didn't stand a chance. That didn't stop him from fighting like his life depended on it, which made sense. It did.

We scrabbled across the floor, crashing into the coffee table. I heard the sound of something breaking, which sucked because you don't want to leave a trail at times like this. Now we'd have to torch the place. That pissed me off, so when I got the chance I let him have it, shoving my knee hard into his balls.

Hands screamed, going limp as I straddled him, catching the front of his shirt to jerk his head up.

"Your call how bad this needs to be," I snarled. "Play nice and it won't hurt so much."

He answered me with a head-butt and my nose crunched. Grunting, I slammed his head down into the floor, then caught him across the cheek with a full-power punch. Sweet fire tore through my knuckles, balancing the pain of my nose and clearing my mind. I hit him two more times, then thumped his head against the thin carpet before I realized Gage was shouting.

"Jesus, Painter! He's out again—let it go!"

I turned to glare at him, snarling.

"Stop," Gage said, his voice like ice. It cut through the haze and I dropped my arm.

"Shit," I said, coming back to myself. I looked down at the man's mashed and bloodied face. "Ah fuck. Sorry about that."

"You got some anger management issues," Gage observed, frowning.

"He broke my fuckin' nose," I said, poking at it tentatively. Ouch. Then I looked around. Fucking hell—there was blood all over the floor, shit broken . . . "This sucks."

"Yeah," Gage said, frowning. "Gonna have to burn everything. I'll make it look like an accident, though."

"Sorry about that."

He shook his head. "Don't apologize—getting out clean was a long shot, and once you started bleeding it was all over. That's on him. No worries."

I stood slowly, then looked from Gage to the unconscious, broken man lying on the floor. "No offense, bro, but telling me no worries when we're gonna torch a guy's place before killing him is kinda fucked."

Gage snickered, so I flipped him off. That set him laughing for real and then I joined him, because it really was kinda funny in a sick way.

"I'll go grab the tarp," I told him, standing stiffly. "And the duct tape. Knowing our luck, the fucker'll wake up halfway to Bellingham and try to crash the car."

"Can't blame him for fighting back," Gage said, shrugging. "I mean, he knew the minute he saw my face that we'd have to kill him. He's a snitch but he's not stupid."

"Smart fuckers don't snitch."

"Fair enough."

"Who ya workin' for?"

I stood in the back of the room, watching as Rollins—the Bellingham sergeant at arms—smiled down at Hands. I'd met him a few times and he'd never struck me as overly sane, but watching him work on Hands?

Yeah, this was some fucked-up shit.

I'd pulled in around nine that morning, and we'd been questioning the snitch for close to five hours now. He hadn't broken, which blew me away. The things Rollins could do with a razor blade . . . let's just say the fucker scared me, and I don't scare easy.

Hands was tough, though—he obviously knew we had to kill him just as soon as he talked, which meant we couldn't get the information with false promises of safety. This was about making him suffer enough that he *wanted* to die. We wouldn't let that happen until we'd gotten what we wanted and he had to know it.

Clearly the snitch wanted to live. A lot.

He screamed again as Rollins carefully peeled back the skin on his arm. For an instant I felt sick to my stomach, but I managed to steady it. He set Bolt up, sent him to prison. Not like he didn't deserve it.

"Jesus, just fuckin' talk already," Rance muttered, frowning. "Hate this shit."

The screaming continued, and then it abruptly ended. Fuck. He'd passed out.

"How far you wanna go with this, boss?" Rollins asked, stepping back and cracking his neck. Blood dripped from the gloves covering his hands. "You know I can break him, but I got a feelin' it'll take time. He's strong."

Rance cocked his head, considering. He had all the time in the world, but I was under a ticking clock. Pic'd told me to stick around, hear what Hands had to say . . . But we'd staged that fire at the fucker's place, which meant I really should get my ass back to Idaho sooner rather than later. I wasn't overly worried about them connecting me with Hands, but you never know . . . Best to play it safe—especially now that I had Melanie waiting for me.

"What're your thoughts, Painter?" Rance asked. I considered my choices. Complicating everything was the fact that I'd been awake for nearly thirty hours now, which meant I either had to pop something soon or crash.

"I need sleep," I admitted. "Maybe you could keep trying while I catch a nap . . . I know Pic wants me to hear what he says, but I'm dead on my feet. It'll take me a good six hours to get home, though, and I need to make it there tonight."

"There's a bedroom upstairs," Rance said. "You can rest for a while and we'll see how things go here. I'm not sure this fucker's information is worth keeping him alive long-term. The sooner we get rid of the evidence the better."

"Works for me."

I gave Hands one last look, then walked out the door. The Bellingham Reapers didn't have a full clubhouse like the Armory, just a house outside the city on some acreage. Right now it was mostly deserted, but upstairs I found Jamie, Rance's old lady. She was probably around thirty-five, and the woman was fucking gorgeous. I'd popped wood the first time I met her a couple years back. Then I'd watched as Rance all but murdered a prospect for checking out her ass, which pretty much killed any lingering interest I might've had.

She gave me a sympathetic smile. I don't know how much club

business Rance told her, but she had to have heard the screaming. Not only was she hot, she was a damned good old lady—whatever she might be thinking, she wasn't giving away shit.

"You should let me take those clothes," she said, nodding toward my shirt and pants. I looked down, startled to see they were covered in dried blood. Fuck. Must be more tired than I'd realized—hadn't even occurred to me that I might need to clean up.

"Bummer. I really liked these jeans."

She gave a gentle laugh, rolling her eyes.

"Let me find you something clean to wear," she said. "Then go upstairs and shower. Leave your things in the bathroom and I'll take care of them. There's a bedroom right across the hall—just make yourself comfortable. Sound good?"

Sounded like heaven.

Half an hour later, I was clean. The clothes Jamie gave me fit surprisingly well, and she'd even left a sandwich, chips, and an apple (cut up and everything, like I was a little kid) on the bedside table for me. I wolfed them down, then lay back on the bed for some much-needed rest.

I'd just started to drift off when my phone chimed.

MELANIE: How's it going?

I considered just turning it off, letting myself sleep . . . but then I thought about her soft lips and sweet tits, and I woke right back up again.

ME: Good. Was up late last night. Wiped. How did the carnival go
MELANIE: They won't be asking me to paint faces next year. Ive decided to count that as a win.

I smiled, thinking about those poor ladybugs of hers. They say love makes you blind, but nobody could be *that* blind. One of my first art teachers told me everyone has the power to paint something beautiful—obviously she'd never had Melanie Tucker in one of her classes.

ME: Thats prob for the best.
MELANIE: Hey—thought you were on my side
ME: I didn't report you for crimes against humanity did I?
MELANIE: Ha ha. You suck.
ME: You have no idea . . . I'll be heading back to CDA, prob get there late tonight. Want me to show you just how good I can suck?

She didn't answer, and I smirked . . . then my cell chimed.

MELANIE: You should warn me before you text things like that. Jessica tried to steal the phone when she saw me blushing.
ME: You at home?
MELANIE: Yup. Working on a paper
ME: Go to your room

Would she take the bait? Long seconds passed. Nothing. The phone buzzed again.

MELANIE: I'm on my bed . . .
ME: What are you wearing?
MELANIE: Are you sexting me?
ME: Do you want me to?
MELANIE: I want everything

And suddenly those borrowed jeans weren't fitting so well after all. I reached down, unbuttoning my fly.

MELANIE: I'm wearing a pair of boy-cut panties with lace insets at the side. Baby blue.
ME: What else?

Please say nothing, please say nothing . . .

MELANIE: That's too easy ;) You first.

I looked down at my borrowed clothes, considering how to answer. Telling her that all I had on were castoffs because my own clothes were covered in a dead man's blood seemed less than romantic.

ME: Jeans and a shirt. Not gonna lie—I opened my fly when you said you wanted everything.
MELANIE: Are you hard?

If I hadn't been before, I sure as shit was now.

ME: Every time I talk to you.
MELANIE: Aren't you just romantic?
ME: So what else are you wearing?
MELANIE: Whats it worth to you?
ME: Dinner at my place when I get back—I make truly excellent ramen
MELANIE: How about dinner at your place but I cook? I make excellent foods that aren't ramen
ME: Deal. Now tell me what you're wearing
MELANIE: Nothing . . . and my nipples are hard. I was rolling one of them between my fingers but then I had to stop. Texting you one handed is tough

Oh Jesus. The blood was rushing downward, taking my ability to think with it.

ME: Wouldn' tmind a picture of tha

Fuck. I'd lost the ability to type, too, and not even autocorrect could save me. This girl was dangerous. Reaching inside my briefs, I caught my cock, giving it a rough squeeze. If I closed my eyes I could almost imagine it was her hand instead of mine. I would never—for the rest of my life—forget the instant her tongue touched me the first time. She'd been so hesitant, so careful . . . Turned me on and drove me crazy, because it wasn't enough. I'd had to teach her how to do it harder.

My girl was a damned fast learner, too.

MELANIE: I don't send pics to strange men.

Goddamn it. She was right, of course. Stupid to send pictures, especially to a known asshole like myself.

ME: Guess I'll just have to use my imagination. I know a way
    you won't have to stop touching yourself to talk to me . . .
    call?

That was it. I waited for a minute, then another, imagining Mel playing with her nipples . . . fingering her pussy . . . Now there was a pretty picture. I hooked my thumb under the waistband of my briefs, lifting my hips so I could push them down. Then I grabbed my cock again, jacking it slowly as I waited for her to respond.

The phone rang.

"Hey you," I said, my voice hoarse. "Please tell me you're still naked?"

Melanie giggled. "Well, I'm not *totally* naked—still have my panties on. I feel kind of silly doing this."

"Don't," I told her, dead serious. "This is right up there near the top on my Dirty Fantasies About Melanie List."

"You have a fantasy list about me?" she asked, her voice catching. Shit, did she think I was a perv? Probably. Made sense that she would, because I definitely qualified.

"While I was in prison," I admitted. "Thought about you all the time. Been thinkin' about you from the first day we met, although I tried to keep it under control. Then they locked me up and you started writing. Once you sent me a picture, I was fucked. Decided I'd best roll with it at that point."

"So what sorts of things did you fantasize about?" she asked, her voice lower. Huskier. My fingers slowed, sliding upward to catch the sensitive skin right below my dick's head. *Shit*, that was good. Her tongue would be even better.

"Long list," I told her, sinking back into the pillow. "Used to think a lot about your mouth."

"Really? And what was I doing with my mouth?"

"Let's just say I enjoyed the blow job," I replied, opting not to share that the full fantasy involved fucking her face with her pigtails as handles. See? I'm not a total tool.

"Well it seemed like a good idea at the time. Friday was incredible, by the way. Just thinking about it makes me so . . ." She giggled. "Okay, talking like this feels weird—like I'm in a bad porno."

"Melanie, believe me when I say it's a very, very high-quality pornographic production," I replied, catching my pre-come with my fingers to use as lube. "I like it so much I've got my dick out and I'm jacking off while you talk. Not sure how long I'll last here, but probably not more than a few more minutes, so please finish that fucking sentence."

"Okay," she said, and I heard the smile in her voice. "Just thinking about it makes me so wet."

I bit back a groan.

"How do you know you're wet?" I asked, barely more than a whisper.

"Because I'm touching myself," she said. "I started with my clit, then started to move lower. Now I'm going back and forth between my clit and my . . ."

Her voice trailed off as burning, twisting need tore through me. The hand on my cock moved faster.

"Jesus, I want back inside you," I admitted. "You got the tightest pussy I've ever felt, Mel. Never been with another girl who felt half as good."

"You're not too bad yourself," she whispered, her voice starting to sound strained. "I used to think about you, too. Before, I mean. I used to lay in my bed and read your letters, and then I'd do exactly what I'm doing right now—touch myself."

My hips arched up. Oh shit. Close now. Just had to hold on to the fantasy that it was her fingers doing the work, and not mine.

"Did you make yourself come—when you were thinking about me, I mean?"

She didn't answer for a minute, but I heard a little gasp.

"Yes," she said, her voice rough. "I'd touch myself and come so hard, thinking about you. Imagining what you'd feel like inside me . . . What it would feel like if you took me from behind. Whether you'd tie me up. Oh my God, I can't believe I just said that."

Fucking hell. *Mel had a kinky side.* I must've done something absolutely incredible in a past life to deserve this, because I sure as shit hadn't earned it in this one.

"I could do that," I said, my voice husky. "And a hell of a lot more."

"Oh," she said, her voice breathless and uncertain. "Painter?"

"Yeah?"

"Are you like, into bondage? Because I know I said I've thought about you tying me up, but I'm not really—"

I burst out laughing. She went silent and then I realized she was probably embarrassed. Shit. Needed to be more careful.

"Mellie, I'm into *you*," I told her. "We can play whatever games you want, but that whole formal bondage thing isn't my kink. There's a lot of territory between having fun tying a girl up and whipping her to get off. We'll do whatever you want, and I guarantee that so long as you're naked, I'll be happy."

"That sounds good," she said, still breathless. "Just so you know, if you were here I'd be licking the underside of your cock right now. You know that little notch? I didn't get to explore it as much as I'd like yesterday morning . . . and I've never tried deep-throating a guy before, but I wouldn't mind giving it a shot with you."

Better.

Than.

Christmas.

"Are you still fingering yourself?"

"Yes," she whispered. "And I'm getting closer. It feels like I'm all heavy down there, like there's a string inside me spooling up between my legs . . . pulled tight . . . it hurts but it feels so good and I really, really don't want it to stop."

I was gonna get calluses on my hand at this rate. Goddamn it, but I wished that was her jerking me off instead of me. I was close, though—the pressure was tight in my balls, making it hard to think. Making it hard, period.

"What are you doing with your fingers?" I asked.

"I'm moving one in a circle, right over my clit . . . I'm pushing down and going faster, because I'm really close. I'm so wet I can feel it running down my crack—ugh. Did that sound gross?"

I licked my lips, holding back a moan.

"No, it sounds hotter than fuck," I admitted. My balls were a pressure cooker, full of hot come just for her. I'd fill her up, keep her prisoner in my bed, just for me.

Suddenly the whole slave-girl thing was sounding more interesting.

"I'm so close," she whispered. "Tell me about—"

She screamed abruptly. I heard shouting and a loud noise.

Then the line went dead.

MELANIE

Kit Hayes exploded into my bedroom, followed by Jessica. They were screeching and shouting, oblivious to the fact that they'd caught me in the act. I squawked in shocked horror, dropping the phone. Thank God I'd been under a blanket—wasn't sure I could live it down if they'd caught me bare assed, wanking like a total perv.

Not after the whole shower thing . . . not to mention flashing my unpainted boobs at Taz.

Oh God. It was already way too late.

"What's wrong with you?" I demanded, clutching the covers to my chest. "Have you lost your minds?"

"Dad and London got married!" Kit shouted, eyes wide. A grim-faced Jessica nodded, confirming the declaration.

"Married? But they were planning a wedding for December . . ."

"Dad said he didn't trust me and Em with a bachelorette party," Kit spat out. "We made a huge mistake by asking if we could use The Line—that tipped him off. He says he and London didn't want any fuss, so they just went down to the courthouse and got a license. They did it this morning, at the wedding chapel. *Nobody* was there. Em's in *another state*."

"I cannot believe her," Jess added. "Loni had no right to do this without us—so irresponsible and selfish. She was only thinking about herself."

Oh, seriously? Now *Jessica* was lecturing people about responsibility? That was ridiculous on too many different levels to count.

"That's unfair," I insisted, even though I was a little miffed, too—I'd been looking forward to the whole bridesmaid thing. "Loni is always taking care of other people. She works all the time, she puts up with our shit . . . she's already done the whole wedding thing once and it didn't end well. We can't blame her for wanting to take care of it and move on."

"Of course you'd take her side," Jess snapped. "You've *always* taken her side. I haven't forgotten that you're the one who ratted me out to her last summer. If it wasn't for my fight with Loni, I wouldn't have run off to California and maybe—"

I sat up, narrowing my eyes at her.

"You've got one hell of a nerve, trying to blame me for that," I said coldly. "It's not my fault that you . . ."

My voice trailed off as I realized they were both staring at me. What? A breeze hit my bare nipple, and I realized I'd let go of the blanket.

Well, wasn't *that* just craptastic.

"You were on the phone with Painter, weren't you?" Kit asked, eyes going from angry to speculative to flat-out dirty in a matter of seconds. How did she do that? "Oh my God, look at her blushing! You were having phone sex when we came in here!"

"Phone sex!" Jess screeched, completely forgetting her rant. "How slutty is that! I'm so proud of you—first you're fucking him in the shower and now you're getting off over the phone. For the record, I still don't think he's a good choi—"

"Wait, you fucked Painter in the shower?" Kit asked. I groped for the blanket, wondering what I'd done to deserve this torment. "So does that mean you're together now?"

I shrugged.

"I'm not sure," I admitted, frowning. "He's busy doing stuff for the club somewhere, but we're exclusive. At least, that's what we agreed before he left."

Kit frowned, sitting down next to me.

"Painter's not really good at the whole exclusivity thing," she said. "I know I warned you off him, but that's obviously a moot point and I want you to have fun . . . still, you need to be careful. You can't take him seriously."

Great, now Kit felt qualified to lecture me, too.

"You know, I'm really tired of everyone telling me what to do all the time," I announced, not bothering to hide my anger and frustration. Kit pulled back, eyes wide. I glared at her. "You need to learn some boundaries. Both of you."

"I'm sorry, I didn't mean anything—"

"You push into my bedroom without knocking, you're telling me who I can sleep with, and you're even pissed at Loni and Reese for getting married. It's their wedding, not yours, and I totally understand why they didn't tell you. You couldn't just be happy for them. No, you had to try and force them into things they didn't want. No wonder they got married by themselves!"

Jessica was inching away, mouth open.

"I'm sorry, Mel."

"Don't be sorry," I said, shaking my head. "Just maybe try to think about how other people feel once in a while. Both of you. I'm sick of it. And that was a *private* call, which means it's none of your damned business who I'm talking to, or why."

Kit looked down. "You're right. We should've knocked."

I couldn't help but notice the apology didn't cover her attempted lecture or acknowledge that perhaps her father had a right to make his own decisions. That was his problem, though—I'd already said my piece.

"We'll be downstairs," Jess said. "And you should probably get a lock for your door . . . especially if you're going to be having sex in here. Realistically, we both know I'm going to forget to knock the next time I get all excited."

Music burst out of Kit's phone and she grabbed it, looking down.

"It's Em," she said, shooting me a furtive glance. "Let's go, Jess. We have plans to make. She's already started driving over from Portland and we have a lot to get done before she reaches Coeur d'Alene."

"You're throwing a party, aren't you?" I asked. Kit had the grace to look guilty.

"A surprise bachelorette party," she admitted. "Tonight. I'm sorry. I know what you said about boundaries is probably true, but there's no way Em and I can let this pass. We have to welcome London to the family *right*. It's our job."

"You're welcoming her by pissing off your dad?"

Kit shrugged. "If you had any idea the shit Dad pulled on me and Em when we were younger, you'd get it. We can't let him get away with this—we just can't. It's the principle."

"You sound crazy."

Kit sighed. "Yeah, I know. But he started it."

They left the room and I started looking around for my phone. It'd gone flying, and it took me a good five minutes to find it wedged between the futon and the wall.

Six missed calls from Painter and one from Reese.

Shit.

He answered on the first ring.

"Are you okay?" he asked, his voice terse.

"I'm fine," I said, and I heard his sigh of relief.

"Okay, give me a minute to text Pic—I messaged him that something was wrong at your place. He's already on his way to rescue you."

"Oh shit. I'm so sorry. I can explain—that was Jess and Kit, and they—"

"Of course it was Jess and Kit," he muttered. "Give me a sec, then I'll call you back."

He hung up, and I reached for my bra. I didn't know about him, but the mood was certainly dead for me. I'd just pulled my shirt on when the phone rang again.

"I'm so sorry," I said again. "They pushed into the room and scared the hell out of me, and then I couldn't find my phone and I guess we're having an emergency bachelorette party tonight for London because she got married."

Silence.

"You wanna run that by me again?" he finally said.

"Apparently he didn't have time to tell you . . . Reese and Loni got married this morning. All by themselves—I guess they didn't like how people kept making plans for them, so they just up and tied the knot without telling anyone."

Painter burst out laughing.

"I'll bet Kit and Em are pissed as hell," he said. "They had all kinds of crazy-assed shit in mind."

"I don't know about Em, but Kit seems pretty upset. Oh, and just so you know, the girls figured out what you and I were doing and started giving me shit, so I yelled at them. Now they're hiding downstairs."

He started laughing again.

"That's almost worth the heart attack you gave me."

"I'm really sorry about that," I murmured. "They scared me."

"They're scary girls," he said. "I don't suppose you want to pick up where we left off?"

I considered it, but the thought of Jess and Kit down below . . . it wasn't working for me.

"No more phone sex until I get a lock for my bedroom door. I don't think I can take another scare like that."

"I'll do it first thing tomorrow."

He sounded so determined I couldn't help but laugh.

"Would it make me sound like a crazy girlfriend if I asked what time you'll be back tonight?" I wanted to take the words back as soon as they left my mouth. I'd meant it as a joke, but guys like Painter didn't have girlfriends. He'd told me himself he didn't date. Now he probably thought that I thought he was my boyfriend and . . . "I didn't mean it that way."

"Mel?"

"Yeah?" I asked, closing my eyes against whatever he might be about to say.

"I wouldn't mind having a girlfriend like you."

My pulse sped as I careened from freaked out to elated. I wanted to jump up, maybe do a fist pump or two. Instead I somehow managed to keep my voice casual.

"I wouldn't mind having a boyfriend like you, either."

"If I ask Pic to give you a key, will you sleep at my place tonight?" he asked. "I'll be getting in late. Really late, probably not until early next morning, but I'd like knowing you're in my bed, waiting for me."

"Sure," I said, feeling all warm and happy. "I'd like that, too."

CHAPTER THIRTEEN

"Jess seems to be recovering from the shock," London said, her voice dry. We were out at Bam Bam and Dancer's place—they were another of the club couples—because the Hayes girls hadn't been able to book The Line on such short notice. My private theory was that it wouldn't matter how much notice they'd had. One thing I'd learned from watching the Reapers the past year was that if Reese wasn't on board, it didn't happen.

Except this party was definitely happening.

Kit, Jessica, and Em had made the best of things, somehow throwing the entire thing together during the time it took Em to drive over from Portland. They'd tried to suck me into it, but no way I wanted to get involved. Reese and Loni *had* to love them— they were blood relations. Seeing as I was something of an add-on, I didn't feel like risking it. (Not only that, as a person with a soul, I hated putting Loni on the spot like that.)

I'd spent the afternoon working on my paper instead, right up until the moment that Jessica tricked me into driving to the grocery store with her. She'd dragged me out to the party instead, which even I had to admit was turning out to be fun. Or at least, it'd been fun until the strippers showed up.

Now Jess was sprawled across a stripper's lap with one arm around his neck, laughing like a crazy woman. A second guy was doing the same with one of the old ladies—Marie—while Kit took pictures with a glee bordering on the obscene. Then a third danced up to Jess, waggling a gold lamé banana hammock in her face.

(Okay, so maybe we weren't bordering on the obscenity line so much as dancing over its grave.)

"London's turn!" yelled Darcy, one of the old ladies about London's age. Her man was part of the Silver Bastards, the same club that Puck was part of. I'd only met him a couple times, but based on that it was safe to say that the Silver Bastards were every bit as scary as the Reapers. Dancer and Kit grabbed London by the arms, dragging her over as Jess jumped off her guy to make room for Loni.

"Smile, London!" Kit shouted, taking a picture as they dumped her into his lap. Loni bounced right back up again, grabbing a throw pillow and launching it at Kit. Jessica leapt to her defense, pitching another pillow toward London, and then it was on.

Battle royale.

(It's worth mentioning at this point that we'd had a lot of alcohol. Jell-O shots. Fireball shots. Some kind of pomegranate martini punch shit that Em mixed up and was serving in big bowl. It tasted like candy, but I'd stopped drinking after my second glass, when my cheeks started to go numb. Unfortunately that'd still been enough to make me seriously buzzed.)

A pillow smacked me in the head, knocking me down to the floor. I landed on top of Banana Hammock Man, putting a hand on his waxed, muscular chest to push myself up, confused as hell.

"Hey," he said, giving me a sexy smile. "You wanna go hide together under the table?"

"Smile!" Jessica shouted out of nowhere. *What the?* I looked up to find her snapping pictures of me on top of him.

"Oh, you little bitch!" I shouted, scrambling off. He gave a startled shout of pain. *Shit*. I'd just used his banana hammock like a gold lamé springboard, poor man. "I'm so sorry."

He moaned pitifully, rolling over to curl up on his side. Meanwhile, Jessica was skipping across the floor, waving her phone triumphantly.

"Jessica, you delete those fucking pictures right now!" I screamed.

She tore across the room and through a set of French doors that opened onto a deck. Then she was over the side, sprinting across the meadow that backed against the house.

"I'm going to kill you!" I shouted, ignoring the laughter from those watching us. She turned her head to taunt me, flipping the bird as she ran.

"Come and get—shit!" the words cut off as she suddenly disappeared. Not disappeared, as in tripping and falling. I mean *disappeared*. One minute she was there and the next she was gone.

"Jess!" I shouted again, anger turning to fear. She hadn't been that far ahead of me. I kept my eyes open, stopping just short of where she'd been, approaching slowly. It seemed unlikely that she'd been teleported away by aliens, but you never know . . .

"Jessica?" I called, hesitant.

"Down here."

Looking around, all I saw was grassy meadow. "I don't see anything."

"There's a hole in the ground," she said. "You're right over me—I can see you. Look down."

I looked down, and sure enough, there was a hole in the ground, maybe a foot wide . . . foot and a half, tops. I dropped to my hands and knees, peering down. It was dark, really dark. I could hardly see her, but she seemed to be down there a ways. Shit.

"What the hell is that? It looks like a cave."

"Sure looks like it."

"Do you see a way out?" I asked, looking back at the house anxiously. Our watchers had lost interest in us. I dug in my pocket for my phone, hoping I had service.

"Step back," Jessica told me. Frowning, I followed her instructions, mouth dropping as her head and shoulders popped out above the ground.

"How did you do that?"

"I just stood up, silly," she replied. "I would've sooner but I needed to text *this*."

She gave me a wicked grin as she held up her cell phone, showing off the picture of me on top of Mr. Banana Hammock.

"If you tell me you sent that to Painter, I'm going to kick your head off like a dandelion," I hissed, glaring at my best friend. *Former* best friend.

"Settle your panties," she said, rolling her eyes. "Do I look like I'd send it to Painter? No, I sent it to Hunter, Em's old man. I may have sent it to Reese, too. Hard to remember. I know I sent him the one of London."

A very, very dark suspicion reared its head.

"Jessica . . ."

"Yes?" she said, fluttering her lashes at me innocently.

"Are you and Kit using the party to collect blackmail material on all the women in the club?" I asked, my voice carefully level. Jessica frowned, and I swear she looked almost hurt.

"Of course not," she said, pushing herself up and out of the hole. "Blackmail means you want money or something, right? We're just doing this for fun, Mel. I'm not trying to take your money. I'd never blackmail you or *any* of the other girls."

She shook her head at me sadly, conveying profound disappointment in my lack of trust.

"I'm going to find Dancer. She should know about this cave thing— I got out just fine, but some little kid could get stuck down there for real."

The pillow fight had ended by the time we got back, apparently transitioning into a water fight. Either that or Dancer was using a hose in an attempt to control the herd of drunken women currently dancing in her backyard.

"Jessica!" Kit yelled as we came back. "You're here—good news! We're already getting responses on our pictures!"

Fuck, how many people were they sending them to?

"Reese is going to strangle me," London said, coming to stand next to me. Her white T-shirt had gone totally transparent, showing off a gorgeous black bra.

A spray of water hit me in the face, then splattered down across my chest.

"You're welcome!" Dancer shouted, laughing. I shook my head like a dog, trying to get some of the water off. Bad idea, because I still wasn't totally steady on my feet. *What the fuck was in that punch?* Dancer and London caught me, one on each arm.

"Thanks," I managed to say, watching as Dancer aimed her hose again, spraying down another woman I didn't recognize.

"Why are you hosing everyone down?"

"Damage control," she said, her words slurring ever so slightly.

"Damage control?"

"Yeah, the girls have been texting pictures of us with the strippers to the men. I got a tip-off—Bam Bam, Horse, and Reese are coming to break it up. I guess once we started groping random naked guys they'd had enough of the bachelorette party."

"So you're spraying everyone with water because . . . ?"

"Because guys get off on girls in wet T-shirts," she said, as if the answer were obvious. *What?* "There isn't a man alive who doesn't secretly pray that when women get together, we have pillow fights followed by wet T-shirt contests. Bam has a thing for mud wrestling, too, but I'm drawing the line here—gotta keep it classy. By the time the guys get here to claim their old ladies, we'll be ready for them. I already paid off the strippers. If they're smart, they've already left."

Wow. Just . . . wow.

"That's impressive," I admitted. She nodded sagely, accepting my praise as her just due.

"Not my first rodeo, baby girl."

Jess came up behind me, throwing her arms around me for a big hug.

"You'll get this old-lady shit figured out, no worries," she said, ruffling my wet hair.

Wait. I wasn't an old lady.

I didn't want to be old. Or a lady.

Pushing Jess off, I turned to Dancer, but she'd already gone off to spray someone else. London was missing, too. Marie was nearby, though.

"Hey," I said, lurching toward her.

"Hey," she said back, grinning like an idiot. Her eyes were big and sparkly and her cheeks were all flushed. At least I wasn't the only drunk one here.

"Am I an old lady now?" I asked. She blinked.

"What?"

"Painter asked me to be his girlfriend, so does that make me an old lady?"

Marie's eyes widened. "Painter seriously asked you that? Holy shit. Hey, Soph—Painter asked Mel to be his girlfriend!"

Ruger's old lady, Sophie, turned toward us. Her long hair was plastered against her head and back. Totally soaked. She looked between me and Marie, obviously surprised.

"Really?" Sophie asked. "Wow, never saw that coming. Like, he used the word 'boyfriend'? That's hysterical."

I frowned, because it wasn't funny at all, let alone hysterical. No wonder Painter was always heading out of town on club business— I would, too, if I had to put up with this shit.

"He's a really nice guy, you know," I said, glaring at them. They looked at each other and burst out laughing. *"Hey!"*

They laughed harder. For the very first time in my life I gave serious thought to punching someone in the face. Totally would've done it, too, if the world hadn't started spinning on me.

"Sorry," Marie finally managed to say. "I can think of a thousand different descriptions for our guys, but 'nice' generally isn't one of them. And no, you aren't an old lady yet—being someone's old lady is more than being their girlfriend. It means the whole club has accepted you as an official partner, and they support the relationship. Maybe you'll be an old lady at some point, but that's something Painter would talk to the club about first."

Sophie nodded. "They have some sort of supersecret process for it. Ruger won't tell me shit about it, but I think it mostly involves an announcement and then drinking beer together. But they can't possibly tell us that, you know? Gotta keep the mystery . . ."

"Oh," I said, swaying. Chair. I needed a chair or something. Standing was way too hard. I looked around, spotting an empty folding chair near the wall. I wandered toward it, slumping down as my phone buzzed.

PAINTER: What the fuck is going on? Hunter just texted me a picture of you climbing around on some naked guy.

Oh *shit*.

ME: It's not what it looks like.
PAINTER: You got one hand on his chest and the other on his dick
ME: I swear, Kit and Jessica set me up. Em may be in on it too. Kit and Jess together are like some nasty demon bigger than its indiviudiual parts. They get together an things like this happn. I think we need one of those priests to come and cast the devls out

He didn't respond right away. Finally my phone buzzed again.

PAINTER: Drunk?
ME: There was something in the punch . . .
PAINTER: Where are you?
ME: Dancers house. It's the bachelorette party
PAINTER: Got it. FYI—don't ever drink Dancer's punch again. I'll send someone to get you, okay?
ME: ok

"Babe!" Marie shouted, distracting me. She ran toward the front door, jumping up and wrapping her legs around a giant man who'd just stepped inside. Horse was a big guy—even taller than Painter—and Marie looked like a little monkey hanging off him.

Reese stepped in past them, taking in the scene.

Kit was sitting on the floor, giggling as she flipped through her phone. Em gave him a thumbs-up as she finished chugging a big cup of punch. Jess had disappeared completely. Reese stalked over to the entertainment center, turning off the music with a flick of his finger. Silence fell, and then Em gave a loud burp.

"Excuse me," she said, wiping her mouth delicately with the bottom of her shirt.

"Fuckin' girls," Reese said, shaking his head. "You're going to kill me."

"Hey," London said, coming up to wrap her arms around him. She kissed the side of his face, which seemed to soothe Reese. Kit stood slowly, then walked over to stand right in front of her father.

"This is what happens to people who get married secretly," she said, poking a finger into his chest. "Don't do it again."

A smile quirked the edges of Reese's mouth. Then he dropped his hand down to give Loni's butt a squeeze. *Ewwww* . . . Kit and I exchanged a look, and I could tell she was thinking the exact same thing that I was. *Old people shouldn't be having sex.*

"If I promise I won't get married again without telling you, will you stop destroying people's lives in search of revenge?"

Kit considered his words carefully.

"I'll try," she said, nodding. "I suppose you're forgiven. *This time.*"

"Wow, I'm just so fuckin' relieved to hear that," he replied. "Now I won't have to cry myself to sleep tonight."

PAINTER

I needed to slow down.

Every time I thought about Mel and that fucking stripper, I found myself pushing the bike's speed higher. Couldn't quite decide what I should do first when I got home—strangle the Hayes girls or slit Mr. Banana Hammock's throat.

The picture of them together was burned on my brain. Hunter'd sent it to fuck with me, of course. Bastard still hated me for what I'd done to Em. Fair enough, because I fucking hated him, too.

Almost as much as I hated the stripper.

But not quite.

Her *hand* had been on his *dick*.

Reese had messaged me a couple hours ago, letting me know he'd dropped Mel off at my place for the night. Good to know she was safe. I'd slept for a while in Bellingham, but I was still pretty fuckin' exhausted and it was a damned long ride all the way back to Coeur d'Alene. I had to be careful, too—leaving the state without permission was a parole violation. That meant no speeding, no splitting lanes . . . I didn't even stop at rest areas, just pulled into truck stops when I needed a break.

Last thing I needed was a parole violation putting me in the same state as a murder victim. Torres should be able to cover for me back home, but if a Washington cop pulled me over, there'd be a paper trail not even he could disappear. Never used to worry about shit like that, but knowing Mel was warm and waiting in my bed? Changed shit. Changed shit in a big way.

I'd just passed the Spokane airport—still a good thirty miles from the Idaho border—when it happened. I'd flown over the crest of the hill into the city and changed lanes to pass another car when I saw the lights behind me. For an instant I convinced myself they were after someone else, because, swear to fuck—I hadn't done anything wrong. Nothing.

Then he was right behind me and it was all over.

I pulled over and waited for the cop . . .

Fuck.

"Good evening, sir. Do you know why I pulled you over?"

"No—I wasn't speeding," I said, trying to figure out how a woman who was five and a half feet at most had the balls to pull over a biker twice her size. Kind of pretty, too, although hard to make out much of her figure under what I assumed was a bullet-proof vest.

"You didn't signal when you were passing the white minivan," she said.

No fucking way. I'd signaled . . . Was the bitch messing with me? Her face was serious, blank. I didn't get that hostile vibe that I got from so many male cops, though. *Probably a legit stop.* Still, this was gonna complicate things if they ever made me as a suspect in the Hands situation.

But what were the odds of that? The only ones who knew were my Reaper brothers, and if the Nighthawks found out, the cops would be the least of my worries.

"I don't doubt what you're saying, but I'm pretty sure I used the signal," I said, giving her a nice smile as I handed over my paper-work. "Maybe there's a problem with the bike."

She smiled back—nice. Took the bait. Might talk my way out of this one yet . . .

"It's possible. Would you like me to look while you test the lights?"

"That'd be great," I told her. "Thanks."

"Sure," she said, stepping back. I turned on the bike and flipped the signal.

"It's on."

"No good," she replied, shaking her head. "It's not working. I need to run your license and registration. Please stay seated on the bike with your hands on the handlebars while you wait."

Fucking hell—must've blown a fuse. I watched the occasional car fly by while she ran the license, wondering if I'd get a ticket. Took a good ten minutes before she came back, her expression cooler this time.

"Mr. Brooks, it says you're under supervision," she said. "Is your parole officer aware that you're out of state?"

"Yes," I lied. If anyone called Torres, he'd confirm it. Of course, his payoff would have to go up—cost of doing business.

"I'm going to let you off with a warning. But I don't want you riding farther tonight without lights."

"Has to be a fuse," I told her. "I've got some extras. If it's all right with you, I can probably swap it out pretty fast."

"Sounds good," she said. "I'll hold a light for you."

Sure enough, the fuse had blown. Changing it out was easy enough, and ten minutes later I was on my way home again.

Back to Melanie.

MELANIE

The first light of dawn had filtered through the windows when I woke up. It took me a minute to figure out where I was—Painter's bed. It smelled good. Like him. I smiled, rolling to the side as I stretched.

Reese had given me a ride last night, along with Kit, Em, Jess, and London. He'd been pissy as hell, although it was clear I wasn't his target. Neither was Loni—he'd taken one look at her boobs in that wet shirt and all was forgiven. (Dancer was a genius.) He'd given me a ride to Painter's place, unlocking it for me and making sure I was safe and settled before moving on to Jessica's stop.

My clothes were soaked, so I'd changed into one of Painter's shirts to sleep in. Because I'm a creeper, I'd grabbed a dirty one he'd had hanging on the back of the bathroom door. It smelled like him, which made me feel all warm and safe.

At least, that was my drunken logic last night.

Now I noticed that there were greasy, black streaks on my arms. They were all over the bed, too, and my stomach tightened into a knot.

Maybe the dirty shirt had been hanging up so it wouldn't touch anything else . . . *oopsie*.

The bedroom door opened and I looked up to find Painter watching me. Crap, he had nasty bruises under both his eyes, and his nose looked a little off-kilter. Had he gotten in a fight?

"Are you okay?" I asked, forgetting about the greasy mess as I stood to walk over to him. He pulled me into his arms roughly and then his mouth covered mine, tongue plunging deep. It wasn't a sweet, gentle kiss. Not at all—this was a branding, a reminder that even when we were apart I still belonged to him. Then his hands were on my ass and my legs were wrapping around his waist. He turned, shoving me into the wall as his hips ground into mine.

I'd never been so turned on so fast—clearly my body recognized him and wanted to make him welcome. Good thing, too, because he pulled his hips back just enough to loosen his fly, and then he was shoving deep inside, so hard and fast that it hovered between pleasure and pain. Then he bottomed out and I gasped, clutching at his shoulders for balance.

"Jesus, Mel," he gasped, pulling his head back. "I like seein' you in my place, wearing my shirt."

I opened my mouth to apologize for the mess on the bed, but he swiveled his hips, grinding deep inside me and I forgot all about it. His hips swiveled again, pushing his pelvic bone hard against my clit, and I moaned. Oh God. How could a girl be expected to think under these circumstances?

After an eternity and no time at all, Painter started deepening his strokes, reaching new places inside me. Tension built, faster and harder than it ever had before. Somewhere in the back of my mind, I was aware of the birds singing outside, of the smell of coffee, and the fact that I was a greasy mess from his shirt and soon he would be, too.

None of that mattered, though.

All that mattered was the fact that I was close—*so close*—to shattering into a million pieces. I caught the back of his head, pulling his mouth down to mine for another kiss. His tongue plunged deep again and my entire body clenched tight, hovering right on the edge.

Then he pulled back before filling me again, followed by a hard grind that threw me right over the edge. I stiffened and shuddered as waves of explosive release crashed through me.

Painter ripped out of me and then I felt the hot spurt of his come hitting my thighs.

We stayed that way for a minute, trying to catch our breath. Then he turned and carried me over to the mattress, lowering me down and covering me with his body. My legs still wrapped around his waist as he looked down, touching my cheek softly with one finger. Then he raised it, showing off a streak of dirty black.

"Mel?"

"Yeah?"

"Any particular reason you're covered in motor oil?"

I bit my lip, offering a soft smile.

"Bachelorette party," I whispered softly. "They really grease up those strippers, you know? Any particular reason you've got big, nasty bruises all over your face?"

"Bachelorette party," he whispered back. "I get real pissy when I see my girl's hand on another guy's dick. So pissy I walked into a wall."

"You know I didn't touch that guy on purpose, right?" I asked. "I mean, he was really nasty."

"Glad to hear it," Painter growled, then kissed me hard. I forgot all about the strippers.

An hour later, I'd come two more times, once from him going down on me and once when he fucked me from behind, fingering my clit.

Now we were cuddled up together, bodies naked and covered in black oil streaks that didn't seem to bother him a bit, so I decided I wouldn't let them bother me, either. I traced my finger through the marks on his chest, seeing that one side had been darkened by a bruise.

"How was your trip?" I asked. He frowned.

"I can't talk about club business, Mel."

I rolled my eyes. "Like I care about the details? I just wanted to know how you're doing and whether things went well, despite these marks all over you. You know, because I care?"

His face softened.

"Sorry. I guess it went okay, but it still sucked because I wasn't here with you. The bruises are from a stupid little fight, didn't mean a thing, so don't worry about it. I did get pulled over by a cop in Washington, though. Turn signal wasn't working right."

"That's no good," I said, wrinkling my nose. "Was it an expensive ticket?"

"Yes and no," he said, leaning over to kiss my neck. "I got off with a warning—just a popped fuse and I was able to fix it right on the spot. But technically it's a parole violation. I've got an understanding with my PO, but he'll probably have to ding me just to cover his own ass. Maybe a few days in the county jail. No big deal."

His tongue flicked out, tracing my collarbone, but I pushed him back—we needed to talk about this jail business.

"How can he just lock you up again?"

Painter sighed, then rolled off me to look at the ceiling. I turned on my side, watching him carefully.

"The judge ordered up to thirty days of discretionary jail time in case I get out of line," he said, his voice careful. "My PO can use it whenever he wants. But they can't send me back to prison without a parole board hearing. Jail's just a smack on the wrist."

I stared at him, stunned.

"You think going to jail is a wrist slap?"

"Compared to finishing out my term? It's nothing. I still got two years of my prison sentence left, Mel."

The words hit me like a blow.

"Two years?" I whispered. "They could send you back for *two years*?"

"Babe, I could get murdered by ninjas, too," he said with a laugh. "Doesn't mean it's going to happen. The club has a lot of influence with the probation department here in town—my conditions are seriously loose. I'm not supposed to leave the state, but it's up to the PO when or how I get punished for that. We've got him in our pockets. Trust me, it'll be fine."

I stared at him, wondering what was going on in that head of his, because none of this was making sense to me.

"So the only thing standing between you and prison is one guy? What if you piss him off? Is it really worth the risk to be traveling when you've got that hanging over your head?"

He winced, reaching up to rub his chin. There was one hell of a scruff developing there and for an instant I felt my attention wander. I wanted to touch it. Maybe rub my face against it . . . *Suck it up, Mel. This isn't playtime.*

"This is all new to me," he said, reaching up with one hand to cup my cheek. "I've never really worried about risking myself before."

"You never worried about *going to jail*?"

"Prison. Jail is for sentences under a year, prison is for longer-term shit."

"You didn't answer my question," I snapped. "If you don't want to talk for real, then don't talk. But don't play word games with me."

"Okay, you want the truth? I've been in and out of juvie, jail, and prison since I was twelve years old. It is what it is—you play the game, sometimes you go down. Until then, I'm not going to let my whole fuckin' life be about sucking up to the parole board."

I sat up, glaring at him. "Are you for real? You don't care about *sucking up to stay out of prison?* Painter, you're smart and you're fun and you're one hell of an artist, so why are you living like this if you don't need to? Out of habit?"

He sat up, too, glaring right back at me.

"You have no right to an opinion. This is my life and I'm gonna do what I have to do, for my club. Just 'cause I love you doesn't mean you have a vote. Me and my brothers vote. Old ladies listen and do what they're told."

We blinked at each other, his words falling between us like charged grenades. So many things in that sentence. I couldn't decide whether I was pissed or . . .

"You love me?" I asked slowly, cocking my head.

"Yeah, I do," he said, still glaring. "You're all I think about and you're in my bed—that's not like me, Mel. I don't do shit like this. I'm gonna talk to Picnic about you, bring it up with the club. I want you to be my old lady."

I couldn't think of what to say—he'd caught me utterly off guard—so I spat out the first thing that came to my mind.

"But I'm not old."

Painter gave a reluctant smile, reaching over to cup my breast, tweaking my nipple in the process. I gasped as his hand slid lower between my legs.

"You're not always a lady, either," he whispered, moving in on me. "But you're mine. That's all that matters, okay? Let me worry about the rest."

Then he was on top of me again and my brain shut off.

I never even noticed how he ducked the prison questions. That's how good he was.

PAINTER

I pulled up to the Armory just before six that night. Pic had called everyone in for a meeting to discuss the Hallies Falls situation and get an update on Hands. Pulling out my cell, I dropped it onto the counter before heading into the chapel. All the brothers were there, even Duck. He'd been having trouble with his joints—Ruger'd told me quietly that they were concerned he might not be able to ride much longer.

He'd always be a brother regardless, but once a man stopped riding he usually didn't last very long.

"Grab a seat," Pic said, nodding toward a spot in the center they'd left open for me. Usually I tried to hang back, but seeing as Pic called the meeting to discuss what'd happened over the weekend, I expected to do a lot of talking. "So, Painter's got a full report for us—let's start with the Nighthawks and then move on to the other issue. All yours, brother. Welcome home."

I gave him a chin lift, then launched into my story.

"Gage is making good progress," I told them. "Marsh—that's the president—has a sister he's fucked in the head over. I don't know what their relationship is all about, but it's weird. Anyway, the sister—Talia—is fucking around with Gage, which got us an invite to a party there."

"What's this Talia like?" Horse asked.

"She's a total bitch," I told him. "But she's hotter than hell. Gage doesn't like her, but at least he can bang her without a bag over her head."

Duck gave a knowing laugh. "He's always gone for the wild ones."

"Yeah, well I don't think he's going for this one, not more than he has to. On a more serious note, though, things aren't good in that club. They're split down the middle between Marsh's people and the older brothers—the ones who came in before Marsh took over. I got the impression Marsh was scoping us out, like he had work for us."

Horse and Ruger shared a look, and I saw surprised faces all around the table.

"Oh, it gets worse," I continued. "Their prospects are a fuckin' joke. They're bringing them in fast. Met one kid who doesn't even own a bike yet."

"Goddamn it," Duck grunted. "We can't let it stand."

Hard to argue with that.

"Yeah," I agreed. "But we want to be careful about the timing— can't let the whole network fall apart when we cut off the head."

"Fair enough," Pic said, leaning back in his chair. He crossed his arms, his face growing more serious. "So now that we've covered that, let's talk about the real issue. Tell everyone about the snitch."

"It was a guy called Hands," I said. Bolt sat up abruptly as our eyes met across the table.

"Same Hands who set up Bolt?" Ruger asked, his voice cold.

"Yup," I said, my voice grim. "At least according to Gage. That shit went down while I was gone. We spotted him at the party. I managed to knock him out in what looked like an accident, and then I helped one of the prospects haul him home. He never laid eyes on Gage, so no chance he tipped off Marsh."

"You should've called me," Bolt said, his voice cold.

"Gage said we couldn't risk a call, not when we planned to take him out," I said bluntly. I didn't mention the part about Bolt losing his shit.

"You think they suspect you set him up?" Pic asked. I shook my head.

"No way—it looked like one of their prospects tripped me. Not only that, I've got a witness that he was safe and sound asleep when I left him. Don't think it'll be a problem. Anyway, we went back after the party and picked him up, then I drove him over to Bellingham in a rig Gage managed to scam up somewhere. They questioned him there."

Bolt narrowed his eyes.

"Rollins?" he asked.

"Rollins," I confirmed. Bolt smiled slowly, a smile so dark I could hardly hold his gaze.

"Bet that was ugly."

"Yeah," I told him. "It was real bad. I'm sorry we couldn't call you, brother, but I promise you this—we took care of him for you. Hands wouldn't talk at first. Guess he was still holding out hope he might get out alive so long as he protected the information. After a few hours I took a break to grab some sleep. Eventually he broke, and they woke me up so I could hear what he had to say for himself."

"And?"

"Well, he's been feeding the feds information about clubs in the region," I said. "Apparently that's not new information, but this is. He's working with Marsh."

"Marsh knows what he's doing?"

"Think so," I said. "Not sure how much Marsh trusts him, but he knows that Hands is a snitch. Real question is whether Marsh is using him or he's using Marsh. Or *was* using Marsh . . . Rollins finished him off not long after that."

Pic nodded thoughtfully. "Rance taking care of the mess?"

"He's got it covered," I said. "They gave me a ride back to Hallies Falls so I could pick up my bike, and then I started back home. Speaking of, I had a little complication."

"What's that?" Pic asked, frowning.

"Fuse blew out on my turn signal and I got pulled over," I admitted. They all stared at me, then Ruger gave a little snort. Horse laughed outright, and I saw smiles all around the table. Cocksuckers.

"You get a ticket?" Picnic asked.

"No, just a warning. She even held a flashlight for me whi—"

"She?" Duck asked, smirking. "So in the last twenty-four hours, you kidnapped and helped murder a guy, crossed the state twice . . . and you got pulled over for not using a turn signal by a *girl* cop? Christ, Painter. Only you."

I flipped him off.

"So she gave me a warning—I'll have to share that with Torres at my next appointment, I guess."

"For the best," Picnic said, frowning. "He'll probably throw you in jail a couple days for being out of state, but if word filters back that you left Idaho and he didn't do anything, they'll start looking at him. We can't afford that kind of attention."

"No big." I shrugged.

"Any questions for Painter?" Pic asked the table at large.

"Was the cop hot?" Horse asked, smirking at me. "Did she give you a full pat-down?"

"Any *real* questions for Painter? No? Okay, then that's it for now, unless someone has something else to bring to the table."

This was it, I realized. Time to talk about Mel. Fuck, they were gonna give me so much shit . . .

"I got something."

Pic cocked a brow. "Killin' a guy wasn't enough for you?"

I shrugged. "It's been a busy couple of days. Seriously, though— I want to talk about Melanie."

Silence fell across the table. I looked over to find Duck smiling his big, shit-eating grin at me.

"So, I want her to be my old lady," I said, watching Pic's face. If anyone gave me trouble, it'd be him.

"You sure?" Pic asked. "She's a nice kid, but she doesn't really know our life. Might be better to give her a little more time first. This is happening fast."

"But it hasn't happened fast," I reminded him. "I've known her for more than a year and we wrote letters that whole time. She's pretty, she's smart—the whole package. I'm taking her."

Pic looked around, and I waited for someone to say something.

"I like her, and it's not like it's a huge surprise," said Ruger. "I mean, he did loan her his car for a goddamn year. She pussy-whipped him long distance—that takes talent."

Horse laughed, and I took a deep breath, wondering how long they were going to drag this out.

"She'll probably be good for him," Bolt said more seriously. "You're smart, Painter, but you're fuckin' reckless. You can't do the club any good back in prison—maybe having an old lady will motivate you to be more careful. Give you something to lose."

He would know—he'd lost his woman, Maggs, for a while. They were back together now but it hadn't been easy.

"It's a good point," Pic said. "You may see yourself as cannon fodder, but you're not. Wouldn't hurt if you were a little more settled. It's fine with me."

"Now what, a group hug?" Horse asked, rolling his eyes. "Enjoy your girl, try not to break her. I don't think you should patch her just yet, though—give her some time to adjust. Get used to all of us. Save both of you a lot of hassle down the road."

"He's right," Pic said. I frowned, not liking where this was going. "It's probably for the best if you take it slow. Your call, but if you care about her, you'll give her time to adjust. Any more business?"

Nobody spoke, so he raised his gavel, hitting the table with a sharp whacking noise.

"Fantastic. Let's get out of here. Loni's got dinner waiting at home and I'm fuckin' starved. Not only that, Kit's staying over at a friend's place tonight, which means I'll finally get some time alone with her. Girl's hardly been home a week, but it feels like a year. Painter?"

"Yeah?" I said.

"I hope you and Mel live happily ever after and all that shit, but don't have daughters. That goes for all of you—no more daughters in this club. I can't handle it."

"She ever going back to Vancouver?" Duck asked. Pic shrugged.

"Dunno," he admitted. "She says she is, but all of her classes are online this semester. I think there's shit going on she hasn't told me about but I'm not gonna push her. She's been stoppin' by to see that cowboy a lot—the one the bull tried to kill."

"What's the story there?" I asked. "She into him or something?"

"Hell if I know. Doubt even she does. Whatever. At least the guy's still alive. Now, if you don't mind, I want out. Loni made dumplings, and if they're cold by the time I get home I'm shooting one of you. I'll let you decide who."

Duck snorted, and that was that.

CHAPTER FOURTEEN

ONE MONTH LATER

> PAINTER: Wanna meet for dinner?
>
> MEL: Sure
>
> PAINTER: My place—I'll buy if you'll cook
>
> MEL: So you don't want to meet for dinner so much as have me cook for you
>
> PAINTER: No—I want to fuck you, too. See? I'm about a lot more than eating
>
> MEL: Complicated guy!
>
> PAINTER: Damned straight. see you at my place

MELANIE

"Painter has never dated anyone longer than a week, let alone a month," Em said in my ear. I was standing outside his apartment, holding the phone cradled against my shoulder while digging through my purse for the key. "I think he's really serious about you."

"He acts serious," I said. "He even says he loves me, but aside from that one time he's never mentioned anything about me being his old lady or anything. And he doesn't tell me where he's going when he takes off on trips, just says it's club business, like I should know what that means already."

My fingers found something solid and pointy. *Ha!* I pulled my keychain out triumphantly.

"I keep forgetting how much you don't know about club life," Em replied, sighing. "They don't talk about their business. Ever. It's just the way it is, not something personal that has to do with you."

"Never?" I asked, finding that hard to believe. "But what about you and Hunter? Do you seriously mean to tell me that he's gone all the time and you have no idea where?"

"This is . . . a sticky thing," she said slowly. "Let's talk hypothetically. Women aren't supposed to know this stuff. We're supposed to be good old ladies and support our men and just trust that they know what they're doing and that they have our best interests at heart. In reality, I think a lot of guys talk to their women—pretty sure my mom was in on most of the club's business, although I don't know about Loni. How much they share depends on the relationship and how involved she is with club life. Consider this, though— do you really want to be in a position where you'd have to testify against Painter?"

"Damn. Never thought of that."

Clearly I'd never thought of a lot of things. Opening the door, I walked through the studio to the stairs leading upward.

"Well, keep it in mind," she said. "Unless you're married, they can compel your testimony. You could lie to protect him—and that's expected of an old lady, by the way—but isn't it better if you truly don't know anything? That way they can't trick you into giving him away."

"Does it ever bother you?"

She laughed.

"Narrow it down for me—does *what* bother me?"

"The fact that you might have to lie to protect Hunter?"

"No," she said, her voice matter-of-fact. "I'm sure it helps that I grew up in this life, but I trust that whatever Hunter does, he has a good reason for doing it. I've learned to trust his brothers, too, which means that when he gets a call in the night from one of them, I know it's important. But me knowing all the details can only hurt him, and I want him safe. See how it works?"

"I trust Painter," I said slowly. "But I'm not sure I trust his club. I'm sorry—I know we're talking about your dad's world here, but this is really strange to me. I keep feeling like I have to turn off a chunk of my brain to be with Painter."

"You don't have to turn off your brain. You just need to learn what's actually important and how to tune out the things that aren't."

"Wait—you can't tell me that your man disappearing in the night and not calling for days isn't important."

"Of course it's important," she said with a laugh. "When Hunter takes off, I worry about him. I think about him and I miss him. What I don't do is spend too much time trying to figure out what he's up to, because nothing good can come of it. Instead I put my energy into the things that matter. My job. Taking care of business around home. People always talk about how guys in clubs are controlling, but I pay all the bills and run our money. He doesn't have time."

I dropped my bag on the table, then walked into Painter's bedroom. My favorite shirt—without the motor oil this time—was laid out and waiting for me. Over the past few weeks I'd learned that me wearing his clothes was a huge turn-on for Painter. This worked, because it was a huge turn-on for me, too.

"It's a lot to think about," I told Em. "But I should get going— he'll be here soon and I want to get ready."

"Have fun," she said with a knowing chuckle. "And stay safe. I'm not sure I could handle a little Painterling running around just yet."

"Take it back," I hissed. "God, can you imagine? I'm not even twenty-one yet. Getting pregnant would suck so bad."

She didn't respond right away, and I frowned. "Em?"

"Hey, sorry," she said. "I just got distracted. Have a good time with Painter tonight, okay? And don't worry about things you can't change. The club is what it is. On the surface they sometimes don't look that great, but over time I think you'll come to appreciate having them behind you. Bye!"

"Bye."

I turned on some music and then stripped down so I could wear his shirt. It was long on me—almost like a dress. Visions filled my head of cooking while he came up from behind, catching the fabric, slowly raising it . . . Oh, nice. Very nice.

The door slammed downstairs.

"Mel, you up here?"

Putting a little sway in my step, I sauntered out of the bedroom, then stopped cold. Painter was carrying a big bouquet of red roses. Like, a huge one. My eyes went wide.

"Had a good day today," he said, grinning at me. "Guy called me—custom client from the Bay Area. He wants a full-sized portrait of his bike and he's offered me a fuckin' fortune to do it. But that's not even the best part. He owns a gallery down there. Says he might be interested in doing a show of my work. I've been runnin' around all afternoon buying supplies."

"Really?" I squealed. "Oh my God, that's incredible! I'm so happy for you."

I rushed to hug him, nearly knocking him down in the process. The groceries and roses fell to the floor as he kissed me hard and deep.

"Bedroom?" I whispered when he finally gave me a break.

"Food," he said, offering a rueful smile. "Today's been crazy, and on top of everything else my phone ran out of power right after I messaged you—haven't eaten anything since that donut I had for breakfast."

Sighing, I stepped back because the man really did deserve a chance to eat. The roses caught my eye.

"You don't happen to have a vase or anything, do you?" I said shyly, picking them up. Not much damage from the fall—a couple bent petals here and there . . .

"What makes you think those are for you?"

I froze. "I'm sorry—I thought that—"

He started laughing, then caught my face in his big hands. "Of course they're for you."

Then he gave me a soft, sweet kiss.

"I'm gonna get changed," he said. "There's fixings for tacos in the bag. Think I remembered everything."

You know those rare moments in life when everything is perfect? The first half of that evening was one of those beautiful times . . . There's no real way to describe it, because nothing special happened. We ate dinner together and then he had me come down to the studio so he could sketch me in his T-shirt and nothing else. Naturally that led to other things, and we were just getting to the good part when someone knocked on the door.

"Shit," Painter muttered, reaching for his pants. He threw me a sheet that he used as a drop cloth and I pulled it over my half-naked body as he walked to the door. "Yeah?"

"This is Kandace Evans," a woman's voice rang through. "I'm your new parole officer. Please open the door."

"I thought your parole officer was a guy," I whispered.

Painter frowned. "He was. Be ready to call Picnic, okay? I got a bad feeling about this."

He ran a hand through his hair, then stepped over to peer through the peephole.

"I'm opening the door," he announced, turning the dead bolt. A tall woman with dark hair pulled back behind her head waited outside. Behind her were two cops. The look on her face wasn't friendly.

"Levi Brooks?" she asked, looking him up and down. Painter crossed his arms over his bare chest.

"I'm Levi."

She peered around him to look at me. "And this is?"

"Melanie Tucker. My girlfriend."

She stepped inside, staring me down.

"What're you hiding under the sheet?"

I coughed, looking away. "Um . . ."

"She's naked," Painter said bluntly. "You caught us in the middle of something. I don't know you. Where's Torres?"

The woman turned back to him, expressionless.

"Chris Torres is on administrative leave, pending further investigation."

"Why?" Painter asked, frowning. This couldn't be good news for him . . . *shit*. I needed to get dressed and find my phone. Call Reese. There was something seriously fucked up going on here.

"He and four others have been accused of taking bribes, including his supervisor," she said, her voice cold. "His files have been reassigned to me. I've reviewed yours, and it's very clear that he's been giving you a pass. Where were you this morning, Mr. Brooks? Around eleven a.m.?"

"Work."

"No, you weren't," she said, and I caught a hint of triumph in her voice. "I checked. And you just lied to me about it—that's a parole violation. Your second violation, because according to your file, you were pulled over out of state without permission, yet Torres only sent you to jail for the weekend. You'll be spending more than a few days inside this time. I still have nearly a month of discretionary detention time left and I plan to use it. Now. The officers are here to take you into custody."

"You're just taking him away?" I asked, stunned. "You can't just do that—he *was* working, it just wasn't down at the shop. He had to get supplies for a commission."

"Parole is a privilege, not a right," she replied, her voice smug and satisfied. "The Reapers have been holding themselves above the law for way too long now. Time for that to end, starting with Mr. Brooks. We'll be searching the entire apartment as well. You'll need to leave."

"But . . ." I looked to Painter, feeling almost panicky.

"Call Picnic," he said, his voice firm and reassuring. "He'll get it all figured out. Go up and get dressed and grab your stuff. I've given up my right to a search without a warrant, but you haven't."

"I'll send an officer with you," the parole officer said. I narrowed my eyes at her. I didn't like this woman. Not even a little bit.

"I'd like to see some identification first," I said.

She strutted over to me, holding out a badge.

Kandace Evans, sure enough.

"That name looks familiar," I said, frowning. Kandace cocked her head.

"You probably read about my brother, Nate," she said, her voice cold. "He disappeared a little over a year ago. We don't know what happened, but he was investigating the Reapers and then suddenly he was gone. Isn't that an interesting coincidence? Now get your things and get out of here. Run off and tell Reese Hayes that I've got his boy here, and he won't be the last Reaper to go down. Then I'd suggest you find a new boyfriend. This one's future isn't looking bright."

FOUR WEEKS LATER

I ran for the bathroom, hoping rather desperately that Jessica was still sound enough asleep that she wouldn't hear me barf. Again. Today marked the fifth time that I'd woken up puking . . .

At first I'd been in denial.

Maybe it was just stress—my boyfriend was in jail, after all. She'd dragged him off and locked him up and there wasn't a damned thing anyone could do to stop her. That kind of stress lowers your immune system's ability to fight off bugs. That had to be why I was so tired out all the time and why I was having strange hormonal swings . . . and no period . . . and the throwing up . . .

Unfortunately, after a life like mine (drunk dad, missing mom— *Go team!*) you can't afford denial long-term. Not if you want to survive. That's why I'd stopped by Walgreens last night and picked up a couple pregnancy kits (two different brands, because if they carried news that would explode my life, I wanted to be damned sure). I planned to take them just as soon as I stopped puking long enough to pee.

Ten minutes later I sat leaning against the tub, staring down at the two sticks on the floor. One of them had a bright blue plus sign.

The other had a picture of a baby on it, like they thought I wasn't smart enough to read the results without illustrations.

This couldn't be happening. I *refused* to accept this as my reality. True, we hadn't always used a condom, but he'd never actually come inside me, either. I mean, what were the odds?

The sticks pointed toward me accusingly.

Okay, in my case apparently the odds were 100 percent.

"Hey, you almost done in there?" Jess shouted through the door. "I have a test this morning—I need to get showered. Not much time left."

I ignored her because I didn't care about her test. I didn't care about school or friendship or anything, because I was pregnant and it was real and there wasn't a damned thing I could do about it . . . except I could. I could just make this problem *go away*.

Nobody ever had to know.

It could be my little secret, just a quick visit to the doctor and *poof!* Problem solved. Running a hand over my stomach, I tried to picture a baby inside. I couldn't feel it yet, but there was definitely a little more pooch around my tummy lately. I had a kid in there. For real. An actual, live baby inside *me*.

In that instant, I knew that I absolutely couldn't kill it.

No fucking way.

"Open the door, Mel!" Jess called again.

I closed my eyes and leaned my head back against the tub, trying to wrap my head around the situation. Okay, so I was going to have a baby. Counting down the months, I figured out that it would come this summer, after the semester finished. That was something . . .

The door rattled again.

"Mel, if you don't say something right now I'm breaking in," Jessica told me, sounding worried.

"Don't be silly," I replied mildly. This was all so unreal . . . "There's a skeleton key on top of the ledge over the door. That should work."

I heard more rattling noises, then the door was opening and Jessica walked inside. She looked down at me, frowning.

"What the hell are you doing?"

"Sitting on the bathroom floor."

"Um, Mel?"

"Yeah?"

She knelt down slowly in front of me, picking up one of the sticks.

"Is this what I think it is?" she asked, her voice a whisper.

"That depends on what you think it is," I told her, feeling distant and detached. Was I in shock? I must've been in shock. Fascinating.

"It looks like two positive pregnancy tests."

"Oh yeah. Then it's definitely what you thought it was."

"And these are yours?" she asked carefully, looking at me like I was a very fragile glass that might shatter at any minute. I sighed, then turned my head to meet her eyes.

"They're mine," I whispered, feeling tears start to run down my face. "Shit, Jessica. How could I be so stupid? I know better. I'm smarter than this."

Scooting over close to me, she pulled me into her arms, running a hand over my hair. "Oh, Mellie. We'll get through this—I promise. We'll get through it together . . . Whatever you decide to do."

"I'm not killing it," I said quickly. "I don't want to kill it."

"Then you won't kill it," she told me, her voice firm. "And if someone has a problem, you can send them to me. I'm the crazy one, remember? I'll just cut them—problem solved."

Then she crossed her eyes and stuck her tongue out at me.

Suddenly I felt better.

This was scary—terrifying—but I didn't have to do it alone. Jessica was here, and despite her crazy, flaky ways, there was one thing she *never* flaked out on. Kids. She loved those kiddos at the community center, put her heart and soul into teaching and mentoring them.

If I had Jess to help me, I'd be okay.

"I'm headed over to the jail today," I said quietly. "Do you think I should tell him now?"

Jessica frowned.

"Do you have any idea how he's going to react?"

"None. We've never talked about kids or anything."

"Well, maybe you can feel him out today," she said. "Get a sense for where he stands on the subject. If the moment's right, tell him. Otherwise just wait until you're ready. I know this probably feels like the end of the world, but you have months and months to figure things out. You don't have to do it all today."

She was right.

"Thanks, Jess."

"No worries," she replied, tucking in close to me. "You know, I always pictured this conversation going the other way."

"What do you mean?"

"I'd always assumed I'd be the one who accidentally got knocked up," she said with a laugh. "Although I'm glad it's you. I'm not ready to go through pregnancy and birth and all that shit."

"How do you always manage to say exactly the right thing and exactly the wrong thing, all at the same time?"

"Just a gift, I guess. Everyone has their talents."

No matter how many times I went to see Painter at the county jail, I never got used to being searched—made me feel dirty. Like there was something wrong with me, because I was visiting someone inside that place where decent people shouldn't go.

In the weeks since he'd been locked up, I knew the club was working to figure out what the hell had happened with his parole officer. If they had the full story, nobody was telling. Officially he was still on administrative leave, although I'd heard rumors that they might be pressing charges against him.

I just hoped Painter wouldn't get caught up in it.

On the bright side, today was my last visit out here—they'd be releasing him tomorrow. According to Reese, none of this was normal and I shouldn't worry about Painter.

Of course, he wasn't the pregnant one.

By the time they finally brought him in to see me, I was so nervous that I'd started trembling.

"Hey, babe," he said, his voice warm as he came to sit across from me at a table and stools painted bright orange. They were all bolted into the floor, presumably so none of them could be used as weapons.

Lovely.

"Hey," I whispered, smiling at him. We weren't supposed to touch, but sometimes he stretched his foot out toward mine under the table. "How's it going?"

"I'm ready to get out of here," he said, flashing me a smile. "I miss you. Miss riding my bike, too. Hell, I even miss that cockwad Puck. Fucker's been down to see me twice a week. How's that for rubbing it in?"

That got a laugh out of me, because I knew how much those visits meant to him.

"So I wanted to talk to you about something," I started.

"What's up?"

"About club life." Hmm . . . how to say it? "Everyone says this isn't the way things normally work—that this parole officer's out to get the club or something. But I also know you have brothers who've served time. What about their families? I know most of them have old ladies and kids and stuff. What do guys like that do if they have to go to jail?"

"Whatever it takes," he said, cocking his head. "Why do you ask?"

"I was out at Dancer's house the other day," I told him. "And I was looking at the pictures of their kids. They've got a really nice family. How does Bam Bam manage to pull off the fatherhood thing and still do what needs to be done for the club? Seems like it would be such a hard balance."

Painter narrowed his eyes at me.

"Why don't you ask me the real question," he said, his voice serious. I took a deep breath.

"Do you want to have a family someday?"

Painter leaned back in his seat, eyes studying my face. Then he slowly shook his head.

"No fuckin' way."

Something twisted inside. I'd like to say it was my heart breaking, but odds were high it was heartburn. I'd been having that more and more lately.

"Never?" I asked, my voice small.

"Mel, I grew up in the foster care system. I was one of the lucky ones, because I got beat up, but I never got raped. Watched kids get raped, though. Watched kids pimped out. Ran away when I was eleven with a couple other boys and lived on the streets after that, right up to the point that they threw me in juvie. Wanna guess what I did to get locked up?"

I swallowed. "What did you do?"

A bitter smile twisted his face. "Not a goddamned thing. They throw you in detention if they don't have anywhere else to put you. I had a bad reputation—troublemaker. None of the foster families would take me. Spent six months inside before they found me a new place, but by that point I'd already figured something out."

He leaned closer, eyes intense.

"If you're gonna do the time anyway, might as well do the crime."

Then he sat back, crossing his arms in front of him.

"No fuckin' way I'd bring a kid into this world. Wouldn't risk doing that to him, and I already know I'd be a shit dad. I don't even like kids. They smell weird, they do crazy things, and they're always jumping out of nowhere. You want a baby daddy, you better look somewhere else."

I swallowed again, staring at him.

"Okay, then. Good to know."

He smiled at me, and this one reached his eyes. "Can't wait to see you tomorrow, babe. Hold you. It's gonna be great."

"Sure," I said faintly. "Great. We'll have a spiffy good time. If you could excuse me, I need to hit the bathroom."

Painter frowned. "You okay?"

"Fabulous," I said, smilingly tightly. "But I really need to pee. I'll see you tomorrow, okay?"

Then I got the hell out of there.

CHAPTER FIFTEEN

ONE DAY LATER
PAINTER

Mel wasn't waiting for me outside the jail.

Okay, so I wasn't exactly expecting her to be . . . I knew she had class, and I didn't want her to miss school. Still, some part of me obviously wished she'd blown it off, because I found myself looking for her, even as Picnic walked toward me, flanked by Horse.

"Good to see you wearing something that isn't orange," Pic said, pulling me into his arms for a rib-crushing hug. "You do okay in there?"

"Fine," I said, glancing back toward the door, where a corrections officer stood watching. "You ever figure out what the fuck happened with Torres?"

"We'll talk about it in the chapel," he said, lowering his voice. "The brothers are all waiting for you. Oh, and the girls are planning a party for you tonight—should be nice. Mel's been real solid while you were in here. Might be time to go ahead and talk to her about the old-lady thing."

Forty minutes later we were all in the chapel. Took another ten to get settled enough to talk, what with all the hugs and shit.

"Okay, let's get moving," Picnic finally said. "Painter, grab a seat. There's a lot going on and we gotta fill you in."

To my surprise, Duck pulled out his usual chair for me, patting me on the shoulder.

"Enjoy the moment, brother," he told me. "There's a hard road up ahead, no question."

"Christ, don't play mind games with him," Ruger snapped. "You're a bastard, Duck."

"No, Boonie's a bastard. I'm a Reaper," Duck replied, chuckling at his own lame joke. Horse rolled his eyes as Bolt snorted.

"Enough," Pic said. "Let's get moving on this, okay? The girls have food going and it smells too damned good to sit in here all day. Not only that, London just messaged me. She's on her way out with Melanie, and somethin' tells me Painter will be real interested in seeing her again."

"The dick goes inside the girl," Horse said helpfully. "Not your hand. Got it?"

"Shut the fuck up," I said, grinning. I had a whole new list of fantasies to work through now that I was out again.

"Okay, here's the story," Pic said. "Apparently they'd been watching Torres for a while. The Evans bitch is out to get us—always suspected the club was behind her brother disappearing—and when she learned about the investigation she was all over it. She'd been setting him and several others up for at least six months before they pulled the trigger on it.

"Torres is still on administrative leave, but they'll be pressing charges against all of them. Apparently they had a hell of a payoff system set up. The good news for us is Torres is stupid, but we aren't. That means there's no trail leading to us and they got plenty to convict him without the Reapers. He knows better than to cross us, so I think we're in the clear there."

"Guess that's something," I said. Pic shrugged.

"Well, the real problem is the rest of your parole. You're out of chances now—she's looking for Reaper blood, and you're vulnerable. She's convinced the club killed her brother."

Several of the guys exchanged glances. Technically we hadn't killed the guy . . . just delivered him to the cartel leaders he'd screwed over, so they could kill him. That shit was on him, ultimately—not like we told him to double-cross a fucking drug cartel.

"Anything we can do about her?" I asked.

"We're working on it," Bolt said. "Sooner or later we'll find a way, but until then you need to be damned careful. Got it?"

"Yeah, I got it," I replied. "For the record, this sucks."

"It is what it is," Pic said. "Now on to other business. Wanted to give you an update on Gage. His situation's good. He's been hanging around with the Nighthawks a lot, so much that they're already dropping hints about him prospecting. Not only that, they gave two of their prospects patches while you were locked up."

"Not a huge surprise, I guess," I murmured. "Still a damned shame to see a club go down like that. Think they're gearing up for war?"

"Looks that way," he affirmed. "Gage is doin' great there, but they've been asking about you. He told 'em you got locked up again, so that's one loose end tied off."

"Still say we should just ride in there and take over," Duck grunted. "They're a support club. Time to assert some fucking authority."

"Not until we have a handle on the situation north of the border," Pic said. "The Nighthawk Raiders are only a symptom of the real problem. We'll take out Marsh once we get the pipeline secured. Took us five years to build that trade up. Can't afford to start over—too many people waiting to swoop in on our territory. We go after Marsh direct without securing the border and we might as well hand Hallies Falls over to the cartel with a fucking bow."

Duck grunted. "You worry too much about money. This is about respect."

Picnic sighed, pinching the bridge of his nose between two fingers.

"Anyone else?"

"Sorry, Duck," Bolt said. "But I'm with Pic on this. You're right—it's a matter of respect. But it's also about business."

"Painter, what about you?" Pic asked. That surprised me—I

gave my reports and occasionally offered a comment, but meetings like this were usually about the more established guys making
decisions.

"The Nighthawks are rotten," I said slowly. "We can take them
out anytime we want, easy. We do it right, we slide into the void and
take over their trade, which is good for us. I agree that we have to
maintain respect, but a few more weeks won't make much of a difference. Give Gage time to work."

"All in favor?" Pic asked. Everyone but Duck grunted an affir-
mative. He just growled at us, then rose from his chair to lumber off
toward the bar.

"He seem grumpier than usual?" Horse asked.

"Been havin' a rough time," Pic said, his voice low. "Goin' to the
doctor a lot lately. Somethin's up, but he won't tell me what. Stupid
fucking stubborn asshole. Painter, you got a minute? Want to talk
to you—in the office."

"Sure," I said, rising to follow him out into the hall. His office
was across the way, and something about getting called into it reminded me of when I'd gotten in trouble at school. There was a
principal-ish feel to the place, even though the walls were papered
with posters advertising headliners at The Line.

"What's up?" I asked, settling into the chair in front of his big
desk. He sat down in the chair behind it, one of those old-fashioned
wooden ones with spindles on the back and rollers on the bottom.

"Just wanted to check in with you," he said. "Now that we've
talked things out. You doin' okay?"

"Fine," I said. "I mean, Mel was a little weird yesterday when
she came to see me, but this has been a lot for her to take in. We'll
figure it out tonight."

Picnic frowned.

"There's something going on with that girl," he admitted. "Jess
called Loni last night, made her drive into town. She spent half the
night at their place, and she won't tell me why. She insisted there's
nothing wrong with Jessica, so I asked her about Mel and she got
real quiet. Loni doesn't lie to me—not after all the shit that went
down—but sometimes she just won't say anything. Not sure what's

going on, but you need to figure it out and take care of it. Let me know if you need any help."

"Yeah, sure," I said. My phone buzzed, and I pulled it out, seeing a text from Mel.

MELANIE: Just pulled up. You around?
ME: Be right out

"That's Mel," I said, feeling a stupid grin cross my face. God, I was turning into a dumbass. "She's outside."

Picnic gave a short, snorting laugh.

"Go get your girl," he said. "Probably time to patch her anyway. That'll settle her down."

Probably makes me sound like a pussy, but it took everything I had not to run to the parking lot. I was eager to get laid, of course, but it was more than that. I wanted to see Mel. Hold her . . . Know that she was still safe and that she still belonged to me.

I managed not to tear off across the gravel like a kid when I saw her, but I walked fast. Fuck, but she was beautiful. She was gorgeous when I'd seen her inside, too, but the lights in there were shit. Made everyone look yellow, even my beautiful girl.

She gave me a soft, hesitant smile, like she wasn't sure whether I'd be happy to see her or something. Never been happier to see anyone in my life.

"Melanie," I said, catching her close for one of those deep kisses that felt like it could go on forever. Vaguely I knew that people were watching us, but I didn't give a shit. I never gave a shit, actually— we liked to live life in the open here at the clubhouse. Mellie was still new, though. Didn't want to scare her off.

Her hands were around my neck, burrowing into my hair as she climbed up my body. Fuckin' loved it when she did that, for a variety of reasons—not least of these was I'm a hell of a lot taller than her and we didn't always fit together quite right. Easier to boost her up than hunch over every time we were together.

The kiss was amazing, but sooner or later we all have to breathe.

"Hey," she whispered, framing my face with her hands as she searched my eyes for something. I wasn't sure what, but she looked almost scared. Pic was right—something was off here. "I'm crazy about you, did you know that?"

"Pretty fuckin' crazy about you," I murmured, kissing slowly down her neck. She shivered and my dick made a serious attempt to crawl out of my pants.

"Anytime," she said. "But there's something we should probably talk about first . . ."

Those weren't good words. Those were *never* good words. I pulled back, studying her face.

"What?"

"Is there anywhere we could go that's private?"

"Sure," I said, thinking quickly. "We got rooms upstairs, you know. Want to use one?"

"All right," she said, her smile tight. I let her slide slowly down my body, teasing my cock. Not even that was enough to distract me from the shadow I'd seen in her eyes.

We caught some shit as I dragged her through the clubhouse. The brothers all knew why I was so hot to get her alone, and for a minute I thought Horse might try to cock-block me, because he's an asshole like that. Apparently the look on my face was enough to warn him off.

On the third floor was a series of rooms anyone could use. Most of the time they were for overnight guests, but guys crashed out here sometimes if they were between places. Also good for when we wanted privacy with a woman, although half the time nobody bothered. Wasn't like we had any secrets from each other at this point, and that went for sex as well as everything else.

By the time we reached the third floor, I could hardly hold myself together I was so horny for her. We were only halfway down the hall when I lost it, catching her and lifting her against the wall. Then our lips were tangled together and I was grinding my cock into her cunt up against the wall. She'd worn this pretty little yellow sundress that just begged to be shoved up and over her head.

Or maybe her back . . . Struck with inspiration, I lowered her, then spun her around until she faced the wall, hands out to brace. An instant later I had the dress up, baring her very cute, very tight little ass to discover a bright red thong, proving that God exists and he obviously wants me to be happy. I ripped open my jeans, whipping out my cock as I hooked the thong with one finger and jerked it to the side.

Then I was inside.

Mel was better than I remembered. I mean, I knew she'd be hot and wet and tight around me, but this was a whole new level of amazing. Slamming deep, I heard her gasp as she pushed her butt back toward me, back arching. The whole time I was inside, I'd pictured us making slow love once I got out. I'd planned to explore every inch of her body, to worship her and show her just how much I cared about her.

That's not what this was.

My hands were tight around her waist as my hips jackhammered home, carrying us fast and hard toward the explosion boiling deep in my balls. I hoped to hell she was as into this as I was, because I didn't think I could slow down and I sure as shit wasn't going to last long. Mel was gasping with every stroke, though, pushing back at me and squeezing down hard. Either she was just as close as me or she was one hell of an actress.

"This is probably gonna be kind of fast," I managed to gasp, slamming in deep. She clenched tight, and I froze, desperately trying to hold back.

"Don't worry about me," she said. I shook my head, even though she couldn't see it. I'd be damned if I'd come before she did. Sliding my hand down and around her stomach, I found her clit, catching it between my fingers. Her entire body seized, squeezing my dick so hard it almost hurt.

Almost.

"Close, baby?" I whispered. Mel nodded her head frantically, wiggling her hips around my cock like a butterfly stuck on a pin.

Christ, that felt good. Powerful. Fuckin' loved this control I had over her, my very own woman to keep forever.

My hips started thrusting again, and I tried to keep it slow. I seriously tried, but no way I could control myself under the circumstances, not when she made those little noises. My fingers moved faster, playing her until she started gasping. Suddenly every muscle in her body went tight and then Mel moaned long and loud.

Finally.

She sagged as I clutched her hips, letting myself go, pounding as hard as I could, feeling it build deep inside until I couldn't hold back the explosion a minute longer. At the last instant I pulled out, spraying her ass and back with my come. Thought my head might explode, felt so good. Slowly I came back to myself, staring down at the length of her back.

My girl, covered in *me*.

I reached down, tracing a finger through it to paint a pattern on her back.

Property of Levi Brooks.

Mine. All mine.

MELANIE

That. Was. Amazing.

Pushing myself up, I felt Painter's arm wrap around my waist, pulling me into his body. Then he was kissing the top of my head, running his hands up my stomach to cup my breasts.

"Missed you," he whispered into my ear.

"Missed you, too," I managed to reply. It was hard to think, like he'd somehow shorted out my brain with pleasure. I opened my eyes, looking down the hallway, wondering if we'd had an audience.

Nope, just us.

Good. This was going to be hard enough as it was.

"We have to talk," I gasped as his teeth caught my ear.

"Talk later," he whispered. "I want to eat you out."

My whole body shuddered, but I managed to tug away from him. Turning, I looked up at him.

"We have to talk," I said again, firmly. His eyes flickered, a wary look stealing over his face.

"Okay."

The room was small—just a full-size bed and an old desk. I walked over and pulled out the chair, because I needed to be facing him when I did this.

Needed to see the look on his face.

Painter took a seat on the bed, facing me, leaning forward over his long legs, elbows on knees.

"What is it?"

I swallowed. I'd rehearsed this in my head all night. Then I'd practiced with Loni and Jessica, who'd taken turns giving me hugs and promising me that no matter what, I wouldn't be alone. I knew they'd be there for me, but would Painter?

Taking a deep breath, I put it out there.

"I'm pregnant."

His face didn't change for an instant. Then his eyes narrowed, looking down at my stomach like he expected to see something.

"Are you sure?" he asked slowly.

"Yes," I said shortly. "I took four tests, I'm missing my period, and I've been throwing up almost every day."

Painter's eyes narrowed.

"Is it mine?"

I blinked. "Excuse me?"

"It's a fair question—is it mine?"

"Yes, it's yours," I said, feeling my heart sink. I knew he didn't want kids, so I hadn't exactly expected him to be all happy about this. Still, it never occurred to me that he'd react like *this*.

"You sure?"

This wasn't going well. Shit. *Shit.* "Seeing as you're the only guy I've been with in the last year, yeah, I'm sure. And fuck you very much for thinking I'd cheat."

He sighed, then reached up, rubbing the bridge of his nose.

"This is why you were talking about kids yesterday. How long have you been hiding it from me?"

"I wasn't hiding anything," I snapped. "I only confirmed it yesterday morning. I planned to talk to you when I came to visit, but you were really negative. I figured I should wait until we had the time to talk things through."

"Have you decided what you want to do?"

"Do I want an abortion, you mean?"

He looked straight at me, his face unreadable. "It's one of the options."

"No, I'm keeping it," I told him shortly. "By myself if I have to. I've only known about this baby for a day, but I already love it. Him. Her. Whatever it is, I'll be the best mother I can. I won't be like my own mom—I'm going to stick around and do this right."

"And what do you expect from me?" he asked, still expressionless. I closed my eyes, feeling my heart twist.

He'd warned me.

He'd told me that he hurt girls, that us being together was a bad idea.

They all had.

"Nothing, I guess," I said, slowly rising to my feet. Walking toward the door, I turned back to look at him. All big and rangy. Sexy. Beautiful.

Toxic.

"I guess I don't expect anything. Go play biker with your brothers, Painter. Go do your club business because I guess that's way more important than the child you helped create. Fuck you."

With that I walked out the door.

He didn't follow me.

CHAPTER SIXTEEN

PAINTER

Pregnant.

Melanie was *pregnant*.

I sat on the bed, head down between my legs, wondering how the fuck this had happened. Okay, I knew exactly how it happened . . . I wasn't a moron. I'd realized how stupid it was to screw her without a condom, but I'd always pulled out before coming and she was just so damned sexy.

I needed to go after her, to tell her that it was going to be okay and I'd take care of her and we'd live happily ever after—but I didn't even know what happily ever after looked like. All I knew was that I'd be a shit dad and she was way too fucking young for this.

She deserved an easier life.

Standing slowly, I started downstairs, trying to figure out my next move. I just couldn't wrap my head around it. Melanie was knocked up. With a kid. *My* kid.

A kid I'd made clear I didn't want.

Why the fuck had I said that? I'd wanted to take back my words about ten seconds after they left my mouth but the damage was done. The look on her face had been worse than a punch to the gut.

There was something wrong with me. Deeply wrong. I needed to man up, pull my shit together, and figure it out.

Right.

I could do this.

Leaving the room, I headed for the stairs. Not sure what I expected to find when I reached the bar, maybe London coming at me with a knife or something. They'd planned a big party for me, and London was in charge of all the food—suppose she could just poison me.

Instead I met Banks halfway up the stairs, his face grim.

"Church. Now," he said. "We've got a situation."

His tone cut through the haze in my head. Church. Okay, I could deal with that. I'd fucked up with Mel, but I could fix it. I just needed a little time to make a plan.

Some time and some space.

Yeah. That'd work.

A little time and space, and then I'd go find her.

"Gage called," Pic said, standing at the head of the table. There was a tension in the air, a sense of violence looming that infected all of us. Felt good, because a crisis meant I had an excuse not to think about Melanie being knocked up. Nothing like a good fight to clear your head—wisdom that'd served me well over the years.

At least until I got arrested.

"He's headed down to Ellensburg this afternoon with the Nighthawks," he said. "Marsh is apparently on a rampage—he's convinced that Hands betrayed him to the feds. Someone gave Marsh a tip that Hands would be at some classic car rally tonight, and he's determined to find him and take him out."

I frowned.

"Where the hell is that coming from? Makes no sense at all."

"Fuck if I know," Pic said, his face tense. "But I guess Marsh has been using more and more. Gage says he's paranoid as fuck. Just walked into the clubhouse and ordered everyone onto their bikes,

Gage included. He managed to call when they made a stop, but only had about a minute to talk—said they're asking about you, Painter. Marsh wants reinforcements, wanted to know if you could come."

"The fuck?" I asked, confused. "I've only met him once. Why the hell would he want me?"

"Why the hell would he drag along Gage?" Pic asked in return. "Not like he's got strong ties, either. Obviously the guy's lost it. We've got a big problem, though, because if he makes too much trouble at the car show, the cops will get him and then our entire network's in trouble. We're looking at some dangerous shit here— Gage needs backup."

"We can head over in a pack," Horse said. "Like we're going to see the show, just happen to run into him. He may be fucking us over, but he doesn't know we're onto him. Just a friendly visit between two clubs."

"Probably the best idea," Pic said.

"That covers the show," I said. "But what about protecting Gage afterward? If Marsh has gone paranoid, what's to say he won't decide he's a risk and put a bullet in the back of his head?"

Nobody at the table spoke.

"Let's pull him out," Ruger said. "Give him cover down at the show, then have him ride for home."

"Marsh could send someone after him," Duck pointed out. "We extract, we need to give him an escort. Either that or blow his cover, which risks a confrontation."

"Marsh knows me," I said, thinking fast. "He asked about me. I can go in, stick with Gage, and it won't set off any alarms. Then whatever happens, Gage won't be alone."

They all fell silent.

"The Evans bitch is determined to send your ass back to prison," Bam Bam said slowly. "It's a big risk, Painter. It was one thing, sending you out when we had Torres in our pockets, but this . . . The rally will be crawling with cops, events like that always are. They only cut you loose today—maybe you should sit this one out."

Mel's face flashed in front of my eyes. I needed to go find her, figure the situation out . . . but what the hell was I going to say? I had too much energy trapped inside, too much frustration and fear and a sick feeling, all mixed up with the sinking certainty that I was going to fuck this parenting shit up in a bad way.

You'll be a terrible father and you know it.

"We all know I'm the best one to go," I said, pushing her out of my mind. I couldn't think about all that right now—she'd be fine. We'd figure it out later. "He shouldn't have to do this alone and I'm the only one who can get in there without blowing our plan to hell. We have to protect the pipeline."

My brothers shared looks across the table.

"This have anything to do with whatever the fuck's been going on with Melanie?" Picnic asked bluntly. "Saw her tearing out of here, crying her eyes out. Loni chased after her. You got a death wish or something?"

"No," I said, shaking my head. "I mean, yes. Me and Mel have an . . . issue. But trust me, it's not going anywhere. I need some space to clear my head and no fuckin' way we can leave Gage hanging high and dry. It's a risk, but we all take risks every day. Isn't that what the 1% patch means?"

Picnic sighed.

"Okay, guess it's your call," he said. "Anyone else?"

Nobody else said anything, and for once nobody gave me any shit. We were all too busy imagining what might lie ahead of us and whether Gage would make it to Ellensburg safe.

It was a legitimate concern.

If Marsh wanted to execute him, he'd probably lure him out with a story just like this. Made sense, too—it's what we'd do in his place. And I'd call Melanie just as soon as I got back. Maybe I didn't want kids, but life was twisty like that. We'd figure it out.

I loved her.

That would be enough. It had to be.

"Okay, I want to roll out in the next twenty minutes," Pic said. "Party's canceled, obviously, but I want all the girls safe at the Armory. Duck, you'll hold things together here. We'll leave you the prospects and"—he shot a look around the room—"Banks. You stay here, make sure they're safe. Probably paranoid, but if they wanted to lure us out for an attack, this would be a great way to do it."

"Mind if I call Puck, ask him to stick around?" I asked. "He was heading over for the party already. I'd like him to keep an eye on Mel."

"Good plan," Pic said. "Not just him—I'll talk to Boonie, too. I know some of them were hoping to make it tonight anyway. I'd be more comfortable knowing London's safe. I'll call her, tell her to get her ass back out here, along with Jess and Mel. Now, anything else?"

Nobody spoke.

"Okay, then. Pull your shit together, brothers. Let's not fuck this up."

MELANIE

"We'll start with toothpicks," Jessica said darkly, stirring her coffee. "Underneath his fingernails, one by one . . . Then I'll use the pliers to rip the nails off before we skin his balls. All I need is twenty-four hours. He'll be begging for his life, and then *blammo!* I'll cut out his kidneys with his own fucking knife, we sell them on the black market and set up a college fund for the baby. Problem solved."

I reached for a tissue, wishing I was even slightly surprised by how bloodthirsty she was.

"You can't kill Painter," I said, blowing my nose loudly. "Even if he deserves it. He's this kid's daddy. I'm not going to hate him, because that's not what's important here. The *baby* is important. I need to figure out a plan, make sure that I have every last thing figured out because if I don't—"

"Stop," Loni said, reaching across the table to catch my hand. She gave it a tight squeeze. "Mellie, look at me."

I met her eyes, wishing my real mom were here. London tried her best, but deep down inside I just wanted to crawl into my mother's arms until she made everything better. Why'd she have to take off like that? Why'd she leave me?

My hand stole down to my stomach, rubbing softly. I'd never do that to my baby. Never. I'd die before I abandoned her.

I love you already, baby. Mommy's here.

"You're going to be okay," London said, her voice firm and strong. From the table her phone buzzed again, but she ignored it, 100 percent focused on me. "Whatever happens with Painter, me and Jessica are your family. We'll be here for you. I promise. Do you understand?"

I nodded, feeling a little stronger.

"I'm great with kids," Jess broke in. "Probably because I think like them . . . Mixed blessing. But Loni's right—you aren't alone in this. I hope he pulls his head out of his ass and does the right thing, but if he doesn't you're better off without him."

"And what's the right thing?" I asked. "Like he's supposed to marry me or something? I'm not ready to be married."

Wasn't ready to be a mother, either.

"The right thing is pulling his shit together and fathering his child," Loni said bluntly. "I know you're worried about raising a child in the club, but Reese did it, and he did it well. Bam Bam and Dancer are great parents. It's possible, but only if Painter makes that choice—that's on him, and nobody else. I'd love it if you two managed to work things out romantically, but even that isn't the issue here. Taking care of your baby is the issue and you don't need him to do that."

She was right.

"I can do this, can't I?" I whispered, looking between them. Jessica smiled and nodded.

"You're the strongest, smartest person I know," she said. "And even when things get hard, you keep fighting. That's a lot more than you and I got from our mothers."

Loni's phone went off for what had to be the tenth time.

"You know, if I wanted to answer the fucking phone, I would've already," she said, her voice soft, yet somehow deadly. As if to taunt her, the phone buzzed again. Abruptly, she picked it up and threw it across the room, shattering it against the wall.

What the hell?

Jess and I gaped. Loni stared back at us, then gave a little shrug.

"Just because I'm not threatening to skin Painter's balls doesn't mean I'm in my happy place. I'll call Reese when I'm damned good and ready."

"Loni, you sort of kick ass," I whispered. She gave me a grim smile.

"I have my moments."

A loud pounding noise filled the air—someone at the door.

"If he has even an ounce of sense, that's Painter with two dozen roses and a ring," Jess growled. Loni and I shared a glance.

"I'm not ready to get married," I reminded her.

"It's not about you saying yes, it's about him offering."

The pounding came again, so I dragged my rear out of the chair and walked over to the window. I don't know who I was expecting— maybe Painter, or even Reese.

Instead I saw BB, a big lumbering bear of a prospect.

"What is it?" I asked, opening the door.

"We need all of you back out at the Armory," he said. "Picnic tried to call but nobody answered."

Loni came to stand behind me. "We're busy."

He shook his head. "No, ma'am. Something's going on and they want all the women out there where it's safe. You have to come with me."

"Oh shit," Loni said, her face going pale. "Okay, girls, grab a change of clothes. I'll drive."

PAINTER

I rode to Ellensburg twenty minutes behind the pack, figuring it would be safer. They'd be more likely to attract police attention than a lone rider would. Not only that, if they arrived first they could scope out the situation with Marsh, warning me off if Gage couldn't. Hopefully it wouldn't come to that—when I'd messaged him saying I was on my way he hadn't given any indication that there was trouble, but he didn't answer when I called, either. Just a texted acknowledgment. Could've been anyone sending it.

The three-hour ride gave me plenty of time to think about the situation with Melanie, though. I'd fucked it up. Fucked it up big-time and was almost certainly making it worse by going to Ellensburg instead of dealing with her right now. I couldn't just leave Gage hanging, though . . . and much as Mel meant to me, talking to her now or talking to her tomorrow wasn't a matter of life and death.

Gage might not have that luxury.

When I finally pulled into Ellensburg, I found a string of messages on my phone between me, Gage, and Picnic.

GAGE: Downtown at the Banner Bank Tavern. They have a beer garden on one of the side streets—closed to traffic. Marsh and his crew are drunk as fuck and he's tweaking. Paranoid. Got six cops watching us. Worried that Marsh will blow it

PICNIC: Across the street. Don't want to come over unless we need to. Think it might set Marsh off?

GAGE: Hang back for now. Painter you anywhere near yet?

PICNIC: He's behind us, should be here soon.

GAGE: K

That last message was ten minutes ago, so things must still be under control . . . or else they'd fallen to utter shit and they were too busy fighting to message me. Either way, I needed to get my ass over there ASAP.

Ellensburg was a relatively small town, so it wasn't that hard to find the bar. Took a while to get there because the streets were choked with what felt like a thousand hot rods. Had to leave my bike parked down the street, too—didn't much like that. Although to be fair, the bike was probably the least of my worries today.

Walking toward the bar, I saw Pic and the others across the

street, looking over a line of custom choppers. They stood out from the crowd, of course—a motorcycle club in full colors always did— but they were keeping as low-key as possible. Pic caught my eye, but we didn't acknowledge each other. Then I reached the old Banner Bank building, all brick and cut stone from the town's earliest days. The bar made the most of the historic atmosphere, done up to look like an old-time saloon. I passed all the way through and out the side door to the beer garden, a fenced-off area they'd set up on the street.

Loud music played and a few people were dancing in the center of the tables. A girl caught my eye, jumping up and down, waving at me.

Sadie.

Fucking great.

"Levi!" she shouted, running to meet me. Just past her I saw Talia hanging all over Gage. Marsh and the others were off to one side, taking up more than their fair share of tables. At least they were somewhat isolated . . . A quick glance showed me that a group of cops was gathered just outside the fenced area, watching the Nighthawks closely. More seemed to be inside, although they weren't in uniform. They gave off that law enforcement vibe, though, and I saw the way they clocked me the instant I walked in.

Not only was Marsh drunk and tweaking, the fucker was doing it at a cop bar.

Christ.

"Good to see you," I told Sadie, pulling her in for a hug. She tried to kiss me, but I managed to turn my head just enough that she'd miss my lips. Even if it wasn't for Mel, I didn't think I could touch her—not after seeing her barf like a fountain. "Gage said he'd be here, suggested I come over to join you guys."

"Where have you been?" she asked, frowning. "You just disappeared that night."

"Jail," I said shortly. Might as well stick to the truth. "Violated the terms of my parole, so they locked me up to teach me a lesson."

She reached up, rubbing a hand up and down my chest.

"Sounds *dangerous*."

"Levi!" Gage shouted, waving me over. Thank fuck. I sauntered over to him, Sadie in tow. He welcomed me with a hug, taking the opportunity to whisper a warning. "Shit's ugly. We gotta contain Marsh or he's gonna blow everything."

Pulling back, I surveyed the group, nodding to the Nighthawk Raiders' president.

"Nice to see you again," I said. "Looks like a good time."

Marsh smiled at me, but I saw something dark behind his eyes. Talia slithered up, then plopped herself on his lap.

"Were you really in jail?" she asked me, reaching for Marsh's drink, chugging it.

"Yup," I said. "Got out this morning. Parole violation."

Her eyes widened.

"What'd you go down for?"

"Weapons charge," I said shortly. Marsh frowned.

"How long was your sentence?"

"Three years."

"That's too long for a weapons charge," he said, narrowing his eyes.

"It's complicated," I said, which was the truth. "Let's just say it could've been a hell of a lot worse. Had priors, too."

An overworked waitress came hustling up to us.

"You guys need anything?" she asked.

"We needed something half an hour ago," Talia said, standing back up. She stepped forward into the woman's space, thrusting her chest out. "Where the fuck have you been?"

"I'm real sorry," she said. "We're just slammed. I'm sure we can—"

"We deserve a free round," Talia said. "This is your fault, not ours."

Gage shot me a look.

"Baby, let's go dance," he said, reaching for her hand. "I want to feel you up against me."

"I'm busy," Talia said, and while she didn't flip him off, she might as well have. She glared at the waitress. "Are you going to get us the drinks?"

The woman glanced at Marsh, then nodded her head quickly. "Sure, I'll be right back."

She backed away, making for the bar door.

"See, it's all about how you talk to them," Talia declared, and Marsh started laughing. "I'm ready for that dance now."

She grabbed Gage's hand, dragging him toward the dance floor. My eyes followed them. Ah fuck. There was a big guy wearing a bar T-shirt talking to the group of off-duty cops, pointing toward our group. Bouncer.

The men stood up and started walking toward us. I needed to do something. Fast.

"Marsh," I said in a low voice, leaning into the seated man. "We gotta get out of here."

He stood slowly, stepping into my space.

"Did you just give me an order?"

Seriously? The cops were coming and he wanted to play bullshit games?

"No, but those guys are police, and they're headed this way," I said urgently. "This is trouble none of us needs."

Marsh narrowed his eyes. "How do you know they're cops? You're working for them, aren't you?"

From the corners of my eyes, I saw his crew crowding in. Then Marsh was on me, his fist catching me hard in the stomach. I lunged for him, a sudden rush of adrenaline pushing me through the pain as people started shouting all around us. The Nighthawk brothers jumped in, punching and kicking me from every side. I was vaguely aware of Gage shouting, trying to reach me. More hits and then I went down, catching a foot in my kidney.

In an instant, the cops were on us and Marsh forgot all about me. I watched as he pulled out an ugly knife, then launched himself at one of them. Ah, *fuck*. Suddenly Gage was next to me, catching me by the arms to drag me back. A body flew by, knocking him over. I saw a flash of bright red blood spray through the air. Catching a chair, I started to pull myself up when someone hit me over the back of the head.

I pitched forward, and in the instant before I hit the ground I thought about Melanie. About our baby.

About the fact that I was almost certainly going back to prison. I'd fucked up. Bad.

CHAPTER SEVENTEEN

TWO WEEKS LATER

Dear Painter,

I got your letter asking me to come and see you before they send you back to California. I've thought about it a lot, and I even drove down to the jail once. I sat in the car for half an hour and then I turned around, because I'm just not ready to talk to you.

I don't know when I'll be ready.

I understand that you panicked—when I found out about the baby, I panicked, too. I cried on the bathroom floor because I was so scared. It's a terrifying thing, to suddenly discover that you're going to be a parent. But here's the thing . . . you didn't only panic. You took off and did something that you knew could land you back in prison. That was a choice you made and there are serious consequences. Now I'm having a baby by myself and you're going to be gone for two years. Do you realize that we've only spent a few weeks together, total, in the entire time I've known you?

You asked if I would consider waiting for you. No. I have one person in my life right now who really matters, and that's the one growing in my stomach. Four weeks spent together full of unanswered questions and secret trips away from me isn't enough to build a life on. It isn't fair to me or our baby to sit around waiting for a man who ran away from us. And yes, you say you regret it, but you also did something guaranteed to separate us. You don't even have to choose to ignore your child. You're gone by default.

And I think that's what you really wanted anyway . . . to have this problem go away.

Now it's gone.

I don't hate you. For what it's worth, I'm sad. I'd say you broke my heart but that's not true—I can't afford a broken heart. I'm a mother now, or I will be soon. If I'm going to take care of this baby, I can't afford to put any more time and energy into a man who will always put his motorcycle club first.

I deserve someone who puts me first. So does our child.

Melanie

TWO MONTHS LATER

Dear Melanie,

I hope you're doing well. I was disappointed that you didn't come see me while I was waiting in the Kootenai County jail for my parole hearing, but I also understand. I appreciate the letter you sent, and I agree with you. You have every right to stay away from me and I don't blame you for being pissed.

I'm pissed at myself, too.

Now I've had a lot of time to think about what I did. You may not be interested in hearing this, but I'm sorry. I'm sorry for all kinds of things. I should've been supportive when you told me about the baby. There's no excuse, but I did want to explain. I had a shit time growing up and kids scare me. But the more I think about a baby with your eyes, the more I want it. I hope that you'll give me a chance to be a father when I get back out of here.

I'm also sorry that I got myself thrown back in prison when you needed me the most. I'm sorry I won't be there when the baby is born, and that when you're tired and you need help I won't be around.

I'll never forgive myself for that.

Puck tells me that Jessica and Loni are helping you out a lot and that you're doing good. He's selling my bike and will get you the money as soon as he can. I hope you'll consider using some of it to come and see me when the baby is born—maybe bring him to meet me. (Or her, if it's a girl. I guess I assumed it was a boy, but I don't care either way. I just want to meet him.) If not that, I hope you'll send me pictures.

Maybe my life would be different if I'd had a dad. Maybe I wouldn't be such a fuck-up. I promise you that if you give me a shot, once I get out I'll be a real father for our child.

I still love you,
Painter

SEVEN MONTHS LATER

Painter,

So, I bet you never expected to hear from me, huh? Hunter was pissed when I told him I wanted to write to you, but then he and I talked about it some more, and when I explained why he understood.

It's because we know what it feels like to lose a child.

I know your situation is different, because your baby is alive and well, but it probably feels like you've lost her. Maybe hearing more about her from me will help. (Hopefully you already know all this anyway, but I didn't feel comfortable asking Melanie about it under the circumstances.)

Anyway, baby Isabella is beautiful. I'm sticking in some pictures from the hospital. Kit and I are both very excited—we asked Melanie if we can be her aunties and she said yes. When we heard she was in labor we wanted to be there, although we weren't in the room. We waited out in the hallway, which made for some very interesting people watching. Lots of excited grandparents, that kind of thing. Jessica and London were inside with her. I drove over and kept speeding because I was afraid I'd miss something, but it turned out I had plenty of time.

I don't know how much you've heard, but things got scary for a while. Izzy (that's what we're calling her) wasn't progressing right and then she went into distress. They had to do an emergency C-section and the baby ended up getting miconium (that's poop—I probably spelled it wrong) in her lungs. She ended up in the NICU for more than two weeks and got pneumonia. Even now we have to keep a close eye on her and we've all been taking shifts watching over her.

She's got apnea, which means she sometimes stops breathing. (There's an alarm that's supposed to go off if it happens, but it's hard to trust a machine with something so important.) It's really scary. The good news is that they think she'll grow out of it and it won't be a big deal. Melanie has been incredibly strong. The same day as her surgery she got out of bed and climbed into a wheelchair, then made us take her down to the NICU to see Izzy. Didn't give two shits that she'd just had surgery, or that the doctor told her she had to stay away.

That girl's a fighter, and she's going to be a very good mother.

I should get going now, but I hope you're doing all right. Hunter says he hopes you eat shit and that you're a douche, but he was smiling while he said it. He also sends his respect.

Take care,
Em

SOUTHERN CALIFORNIA, STATE CORRECTIONAL FACILITY
MELANIE

I wasn't ready to see him.

I'd been pumping myself up for weeks—I'd even called Jessica early that morning for a last-second pep talk before I left the hotel room. She'd reminded me of all the reasons I wanted Izzy to know her daddy, but now that we were really here, in the visiting area, I couldn't remember any of them.

All I could think about was how much he'd hurt me the last time we talked.

I glanced around in near panic, wondering if I should just leave. The guard standing next to me—the one who'd escorted us in—caught my eye.

"They'll be here in a minute," she said in a low voice, offering a reassuring smile. She didn't look like she should be working in a prison. The woman was probably around Loni's age, and while she wasn't exactly model gorgeous she wasn't unattractive, either. She looked down at Izzy, her face softening even more.

"I'm sorry I had to search the diaper bag," she added. "You wouldn't believe how many people try to sneak contraband."

"I understand," I said quietly, although the reality was I could hardly wrap my head around it. How had I fallen into a world where people expected me to load my daughter's diapers with drugs?

"You ready?" Puck asked, his face grim and blank as always.

Painter's best friend made me uncomfortable, but I couldn't deny he'd been a huge help. Sometimes it seemed like I couldn't turn around without finding some biker checking up on me. This was good and bad—I needed the help, but I hated feeling dependent. Much as I blamed Painter for what happened, I blamed the Reapers, too.

They'd dragged him down into this.

Them and their "club business."

We stood awkwardly with the rest of the visitors, ranging from other young mothers with kids to people in their fifties and sixties. A few of the women could've passed for hookers—for all I knew, they were.

Do prostitutes visit their pimps in jail?

That was a dark thought, but darker still, how many women were forced into prostitution to support their kids once their fathers were locked up? I looked down at Izzy, sleeping peacefully in my arms, and knew I'd do anything to take care of her. Anything at all.

A door at the far end of the room opened, and then men wearing orange jumpsuits started walking in. A little boy next to me shouted "Daddy!" as he tore off toward a scary-looking Hispanic guy covered in gang tattoos. He smiled, swinging the boy up in his arms, holding him tight as he kissed his hair.

Then Painter came in.

My breath caught, a thousand different emotions fighting for control. Anger. Love. Hurt . . . Some detached part of me noted that he looked better than ever, although his face was harder than ever. His hair had grown out, hanging down to his shoulders loosely. Pale blue eyes searched for us, dropping instantly to the precious bundle of life in my arms.

He stopped walking, then swallowed.

"C'mon," Puck said, reaching down to touch my elbow, urging me forward. I stepped toward Painter, our eyes locked on each other. Then I was standing in front of him, tense and uncomfortable. Puck wasn't with me, I realized. He'd stepped back, offering what privacy he could under the circumstances.

"Hey," I said softly.

"Hey," Painter replied. "Thank you for coming."

This was even harder than I'd imagined.

"I wanted you to meet her," I told him, feeling uncertain. "You should know your daughter."

He looked down, taking in the tiny, sleeping face. She'd been born with a head full of pale blonde fuzz. I'd put a little white headband on her with a flower on it—it matched her sundress, a gift from Loni.

"Can . . . can I hold her?" he asked softly.

"Sure."

He put his arms out and I handed her over carefully, catching my breath when our skin touched. It was still there, the awareness between us. Intense and electric. Izzy startled, her little hands lifting up as her eyes opened.

Pale blue, just like his.

They stared at each other, father and daughter, and something inside my chest broke. He reached a finger toward her and little Isabella grabbed it tight, making a soft, gurgling noise.

"She's perfect," he whispered, and even though we were surrounded by people it felt like we were the only ones in the room. Just me, him, and our daughter . . .

"Do you want to sit down with her?" I asked.

"Yes."

I looked around, finding an open table. "Let's go over there."

Painter walked over slowly and carefully, holding Izzy like she was made of spun glass. He seemed to be whispering to her, and any doubts I'd had that he'd love her disappeared. He'd already fallen for her—fallen for her just as hard and fast as I had the first time I saw her in the NICU.

"Em sent me pictures," he said, once we were settled at a table. "She told me about when she was born, too. It sounds like you did an amazing job."

"I tried. The C-section was rough—I really wanted to do it all natural, you know? They say that's better for the baby. But I just couldn't. I tried and tried, but she wasn't coming."

He looked up at me, eyes intense.

"She's *perfect*," he said again, emphasizing the word. "You did everything right, Mel. They told me about all you went through, fighting for her. I can't imagine anyone ever doing better."

Blinking rapidly, I fought back the tears prickling at my eyes.

"I wish you could've been there," I whispered.

"I wish I could have, too."

Izzy gave a little squawk. His eyes flew back to her, widening in something like panic. She raised her arms, stretching them high as she yawned. Then her eyes narrowed as her nose scrunched. I knew that look.

"What's wrong with her?" he asked quickly, his voice almost panicky.

"She might have gas," I said. "Or she could be pooping. Just give her a minute."

Izzy didn't need a minute, though. A series of loud, wet, squelching noises exploded outward. Painter's face twisted, a combination of shock and horror—like he half expected her head to spin around or something. He looked back at me.

"What do we do?"

I laughed—couldn't help myself.

"Just give it a couple minutes," I told him. "Make sure she's done. Then I'll go change her."

PAINTER

Melanie's ass twitched as she walked away with Isabella. My daughter—how unreal was that? I could see the differences in Mel's body since the pregnancy—she'd filled out. Her boobs were bigger, too. A lot bigger. I'd missed her so fucking much since I'd gotten locked up. This was different than it'd been before. Worse. Not that spending time in a cell is ever good, but knowing I was missing out on something so amazing—so *important*—turned it into pure torture.

And this time I didn't even have letters from her to get me through.

I hoped it wouldn't take long to change Izzy. We had only a limited time for visitation, and I didn't want to waste any of it. God only knew when—or if—she'd ever make it down again. Christ, I loved the kid more than I ever thought was possible, and now I might not see her again for months.

"How's it going?" Puck asked, his voice low as he eased into the seat across from me. I shrugged.

"Well, aside from the fact that I'm in prison and I missed the first five months of my kid's life, it's fuckin' great. How are things on your end?"

Puck gave a slow smile. "Better than yours. I've been keepin' an eye on her for you."

"Thanks," I said. "I fucked up bad this time, bro. Real bad."

He nodded. "Yup."

I bit back a laugh, leaning forward over my legs.

"Love how you always try to make me feel better."

Puck cocked a brow. "Like you want me blowin' smoke up your ass?"

"Fair enough. How was the trip down?"

"Good," he said. "Weird, traveling with a baby, but she was good. Cried a little bit during takeoff. Mel had to nurse her on the plane. Think that made her a little uncomfortable."

Frowning, I gave him a hard look. "You check out her tits?"

"Yeah, because I've got a milk fetish," he said, rolling his eyes. "You're a sick motherfucker, you know that?"

That made me laugh again, and he joined me.

"So you keepin' safe in here without me?" he finally asked.

"It's tougher this time," I admitted. "But I got Pipes at my back. This shit goin' down in Hallies Falls has him worried and a lot of the alliances have fallen apart. We lean on each other a bit. And of course there's Fester . . . He was real happy to have me back."

Puck snorted. "How is the Prince of Perverts?"

"You'll be shocked to hear he's still a disgusting little twat," I said. "But get this—they've started a new art program. I'm helping

teach it, and he's one of my students. He's not half bad, so long as
you keep him focused. A little more interested in anatomy than I'd
like. Sort of obsessed with how muscles and joints come together . . .
and what they look like ripped apart."

"Have fun with that," he replied, smirking. I flipped him off
and we both sat back, staring at each other. There was a whole
lot more I could say, but what would be the point? Nothing ever
changed on the inside. "Not gonna lie—glad I'm not in here with
you."

"Fair enough."

"Got some updates for you," he said quietly. "I know you heard
some of this, but figured I'd fill you in on the rest. They tell you
Marsh was carrying a shitload of meth?"

"Yeah, Pic mentioned it, back up in Coeur d'Alene," I said.

"Well he finally pled out. Between stabbing the cop and the
drugs he was carrying, he's going away for at least three years.
Maybe more, depending on his behavior—guy's not exactly known
for holding his shit together under pressure."

"That's good news. And the rest of them?"

"They locked up two others. Talia's in the wind, nobody knows
where. Marsh is pissed—he's blaming you for what went down, not
that it matters."

"Good riddance."

"Yeah. Gage is still in Hallies Falls. Helping those who are still
left rebuild. Those who are worth keeping, that is . . . There's been
some talk of them patching over as Reapers."

"Might be for the best," I said, thinking of Cord and the other
brothers who'd been so unhappy under Marsh. "Pipes has filled me
in some, but his intel is limited. We're too far away to stay in touch,
you know?"

Puck nodded.

"Well, I got good news, too," he said. "Pic wanted me to go over
it with you, actually. They still have your work hanging in the custom shop, and that guy who talked to you about painting his bike
has been in a couple more times. Apparently he's friends with an art

dealer, and he showed him some pictures of your work. They're interested in doing a gallery show."

"Huh," I said, not quite sure what to do with that information. Puck cocked his head.

"Thought you'd be more excited."

"I am. I mean, I think I am. But I'm not quite sure how it would work . . . Don't have very many pieces, and it's not like I can do more from inside. And he knows I'm locked up—I wrote to him already, telling him I'd have to pass on the commission."

Puck coughed. "This is where it gets weird. I guess you being in prison—you know, hardened felon, motorcycle club, and all that shit—makes you more interesting. Guy says the dealer got off on it, called you dangerous."

I snorted.

"This crap for real?"

"Apparently. He wants to come see you. Pic got in his face, said we'd reach out to you first. Doesn't want you treated like some kind of sideshow freak, you know? But it could be money—Mel's not exactly rolling in it. You start pulling money in, that'll make a big difference."

"Do it," I said shortly.

"Do what?" Mel asked, coming up to us. Izzy was wide awake and alert, and she'd been changed into fresh clothes.

"There's a guy who wants to put on an art show with some of my work," I told her. Her eyes widened.

"That's great news."

"Maybe. I'm not gonna get too excited until we see how it plays out. Can I hold Izzy again?"

"Sure," she said. I reached out for the baby, the back of my hand brushing the lower side of her boob. Her eyes flew to mine, and she blinked rapidly. Tears? No, not quite, but her eyes were red and definitely sad. I pulled Izzy close, leaning down to take in her soft, baby smell.

It hit me that after today, I might never experience that smell again. Christ. This was so much worse than I'd ever imagined life could get . . . felt like my guts were being ripped out, every second with her precious and perfect and speeding faster than should be possible.

"Puck, can you give us a minute?" I asked him. He nodded, ambling toward the vending machines. Melanie sat down across the table. I'd been hoping she'd sit next to me, but no luck.

"I already apologized in my letters," I started. She held up a hand.

"This is hard enough without listening to your justifications," she said, her voice carefully blank. "I don't want to hear it."

"I'm going to be a good daddy."

"You can't be," she replied harshly. "You're not there and you won't be for another year and a half."

Taking a deep breath, I forced myself to stay calm.

"I realize that," I said slowly. "But once I get back, that's going to change."

"We'll see."

"No, I mean it. I'm going to be there for both of you. I promise."

She looked at me steadily, then glanced around the room. Other families sat at tables, other fathers holding their kids, playing games with them or coloring. Reading stories together.

"How many of them have made those same promises?" she asked, her voice sad. *Fuck.*

"Words can't fix this—I get that. But once I'm out, you'll see for yourself. I'm going to take care of you and Izzy."

She looked away for long minutes. The baby gurgled again, then stretched her little body, kicking out with her legs. Then Izzy smiled at me and the whole world disappeared.

Yeah, sounds stupid, but it's the fuckin' truth.

"I'll take care of you," I whispered, leaning down to kiss her soft cheek. "I promise. Your mama doesn't believe me yet, but I'll show her. I'll show both of you. Daddy's here, baby girl."

"For now," Melanie muttered. I didn't say anything—after all, what the hell could I say?

She was right.

MELANIE

Izzy started crying when we finally pulled away from the prison. The visit had been four hours long, but it felt like forty minutes. That's how fast it was over. I couldn't blame her for it either—I felt like crying, too.

"She doing okay?" Puck asked, one big hand draped over the top of the steering wheel.

"Fine," I said. "Although she'll probably want to eat soon."

"I'm hungry, too. We can pull off and grab something on the way back to the hotel. Unless you want to do something while we're down here? Got some time to kill this afternoon."

"What, like go sightseeing?"

"If you want."

I considered the idea, but the thought of doing touristy things with Painter's best friend and a newborn didn't exactly strike me as fun. "No, let's just go to the hotel. Izzy could use a nap and I'd like some space."

"You got it."

He turned on the radio and we settled in for the drive. The look on Painter's face as we left haunted me. I wanted to hate him for what he'd done, but the pain he'd suffered when he handed Izzy back to me was real.

He loved her.

I wasn't sure that he would—he didn't want kids. He'd chosen prison over our daughter. Not that he'd sat down and checked a box marked "prison" instead of "fatherhood" on a test, but he'd known damned well that his parole officer was out for blood when he left the state.

But he truly loved Izzy. I'd seen it.

"I'm going to start sending him pictures," I told Puck abruptly. He shot me a quick glance, then nodded.

"He'd probably like that."

And that was it.

I liked Puck, I decided. He was big and scary, with a nasty scar across his face and all the social skills of an ax murderer, but he knew when to keep his mouth shut.

"Thanks. Thanks for bringing us down here."

He glanced toward me again.

"Anytime, Mel. Anytime."

CHAPTER EIGHTEEN

"Cake?" Izzy asked, her voice hopeful. I looked at the pyramid of brightly frosted pink cupcakes with little princess cutouts on them and sighed.

London and Jessica seemed determined to bury me in a mountain of pink, something my daughter was all too happy to encourage. Not only were the cupcakes pink, the plastic tablecloth, the cups, the plates, the napkins, and the balloons were all pink, too. Specifically, the kind of neon pink that almost makes your eyes bleed, with princesses and unicorns, because God is cruel.

Even worse was the disturbingly poofy dress Painter had given her. Okay, so even I had to admit it was cute, a little tutu thing with a bright tulle skirt attached to a lightweight cotton one-piece. It even had "Princess" written across the front in silver sparkles. Would've been cuter if it hadn't been so damned pink, though. Sometimes it felt like an Easter bunny had barfed all over my life, because everything was pastel and pretty.

Thus are the joys of having a daughter.

In the distance I heard the roar of Harley engines and looked up to see Painter and Reese Hayes pulling around the corner to the parking lot. The sound was enough to break through Izzy's cupcake-induced trance, something I wouldn't have bet was even possible.

"Daddy!" she shrieked, taking off across the lawn toward them. It was a gorgeous day for a birthday party in the park—would've been perfect if *he* weren't coming. But I also knew how much he was looking forward to sharing a birthday with her.

Too bad it meant I couldn't relax and enjoy the party like I wanted to. Asshole. Ever since he'd gotten back, he'd been nice. Too nice. It felt like a game, a show he was putting on to prove that he'd really changed and I should forgive him. This was fine and dandy, but ultimately it meant jack shit because Painter still danced on the wrong side of the law, and we both knew it. I couldn't afford to get used to having him around, or depend on him. It'd destroy me if—no, *when*—the next crisis hit. Izzy couldn't afford for me to be broken.

Just because he wasn't in prison right now didn't mean there wasn't a cell in his future.

"You ready for this?" Jessica asked, coming up next to me. She knew exactly how I felt about the situation—I couldn't exactly talk to Loni about the Reapers, but Jess was a different story.

"Yup," I said, pasting a happy smile on my face. "It's gonna be great. A blast. Too much fun."

"You're overdoing it," she replied, bumping my shoulder with hers. "Just try to relax. It'll be over in a few hours and then you'll be back home again with Izzy."

I closed my eyes, fighting off a wave of panic.

"No, I won't."

"What do you mean?"

"Painter is taking her for a sleepover tonight," I said, feeling my smile solidify into something that couldn't have been pretty. "He's been wanting to for a couple months, so I set him a series of conditions. He met them. I never expected him to meet them."

Her eyes widened. "Why haven't I heard about this before now?"

I shrugged.

"Never thought he'd actually do it," I admitted. "When he asked me to come over and check out his place, I was stunned. It's totally childproofed. He's even got a toddler bed for her, and he bought all her favorite foods. Loni's scheduled to be on call if he needs help, and of course I'll be watching my phone. Izzy's all excited about it—we packed a whole suitcase full of stuffed animals to take to Daddy's house."

"Wow," she said. "Didn't see that coming."

I watched as Painter pulled Isabella up onto the bike with him, letting her pretend to drive it. God, she looked more like him every day—that white-blonde hair of hers shined in the sun like a beacon, and if anything the blue of her eyes had gotten brighter. Not only that, she loved to finger-paint. Okay, all kids that age love to finger-paint, but even the preschool teacher at her daycare said she showed signs of talent. Wasn't sure how I felt about that.

"Relax," Loni said, wrapping an arm around my shoulder and giving me a hug. "It's just a party and a sleepover. He'll do fine."

"That's what scares me," I admitted. "What if she likes him better than me? All he ever does is fun stuff with her. I'm the one stuck doing the real work and telling her no. At this rate she'll hate me by the time she's twelve, and then he'll get married someday and she'll want to go live with him and her new stepmom and I'll be all alone and—"

"Mel!" Jess said, snapping her fingers in front of my face. I looked at her. "Pack up the crazy, babe. She's only two."

I blinked at her.

Shit, she was right. *You're losing it.*

"I have a date tonight," I admitted. "I'm a little freaked out by that, too . . ."

"A date?" Loni asked, staring at me. "Seriously?"

"Hey, it's not that weird," I said, frowning. "I date."

"Twice," Jessica said. "You've gone out twice since Izzy was born, and both times you cut it short to come home and check on her. It's unhealthy—you deserve a life. And Painter should take on some of the responsibility. She's his kid, too."

In the distance, I heard Izzy screaming excitedly as Painter swung her up and onto his shoulders. Then he and Reese started across the grass toward us, laughing and talking along the way. Reese had been great, I had to admit. He and his daughters had welcomed me into the fold like one of their own, so much that I had to work hard to keep my distance or I would've gotten sucked into the Reapers' extended family.

It wouldn't have been all bad, I knew that . . . The girls had offered to babysit for me time and again, and I knew they meant well. But every time I saw the Reapers colors, I thought about Painter missing Isabella's birth. About the endless nights sitting up with her in the NICU, still recovering from surgery. Then we finally made it home, and I'd spent weeks alone in the dark, holding her, terrified to sleep because the only thing standing between my baby and death was an electronic monitor that was supposed to go off if she stopped breathing.

I didn't trust that monitor.

Not after the night I woke up needing to pee, only to find Izzy had turned blue from lack of oxygen. Fucking machine was useless. I'd never been so alone or afraid in my life, and it felt like forever before she grew out of it. Rebuilding my life hadn't been easy, but I'd gotten there. Mostly. Eventually I made new friends. I wasn't the only single mom in the nursing program at the college. Having Izzy had delayed my education some, but I'd done pretty well on my own.

Better than well, actually.

Now I had my own apartment, a decent job, and health insurance. No more state assistance, either—that was a nice change. Most of my childhood had been spent on welfare, and I remembered all too well how people looked down on me and my mom for that. They'd looked down on my dad, too, but I didn't care about that. He was just the drunk in the living room.

"So what's the plan?" Reese asked as they reached the picnic shelter.

"Cake!" Izzie shouted. "Cake cake cake cake! Izzy cake!"

"Sounds like we're having cake," I said dryly, shaking off my darker thoughts. "I'll grab the matches."

"Got it," Reese said, pulling out a Zippo. He didn't smoke, so I'd never quite understood why he carried it—guess the ability to set fires at any time is a useful one. He handed it over to Loni, who lit the candles as I pulled out my phone to record the moment. Painter swung Izzy down and plopped her in front of the sticky pyramid.

"Happy birthday to you . . ." we all sang, with Isabella singing the loudest. She clapped her hands, and when we finished she lunged for a cupcake, grabbing the one with the candles still flaming.

"Shit," Painter said, jumping forward to catch it. Izzy turned on him in a rage, smacking his arm.

"Mine!"

"Isabella, that's not okay," I said firmly. She glared at me.

"Izzy cake."

"You can have the cake when you say sorry," I told her. Her glare turned dark and she looked even more like her daddy, only this was funny instead of scary. Jess snorted. "No inappropriate feedback, please."

Painter shot me a look. "It's her birthday, Mel. Don't be a hard-ass."

Oh no. No fucking way—he didn't get to undermine me like that. Not to mention his language . . .

"Izzy can have the cake when she says sorry for hitting you," I said. He set the cupcake down in front of her, deliberately. I cocked my head, glaring at him.

"Isabella, say sorry," Jess said, catching her attention. "Say it with Auntie Jess?"

The little girl looked at Jessica and smiled. "Sowwy."

I sighed in relief, realizing this could be a sign of things to come—Izzy was a smart kid. Too smart. If she realized she could play her parents against each other, we'd be screwed by the time she hit middle school.

I felt another wave of near panic hit—if I couldn't control a two-year-old, how was I supposed to control a middle schooler?

"Okay, princess. Cupcake time," Painter said, swinging a leg over to straddle the bench next to her. She beamed at him, shoving it into her mouth without paying the slightest attention to me. It was always like that . . . Izzy was daddy's girl, through and through.

I hated it, and I sort of hated myself, too.

What kind of crazy woman is jealous of her own daughter?

• • •

"She's gonna do fine," Painter said, giving me a cool look. We stood next to each other under the picnic shelter, watching Izzy play chase with Jessica on the playground equipment. He'd lost all the smiles now that we were alone. Prison had impacted him even more deeply this time. He'd gone darker, more still. His art was darker, too. From what I'd seen in his studio, there was a new power to his painting, but also a new sense of danger.

No wonder his works were selling like crazy.

Seemed a little unfair, actually. Painter committed crimes and went to jail, and all it did was titillate potential buyers. I busted ass and worked hard, but I still couldn't afford a new car. The fact that he'd offered to buy me one just made it sting more.

Asshole.

"You promise you'll call if she gets scared?" I said, hating this entire situation.

"Sure," he replied. "But she won't. She loves my place, and it's not like she's never been away from home—she's spent the night with London and Reese. She'll do fine. You need to stop worrying."

"Okay," I whispered, defeated. "I'll be out this evening, but I'd still really appreciate it if you let her call me at bedtime. I want to say good night."

"Out where?" he asked casually. I shot him a look.

"With a friend."

"Date?"

"None of your damned business," I snapped. Shit. Why had I done that? Way too defensive, which was a dead giveaway.

"Anyone I know?" he asked, his jaw tight. I turned to him, raising a brow.

"You screw everything that walks," I spat out. "How dare you question me?"

"Jealous?" he asked, eyes hard. Scowling, I flipped him off subtly. He raised a brow.

"You want me to stop screwing around, come over with Izzy

tonight and I'll be happy to limit my fucking to you, Mel. Anytime you want under me, the door's open."

The words sent a wave of heat through me, and I'm pretty sure my nipples went hard as rocks. He gave a mocking ghost of a smile.

"Still remember how you taste, baby—not to mention how that cunt of yours felt wrapped tight around my cock. Do *not* fuck with me, Mel. I'm not some little boy you can play games with."

I stepped back, eyes wide.

"You shouldn't talk like that," I managed to say. His smile turned nasty.

"Mel, I've done everything you've asked," he said. "And there's not a damned thing on earth I wouldn't do for Isabella. But I'm sick of jumping through your hoops, only to have you go full bitch on me when I want to see my daughter. She's my kid, too."

"Do you lay awake nights trying to think up new ways to be an asshole?" I asked. "And I've never asked you to do anything for me. I'd be just as happy if you disappeared. Me and Izzy were doing great before you came back and decided to play daddy."

Something flared in his eyes, and then he stepped into my space. I tried to back away, then felt the picnic table hit my butt, blocking me.

"I'm not playing anything," he said, the words low and hard. "I fucked up. I know I fucked up, I've apologized for it, and I've done my best to make up for it. I'll never get that time with her back, and I'll regret that for the rest of my fucking life. But no goddamned way I'll let you or anyone else get between me and my girl, Mel. I appreciate all you've been through and I'm thankful that you're Izzy's mom, but don't think you'll get rid of me. You'll *never* be rid of me, Melanie. For the rest of your fucking life, I'll be here because we share a kid. So stop being so nasty all the time."

I stood, trembling, as he raised his hand to my hair, pushing the short bob back behind my ear. His fingers traced the lobe, sending chills all the way down my spine and between my legs. Memories hung between us, heavy and sweet.

"I liked it better long," he whispered.

"It was too much work taking care of it," I managed to reply, wishing like hell I couldn't feel the heat radiating off his body.

"If you fuck him tonight, think of me," he replied, eyes burning. "Remember what it felt like when I was the one inside you."

How could someone so vile be so sexy?

"Right, because you're always thinking of me?" I sneered. He licked his lips hungrily, then leaned over to whisper in my ear.

"Every single time, I pretend it's you under me. Doesn't matter who it is, I close my eyes and it's always your face I see, Mel. You give the word and I'll fill that hungry cunt of yours."

I closed my eyes, desperate for some space.

"You can't talk like that."

He traced his nose along the side of my face, scenting me.

"Almost a year," he whispered. "Almost a year I've been free, doing everything I can to help you. Financially, around the house. I said something stupid when you told me about Izzy, and then I got reckless. I paid for that by losing the first part of my daughter's life. I won't lose any more. I'm done trying to make you happy, Mel, so here's the new rules. You can fuck around all you want, but you stay the hell out of my world. You come back inside, I'm taking over. Got it?"

My eyes snapped open again, and I jerked back so hard I would've fallen across the table if he hadn't caught me.

"What?"

"You heard me," he said, his face like stone. "New game, Mel. I'm done riding bitch so you can feel good. Consider yourself warned."

With that, he turned and walked away.

SIX MONTHS LATER
KOOTENAI MEDICAL CENTER EMERGENCY ROOM

"Todger's back," Sherri said, nudging me with her shoulder. "Drunk off his ass and hasn't been cleaned up since the last time he was in here. Rock, paper, scissors to see who has to deal with him."

I nodded and we counted to three. She went with paper, I was rock. Crap.

"Lucky bitch," I said, rolling my eyes. She laughed, offering me a little finger wave. Todger was harmless enough, even if he did smell like a dead fish. The guy had been in and out of the ER for years, just one of the many mentally ill homeless guys we saw regularly. About six months back he'd found some temporary housing, but the last time he'd been in, he'd confided in me that the CIA had planted bugs in the apartment and that he wasn't safe there. So far as I knew he'd gone back to sleeping under the bleachers down at Memorial Stadium. "Cops bring him in?"

"No, the warming station called an ambulance," she said. "He started seizing on the floor, sounds like DT's to me."

I raised a brow. "Seriously? He's trying to sober up?"

"Who knows with Todger? Anyway, you better get in there and check on him. We put him in a room, but Dr. Ives is busy with a real case and Dr. Baker is grabbing some food while she can. Said Todger would still be there when she gets back."

Fair enough—Todger was a frequent flier at the ER, but what he really needed was long-term treatment. When I'd first started, I'd pestered the hospital social workers until they found him something, feeling all proud of myself. They'd warned me that it wouldn't stick, and it hadn't. He'd lasted less than a week before he walked away from the program, saying he didn't like the psychiatric drugs or the people telling him what to do.

Based on his smell, I figured he didn't like being forced to bathe, either.

"I'll check on him," I said, sighing. Taking a quick sip of my coffee, I left the nurses' station and headed toward his room.

"I owe you one!" Sherri laughed, and it took everything I had not to flip her off. Knowing my luck, some administrator would see me and I'd get reported.

I smelled him before I saw him. For a small-town hospital, we got more than our fair share of homeless, so I'd gotten used to patients who reeked of feces and stale alcohol. Frankly, it was better than the smell of blood and rot, which scared the hell out of me. At least you can wash off shit and Todger wasn't likely to die on me. I stepped into the room and reached for the curtain.

"Todger, I hear you're back—"

He hit me from behind.

It took a split second to orient myself and then I was fighting. Unfortunately, that was just enough time for him to get his hands around my throat. *Oh my God, is this really happening?* Sweet, stinky Todger was attacking me, choking the life out of me and I couldn't even scream for help. He slammed my head against the floor, sending bright bursts of pain exploding through my skull.

I kicked out, desperate to throw him off. My feet caught the computer cart, sending it crashing across the slick tiles. It slammed into something and then metal crashed to the floor, clattering loudly.

"I'll kill you, bitch," he hissed in my ear, slamming my head to the floor yet again. "I'm onto you. You've been feeding them information about me too long, but now you'll pay. You'll die!"

The last words rose in pitch, and then he started a long, high keening as his fingers tightened around my neck. Loud shouts penetrated the fog in my head, and then there was a flood of people in the room. Orderlies were pulling at him, prying his fingers off my throat as they dragged him away. Somehow I found the strength to scramble backward, huddling against the wall as I watched Sherri in action, an avenging angel with a hypodermic needle. She darted in, injecting him fast and hard.

Todger continued to fight, but I knew the meds would kick in fast. The reality around me seemed distant and hard to follow— shock. Then Sherri was next to me, coolly assessing as I caught snatches of conversation in the distance.

"Check on her."

"Restraints . . . never saw this coming."

"He's been getting worse for months . . . call psych . . ."

"Melanie?"

I focused in on Sherri's face, blinking.

"You're in shock, babe. Stick with me, okay?"

"I'm fine," I managed to whisper, trying to focus. My head

hurt . . . a lot. But nothing else. No broken bones, nothing like that. "I'll be just fine. No worries."

Sherri gave a short laugh.

"Always the hero, aren't you?" she said, although I caught a hint of fear in her voice. "On the bright side, maybe we'll finally get an inpatient bed for Todger. At least for a while."

"He'll be right back out," I managed to whisper, offering her a weak smile. "Probably won't even remember what happened."

That made her laugh.

"Sad but true," she said. "Just watch, they'll turf his ass five minutes after the hold ends."

"All in a day's work," I said ruefully, shaking my head. Big mistake. Rolling over, I puked all over the floor.

Wasn't that just great—he gave me a concussion.

Pisser. The next couple days were gonna suck.

PAINTER

I leaned over the pool table, lining up my shot. The game had started as an excuse to wrap myself around the cute little redhead who'd been flirting with me across the bar for the last half hour, but she'd turned out to be a surprisingly good player. Suddenly I'd found myself with a real challenge. Turned me on, had to admit.

About fuckin' time, too. Most of the women I met these days were boring. I liked getting my dick sucked, no question, but I still tended to close my eyes and picture Melanie in their place. My cock never seemed to get the message that she wasn't interested in us anymore, no matter how many times my brain explained this reality.

Fuckin' ridiculous. All of it.

Pulling back the cue, I took my shot. The ball hit with a satisfying crack, sending the green solid toward the back corner pocket. Red pouted prettily, then sashayed over to give me a kiss. I'd just covered her mouth with mine, reaching around to grab her ass, when the phone in my back pocket buzzed.

I considered ignoring it.

Christ, but I *wanted* to ignore it. Unfortunately, one of the downsides of club life is always answering the damned phone, because a brother might be in trouble. Giving Red's generous ass one last squeeze, I pulled away to grab my phone.

Melanie.

She never called, not unless it was about Izzy, and I couldn't think of a single reason she'd be in touch at midnight on a Friday if it wasn't an emergency.

The pretty redhead ceased to exist.

Catching Puck's eye, I mouthed *Melanie* as I made for the bar's open patio, away from the music.

"Hey, what's up?" I asked, feeling anxious.

"Painter? Are you there?"

"Just a sec," I told her. "I'm heading outside where it's quiet."

"Okay."

It took a minute, but I finally found a patch of privacy toward the back. "Hey, what's going on? Is Izzy okay?"

"She's fine," Melanie said, her voice sounding strange. Harsh, like she'd been coughing. "Look, I need your help."

Well. That was different.

"All right . . ."

"Here's the situation—my shift was supposed to end at eight, but there was an accident at the hospital. Izzy's with a sitter and they're keeping me here overnight. London's out of town and—"

"No, it's fine," I said, my mind switching modes instantly. I'd heard some guys bitching that their exes were always dumping the kids on them, but Mel wasn't like that. If she'd called, it was because she'd run out of options. "I can get her. What's the situation?"

She didn't answer for a minute, and I went from concerned to suspicious.

"Melanie? What's going on?"

"A patient attacked me," she admitted slowly.

"The fuck?" I asked, chilled. "Why?"

"He's mentally ill," she said quickly. "Probably doesn't even remember doing it. Look, it's no big deal but they want to keep me for the night to make sure the head injury isn't serious. I told them it's not, but you know how it is. Liability."

"I'm coming to the hospital," I said. "I want to see for myself."

"No, it's nothing," she said. I might've believed her if she hadn't sounded like she'd swallowed a truckload of gravel. "I'm fine, but Izzy's sitter has work in the morning and she really needs to get home, to bed. She's at my place. I'll call her and let her know that you're on your way. Izzy's sound asleep—she won't even realize anything happened."

I considered arguing with her, then decided it was a waste of time.

"All right, I'll head there now."

"Thanks, Painter," she replied, sounding tired. "It's been a rough night. Knowing Isabella's covered is a big relief."

"Thanks for watching Iz," I told Marie, Horse's old lady, early the next morning. "She'll probably wake up around seven, and if she's upset that Mel isn't here, you can have her call and I'll talk to her."

Marie nodded, smiling at me reassuringly. No complaints from her, despite the fact that we'd dragged her out of bed at five a.m. Horse was a lucky man. "No worries—we'll have a great time together. Just go make sure Melanie's okay and I'll keep you covered on this end."

"Thanks."

Grabbing my cut, I made for the door, knowing it was too early to go see Mel and not caring—I couldn't hold out any longer, I needed to see her for myself. Puck followed. He'd ditched the girls last night to come with me, because that's the kind of friend he was. Horse had offered to come, too, but I figured two bikers were enough to keep people at the hospital from fucking with us, but not so many we'd have to worry about them calling security on our asses.

We pulled up to Kootenai Medical Center and parked, stopping by Information to find Mel's room. The little old lady manning the desk probably wasn't supposed to hand that out, but a few sweet words and she fell right into line. Sometimes it scared me how easy women were to manipulate.

Make that women who weren't Melanie—she saw right through my shit.

We followed the signs upstairs and found the right hallway. A tall, sexy black chick with braids was at the nurses' station, and I left Puck flirting with her while I looked for Mel's room. The door was shut. I gave a little knock, then stepped inside to find her sound asleep on a bed.

Ah, shit.

She looked like hell. There were bruises all over her face and ringing her neck. No monitors hooked to her, though—that had to be a good sign, right? There was a recliner-looking chair not far from the bed, a weird, skinny piece of furniture that was probably supposed to look normal, but was off just enough that it rang all kinds of "institutional" bells.

I sat down, leaning forward to study her. There were finger marks on her throat. *Finger marks.* Someone had put their hands on my woman, tried to *kill her*, and I hadn't even known it was happening. I felt rage boiling up, starting deep down in my stomach, twisting and tightening every muscle in my body as I braced myself for violence.

Except there wasn't anyone to defend her from. Just Melanie, pale and broken in a hospital bed.

What the fuck had happened?

Twenty minutes passed, and then the door opened. The babe with the braids walked in, looking me over.

"And you are . . . ?" she asked.

"I'm the baby daddy," I said, keeping my voice steady with no small amount of effort. "Mel's kid is my daughter. She called me last night, said there was an accident and she needed me to watch over Isabella. Got that covered, so now I'm here to make sure she's doin' okay."

Her face softened a little.

"Mellie's fine," she said. "She can tell you the details when she wakes up, but we're just keeping an eye on her."

"Hey," Mel whispered. She was fighting to open her eyes, raising a hand to her head. Relief flooded me, although it couldn't fully calm the violence inside. "Sheesh. I feel like death."

"How's it going, Mellie?" the nurse asked. "You remember what happened?"

Mel nodded slowly. "Yeah. Todger—never saw it coming."

Braids snorted.

"None of us did. You have company."

Melanie looked at me, and I cocked my head, forcing my face to stay calm.

"Where's Izzy?" she asked, frowning.

"I spent the night with her, and then Marie came over early this morning," I said, my voice harsher than I'd intended. "She and Horse will take her out to pancakes or something—that'll blow her little mind. Now tell me what's going on here."

"Mellie, you want him out of the room?" Braids asked. "He's here with a friend, but I can call Security on them."

Her gaze was challenging, making it clear she'd stand up for her fellow nurse as needed—apparently Puck's flirting would carry us only so far. Inconvenient, but also good to see. I liked the idea of Mel's coworkers taking her back.

"No, it's good," Melanie said. "I want to get home as soon as possible. Don't want Izzy freaking out."

"I hear that," said Braids. "Soon as we get you cleared, we'll get you on the road. Let me take your vitals and then I'll see if I can find a doctor to clear you."

I probably should've offered to step into the hallway while she did her work, but no way I was letting Melanie out of my sight until I knew the whole story. This situation felt too much like the morning I'd first met her. We'd been at the hospital then, too—London's house had blown sky-high, and Mel had gotten caught in the explosion.

"Hit your call button if you need me," said Braids, making a point of handing her the little remote thingy. I took in a deep, calming breath and offered her a sweet smile and she softened, just like the old lady downstairs. Too easy.

"Why are you here?" Melanie asked after Braids left. I think she was trying to sound tough, but it came off more pathetic than anything else.

"To find out what the hell happened," I told her, studying the bruises. "You look like shit."

"Fuck you."

"Anytime, although you're probably not up to it today. Now tell me the whole story."

She glared at me for a second, so I just crossed my arms and waited her out.

"One of the regulars in the ER—a homeless guy—attacked me."

"Why?"

"He's mentally ill," she said, shrugging. "Paranoid. Probably decided I was trying to do something to him. Off his meds."

"So what happens to him?"

"Oh, they sedated him and hauled him off to Psych. They'll stabilize him and then he'll probably be out again."

"Seriously?" I asked, startled. "No charges, nothing?"

"It wouldn't make any difference," she said, sighing. "System's not set up for people like him. He's sick, not evil. I don't want them pressing charges."

"So they'll just let him out again?"

"Not until he's stabilized. Who knows, maybe he'll realize what he did and stay on his meds this time. It's a fucked-up situation, but I guess anything's possible."

I didn't like this shit. Didn't like it at all.

"So what's to stop him from coming back and attacking you again?"

"Hopefully the medication," she replied. "We'll see. I'm careful, Painter. This was just a random accident, it's not like he's out to get me. He probably won't even remember doing it. Just let it go, okay?"

I stood, pacing across the room as I tried to wrap my head around the situation. "So I have to explain to our daughter that her mama's beat to shit because of some crazy guy, and when she asks whether it could happen again, I just say maybe? No. You need to find a better job, Mel. It's fucked."

"I'll tell her that there was an accident, I'm fine, and it won't happen again. There's no reason to scare Izzy."

"There's a thousand different ways to be a nurse. I don't get why you want to be around crazy people and stabbings and accidents. Why would anyone choose that?"

"Because it's challenging and exciting?" she snapped. "Because these people need me, and every day I'm pushed to the limit of my abilities? Anything could happen and I like that—it's never boring. You of all people should understand that, Mr. Reapers MC. At least I'm fixing the holes in people instead of making them."

I spun around, staring her down. "Excuse me?"

"You're an adrenaline junkie, Painter," she said. "You make damned good money with your art, but you spend all your time on a fucking motorcycle. Donor-cycle, that's what we call them in here, did you know that? You get in fights, you go to jail, all for no reason other than getting off on the rush."

"I've been a goddamned saint since I got out, and you know it. I'm not reckless, I take good care of our kid, and I'm not putting myself at any more risk than you are. Sure, I'm in a motorcycle club, but you're the one who got jumped and beat to shit last night. You're just as much of an adrenaline junkie as me. Admit it."

We stared each other down, and despite the black eyes and ring of bruises, my cock was getting hard. Her chest was heaving and her nipples pointed at me through the thin hospital gown.

"Fuck you," she finally said. I laughed.

"Anytime—we covered that already," I said, feeling strangely relieved. If she was strong enough to fight with me, she'd be okay. "Will you promise me one thing, at least?"

"What's that?"

"If you're gonna work in this place, I want you takin' some self-defense courses down at the gun shop, okay? Ruger teaches them, and he's good at what he does. Maybe learn about guns, too."

She frowned at me. "Why should I need to know how to shoot?"

"Why should you need to know self-defense at all?" I countered reasonably. "Because the world is dangerous and you got attacked. It'll make me feel a lot better. Do it."

Mel's eyes narrowed.

"*Please.*" I added, rolling my eyes. She shrugged.

"All right. Although I was planning to anyway. Take a class, I mean. I never want to feel that helpless again."

I smiled, knowing I'd won whether she wanted to admit it or not. "How much longer are you stuck here?"

"Just until they check me out."

"I'll wait and give you a ride home. We can explain to Izzy together. You look like you need sleep. Want me to take her for the night?"

Melanie's eyes narrowed.

"Yes, that would be lovely. Asshole."

"Bitch."

"I'd say 'Get a room,' but you've already got one. Want me to stand guard outside the door?"

We both turned to find Puck watching us, his dark face grim. I caught the hint of laughter in his eyes, though. Next to him stood Braids.

"The doctor will be here in five," she said. "Maybe the baby daddy should wait outside?"

I laughed.

"Yeah, I'll do that. You're on my bike going home, Mel. It'll be just like old times."

She flipped me off and Puck burst out laughing. I followed him into the hallway, leaning back against the wall, feeling strangely satisfied with myself.

"You get off on baiting her, don't you?"

I shrugged, refusing to acknowledge the point, even if it was the truth. Hell, it was better than not getting off at all.

CHAPTER NINETEEN

ONE MONTH AFTER IZZY'S FOURTH BIRTHDAY
JULY
MELANIE

"You're so hot, Mel," Greg whispered, running his hands down my ass. He pulled me tight into his body, swaying awkwardly to the music, and I wondered if he was really the player Sherri insisted he had to be.

All firefighters are players, she'd told me. *So have fun with him, but don't get your hopes up. You need someone stable. That new security guard keeps flirting with you . . .*

I didn't want to believe her, though. Me and Greg would be perfect for each other—like a storybook. He was also an EMT, and I'd seen him on and off at work for months now. Handsome, built . . . sort of rough and ready in a way that I didn't like to admit totally turned me on, but it did. It *so* did.

He reminds you of Painter, my brain whispered insidiously.

Shut up, bitch! my vagina hissed back. *He's probably got a really nice dick.*

You're drunk. Stop being such a slut.

You're a cock-blocker—we haven't had sex in forever!

I blinked, realizing my brain was 100 percent right—I was definitely drunk, because why the hell else would I be imagining an argument with my vagina in the middle of a dance floor?

Pull your shit together, Mellie girl.

Greg had asked me out to the Ironhorse for a drink (which had turned into many drinks) and now it was nearly midnight. The music wasn't great, but the crowd was into it and I was having a good time—a good enough time that I'd been giving serious thought to going home with him. Well, serious *something*. "Thought" might not be the best word, seeing as things had gotten pretty damned fuzzy after that last round of shots. But I was definitely turned on and it'd been a long time since I'd gotten laid. Not since the dentist . . . ugh. That'd been a mistake.

He was so . . . clean.

Greg nuzzled into my neck, then I felt something warm and sort of icky. Oh. My. God. Was he licking me? He was. He was *licking me*, like some sort of dog. Okay, so maybe going home with him wasn't such a good idea.

All this was processing through my drunken head when suddenly Greg was gone. I nearly fell over as a hard arm wrapped around my waist, jerking me back into a tall, strong body that smelled like leather and just the faintest hint of linseed oil.

"Time to go now, Greg," said a familiar voice. I blinked, trying to figure out what was happening. Greg stared at me, something like horror crossing his face.

"She's yours?" he asked.

"Mother of my kid," Painter replied, his voice hard. "You lookin' to get laid, Greg? You want to fuck my Izzy's mama? Let me guess—you want to do all kinds of dirty shit to my girl. How you think that's gonna end for you?"

Greg's eyes filled with terror, and then he was backing off so fast I'm surprised I didn't hear a "meep meep" and a whooshing noise.

"Sorry, Painter. Meant no disrespect."

Suddenly he was gone, abandoning me on the dance floor like an STD. I jerked away from Painter, rounding on him and jamming a finger into his chest.

"Who the fuck do you think you are?"

He looked down at me, his face grim.

"What's the rule, Mel?"

"What?"

"We got one rule—what is it?"

"That you're an asshole?"

"You stay out of my world," he said. "I've backed away, given you your space. But you stay the fuck away from my world, and that means no bikers."

"Greg's not a biker."

Painter cocked a brow. "He's a hangaround with the Reapers. Or at least, he was. Now that I've seen his hands all over your ass, I got a feeling he won't be hanging around anymore. Never liked the look of that fucker anyway."

I blinked, trying to bring things into focus, both literally and figuratively. This would've been a whole lot easier if I hadn't drunk so damned much booze. Shit.

"How was I supposed to know that?" I asked, frustrated by how much my words slurred. I couldn't hold my own against this fucker if I couldn't even talk right.

"You should've asked," he said. "And now you're gonna pay the penalty."

I blinked, trying to process this, then faster than you could say, "I hate bikers," Painter caught my hips and jerked me into his body. He'd touched me enough over the years that I was well aware the raging attraction between us had never died. Now it roared to life, clouding my thinking almost as much as the vodka. We started swaying to the music, me tucked into him as one of his hands rubbed slowly up and down my back. The other one caught my head, resting it against his chest.

That familiar ache swirled through my stomach, and while I should've been telling him to fuck off, I wasn't entirely sure I'd be able to stay upright if I wasn't holding on to him. If he'd said anything—if he'd even copped a feel—I might've summoned the willpower to stop him. Instead we just danced slowly.

I felt myself falling into him.

It was nice. Way, *way* too nice.

The music changed, another slow song. Painter surrounded me.

No matter what else had happened between us through the years, this never changed—the burning need I felt for him, the desire to rub myself against him and spread my legs and . . . Oh God. It hurt. It actually *hurt*, I wanted him so bad. I should be pulling away, but instead I burrowed my nose deeper into his chest, taking in his incredible scent, my nipples tightening.

One of his hands slid lower, catching my butt, squeezing obscenely. His cock hardened against my stomach, the slow sway of his hips growing more aggressive. We'd gone from swaying to grinding and my body loved every second of it.

Clearly, it'd been too long since I'd gotten laid.

"Jesus, Mel," he whispered, leaning down to nuzzle my neck. The heat of his breath, the softness of his lips contrasting with the hardness of his body . . . It was almost more than I could take. The ache between my thighs was growing, turning into an active need beyond my ability to contain.

This was a *very* bad idea.

I didn't even notice when he started walking me toward a dimly lit table in the back of the bar. Puck was there, along with Banks and a couple of girls I didn't recognize. Painter grabbed the chair in the corner against the wall, pulling me down into his lap, catching my mouth with his before I could even imagine protesting.

This kiss wasn't hurried.

It wasn't hot and desperate and dangerous, just a slow fire building until I completely forgot about everyone around us. When he shifted my hips to straddle his across the chair, I didn't care who might be watching. I was too drunk, and not just on the booze.

His dick pushed between my legs, one big hand guiding me as my hips slowly rubbed against his. The other hand was buried deep in my hair, holding me prisoner as his tongue dove deep inside. The pressure started to build, and all I could think about was how much I wanted the rest of him inside me, too.

Desperately.

"What the fuck is going on here!"

Jessica. That was Jessica's voice. I froze. Here I was, making out in a bar with Painter, and Jessica had just caught us and . . . Oh

God. I'd lost my fucking mind—there was no other possible explanation for what I'd just done. I tried to pull away but Painter held me tight. Then I heard Puck's deep voice.

"Go to hell, Jess," he said. "It's none of your damned business what they're doing."

I managed to bring my hands up, pushing against Painter as hard as I could. His arms loosened, although he still didn't let me up entirely. Looking at Jessica, I saw exactly how bad I'd fucked up written all over her face.

"Have you lost your mind?" she asked, eyes wide. "Both of you! So you get drunk and share a quick fuck . . . Where does that leave Izzy? What the hell's wrong with you?"

Oh God. I was such a slut.

"Get the hell out of here, Jess," Painter said, eyes narrowing. "It's none of your business."

Puck stood, shoving off the girl sitting on his lap as he stepped toward my best friend in a way that could only be described as menacing.

"No!" I said, pushing against Painter again, harder this time. He let me go reluctantly, people turning to stare at us. Oh shit. I was *that* girl—the one who caused scenes in bars.

Fucking alcohol. Hadn't I learned a damned thing from watching my dad?

"Jessica's right," I said, standing up. I bumped into the table in the process, sending an impressive collection of drinks sloshing. "This is a huge mistake."

"Let's go," Jess said, catching my arm. Painter surged up, catching me around the waist and pulling me back into him.

"Stop," he said, his voice cracking like a shot. We all froze. "This is between me and Melanie, so none of you get a fucking vote. Mel, we need to talk. Somewhere quiet. Private. Puck, take care of my tab and I'll catch you later. Sound good?"

"Sure," Puck said. Jess opened her mouth to protest and then Banks stepped into her space, snaking an arm around her upper chest and pulling her into his body. It almost looked like a casual embrace, but when she pushed against him angrily he didn't give an inch. A wolfish smile crossed Banks's face as he leaned down, whispering something in her ear. I couldn't hear what he said, but the expression on her face freaked me out—was that anticipation or fear?

Painter pushed me across the floor, big hands on my shoulders to guide me. Then we were passing through the door, out into the cool night air, music spilling out of the bar behind us.

"What the hell, Painter?" I managed to ask as he dragged me down the street, walking so fast I could barely keep up.

"We're gonna talk this shit out."

I stumbled over a curb. He steadied me, and I glared up at him.

"Your fucking long legs are going to get me killed," I spat. "Slow down, asshole."

Painter answered by swinging me up and over his shoulder. I shrieked, and across the street a group of drunk guys started hooting and laughing at us.

"Jesus, what's wrong with you?" I shouted, not entirely sure if I was yelling at Painter or the guys. He could be a murderer for all they knew.

We reached his SUV, and he balanced me like a sack of potatoes as he dug out his keys. The lock chirped at us happily, and then he was opening the door and dropping me down on the passenger seat.

"Stay," he said, reaching around to grab the seat belt, buckling me in. I scowled as he walked around to the driver's side, trying to decide if I should make a run for it. It was late, though, and I needed a ride home.

Might as well talk to the jerk and get it over with. He climbed in, turning on the truck with a comforting roar. The seats were soft leather, decadent and lush. Apparently the art world was treating him well.

"For an asshole I hate, you have a very nice vehicle," I said grudgingly. Painter gave a short, bitter laugh.

"So glad to hear you approve. Now I'll be able to sleep at night."

"Why do you have to turn everything ugly?"

"Because my balls are blue and my dick's so hard it hurts," he growled, turning to face me. "This is fucking ridiculous, Mel. Why do we keep fighting like this? I want you, you want me, we have a kid together. What's the big fucking deal?"

"You left me alone!" I shouted, glaring at him. "Izzy was so *sick,* Painter. They weren't sure she was going to make it. You don't have a fucking clue what it was like, sitting there, waiting for her to take her next breath, hoping it wouldn't be her last. We needed you. *I* needed you. Am I just supposed to pretend all that didn't happen? That you didn't choose prison over us when we needed you the most?"

"That's not true!" he yelled back. "Yes, I fucked up. I've admitted I fucked up a thousand times. A thousand and one, counting just now. But it's not like I had the fucking choice to come and help you, Mel—they don't just let you leave prison because you say 'pretty please, Mr. Warden, let me out because my girl needs me.'"

"That's *bullshit!*" I screamed at him. "You had a *choice,* Painter. You were on parole, you knew they were out to get you, and you *still* turned and ran off with your club like a fucking coward when I told you I was pregnant. Do *not* tell me you didn't have a choice. You *always* have a choice."

Painter blinked rapidly, then stared straight ahead, hands gripping the steering wheel so tight his knuckles turned white.

"You're right."

The words shocked me. Painter turned back to me, eyes burning with intensity.

"I was scared when you told me about Izzy," he said. "You were scared, too—you told me you sat and cried on the floor in your bathroom when you found out, for fuck's sake. You told me and I didn't know what to say. I'd never wanted a kid, and then you were pissed and you left and I made my choice. I didn't want to face that reality, so I rode with the club instead. I thought the run would clear my head, that we'd figure everything out when I got back. Instead they locked me up and I'll have to live with that the rest of my life."

"Painter . . ."

"I'm still scared sometimes when I look at her," he continued, shaking his head slowly. "She's this little tiny thing and there's so many different ways we can break her, Mel. Even if we don't, there's a whole goddamned world out there just waiting to hurt her when she gets bigger. Mean girls and horny boys and school and the flu and that's just the start. The best we can do is just push forward, one day at a time. I wasn't with you then, but I'm with you *now*. I'm busting ass, building my career, earning money to support her—legal money, by the way—but you want me to go back in time and change history. I just can't fucking *do* that, Melanie. Not even for you."

Blinking, I stared at him, trying to process his words.

"You shouldn't have left us," I whispered.

Painter shook his head, reaching down to slam the SUV into gear, pulling out onto the street.

"Fuck, but you hold a grudge."

"I did what I had to do, by myself. You disappeared. I never had that option, not even when things were at their worst."

Painter slammed on the brake, the SUV skidding to the curb.

"What the hell?" I gasped, clutching the door.

He turned on me.

"You had options," he said, his voice more intense than I'd ever heard it. "Just like I did. I already admitted it—I chose prison. You chose our *child*. You could've aborted her, but you didn't. You took the hard road, and you raised a hell of a child along the way. I will never, ever forgive myself for leaving you alone, but I give thanks every fucking day that you were the strong one, Melanie. I can't imagine life without Izzy. She's the best thing that ever happened to me. Thank you for that."

My breath came fast as we stared each other down. He was right. I'd been damned strong, and I'd been rewarded for that strength with an amazing, beautiful child who deserved the very best of everything in life.

"You're welcome," I managed to say, swallowing. Painter leaned over, catching the back of my head and pulling me in for a rough kiss. This wasn't a seduction—not at all. He shoved his tongue in my mouth, and I felt every bit of his anger and frustration. I wanted to punch him and kiss him and fuck him until he admitted that . . . I didn't know.

What did I want him to admit?

I heard the click of my seat belt, and then he caught me under the arms, jerking me across the center console. Then the steering wheel was in my back as the kiss deepened. Now it was my turn to get aggressive, grabbing his hair and jerking it back—partly to hurt him and partly so I could attack him with my tongue. The fire I'd felt at the bar was nothing compared to the burn coursing through me now. I wiggled, trying to find some way to get close enough to him for more contact, but it wasn't possible.

Finally we broke apart, gasping, our foreheads resting against each other.

"This is ridiculous," he said. "Come home with me. We're good together, Mel. You know we are."

I thought about it. What would it hurt, just one night together? Whatever else had gone wrong between us, there'd never been anything wrong with our chemistry. He caught my hand, raising it to his lips to kiss my knuckles. A stray bit of light from the streetlamp caught on his ring—a Reaper.

His club.

My brain slowly reasserted control as I ran my thumb across it.

"This is why," I said, wishing I could turn off reality and simply go with him. "They'll always come first. You're a good daddy to Iz, but your club is more important than anything else. I want better than that for myself, Painter. I deserve better. That's why I can't go home with you."

With that, I pushed away from him, sliding back across the console awkwardly. He stared at me in the dark, the silence between us so heavy I felt like I was smothering.

Finally he spoke.

"What's that supposed to be—some kind of fucking ultimatum?"

"No," I said, feeling clearer than I had all night. "Not at all. I will never ask you to leave the Reapers for me, Painter. Just like I'll never settle for a man who isn't one hundred percent mine. We want different things. That's why all of this is such a big waste of time."

"That's bullshit."

I don't know what I'd expected him to say, but this wasn't it.

"You're a hypocrite, Melanie," he continued. "You're all about how evil the club is, but who's watching your kid right now so you can go out and party?"

"Dancer," I admitted, wishing like hell I'd just hired the kid down the street. But she'd invited her boyfriend over last time, and while I was pretty sure Izzy hadn't seen anything, I didn't feel like I could trust two horny teens to watch her . . .

"Yeah, and who helped you move into your house?"

"You and Reese."

"Me and Reese and Horse and the prospects," he said. I was starting to get the ugly sense I wasn't going to win this fight. "When your car broke down, who towed it in and had it fixed?"

"Reese," I whispered.

"Yeah, and which one of us wound up in the hospital after that homeless motherfucker went on the attack? Call me crazy, but if I remember correctly that was *you*, Mel. You know, you with your job where you see more blood and guts and destruction in one night than I see in a year?"

"That's unfair and you know it," I snapped. "You forgot one key point—my job is *fixing* those people, helping them."

"And I'm sure Izzy will be very comforted by that fact when you turn up dead because some guy named *Todger* ambushed you in the parking lot," he snarled. "But the good news is that he probably won't even remember what he did, so I guess that makes it all okay, right?"

"I hate you. I wish you'd stayed in that prison," I hissed. "Then I'd never have to deal with your shit."

"Is that what you really want?" he asked. "Me gone—*really?* Because I'm the one who shows up at your place to fix the fucking sink when it's leaking. And the dryer—remember when your dryer broke? I found you a new one on craigslist, hauled it over, and hooked it up. Guess you forgot that part. But if you really want me gone, I can make that happen. I got offered an art fellowship in New York last week—a chance to study with people who know their shit. People who can teach me. They're waiting on an answer,

Mel. It's everything I've ever dreamed of, right there on a fucking platter waiting for me. Is that what you really want?"

"What?" I gasped, stunned. "You got offered a fellowship?"

"Yeah, a damned good one," he said, face still hard. "You know my stuff's selling more and more . . . all those city people love it because it's so raw. It could be a big deal."

I felt like I'd been punched in the gut. Izzy . . . How would I tell her? Oh God. I couldn't wrap my head around it.

"Still hate me, Mel?" he asked softly. I shook my head, because I didn't. Of course I didn't. The thought of him leaving again hurt me, hurt me as much as it had the first time. That was the problem, of course . . . not that I didn't care about him, but that I cared too much. "Do you really want me gone?"

"No," I whispered, and I meant it. "I mean, I want you to have the opportunity, but . . . God, that would kill Izzy. And what about the club?"

"Despite what you seem to think, they're my brothers. They actually give a shit about my happiness." *Unlike some.* He didn't have to say the words. "I can take a leave anytime I need to, did you realize that? BB did when his mom was dying. I'll admit it—I used to worry that they'd kick me out if I wasn't useful. But they're my family, Mel. You should understand that by now. Business is business, but family is what it's really about. Riding bikes with my brothers. The business side is just a means to an end."

Oh God. I shivered, despite the heat blasting through the SUV.

"You're taking it, aren't you? You're leaving us."

Painter laughed, but there was no humor in the sound.

"No, Melanie," he said softly. "I'm not."

"Why not?"

"Because I'd rather die than lose my daughter. This is my home, Mel. My life was shit as a kid. No dad. My mom wasn't worth a damn and once I hit the system it was all over. You think they can offer me anything in New York more valuable than what I already got here? I got a second chance with Izzy, and I will never let her go. *Never.* I'd rather be dead than lose her again."

Sniffing, I realized my eyes were starting to water. Ah hell. I hated it when I cried. Hated. It. And how dare he turn this all back on me? I hated him, too.

Thank God he wasn't leaving us.

"I'm glad you're staying," I managed to say. Painter snorted, then shifted the SUV back into gear. I sniffled a little as he started driving toward my little house in Fernan. It wasn't much, but it had a fenced yard that Izzy loved. Not only that, someday it would be ours.

No landlords to hassle us. No leases to negotiate or rising rent. Never again.

"It was a flattering offer," Painter admitted, turning down Sherman. "But I already lost way too much of Izzy's life. Not to mention I fuckin' hate cities. Way too many damned people. Just like being in prison again."

That made me laugh, a pathetic sound but still better than crying.

"I'm sorry I called you an asshole," I said after a long silence.

"It's okay," he replied. "I *am* an asshole. And what you went through on your own with Izzy and everything, that'll never be okay. But I've grown up since then, and I'm a loyal fucker. One day you're gonna figure out that I'm serious when I say I'm here to stay."

God, but I wanted to believe him. Wanted it too much.

We didn't talk after that, and ten minutes later we pulled up to my place. Loni had grown up here and lived here until she moved in with Reese. Not in this same house, of course. That one had burned down from a gas leak. She'd used the insurance money to rebuild, and had kept it as a rental. Last year I'd gone to her and made her an offer, asking her if I could buy it on contract.

When she'd said yes, I'd hardly been able to believe it.

"Don't forget, I'm taking Izzy to the family party out at the club tomorrow," Painter said as we rolled to a stop in the driveway.

"I haven't. She and I are going to make cookies in the morning. She wants to bring something like the big girls do," I told him. He smiled.

"You could come with us, you know."

I sighed, closing my eyes.

"I'll probably be hungover," I admitted. "I think I'll just stay home. There's a lot of laundry to catch up on."

"Coward."

For once I didn't argue.

"Thanks for the ride," I said, looking over at him. He stared back at me, thoughtful in the darkness.

"This isn't over."

I couldn't think of a damned thing to say in response, because I knew he was right.

It would never be over between us.

CHAPTER TWENTY

SUNDAY AFTERNOON—ONE MONTH LATER

"More pink?" Jessica asked Izzy. The little girl laughed maniacally, grabbing the container of pink sugar crystals and shaking it over the tops of the cupcakes. I'd read an article a couple weeks back that said science has proven there's no connection between children eating sugar and crazed behavior.

Science lies.

"There's more frosting than cake," I pointed out, leaning against the kitchen counter. Sherri sniffed.

"That's the best part," she said. "The cake exists to convey the frosting—that's the only reason you bake it."

"You're not the one who's going to be stuck with a kid jacked on sugar all night."

"Neither are you," Jess said pointedly. "This is Painter's time bomb. Which means you have a night free, and yet something tells me you don't have a hot date. Why don't you have a boyfriend, Mel? You're pretty, you're smart, you make good money, and you really shouldn't be sitting at home alone."

She raised a brow pointedly. I widened my eyes, glancing toward Izzy, wordlessly insisting that we not talk in front of her.

"Don't think you'll get off that easy," Jess said, her voice dark. "Izzy, are you almost done?"

"Yup," Izzy said, smiling at us broadly. The entire lower half of her face was smeared with frosting. No, make that her entire face. She even had some in her hair.

"You need a bath before Daddy gets here," I told her. "Let's go!"

"Daddy said I can eat chips!" she announced proudly, sliding off her chair to walk into the bathroom.

"We're talking about this," Jess warned me. "You're twenty-five now. If you don't exercise your lady parts, they'll get all shriveled. Do you *want* shriveled lady parts?"

"What are lady parts?" Izzy asked.

"Auntie Jessica is making bad choices," I told her primly. "Go hop in the tub. I'll be right there."

Izzy looked confused, then shook herself like a puppy and took off toward the bathroom.

"You can't say things like that in front of Izzy!" I said. "Now, watch—she'll ask me about it in front of Reese—or Painter."

Jess cocked a brow in challenge.

"If you'd get off your ass and find a man, I wouldn't have to say things like that."

I glanced at Sherri, looking for an ally. She was digging through the fridge, then pulling out a beer triumphantly.

"Don't mind me—I'm just settling in for the show," she said with a grin.

I heard the tub turn on in the bathroom. "*You* don't have a boy-friend, Jess."

"No, but I go out. I get laid. Hell, I had a booty call with Banks last weekend. I'm in the game, Mel. So is Sherri."

Sherri raised her bottle, toasting me.

"That new security guard was asking me about you again," she said, waggling her eyebrows. "He thinks you're cute. Wants to take you to dinner. I got his number for you—let's call him."

"Mama! My duckie pooped out something black and icky!" Izzy shouted from the bathroom. Jess raised a brow.

"That doesn't sound good."

I sighed. "I'll be right back. Try not to do anything evil while I'm gone."

Jessica rolled her eyes and Sherri laughed.

I found a naked Izzy standing in the tub, staring down at clumps of some kind of nasty mold floating around on the surface of the tub.

"Yuck," I said, lifting her out. "Where's the duckie?"

"I put it in time-out," she told me, her voice very serious. She pointed to a little biker duck sitting on the edge of the tub. Painter had given it to her—he'd brought it back from one of his runs with the club. Some rally in Seattle.

Picking the duck up, I studied it. Sure enough, there was a piece of something nasty hanging out of the hole on the bottom.

Mold.

"Baby, I'm really sorry, but this bird has to go," I said, bracing myself for a tantrum. Izzy surprised me, nodding her head in firm agreement.

"I don't like poopie ducks."

"There's a lot not to like about them," I agreed.

Grabbing a chunk of toilet paper, I fished the little bits of mold off the surface of the water and hit the drain. Now I'd have to bleach the damned tub, which was always a treat—at least I was an expert. Izzy might be all princess when it came to clothing and colors, but when it came to filth she could hold her own with any boy. (Twice now I'd found little worm houses in her room, carefully built out of plastic cups, dirt, and little curtains made out of tissues. She even tucked them in at night, in little worm beds. Ugh . . .)

"Let's take a quick shower instead," I told her, reaching for a couple washcloths. Izzy watched carefully as I put them on the bottom of the now-empty tub. Lifting her, I set her back inside on the cloths, then stood and grabbed the showerhead. It had a nice long hose specifically for times like this. Painter had installed it after she'd taken a mud bath, and we'd had to spray her off outside.

"Close your eyes," I warned her, gently sluicing the water across the clumps of frosting. It didn't take long—a quick shampoo and rinse, and then we were done. Wrapping her in a towel, I gave her a fast rub before sending her off to get dressed.

"Do I want to know what the duck poop was?" Jessica asked when I walked back into the kitchen. They'd been busy—the frosting was all cleaned up, the table had been washed, and she was carefully setting the cupcakes into a rectangular cake pan.

"Mold," I said shortly. Jessica made a face. "Hey, I'll take that over giving an enema any day!"

"God, do you remember that old guy with the blockage?" Sherri asked. "I've never seen so much shit in my life. It just kept coming and coming . . ."

"You have the most disgusting jobs on earth," Jess declared. "Seriously cannot understand how you do it."

"Speaking of, can you take my late shift on Thursday night?" Sherri asked me. "There's a baby shower for a girl I went to high school with."

"I don't know," I said. "I'll have to find someone to watch Izzy that night—the regular sitter is out of town this week. Maybe Loni can, but she's already watching her on Wednesday, too."

"I'm sure it'll be fine," Jess said quickly. "And if she can't, I'll come over."

"Perfect," said Sherri. "And I'll cover your shift on Wednesday night."

I frowned. "I don't need you to cover my shift—Izzy already has a sleepover planned with Loni and Reese."

"But you still need coverage," she said, grinning wickedly. "Because you have a date. With Aaron. He's taking you to dinner up in Callup and then to a party, seeing as neither of you are scheduled for Thursday morning."

"What the hell are you talking about?" I asked, getting a cold feeling deep in my stomach.

"You texted him while Izzy was taking her bath," Jessica said. "You told him that Sherri suggested you get in touch. He asked you out. It was all very sweet—he really likes you and I think you really like him, too. At least, that's the impression you gave with your text, you wicked little flirt."

"I was impressed," confirmed Sherri. "Didn't know you had it in you."

I stared between them, wondering whether Painter could help me dispose of two bodies without leaving any evidence.

Probably.

"Give me my phone."

Jess handed me one of the frosted pink monstrosities instead.

"Join the dark side, Melanie. We have cake."

"I'm not going out with him—and fuck you, because that cake's pink and I hate pink."

"You don't have to go on the date," Sherri said quickly. "Of course, it will probably be awkward as hell to back out at this point. Really hurt his feelings, you know? He thinks you're interested. And be fair, Mel. He's cute."

I stared at the cupcake, picturing the security guard. Aaron. Aaron Waits. He seemed like a nice enough guy, and Sherri was right—he really was cute. Not as big and tough as Painter, but not all clean-cut and shiny like that damned dentist, either.

"Don't take this as a sign that what you did is okay . . ." I said finally, reaching for the cupcake.

"Of course not," Jess said, trying hard not to gloat and failing miserably. "It's that terrible impulse-control problem of mine, you know? So hard to overcome. I'll totally talk to my therapist about it."

"Don't you dare pull that shit on me," I said, biting down into the pink monstrosity. It was really good—there was just the right ratio of frosting to cake. I hated it when the frosting wasn't thick enough. "You haven't been to therapy for years, and you're perfectly capable of controlling your impulses when you want to."

It was true, and it would've sounded a whole lot better if I hadn't sprayed crumbs along with my words.

"Ta-da!" Izzy shouted, running into the kitchen. She had on her newest princess dress, this one bright green, thank God. She looked like a blonde princess Merida from *Brave*, complete with the corkscrew curls. Seeing as Painter and I both had straight hair, I'd never quite figured that one out, but it was adorable.

"You look great!" Sherri said, pulling her up and swinging her around. "Why are you all dressed up? Do you have a ball to go to?"

"Nope, Daddy's gonna teach me how to shoot a bow and arrow," she said proudly. "I'm all ready. He says a girl needs to know how to defend herself in this world."

"He's weaponizing the child?" Jess asked in a low voice. "Why am I not surprised by this?"

I nodded, wishing I had a bow and arrow. I wasn't quite sure who I'd rather use it on—Jessica or Painter.

Or maybe Sherri.

I just hoped I wouldn't need to use it on Aaron.

WEDNESDAY NIGHT

"Are you sure it's okay?" I asked Loni. "I feel weird asking you to watch her while I'm on a date, because tonight was supposed to be about work. I don't want to impose on you."

Loni rolled her eyes.

"It's fine," she said. "Reese has some club thing happening, anyway. He won't be home until late. And I'm happy you're going out— you're young. You should be having fun, and you know how much I love playing grandma. And Reese will probably get up early with her and make pancakes. Definitely a winning situation for me."

That made me smile, because for a man who complained so much about being surrounded by girls, Reese was suspiciously available whenever I needed a sitter. Izzy had him wrapped around her little finger and she knew it.

God help me once she was a teenager.

The roar of a Harley came from outside, and I shot Loni a quick look.

"Was Reese coming over?" I asked. She shook her head.

"Painter?" she suggested.

"I'm not expecting him."

"Daddy!" Izzy shouted, running into the living room. "I can hear his motorcycle."

She jumped up onto the couch and looked out through the front window. "That's not Daddy."

Leaning over her, I peered out to see Aaron—my date—climbing off a big, black Harley.

"Ah crap," I muttered. "He's a biker."

Loni and I shared a quick look. She knew all about Painter's "no bikers" rule, although she thought it was bullshit. I knew this because she'd told me more than once.

"They've got a club thing tonight," she said quickly. "You should be just fine."

Hopefully.

Aaron rang the doorbell and I went to answer it, forcing myself to smile. This whole thing felt awkward and uncomfortable, like I was lying to him. The pleased look on his face didn't help, either.

"You ready?" he asked. "I brought my bike—the ride up to Callup is gorgeous this time of year. We'll stop along the way and eat dinner at the Bitter Moose. Have you ever been there?"

"No," I admitted. "Never even heard of it."

"You'll love it," he said, and something about his tone put me off. Maybe it was the way he didn't even bother to tell me what kind of food they had, or ask if I wanted to go. "And afterward we'll hit a party with some of my friends. You look great, by the way, but I think you should change."

"Thanks," I said, glancing down at my skirt. *Appreciate the warning ahead of time, asshole.* Ugh. Now I was just being bitchy— most girls would be thrilled to have a guy show up on a motorcycle. For all I knew, Sherri had told him I loved bikers. "Um, I'll be right back. This is Loni, she's kind of like . . . my mom, I guess. And my daughter, Izzy."

Aaron knelt down, looking Izzy right in the eye. "Your mom's friend Sherri told me all about you. She said you like pink things. I brought you something."

With that, he reached into his pocket and pulled out a little stuffed unicorn with a fluffy pink mane and tail.

"It's beautiful!" Izzy sighed, reaching for it. Aaron winked at me, and I felt my snit evaporate, along with my doubts.

"I'll be right back," I said. "Izzy, what do we say?"

"Thank you!"

Maybe tonight wouldn't be so bad after all.

Aaron had been right—it really was a perfect evening for a ride, and the trip over Fourth of July Pass into the Silver Valley was stunning. Despite my misgivings, the date was going well. Better than any I'd had in a long time. I still wasn't feeling the same kind of instant chemistry with him that I felt with Painter, but whatever. No man's perfect.

We'd arrived at the restaurant—which was really more of a pub than anything else—at seven thirty and had a decent dinner. The Bitter Moose wasn't anything fancy, but the place had plenty of atmosphere. Sort of like one of those historical theme restaurants, but this was definitely the real deal. According to the article printed on the little paper menus in the center of each table, it dated back to the gold rush days, when it was a brothel. Later it was a hotel and now the owner lived upstairs.

By the time we finished eating it was nearly nine. The lights had dimmed and the music had gotten louder. Several couples got up and started to dance. To my surprise, Aaron convinced me to join them. It wasn't all hot and intense and sweaty like a real club, but it was fun and when I checked the time a whole hour had passed.

"You want to take a break?" Aaron asked. I nodded. "Water or something heavier?"

"Water's great."

Our waitress had already cleared away our plates, but she'd left the water at the table and I took a deep drink, appreciating how low-key the date was. Felt good to relax. Aaron seemed less chilled, but he smiled enough that I decided not to worry about it.

"So you must've had Izzy when you were fifteen or something," he said, leaning forward so I could hear him over the music. "Because you look way too young to be a mother."

"I was twenty-one," I said, feeling myself flush. "I'll admit, it wasn't planned, but I guess it's worked out pretty well. I can't imagine life without her. Do you have kids?"

He shook his head.

"Hell no. I was married right out of high school, though," he said. "We were way too young—finally split up last year, although I'm still friends with her. Does that seem weird to you?"

"I can't imagine being friends with my ex," I admitted. "We fight all the time—doubt we could agree on the color of the sky. But I have to admit, he's a fantastic dad to Izzy, and he helps me out a lot, too."

"You still have a thing for him?" Aaron asked.

Yes.

"No," I said firmly. "Absolutely not. I just try to stay out of his way. He's . . . intense. But like I said, he's a good dad to Izzy. He's an artist."

Aaron got a funny look on his face. "That's weird."

"No it's not," I said, strangely offended. "He's amazing, a natural talent—he sells his paintings all over the country, and people hire him to do commissions, too."

He held up his hands in mock surrender.

"I wasn't trying to piss you off."

Shit. What was wrong with me?

"Sorry, I guess it just struck me the wrong way."

"No worries," he said, although the look in his eyes was speculative. "You sure you're not hung up on him?"

"It's complicated," I admitted awkwardly.

"Well . . . okay then. I guess I'll get the bill," he said. "We should probably get going anyway. I'm meeting someone at the party around ten thirty—he's got something I need to pick up."

"I want to use the restroom before we go," I said, wishing I'd kept my mouth shut about Painter. The man wasn't even here, yet somehow I couldn't look at Aaron without comparing the two.

"Sounds good. Why don't you do that while I pay," Aaron said, reaching over to catch my hand. "Hey, are we okay?"

"Of course," I said, giving him a smile that wasn't quite real. "I'll meet you out in the parking lot—how does that sound?"

"Perfect."

He gave me a smile that I think was supposed to be seductive.

My return one was significantly less so. Crap, how awkward was that? Here I was, out for the night with a perfectly decent man. Why didn't I feel more for him?

Pisser.

Jessica and Sherri were going to be so disappointed by this one, I realized, because there was no way I'd be going home with Aaron Waits tonight. Hopefully things wouldn't get too weird back at work.

He really was a nice guy.

Of course, the dentist had been nice, too. Ugh.

Callup was a picturesque little town.

Small. Like, seriously small, with an old-fashioned main street lined with all sorts of pretty stone buildings. It looked like something out of a very old newsreel, you know, the kind where you can see a few cars, but mostly horses and there's no sound?

We passed through it slowly and then continued out along an old road for a couple miles before I saw a concrete-block building that'd seen better days. Parked in front of it was a long line of motorcycles along with several guys wearing leather vests. Then I saw a mural on the outside wall, one that looked suspiciously like Painter's work. There was an image of a skull wearing a miner's hat and the words "Silver Bastards MC."

No.

Oh *fuck* no. This was bad—bad, badder, *baddest*.

We had to get out of here, because this was Puck's club, and he was Painter's best friend.

Oblivious, Aaron pulled to a stop at the far end of the gravel parking lot, well away from the line of what had to be club bikes. A guy wearing a prospect's cut started toward us and I realized that I had about thirty seconds before my world imploded around me.

"We have to leave," I told Aaron, without climbing off the bike. He turned to look at me, frowning.

"We just got here," he said, confused.

"No, you don't understand," I said, feeling almost panicky. "This is an MC clubhouse. I can't go in there."

Aaron gave me a sweet, if borderline condescending, smile. "Don't worry—I have friends here. You don't need to be afraid. I'll protect you."

"My ex is a member of the Reapers MC," I told him. "If he finds out I'm here, there'll be trouble."

He frowned. "You didn't mention that before."

"It didn't seem relevant then. Now it does. Let's go."

"No," he said, his voice hardening. "I have to meet my friend and pick something up."

"Then take me back into town and drop me off. I'll wait for you."

"Hey," the prospect said, coming up to us. He looked between us, and Aaron bristled. "We have a problem here?"

"No problem," Aaron said quickly. "I'm friends with Gunnar. My date's just a little shy about the clubhouse. Guess she's not used to being around bikers."

God, what a prick. I opened my mouth to call him on his shit, then snapped it shut again. Clearly Aaron wasn't going to take me back to town, which meant I had to play this through. It might even work—I didn't really know the Silver Bastards, with the exception of Puck. If I got really lucky, he wouldn't even be here tonight.

Or if he was, maybe I could hide in the bathroom or something . . . I'd call Painter when I got home, explain what'd happened. Not that I owed him any explanations, but all blustering aside, I really didn't want to get into it with him over something this stupid. Not after the whole Greg debacle. The fact that I was innocent wouldn't do a damn thing to save me if Painter got his panties in a twist.

Aaron smiled at me tightly. Obviously he wanted me to keep my mouth shut. We'd had a good time so far, but I was starting to think that maybe Aaron wasn't such a great guy after all. Sherri was going to hear about this.

No more blind dates.

"Gunnar's inside," the prospect said, still eyeing us. I climbed off the bike, then stood there like a good little woman while Aaron got off, too. He caught my hand, giving it what I suspect was meant to be a reassuring squeeze as we started toward the door. Several big men stood around watching us and the bikes, and I thought I recognized one of them.

Oh, crapsicles.

That was a Reapers prospect, and where there were Reapers prospects, there were Reapers. I looked more closely at the bikes, starting to feel just a little sick to my stomach. There was Reese's ride, and Horse's. Then I saw a midnight blue custom-painted masterpiece, and knew that I was completely and totally fucked.

Painter was here.

My feet stopped, and I tried to jerk my hand out of Aaron's.

"We have to go," I hissed, eyes wide.

"Not until I get my shit," he said, and while I think he was trying to sound soothing, his hand tightened on mine. "If your ex was really with a club, you'd know it's a bad idea to argue with me in front of them. Just do what I say and you'll be fine—you're totally overreacting here."

"I'm sorry, Aaron, but you have no idea what you're talking about. He's inside, and he can't see me with you," I said. "That's his bike, right there."

Aaron frowned, and for the first time I thought I saw understanding in his eyes.

"Okay, we'll make it fast," he said. "But I can't leave you out here—it's one thing if you're with me, but no way I'd leave a date alone in a place like this. We'll leave as soon as I find Gunnar."

For an instant, I considered making a break for it. Just kicking him in the shin and taking off into the trees surrounding the building, but the only thing stupider than showing up at a Silver Bastards party with a strange guy would be causing a big scene. Instead I forced myself to take several deep breaths, then followed him into the bar. Maybe I could hide in the corner, blend in somehow. God, I hoped I could.

The place was packed.

There were girls everywhere—girls in tiny tank tops, girls in bikini tops, and even a few without anything on their tops at all. I could still remember when my boobs were perky like that. Pre-baby, of course. Sigh. Some were carrying around trays of drinks, while others were perched on the laps of more big, burly bikers than I'd ever wanted or needed to see in my life.

Most of them wore Silver Bastard colors, but here and there I saw Reapers patches. There was Reese, standing not far from me. As I watched in horror, a girl who had to be younger than me sidled up to him, wrapping her arm around his waist and nuzzling his chest.

For an instant my heart froze.

Was he cheating on London?

Fuck fuck fuckity *fuck*, this was bad.

Reese scowled, pushing the girl away roughly enough to make it clear he wasn't interested. She must have been stoned or something, because she immediately turned to another man, doing the exact same thing to him. I didn't recognize him, thank God.

This was a nightmare.

"Gunnar!" Aaron shouted, and a huge man wearing only his Silver Bastard colors turned toward us. He had dark hair pulled back in a ponytail, a dark beard, and rich, sexy eyes that scanned me quickly before offering me a smile that sent a shiver down my spine.

Oh *my*.

Granted, he wasn't as hot as Painter, but still . . . Why couldn't Sherri set me up on a date with someone like him? The thought was ridiculous, of course, because I already had way too many bikers in my life. Aaron started walking toward him.

Still no sign of Painter. Perhaps I'd live to date another day after all.

I put my head down, crossing my fingers. Maybe we'd get through this all right after all . . .

"Good to see you," Gunnar said. "Who's the girl?"

Aaron put his arm around my shoulder possessively, and I could practically smell the smug he radiated. Ah, wasn't that sweet—he was proud to have me as a date. Wasn't that just suicidal of him. *God*. In the distance, I heard the sound of glass breaking, cutting through the music and conversation all around us. I glanced up, sensing danger. Then Reese's voice rang out.

"Hold on, son."

I looked at him, then followed his gaze across the room to see Painter.

Enraged.

He was stalking toward us, eyes full of murder.

CHAPTER TWENTY-ONE

In an instant, Reese was pushing through the crowd, grabbing Painter's arm. I focused on the gesture—Reese was trying to save me. Pulling away from Aaron, I hissed urgently, "We have to get out of here *right now*."

He was too busy watching the show, though, too stupid to realize how much danger he was in. Just like a big, dumb puppy. God, Painter was going to slaughter Aaron. He'd go back to jail, and it would all be my fault. On the bright side, I probably wouldn't outlive my dumbass date by long, so I guess I had that going for me. Why hadn't Aaron *listened* when I told him we needed to leave?

Painter shoved Reese off, then he was in front of us before I could get out a word of explanation. I screamed when he caught the front of Aaron's shirt, jerking him into the center of the room as his fist slammed into his face. He hit him again, and I found myself screaming even louder when Aaron fell to the ground, Painter following him down like a rabid dog, raining vengeance.

"You asshole!" I shouted, shocked and horrified, because this was *hell*. It had to be. I'd fallen through a hole in the world, straight into hell, where all my worst fears were coming true. Suddenly Puck was there, dragging Painter off my date, who was moaning and whimpering on the ground.

Puck let Painter go, and now he stood over Aaron, taking deep breaths, the effort to stop fighting almost more than he could handle.

"Get him out of here," he growled. "Get him out of here before I kill him."

"Fuck," Horse said, grabbing Aaron under the arms. A path cleared between him and the door, and I shrieked wordlessly at Painter, angrier than I'd ever been before. What if Aaron pressed charges?

How dare he pull this kind of shit?

He turned on me, face full of terrible purpose as Reese stepped between us, blocking his path.

"Not happening, son," he said.

"It's none of your business," Painter snapped. Damned right—it wasn't *anybody's* business. Stupid fucking bikers, telling people what to do. I was an adult, free to date whoever the hell I wanted. Painter needed to go straight to hell. I'd take him there, too—he might be the big, tough guy but I was a motherfucking *nurse*. I knew exactly how to kill a man, kill him in ways so terrible he'd be begging for death before I finished.

"*She's* the one who came here," Painter added with a sneer. Oh, fuck him. *Fuck* him.

"I didn't even know where we were going!" I shouted. "It was just a date, you asshole!"

"He's a fucking biker. You broke the rules, Mel. Get your ass over here."

"Not happening," Reese said, his voice like thunder. "I am *not* dealing with this tonight. Painter, get your ass home. Melanie, you're with me."

Something dark filled the room, some sort of swirling tension I didn't understand and didn't care about, because I'd had just about enough of this shit. Painter and I needed to have this out once and for all. Using every bit of my strength, I shoved Reese out of the way, launching myself toward Painter.

"What I do is none of your goddamned business!"

Painter stared at me, a slow and terrible smile coming over his face.

"Fuck it," Reese said. "I'm done with both of you."

I felt a moment of triumph, then Painter took a step toward me, hell in his eyes.

"I'll give you a ride home, Mel," he said, softly menacing. "We can talk when we get there. Privacy, you know?"

Oh shit. I looked around frantically, but the wall of men around me didn't break. They were all there—Ruger, Horse, Banks. Their faces were hard, and I realized in that instant that these men—men who had been so helpful toward me over the years—weren't my friends.

They were Painter's brothers.

"Fuck . . ." I whispered, suddenly terrified.

"Maybe we'll do that, too."

In an instant he caught me, throwing me over his shoulder and striding toward the door. I screamed again, my throat sore as he pushed through the crowd, carrying me through the parking lot. At first I thought we were headed for his bike, but he passed it, crossing the road instead.

I raised my head, staring blindly at the prospects. Two of them had laid Aaron on the ground next to the building, obviously trying to figure out how seriously injured he was. A third stood and stared, something like shock on his face as Painter hauled me into the trees.

Then we were in the woods, surrounded by darkness. His hand came down over my ass, swatting me hard before he dropped me to the ground. If he hadn't steadied me I would've fallen over.

"It's over, Mel. It's all over. You're mine now."

Steadying myself, I smacked his chest, because two could play at that game. "You had no fucking right to hurt him—he didn't do anything to you."

"He touched my woman," Painter snarled. "I've held off. I've given you so much fucking space you could build a goddamned kingdom, but I told you what would happen if you came back to my world. So far as I'm concerned, that means you're mine. I'm sick of this shit. C'mere."

With that, he grabbed me, jerking me into his body for a hard kiss that I wanted to hate, just as much as I wanted to hate him. But there was still that fire between us, one I could never quite kill. Now it was roaring to life.

I wanted him.

No, I *needed* him. Inside me. Over me. Filling me and hurting me and keeping me safe, because my body had decided I belonged to him, even if my mind thought that was complete and utter shit. One hand was tight in my hair, holding my head captive as he ravaged my mouth. The other slid down into my pants, clutching my ass so tight I knew there'd be handprints in the morning. My arms went around his neck and then Painter was lifting me, my legs wrapping around his waist.

He was so hard.

I remembered what his cock felt like when we'd made Isabella. How he'd claimed me and I'd felt so protected and loved, before everything fell apart and I was suddenly alone and scared. I wanted that feeling again—only Painter could give it to me. I'd tried to find someone else, but it was like he'd broken me, destroying every chance for happiness away from his touch.

God, but I hated him for that.

He pushed me up against a tree, grinding his hips deep into mine. It hurt. The bark dug into my back and his cock pushed against me so hard I felt every seam of my jeans, but I didn't care. I wanted more. Digging my fingers into his back, I clawed him, because if he was going to mark me then I was damned well going to mark him, too.

His hips grew more frantic and suddenly it wasn't enough. I broke free, moaning. "Fuck me."

Backing away from the tree, he pushed me down into the dirt. Then his hands were ripping apart my fly and jerking down my jeans. They stuck. I kicked wildly, trying to get them off but it was too slow for him. Jerking me up by the waist, he turned me and shoved me down in front of him. I landed hard on my hands. Then I heard the rip of his zipper and he grabbed my hips, steadying my body as he lined up the head of his erection with the aching, empty space between my legs.

"I am the last man you'll ever fuck," he growled, thrusting into me hard. His cock slammed home in one motion, stretching me as I screamed in agonized need.

It hurt.

I wanted more.

I hated him.

"Missed this," he groaned, jerking his hips back, only to slam into me again. His hands wrapped around my waist, holding me tight as he fucked me harder than anything I'd ever experienced. "Jesus."

Bracing on my hands, I thrust my ass back toward him, wondering how something this hateful could feel so good. How *he* could feel so good, with his big, violent hands and his caveman desire. I'd never been so turned on in my life, every thrust hitting a space deep inside that sent aching swirls of painful need shattering through my body.

This wasn't sex.

It was a fight for dominance, a fight I knew I couldn't win but I was damned if I wouldn't try. Every time he filled me, I squeezed down, hoping to hurt him or hold him or I don't know what. He'd groan in agonized satisfaction and then we'd do it again, over and over and over until I felt like my heart might explode.

Suddenly his hand reached around me, finding my clit, and then I *did* explode.

Exploded and died.

My vision shattered, my pulse pounded, and every muscle in my body clenched hard, taking him with me as he shouted his own release. Hot seed spurted deep inside my body as I sagged forward into the dirt, spent. Painter collapsed on top of me, both of us gasping for air. Slowly reality came back and I felt his softening cock slide free, his come running down the inside of my legs.

That's when it hit me.

We forgot the damned condom.

Again.

PAINTER

Mel looked like shit.

She was covered in dirt, her shirt was torn, and she had this lost, haunted look in her eyes. Christ. Picnic would take one look at her and assume I'd beaten her.

He wouldn't be that far off.

Pic wasn't waiting for me at the clubhouse when we got back, though. Most of the Reaper bikes were gone, and there wasn't any sign of the fuckwad, either. The Silver Bastard prospects were smart enough to keep their mouths shut, although I saw one duck back into the clubhouse.

Seconds later Boonie stepped out, followed by Gunnar.

"Can I have a word?" he asked, eyes flickering to Mel.

"Sure," I said. "Give us a sec."

Mel nodded, almost like she was in shock. I suppose she probably was. Hell, I felt sort of shocked myself, so I suppose it was fair enough.

"What's up?" Boonie cocked a brow, then nodded toward her. "She okay?"

"She's fine."

"You hurt her?"

"No," I said, daring him to challenge me. He frowned, then nodded. "I've got some information for you, about the guy she came with."

I stilled.

"What's that?"

"He's a dealer," Gunnar said, crossing his arms over his chest. "I'm not sure if he was dating her for real or just using her for cover, but he was here to pick up a shipment. We've been working with him for about six months now. Does special orders, that kind of thing. He's bad news."

I nodded slowly, looking back toward Melanie. She was standing next to my bike, hugging herself protectively. For an instant I felt guilty, then shook it off. She was mine. No way I should feel guilty about claiming my own damned property.

"We have a problem?"

Boonie shook his head.

"He's nothing. I mean, he was a decent earner, but he'd never be more than that. He'll keep his mouth shut—he's seen enough to know better than to talk. I had a little chat with him, too. Guess he works at the hospital with her. I suggested that he find another job—fast. He seemed to think this was a solid idea. You won't be seeing him again."

"Thanks," I said. "Sorry about the mess."

"Shit happens," Gunnar said, eyeing Mel again. "You sure she's okay?"

"She'll be fine," I said. "It's not what it looks like."

"That's good, because it looks like you raped her," Boonie said. I shook my head.

"More like we hate-fucked each other. Trust me, she was into it. Sick and twisted, but it wasn't rape."

"Darcy will be relieved," Boonie said. "Think you pissed off my old lady something fierce—she took off right after you did. Got a feeling I won't be gettin' any tonight."

I bit back a grin, because Darcy pissed off was something to see.

"Sorry about that."

He shrugged, then gave me a sly smile.

"Gotta love makeup sex. Good luck with your girl."

"Thanks. Have a feeling I'll need it."

He thumped my back and we said our good-byes, then I started back toward Melanie. She glared at me the whole time, which I found almost comforting. I could handle nearly anything but that strange blankness she'd had right after I fucked her.

That was a little scary.

"You ready to go home?" I asked.

"I've been ready to go home all night. I still hate you."

"You need to find new insults. That's getting old."

"Fuck off."

Grinning, I climbed onto my bike. She climbed up behind me, tucking in tight and wrapping her arms around my waist, tits pressed against my back. For the first time in forever things in my world felt right, twisted as that sounds.

She was mine. She'd always been mine. I'd be damned if I'd share her with another man.

We pulled up to her house a little before midnight. Pic had mentioned earlier that Izzy was sleeping over at his place, but I'd assumed it was because Mel had to work. Much as seeing her with the fuckwad pissed me off, the end result was working in my favor. Turning off the bike, I waited for her to climb off, then followed her toward the house.

"You don't need to come in," she said.

"Yeah, I'm pretty sure I do," I replied. "We need to get cleaned up, and then we need to talk."

"What's to talk about?" she sniped, digging in her pocket for the key. She fumbled and nearly dropped it, so I reached out and took it from her, opening the door. I glanced around the cozy house as we stepped inside. Izzy had taken all the pillows off the couch, lining them up along the wall. On top were all her dolls and stuffed animals, including a little skeleton from last Halloween that she'd fallen in love with. They were covered in blankies, washcloths, and even a few tissues.

"She put her babies to bed before she left for London's," I said, feeling the same sense of peace I always got when I thought about Izzy. God, but I loved that kid. Mel smiled, glancing toward me with a look of shared pride in our girl.

"She always does. Tucks in each one and then she tells them a story. Does she do it at your place, too?"

"Yeah."

"We made a good kid."

"I want us to live together," I said abruptly, running a hand through my hair. "We're a family, Mel."

She stared at me, covered in dirt, hair looking like she'd survived a tornado.

"We're fucked up," she said. "Look at us. There's something *wrong* here, Painter."

"That was the best sex I've ever had," I told her. "Look me in the eye and tell me it wasn't the same for you."

Mel glared at me, but she didn't say a damned thing. I bit back a laugh—busted.

"The sex is good. We've got a kid. You already admitted you want me around—don't think I've forgotten that. So far as I can tell, the only reason we aren't together is that you're so damned stubborn you can't let yourself just accept it and be happy."

"What about Aaron?" she asked. "That's messed up, Painter. You would've killed him. I saw it in your face."

She was right. Almost.

"But I *didn't* kill him," I reminded her.

"That's because Puck stopped you."

"Maybe," I admitted. "But he was with me for a reason. That's the thing about having brothers, Mel—they got you covered when you can't cover yourself."

"Yeah, I noticed that," she said, her voice growing harder. "Particularly the way they all pretended you weren't dragging me out against my will. I was screaming for help and they just watched. That's sick."

"He's a dealer," I said, derailing her. She blinked.

"Who?"

"Aaron. He was using you for cover—he was at the Silver Bastards' clubhouse to pick up a shipment. Drugs—or maybe guns. I didn't get the specifics and I don't care. What I do care about is the fact that if he'd gotten busted, you would've gone down as an accomplice. So far as I'm concerned, I didn't hurt him enough."

She stilled.

"Are you serious?"

"Yeah. That's what Boonie was telling me."

"Shit," she said, collapsing onto the couch. She let her head fall back, staring at the ceiling. "He met Izzy. He gave her a little stuffed unicorn . . . I thought it was sweet."

"Fucking asshole. Where is it?"

She looked around. "I don't see it—she probably took it out to London's. Don't worry, I'll bribe her or something, get it away from her. No way I want that in this house, knowing how he used me."

I sat next to her, propping my feet up on the coffee table. We both needed a shower in a bad way, but we needed to get this shit settled even more. She was on the edge, though. I could see it. Christ, but women were complicated.

"Can I ask you something?" she asked.

"Sure."

"Would you ever do that?"

"Do what?"

"Carry something illegal around me or Izzy?"

I sighed, wondering how to answer. Fuck it, might as well give her the truth.

"I have a gun on my bike. That's illegal—I'm a felon, not allowed to own a firearm."

"Where is it?" she asked.

"Got a hidden compartment for it," I told her. "Ruger rigged it up. You want to see?"

I don't know why I offered, but for some reason it seemed like the right thing to do—maybe if she saw it for herself, she'd believe me when I promised that I wasn't smuggling anything worse.

"Yes," she said, looking a little surprised that I was so comfortable with it—good. Maybe she'd believe I was serious, because I was. I'd never put her in that kind of danger. "I think I would."

"Okay, then."

We went back outside. There wasn't much light, but I carried a little flashlight in one of my saddlebags, along with a first aid kit, a sewing kit, some tools, and a few other essentials—never know what might happen on the road.

"You're like a Boy Scout," she said, and I heard a smile in her voice.

"Yeah, that's me," I replied, laughing. "Here it is."

I popped open the compartment using the hidden latch, showing her the small semiautomatic pistol inside. It was loaded and ready to go, and there was a spare ammo cartridge, too.

"Note the complete and utter lack of drugs," I pointed out dryly. "For the record—it's not illegal for you to be holding this gun, just me. There's no danger to you if we happened to get caught with this."

"Will you show me how to open it?"

"The gun?" I asked, surprised. She gave a little laugh.

"No, your supersecret compartment."

I closed it back up, looking at her.

"What is this, some kind of test?"

"I don't know. Do you need testing?" she challenged. I sighed, because she probably did want to test me.

"Give me your hand."

Guiding her, I let her feel the little latch for herself, then watched as she opened and closed the compartment several times. Then we walked back to the house, but at the door Mel stopped me, putting a hand on my chest.

"You should leave now," she said. "I can't handle any more tonight. I need to take a shower and then get some sleep, and I'll do that a hell of a lot better if you aren't around. Safer for you, too. Now that I know where to get a gun, I might be tempted to kill you in your sleep."

"All right," I said, and while I wanted to argue, I could see she was telling the truth—Mel was done. Spent. "I have shit to do tomorrow. Important shit. Club business. But when I finish, we're going to talk. I'll come for you tomorrow night."

She shook her head.

"I'll call you when I'm ready to talk," she protested.

"No fucking way. I'll give you tonight, but tomorrow we're settling this. For real."

"Fuck you."

I leaned forward, kissing her on the lips. She softened for an instant, then she was pushing at my chest.

"I already did," I reminded her. Mel frowned.

"Huh?"

"I already fucked you. It was amazing. But then, us fucking always is, right?"

Her face hardened, and she slammed the door in my face.

I couldn't help myself—I laughed.

CHAPTER TWENTY-TWO

FRIDAY MORNING
MELANIE

"He just quit," I heard Brit telling another nurse. "No notice, nothing."

"Who?" I asked, leaning against the counter. It was nearly eight in the morning, almost time for shift change and report. Damned good thing, too, because I was exhausted. I'd gotten shit sleep last night, and then I'd spent the day with Izzy. Because London was an angel, she'd agreed to take her for a second night in a row, but when I'd tried to nap that afternoon after dropping her off out at the Armory, there'd been no joy.

I kept thinking about Painter's promise to come back last night.

I should've called him. Should've let him know I was working and that we'd have to talk a different time. But there'd been some defiant, angry part of me that wanted him to sit around waiting, wondering where the hell I was, because fuck him and his orders.

Twelve hours later I was exhausted and grumpy and wishing like hell that I hadn't set myself up like that—he'd find me sooner or later, and when he did, I'd be too tired to fight him.

"That cute security guard," she said. "Aaron Waits. Damned shame, because he made nights like tonight a whole hell of a lot more fun."

Good, I thought fiercely. I never wanted to see that fucker again.

"You're married," I pointed out. "Not like you could do anything with him."

"Married doesn't equal dead," she replied, giving me a wink. "I can appreciate the scenery without touching it. Only ten more minutes until shift change—I can't wait. I hate nights like tonight. So boring."

She was right. Some shifts were hellish—terrible car accidents, people dying. Those were the kind of nights that stuck with you, haunting your dreams. But tonight had been the complete opposite. Only four patients, and two of them had colds. I'd never seen the place so empty.

"Day shift is screwed," I said. "Because you just know the law of averages has to catch up to them sometime. Some kid is out there right now, playing with matches."

She nodded at me, agreeing. Sooner or later, the patients would come.

But not for us. Not tonight.

"Let's do the report," the charge nurse said, coming toward us. "Not much to talk about."

We filled the day shift in on our patients and then ten minutes later we were all clocked out. There hadn't been much to share with them. Time to go home and catch some sleep before I had to deal with Izzy again. If I got lucky, Reese and London would keep her a few extra hours, let her watch some TV. I might even get a nap.

Painter's big blue Harley was parked outside my house.

I thought about the gun hidden inside. About the way he'd beaten up Aaron. What might've happened if Aaron and I had gotten pulled over, searched.

What a mess.

Taking a deep breath, I opened the door, not bothering to question how Painter had gotten inside. He was a Reaper—so far as I could tell, things like locks and walls didn't apply to them. I mean, he'd walked all over every other boundary I'd ever had, so why should this be any different?

He wasn't in the living room, but I heard music playing from one of the bedrooms. Dropping my keys and purse on the table, I kicked off my shoes and contemplated making myself a cup of coffee before facing him. Of course, that meant I'd have trouble napping should a miracle occur and I actually got the opportunity.

I'd sort of expected to find him in my bedroom, maybe pawing through my underwear drawer. The sound came from Izzy's room, though. Frowning, I walked to her door, pushing it open slowly. He was inside, painting one of her walls. The floor was covered in tarps, and the bed had been pushed into the center of the room. Along the wall he'd done a blue sky over green grass, leaving a large empty hole in the center. Now he was sketching on it with a thick charcoal pencil, although I couldn't quite tell what he was drawing from here.

"Hey," I said hesitantly, not quite sure what to expect. He turned to glance at me, eyes flickering over my scrubs.

"Hey."

I sidled into the room, off-balance. I'd expected to be fighting with him by now—this was weird. "Whatcha doing?"

"Designing a mural for Izzy," he said. "I hope you don't mind—we'd talked about it a while ago. I was waiting for you last night and figured I might as well get started."

Hesitantly, I came closer, trying to read his mood. His face was blank, though, so I studied the outline on the wall instead. It looked like . . .

"Is that a princess riding a motorcycle with a unicorn horn on her helmet?" I asked, bemused. Painter nodded.

"Yup, it's what Izzy wanted," he said. "Hate to break it to you, but she wants the princess *and* the motorcycle to be pink. I'm doing it in regular latex house paint, by the way. I've got a feeling she'll want it changed at some point."

"Hopefully some point soon," I said. "I'm really tired of pink and I'm pretty sure I could vomit unicorns on demand."

He laughed. "Yeah, me, too."

Stepping up to the wall, I traced my finger along the sketch, thinking about what it would look like when he was done. "She's going to love it."

"That's the goal," he said. "She told me that she wants to look at it and remember she has a daddy when I'm not around."

Ouch.

"She loves you."

"I know."

Turning to look at him, I cocked my head.

"I'm really tired," I said. "So I don't have the energy to play games right now. Are we going to fight?"

He shook his head. "No. I was pissed at you last night. For a while I figured you were probably off fucking some other guy, then I realized how stupid that was. London wouldn't tell me where you were—Reese must've mentioned what happened up in Callup, because she treated me like a serial killer. Just in case you ever wonder whose side she's on . . ."

I smiled.

"I got lucky with her," I acknowledged. "When my own mom bailed, she took me in, just like she took in Jessica. She's been a grandma to Izzy, a mother to me . . . but I'll never understand why Mom left. I look at Isabella and can't wrap my head around it, because I'd die before disappearing on her."

Like you did in prison.

"Are you ever going to forgive me?" he asked softly, catching my chin, forcing me to look at him. "Sometimes it feels like you hate me out of habit. It's still between us—that chemistry. Sex isn't the problem. And I'm a good dad to Isabella. I help you out as much as you'll let me. I fuckin' hate your job at the ER, but I'm not telling you to stop doing it because I know it's important to you. So why does it always have to be a fight, Mel?"

Shaking my head, I leaned forward into his chest. His arms came around me, rubbing my back. It felt good. Safe.

"It scares me," I confessed.

"What?"

"That I can care about you this much. You're a mystery to me—

you play with our daughter, you paint her pink motorcycles. You even let her dress you up like a fairy that one time and had a tea party with her."

He groaned.

"How did you find out about that?"

"She told me," I said, biting back a smile. "And she drew a picture. I took it to work and showed everyone. But I think you should be thanking me, because I seriously considered giving it to Reese."

He groaned again, his hand running up my spine to the back of my neck. The muscles there were tight from a long night of work, and as he dug his knuckles in deep, I sighed with pleasure.

"So what's the problem?"

"You beat Aaron up," I said softly. "You really hurt him."

"You could've gone to jail as his accomplice. He deserved it."

"You didn't know that when you attacked him—that was about you being jealous. That's fucked up, Painter."

"Probably," he admitted. "And I was pissed at you last night, too, but I got over it. It's true I lost my shit, but it's also true that I don't do it very often."

"You could go back to jail."

"You could get stabbed by a crazy guy in the ER."

Pulling away, I frowned up at him. "That's different. I'm doing something that helps people, remember? You're . . . running drugs or something. I don't even *know* what you do—you won't tell me."

His face grew serious.

"Mel, I'm not going to lie to you about who I am," he said slowly. "I don't always follow the law, and when my brothers need me, I'm gonna take their backs. But I'm an artist—*that's* what I do for a living. I'm not running guns, I'm not selling drugs. I paint fucking pictures, and then I sell them to rich assholes so they can brag about my 'primitive art' at their cocktail parties. I'll take their money with a smile, pay my club dues, and then I'll always come home to you and Izzy. I *love* you."

I closed my eyes, tasting the words. We'd known each other so long, been through so much. He'd always been there, even when he wasn't. My life had revolved around Painter for six years, from little girl crush to need to hatred to . . . *this*.

"I love you, too," I admitted slowly, opening my eyes to take him in.

He cocked his head, studying my face.

"Usually people don't look so unhappy when they say that for the first time," he said.

"Usually people get to sleep at some point, but it's been twenty-four hours," I replied quietly. "Like I said, I'm too tired to fight, so might as well lay it all out there."

"Does that mean you'll tell me this was all some kind of sleep-deprived hallucination at some point?"

I considered the question, then shook my head.

"No, I've loved you for a long time. I tried to move on, but I can't. Still kind of pisses me off, because there's all kinds of things I don't like about you . . . but it is what is it."

"Some guys would be offended by a declaration like that," Painter said. "But I think I'm gonna count this as a win."

I gave him a smile, then pulled away, looking around the room. There were cans of paint everywhere, big and small. All different colors.

"Where did this all come from?" I asked, waving my hand toward the mess.

"Oh, I picked them up here and there," he said, shrugging. "Been planning the mural for a while. Last night I was pissed off, and when I get pissed I usually fight or paint. I already did enough fighting this week."

"How did you figure out that I was working?"

"Jessica," he said. "I called her."

That surprised me. "Jessica hates you."

"I know," he said. "She didn't want to talk to me at first. I may have threatened her a little bit."

My eyes widened. "Did you hurt her?"

He gave a low laugh, shaking his head.

"Not that kind of threat."

"What kind of threat?" I asked, eyes wide.

"I threatened to call someone," he said. "Maybe send him some pictures, that's all. You don't want to know—trust me."

"Is this about all those years ago, when you and Jess—"

"No," he said firmly, cutting me off. "It's nothing to worry about. Just let it go—when she's ready to tell you, she will. Or not. Either way, I used it against her last night, and I don't regret that at all. I was still pissed with you, by the way—but after a few hours of painting I got over it, and then I was just relieved you weren't with another guy."

I studied his face, taking in the high cheekbones, his crystal blue eyes, and pale skin. "We're really lucky Izzy got my skin. You never tan."

He laughed again. "You're punch-drunk."

I shrugged, then sat down suddenly. Okay, "sat" was probably a stretch—it was more like my legs gave out, but with a controlled landing. Painter lowered himself next to me.

Looking at the cans of paint, I saw a small red one not far away and grabbed it.

"Do you remember that night you taught me how to paint lady-bugs?"

"Vividly. One of the best nights of my life."

"Do you think I could paint one on Izzy's wall?"

Painter stared at me, assessing. "You know, with anyone else I'd say yes, but I'm kind of scared you'll give her nightmares. Zombie mutant ladybugs or something. Maybe if we did it together?"

I frowned, but he had a point.

"Okay, show me."

"Sure," he said, glancing around. There was a pile of smaller brushes near the wall. He leaned over on his knees to grab one, then sat back down. Prying off the lid, he opened the can and handed me the brush.

"Let me find something for you to practice on."

I dipped the brush into the paint, letting the bright red drip slowly from the bristles back into the can. So much had happened over the years together—hard to wrap my head around all of it.

"I'd do it again, you know," I said suddenly. Painter glanced at me, a question in his eyes.

"All of it," I clarified. "I'd do it all over again. Us. I can't imagine life without Izzy. Having her made me stronger—I don't think I'd have gotten this far if it wasn't for her. It was worth it, even all the fighting with you."

Painter smiled, then shook his head. "You would've accomplished all kinds of things, no matter what."

I raised the brush, studying the color. He was right about the ladybugs—if I tried to paint something on the wall, I'd give Izzy all kinds of nightmares. Biting my lip, I studied his face. Then I leaned over and drew a bright red line down the length of his nose.

Painter blinked.

"Why the hell did you just do that?"

"You painted me," I said. "Remember? You practiced on me all those years ago. Now I think you should let me practice on you."

Heat flared in his eyes, and then he dropped his hands to the hem of his T-shirt, pulling it up and over his head.

"All yours, babe."

Biting back a laugh, I dipped my brush again and drew a circle around first one nipple, then the other. I followed this with a broad semicircle across his stomach.

"Look, it's a smiley face."

He rolled his eyes, but he didn't stop me when I dipped the brush again, this time painting a line down the length of his arm. I loved his arms—they were strong, roped with thick muscle. If I had to fall in love with an asshole, at least he was a hot asshole.

"Glad you think I'm hot," Painter said, and I blinked.

"I didn't realize I'd said it out loud."

He leaned forward and kissed me slowly. Oh, that was nice . . . I kissed him back and he caught me by the waist, dragging me over to straddle his body. I deepened the kiss, savoring his taste. How had I ever convinced myself I could live without this? Then Painter was pulling my scrub top up and over my head. Reaching around behind my back, I unhooked my bra without letting his lips go, launching myself back into him with enough force to push him over backward with a thump.

We both burst out laughing, which didn't stop him from grabbing my scrub bottoms and shoving them down, too. I kicked them free, sitting up and reaching for his fly. He scrambled to help me, and then his cock sprang out, hard and ready to go.

This was what I wanted.

What'd been missing, all along. Painter. Admitting it was a relief. Lowering my head, I licked the edge of his dickhead, then let my tongue trail down his length.

"Jesus, that feels good," he muttered. "But if—"

I shot a quick glare at him. "Less talk. If you don't talk, you can't say something stupid and fuck this up."

"Gotcha." He shut his mouth so I opened mine, sucking him down as I started pumping his cock with my hand. His head dropped back and he draped one arm over his eyes, groaning. His other hand burrowed into my hair, guiding me as I moved more quickly.

Eventually it wasn't enough—I wanted him inside. Not that I didn't enjoy the foreplay, but right now I needed to ride him fast and hard. Sliding up his body, my knee hit something and it fell over with a thud.

"Shit," I said, realizing I'd knocked over the can of red paint. "Oh shit!"

I pushed off him as he tried to sit up, which set us off-balance. Grabbing for his shoulder, I missed, and then I fell over sideways, right into the bright red pool.

Painter started laughing.

I tried to push up again, but the tarp was slippery as hell and my hands slid out from under me. Painter laughed harder, so I scooped up as much paint as I could, throwing it toward his face.

It hit with a wet smacking sound.

Now I was the one laughing as he tried to wipe it away. Scooping up more, I flung it at him again, hitting his chest. He lunged for me and I shrieked, scuttling backward through the mess. Then he was on me, and we were wrestling. He was stronger, but I was slippery as hell and his pants were wrapped around his knees, hobbling him. I kept swiping at the paint and trying to rub it on his face, until finally he caught me, rolling me under him for a deep kiss.

Unfortunately, not even a kiss from someone that sexy is enough to overcome the taste of paint. On the other hand, his dick was still hard, and if I had to choose between kissing or fucking, the kisses weren't my first choice. I reached down, grabbing for it. I wanted him inside me . . .

Shit.

Even his cock was covered in latex, and not the pregnancy-preventing kind.

"Condom," I managed to gasp. "Do you have one?"

"Yeah, in my wallet," he said, reaching for a rag. He wiped off his hand, then fished the wallet out of his back pocket. Pulling out a condom, he tossed the leather wallet across the room, presumably to save it from the paint. I watched anxiously as he rolled the rubber down over his erection, thinking back to the night before.

"We forgot to use a condom again last night," I pointed out. "I don't think it's the right time of my cycle to get pregnant, but . . ."

Painter looked at me, his eyes fierce.

"If you're knocked up again, we're getting married."

My jaw dropped.

"You'd marry me just because I was pregnant?"

He shook his head, giving me what I think was supposed to be a reassuring smile, but looked more like a zombie leer, given the red smeared across his face.

"No, we're getting married anyway," he said. "But if you're knocked up, we should probably do it while you can still fit into a wedding dress."

"Holy shit."

He shrugged, then pushed me back down, centering himself between my legs. I gasped as he pushed in, savoring the stretch even as I realized we'd have to take it easier this time—I was still sore.

"Careful," I warned. "You look like a vampire, did you know that? The paint on your face is like blood."

"This whole place looks like a crime scene," he said, winking at me.

"Oh, God. What a metaphor for our relationship."

He laughed. "We'd better take a shower together just as soon as we finish up here. No help for it."

"I think we can make that happen," I replied, wrapping my arms and legs around him. He twisted his hips, grinding into me slowly, and I sighed.

This was good. Really good. Too bad we'd destroyed Izzy's room to get here . . .

"You think this tarp will be enough to protect the carpet?"

He pulled back, then thrust into me again, hard.

"Absolutely not," he said cheerfully. "I'll probably have to pull it up and replace it. Totally worth the effort, no question. Now less talk and more fucking. Please?"

"You got it," I whispered, closing my eyes and letting the sensation take me.

I wasn't quite ready to marry him—not yet. I wanted to be sure we could go more than a week without trying to kill each other . . . But this had potential. Not only that, I'd never have to go on a blind date again.

Forgiving him was probably worth it, just for that alone.

PAINTER

I tiptoed out into the living room wearing only my briefs, because my jeans were soaked through. The paint was still smeared across my body, too, but I'd managed to wipe off my feet. Now I was on a mission to find paper towels.

That's when the door opened and Isabella ran in, followed by Reese and London.

All three froze.

"What did you do?" London asked, her voice a hoarse whisper. I frowned—a little paint never killed anyone. Izzy screamed and started to cry. London gathered her up, staring at me in horror.

"Where is she?" Reese asked, his voice grim.

"Mel? She's in the bedroom. I was just getting some towels to start cleaning up the mess. We'll probably have to pull out the carpet, though."

"Jesus fuckin' Christ," Reese said. "Loni, get that kid out of here."

I frowned, then caught a glimpse of my arm . . . dripping red.

"Wait!" I said. "This is *paint,* not blood. What the hell did you think, that I killed her?"

London nodded slowly, and I realized she was serious.

"No," I told them, outraged. "I *love* Melanie—I'd never hurt her."

"Given how you treated her the other night . . ."

"No, no fuckin' way," I replied, raising my voice. "She might kill me, but I'd never kill her. Mel, get out here. Izzy's home and she needs to see that you're okay."

"Just a sec," she shouted back, and I saw Loni visibly relax. Then Mel walked into the living room, wrapped tight in a bathrobe. Her feet had been rinsed off, but the rest of her was still covered in red. It was even matted into her hair. I winced—we probably should've at least moved to a cleaner part of the tarp.

"Hi," she said, offering a feeble smile. Reese sighed heavily, then looked at Izzy.

"Let's go get some ice cream. I think Mommy and Daddy need a little more time."

Mel nodded, and I thought she blushed. Hard to tell, given the situation. "That's probably a good idea."

"Yup, we definitely need ice cream. Maybe a nice breakfast mimosa," London announced. "We'll be back in an hour. That should give you two enough time to get cleaned up. I want to . . . never see anything like this again."

Then she turned and walked out the door, Izzy gaping at us over her shoulder. Reese sighed again.

"Have fun, kids," he said, following her.

Mel giggled again, and I shook my head. They were gonna crucify me out at the clubhouse for this one.

Guess I should just be glad he hadn't started snapping pictures.

CHAPTER TWENTY-THREE

OCTOBER
MELANIE

"You look adorable," Duck said, kneeling down next to Isabella. She was dressed up like a princess, of course, and the little purse she carried was already stuffed full of candy.

We were out at the Armory for their annual family Halloween party. Later it would turn into their annual grown-up Halloween party, and I had a feeling the costumes would be getting significantly skimpier. For now, though, we were surrounded by crowds of cute kids going slowly insane as they ate their weight in processed sugar.

"I'm a biker princess," Izzy said proudly. "Just like on my wall. Daddy helped me paint it."

"Well, here you go, princess," Duck said, pulling a dollar out of his pocket and handing it to her. He glanced at me and shrugged. "Uncle Duck didn't remember to buy candy."

"There doesn't appear to be a shortage," I said dryly, looking around the courtyard. The air was crisp, but it was one of those perfect October afternoons—sunny, with the smell of fall filling the air. Rows of tables were full of food, and they'd already started the bonfire. I couldn't help but notice there were a disproportionate number of little bikers wearing their own MC cuts. Painter came up behind me, sliding a hand around my waist as he kissed the back of my neck.

"You hittin' on my girl?" he asked Duck. The old man shrugged.

"Maybe," he replied. "But I can't decide which one. Mel's pretty, but this little princess of yours will probably be even prettier once she grows up."

"If you wait for me, I'll marry you," Izzy told him gravely. "But only if you let me bring my unicorns to live at your house. And I'm having an operation later this week, so you should bring me Popsicles, too. Daddy said I can have as many as I want."

Duck shot me a glance. *Tonsils*, I mouthed. He pretended to consider her offer, then nodded.

"We got a deal," he said, offering her his hand for a shake. "I'll start buildin' you a unicorn stable right away."

"Hey, Melanie!" London shouted. I looked up to find her waving at me from the food tables. She was in her element, bossing everyone around as she got the meal ready. "Can you give me a hand? I need someone to cut the pies."

"Sure," I yelled back, then looked down at Izzy. "You keep an eye on Daddy for me, okay? Make sure he makes good choices."

Painter nipped the back of my neck. Smacking him, I headed over to London, who handed me a knife.

"Is this for Painter or the pie?" I asked.

"I haven't forgiven him yet. Could go either way," she said, winking. "Cut each one into eight pieces, except the big ones from Costco. We can get twelve out of those."

I started in on the pies, noting that one of them was huckleberry—I wonder who'd brought that? I needed to make friends with them ASAP.

"Can you hand me that towel?" someone asked. I looked up to find a girl with skin just a little darker than mine and a head full of springy black ringlets. "I wanted to wipe off this casserole dish."

"Sure," I said, smiling at her. "I'm Melanie—what's your name?"

"Deanna. I'm new around here, just moved to town."

"Oh," I replied, wondering if she was with someone in the club.

"Mel, can you help me grab the veggie trays?" Loni asked. Giving Deanna a quick wave, I followed Loni through the back door and into the kitchen, where she made a beeline for one of the fridges. Pulling out three big veggie trays, she handed them to me and then grabbed a cardboard box off the counter, loading it with packages of hot dogs.

"We've got sticks so the kids can roast their own," she said.

"That's a lot of hot dogs just for the kids."

She laughed.

"Yeah, well once the kids start, the guys will follow. Usually I hate hot dogs, but even I enjoy one roasted over an open fire every once in a while."

"So who's Deanna?" I asked. "I just met her outside—never seen her around before."

"New club whore," Loni said bluntly. "She seems friendly enough—Reese said she showed up a few weeks back. Duck gave her a place to stay."

I raised my brows.

"Her and Duck?"

She nodded. "Apparently."

"Wow, good for him."

An hour later, Izzy had crawled into my lap and was starting to yawn.

"You ready to take her home?" Painter asked. I nodded.

"I think so. It's been a long day. Are you staying at the party?" More people had been arriving steadily, some I knew and more I didn't. Among them were far too many girls wearing "costumes" the size of postage stamps.

"I'll come home with you guys," he replied, and I smiled. *Melanie: one. Halloween tramps: zero.*

"Fucking hell!" someone shouted. I looked up to see a group of men gathering around something near the bonfire. "Call nine one one!"

Painter and I shared a look, then I thrust Izzy at him. She squawked in protest, but I ignored her as I ran toward the fire, pushing forcefully through the crowd of men.

Duck was on the ground, eyes closed.

"What happened?" I snapped, kneeling down next to him, feeling for a pulse. Nothing. No breathing, either.

"He said his chest hurt," Reese said. "We were getting him a chair, and then he fell."

"Reese, call nine one one," I ordered. They all paused, and I realized they weren't used to a woman giving their president orders. Rolling Duck onto his back, I looked up at the circle of men and snarled, "I'm a fucking ER nurse, and that means right now I'm in charge. Call nine one one, and someone get Painter. I need my keychain. Do you have a defibrillator?"

"No," Horse said bluntly. "Never occurred to us."

Of course not.

Rising to my knees, I traced my fingers over Duck's chest, finding the bottom of his breastbone. Centering the heel of my left hand just above it, I braced my right on top of my left and pushed down using all my weight.

His sternum cracked loudly. I felt the crunch of his ribs as I started chest compressions. One. Two. Three—all the way up to thirty, and fast, too.

"Where's my keychain?" I yelled, looking around. Painter dropped down next to me, handing it over. I found the little pouch I always kept attached to it, and pulled out a lightweight pocket CPR mask, slapping it over Duck's mouth to protect myself from any diseases he might have. Then I gave him two powerful breaths, watching for his chest to rise and fall.

Time to start compressions again. I looked at Painter.

"You're going to help me," I told him. "I'll do thirty compressions, then you'll give him two deep breaths. Watch me this next time, then do exactly what I do. After five cycles, we'll trade off—otherwise we'll never make it."

He nodded.

One. Two. Three. Four . . .

I could feel myself tiring already, which wasn't a surprise. Real CPR wasn't nearly as smooth and easy as they show on TV, and the compressions had to be deep if they were going to work. His organs needed oxygen, and every minute that passed, more heart muscle was dying.

By the time we traded off, my arms and back ached. I checked for his pulse. Still nothing.

"Is the ambulance coming?" I shouted.

"Yes," Reese said. "But they're at least another ten minutes out."

Fuck. Stupid old man, having a heart attack in the middle of nowhere. Suddenly Duck vomited and I jerked back, grabbing Painter's arm. "We have to roll him, otherwise he'll drown on his own puke."

Pushing Duck to his side, I let the disgusting fluid mixed with chunks of hot dog drain out of his mouth, then turned him back over. We weren't safe yet.

"Okay, you can start again."

Time seemed to blur after that—an endless cycle of compressions and breaths punctuated with pulse checks. We traded places again, and yet again, over and over until finally I checked his pulse and—

"Stop!" I shouted. "I've got something."

Painter dropped back, panting as I listened for Duck's breath. There it was. I dropped to my butt, exhausted but triumphant.

"He's alive," I said, feeling dizzy with relief.

"Coming through," a man's voice shouted. Reese pushed people out of the way as the EMTs came toward us, carrying their equipment.

"I'm an ER nurse," I told them. "He was down about . . ."

Hell. I had no idea how long he'd been down.

"Twenty minutes," Reese chimed in, his voice grim.

"Does he have a history of heart disease?" the EMT asked.

"No idea," Reese answered. "He's been at the doctor a lot lately, but didn't tell anyone why."

I felt someone catch my arm, pulling me away from Duck's body. Painter.

"Good job," he said softly. I nodded, because he was right—we'd done a hell of a good job. Wrapping an arm around my waist, Painter helped me over to the grass, where I lay down on my back, arm flopped over my eyes. He collapsed next to me, then Izzy ran up, crawling in between us.

"Is Uncle Duck dead?" she asked, obviously afraid. I cuddled her close.

"No, baby. But his heart is sick. They're going to take him to the hospital and see if they can fix it."

"What are his odds?" Painter asked. I considered the question.

"Depends," I admitted. "I have no way of knowing how much damage he has or why he had a heart attack in the first place. If they get him to the hospital in good time—and they should be able to—they'll run a catheter up his groin and check him out. If they find a blockage, they should be able to clear it and put in a stent. It's a common procedure—he could be back home by tomorrow. That's a best-case scenario, though. And he's going to hurt like hell no matter what. I probably broke half his ribs."

"Is it always like that?" he asked.

"Like what?"

"That . . . violent?"

I laughed. "CPR? Yeah. It's not something you do for fun."

"I'm tired," Izzy announced. Me and her both.

"Most of the club will be heading down to the hospital," Painter said. "But I think we need to go home. I'm wiped."

"Sounds like a plan. I'll make a few calls once we get there, see if they'll give me any information. You think you could leave your bike out here, maybe drive us back?"

"Yeah," he said, rolling over onto his elbow to look at me. "They're all going to want to thank you—you're a hero, Mel."

I offered him a weak smile, then shook my head.

"Nope, I'm just a nurse. But remember tonight the next time we have a fight, okay? Because I know about a hundred different ways to kill you in your sleep, bring you back, and then do it all over again."

His eyes widened, and Izzy laughed, clapping her hands.
Best. Kid. Ever.

THREE DAYS LATER
PAINTER

"What the hell are you doing here?" I demanded. I'd just pulled up
to the Armory for an emergency church meeting, only to find Duck
pulling up next to me. I'd been to visit him the day after his heart
attack, so I knew he was doing all right, but it still startled me to
see him here.

"We got church," Duck said, frowning as he lumbered toward
the building. "I always come in for the meetings. Although I had to
drive a fuckin' cage to get here."

"Mel said she didn't want you riding your bike for a couple
weeks," I reminded him. "Nothing strenuous, remember?"

"I know," Duck growled. "And it's fuckin' killing me. But that
new girl of mine has been takin' good care of me. Seems damned
unfair that when she gives me a sponge bath I can't have my happy
ending, though."

"You don't need sponge baths—you could just take a shower,"
I pointed out reasonably. Duck smirked.

"She doesn't know that. Now, let's get inside—Pic said it was
important. Better hear what he has to say for himself."

"Got a call from Hallies Falls," Picnic said, looking around the
table. "Not good news. Gage got attacked earlier today. The details
are fuzzy, but his old lady found him on her living room floor half
dead—all cut up. He's in emergency surgery right now."

"Was it club-related?" Ruger asked.

"Cord thinks so," Bolt said, sharing a look with Picnic. "They
took his colors. Someone wants to start a war."

The words hung heavy over the table. I didn't know about everyone else, but I was running through a mental list of potential suspects and coming up short. Who was strong enough to challenge us right now?

"You think it's the cartel?" Horse asked.

"Probably," Pic said. "Things may be heating up again north of the border. I think we should head over and check things out for ourselves. Rance is on his way, too. He's been hearing rumors on his end, so odds are good it's connected with that shit going down in Vancouver. Thoughts?"

"I'm with you," said Ruger. "We could ride over, pay Gage our respects, and do some poking around along the way. They're still a small chapter—might help them sleep a little better tonight, knowing they've got backup."

"Anyone disagree?" Pic asked. Nothing. "Okay, then. Duck can stay behind. We'll want a couple more bodies here just to cover our asses, too."

"I need to stay," I announced. "Izzy's having her tonsils out tomorrow. Hopefully it won't be a big deal, but they've got to put her under. Promised her I'd be there when she wakes up."

I waited for someone to protest, give me shit about bailing on the run.

"Understood," Pic said. "We'll leave the prospects with you. They can stay here at the Armory, make sure nobody tries to fuck with us on this front. I'll want to roll out in an hour—if you need to run home and grab some shit, now's the time. Assume things could get ugly, so we ride fully armed. Talk to Ruger if you need an extra weapon or more ammo."

He gave the table a sharp rap with the gavel, then stood up. I followed him out, catching his arm.

"Sorry about the run."

"No, it's better to have you here," he replied. "Don't need a brother on the road with us who isn't focused, anyway. And it's not good enough to leave the prospects—I'm more worried about Duck than anything else. I told him not to come out for church, but he still showed up. He's pushing himself already, hates to show any kind of weakness. The prospects and Deanna don't stand a chance of keeping him in line."

"Christ, and you think I do?" I asked, biting back a laugh. "Duck does what he wants. Always has."

"Yeah, and in two weeks he can again," Pic replied. "But the doc said if he doesn't take it easy, he could blow the artery in his groin right out—the one they shoved the catheter through. Once you start bleeding in a place like that, you don't stop until you're dead. Mel worked too hard saving his nasty ass for us to lose him over something stupid."

"Right, and what am I gonna do to stop him?" I said, shaking my head. "The bastard killed more guys in 'Nam than's in this whole club. He's not gonna listen to me."

Pic snorted.

"He killed more guys in 'Nam every time he tells the story," he replied. "I guess if he gives you enough shit, you can have Mel drug his ass. Or tie him down—I dunno. Just keep an eye on him, okay?"

"You're sticking me with an impossible job," I realized slowly. Picnic cocked a brow. "All you guys gotta do is figure out who's attacking the club and stop them. I have to control Duck."

"Note that I didn't volunteer to stay in Coeur d'Alene," he said smugly. "Good luck."

"Painter, get your ass out here!" Duck shouted from the bar. "Let's go talk to the prospects—make sure they understand what's expected of them."

"Did you plan for me to stay here?" I asked with a sudden flash of insight. "Because of Mel?"

Pic shrugged. "That's for me to know. Now you heard the man—get your ass out there. Duck's waiting."

Then Pic offered me a cheery salute. I flipped him off in response, because fuck him.

CHAPTER TWENTY-FOUR

MELANIE

"You want to watch TV?" I asked Izzy, snuggling down with her in my bed. *Our* bed—mine and Painter's. It still felt really weird, even after more than a month of us all living together.

"Yes," Izzy said, her voice small. The surgery had gone well, and now she was slurping down a blue Popsicle like her life depended on it. She'd already had two, but children are lawyers, and she'd taken the "unlimited" clause seriously. At some point I'd have to cut her off—didn't want to risk an upset stomach. Reaching for the remote, I flipped on the small TV sitting on top of my dresser. Izzy sighed in pleasure, and I kissed her forehead.

"Look who came to see you," Painter said from the door. Behind him was Sherri, carrying another box of Popsicles. London had brought some by earlier, and of course Painter had bought about a thousand of them, too.

Apparently Isabella had been extracting promises from everyone.

"How are you?" Sherri asked. Izzy, mesmerized by the television, gave her a thumbs-up. Sherri raised an eyebrow and I shrugged. She laughed. "I guess I'll just go put these in the freezer."

Painter's phone went off, and he stepped out to answer it. I cuddled closer to my girl, resting my eyes for a second. I hadn't slept for shit last night—I knew very well that a tonsillectomy was no big deal, but when it's your own kid going under, you tend to worry.

"Mel? Can you come out into the living room?" Painter asked, popping his head back in. "We need to talk."

Kissing Izzy again, I followed him out.

"What's up?" I asked.

"Duck," he said, his voice grim. "Apparently he's decided he wants to rake leaves. That was Deanna on the phone—Pic told her to call me if he tried to pull anything."

"Are you fucking kidding me? It's way too soon after his heart attack—not only are his ribs fucked, but the artery in his groin can't take that kind of pressure. If it blows, he'll bleed out in minutes. There won't be time to save him."

"No shit," he said, sighing. "I'm gonna run out there, check on him. Will you stick by the phone in case I need any medical advice?"

"Of course. You know, if he's being that big of a jerk, you should have him talk to me. I've seen people bleed out—it's not pretty. There's a lot of blood in the human body, and once it starts spraying from an artery, you're up a creek unless you get damned lucky. He can't fuck around with this."

"What's going on?" Sherri asked, coming out of the kitchen.

"Duck."

"Duck?"

"One of the brothers in the club," Painter said. "The one who had the heart attack—he's decided he wants to do some lawn work."

"Are you fucking kidding me?" she asked. "That was what, three days ago?"

"Yeah, I know," Painter replied, holding up his hands in surrender. "Okay, I'm heading out. Stay by the phone."

"Call me after you see him. I want to know he's all right."

"Sure thing."

He dropped a kiss on my forehead, then grabbed his keys and walked out the door. Seconds later I heard the roar of his bike.

"That's insane," Sherri growled. "Men are so stupid. The ribs alone should be enough to convince him to take it easy . . ."

"Tell me about it. I'm gonna go check on Izzy."

Back in the bedroom, I found Isabella sound asleep in the middle of the bed. The blue Popsicle had fallen down next to her, melting over my sheet. It looked like a Smurf had died there. Grabbing some tissues, I scooped it up and carried it back into the kitchen.

"She's out," I told Sherri. "Want a cup of coffee?"

"Always," she replied. "And we should talk. I have hot new gossip—remember how we're supposed to get a new cardiologist? Well I heard . . ."

An hour later I knew more about the new cardiologist than I ever wanted to know, up to and including his blood type. Literally. He was O negative—a universal donor—which apparently he liked to brag about.

What I didn't know was how Duck was doing. It should've taken Painter fifteen minutes to get out there at most.

"I'm going to call him."

"The cardiologist?" Sherri asked. "Okay, his number is—"

"No, Painter," I said, rolling my eyes. "Although maybe you should call Dr. Love Nuts and ask him out on a date. You're obviously obsessed with him."

She flipped me off as I grabbed my phone, and I returned the gesture out of habit. Hitting Painter's number, I waited for him to pick up.

Nothing.

That was weird.

Hanging up, I texted him, asking for an update. Then I went to check on Izzy again, who was still sound asleep. By the time I came back out, Sherri was rummaging through the fridge, and I realized how late it was getting—nearly seven.

"I've got a bad feeling about this," I told her. "Painter should've been in touch—he promised he'd let me know how Duck was doing. Now I'm worried that something's gone wrong."

Sherri nodded slowly.

"If he was stupid enough to be doing yard work, it's a possibility," she admitted. "You want to run out there?"

I looked at the phone again, then thought about my daughter.

"I don't want to leave Izzy, but I'm concerned."

"You go check on this Goose guy—"

"Duck."

"Whatever. You go check on him and I'll keep an eye on Izzy."

"I shouldn't be leaving her—she just had surgery this morning."

"You do remember that I'm an emergency room nurse?" Sherri said. "Not only that, I've known her half her life. She's as safe with me as she is with you. Probably safer, because I have more emotional distance. If she gets scared, I'll snuggle her. If she has a complication, I'll handle it. She probably won't even wake up while you're gone."

I picked up my phone, dialing Painter again.

Still nothing.

"Yeah, I think I'll go," I said finally. "Painter should've called."

"Git," she told me, flapping her hand at me. "Scoot. Skedaddle. I've got you covered."

Duck lived out toward Rathdrum, in an old house that'd seen better days. He had about twenty acres, most of it prairie. I'd gotten the address from London, who'd told me to call her once I figured things out.

It'd rained that morning and, just my luck, the driveway was a full-on mud pit. Painter'd parked his bike near the gate, next to the rusty old Chevy Duck drove when he couldn't ride. Eyeing the muck, I decided to follow his lead, pulling in next to him.

As I stepped out, my faded Converse squooshed down into the loose earth. Ick. Painter was gonna owe me for this.

So was Duck.

The house was set back far enough from the road that it took me a good ten minutes to walk there, including the time I lost falling on my ass, trying to get back up, and then falling down again—this time on my face. I checked my phone. Still nothing. If I got up there and found Painter and Duck sitting on the porch sharing a beer, they wouldn't need to worry about his catheter wound killing him.

I'd do it with my own bare hands.

The house came into sight, and I was about twenty feet away when I heard the shouting.

"When it's time to kill him, I want to do it!" a woman yelled. What the hell—was that Deanna?

A strange man's voice answered from the back of the house, although I couldn't make out the words. Holy shit. Pulling out my phone, I sent London a quick text.

> ME: There's something wrong here at Ducks house. I don't know what yet but I think you should call Reese

Silencing the phone, I slipped it back into my pocket, then started working my way around the house toward the back. It didn't take long to find a window, which thankfully had been left open a crack. Dropping down, I crawled forward through the wet earth, then slowly raised my head to peek inside.

Ah, fuck.

This was bad. Really bad. Like, pissing-your-pants bad. Painter was sitting in the center of Duck's kitchen in a wooden chair, hands cuffed behind his back. His legs had been tied to the chair's legs and there was a ragged bandanna gagging his mouth. Beyond him, lying across the floor, was Duck. His eyes were closed and there was a massive bruise forming on his face. Even worse, I saw a dark stain near his groin.

Blood or pee.

I had the feeling it was blood, although there wasn't enough for a full bleed out. Not yet. That could change any minute, though. I looked at Painter again. This time his eyes met mine. He gave his head a fast, hard shake, then jerked his chin at me. The message was clear—he wanted me to get out. I lifted my hand to my ear, pretending it was a phone, letting him know I was calling for help.

Dropping back down, I pulled out my cell and sent London another message, copying Reese.

> **ME:** Painter is being held prisoner in Ducks house. I'm outside
> looking in. Duck is down. Send help NOW

The door from the dining room to the kitchen crashed open, and then a big man I didn't recognize walked into the room, followed by Deanna. She looked different somehow—tougher. She walked with more swagger and held a gun. Standing over Duck, she casually kicked him in the balls.

My breath caught as I watched the stain, waiting for it to widen—how much abuse could his artery take?

"I've been wanting to do that for a hell of a long time," she said. The big guy stepped over to her, pulling her in for a hug.

"Sorry, Talia girl," he said. "I know it wasn't easy."

"God, his breath was so fucking bad in the mornings, Marsh," she said, sounding strangely childish, a whiny little girl. "I swear, blowing him was better than kissing him."

"It's over now," he replied, giving her another squeeze. Then he let her go, stepping back over to Painter. He reached out, slapping his face so hard it rocked the chair. "You fucked me up, *Levi.* Five fucking years I sat in a cell because of you. I already killed your friend, and now it's your turn. You got no idea how much I enjoyed cutting him up. I'm gonna have so much fun playing with you."

With that, he pulled out a pocket knife and flipped it open, slowly slicing across Painter's forehead, right along the hairline. Blood welled to the surface, sliding down his face. Fuck, fuck, *fuck!* No way I could sit here and watch them kill him. Like hell.

"Thought I might start by scalping you."

Talia grunted approvingly, and I dropped down below the window, wondering what the hell I should do—Reese would send help, but how long would it take? Most of the guys were out of town . . . Should I call the cops?

No. Painter didn't like cops. But Painter was about to end up *dead*. But hell, even if I called the cops, would they get here in time to save him? If only I had some kind of weapon . . . *like the gun hidden on his bike*. Could I save him and Duck with it? I wasn't sure, but I did know one thing—I wasn't going to save them by doing nothing.

I scrambled along the side of the house, slipping in the mud every few feet. Then I was off and running toward the parked vehicles. The mud sucked at my shoes and I fell twice along the way. None of it mattered. Time was passing—way too much time—and for all I knew they were already dead. After what felt like a year, I finally reached the bike, skidding to a stop next to it. At first I couldn't find the latch because my fingers were all muddy and numb from the cold. Then it fell open and I was grabbing the gun. With shaking hands, I pulled back the slide, thankful I'd taken the self-defense classes after Todger's attack last year.

You can do this.

Grabbing the extra clip, I started back toward the house, praying it wasn't too late. By now I was completely covered in mud, and I'd lost one of my shoes. None of it mattered, though. All that mattered was getting back in time.

Saving them.

But how?

Somehow I forced myself to slow down, to creep toward the window without making any noise—it wasn't easy. Adrenaline sent my heart racing and my lungs pumped hard. Every breath seemed louder than the last, but I forced myself to calm down. Focus.

Pretend you're at the ER, running a code, I told myself. *You're cool, you're professional. Nothing can touch you.*

The thought soothed me.

Reaching the window, I peeked up slowly. Oh God. Painter's face was a mass of blood. *Head wounds bleed a lot—don't panic!* Marsh stood over him, casually stretching like a man after a hard day's work. Then he glanced over toward Deanna.

"You want to do the next one?" he asked. She shrugged, and I tried to read her expression. If anything, she looked almost bored.

"I think you should just shoot him," she said, pulling out her gun. "I know you like to play with them, but we don't have a ton of time. His bitch will probably miss him sooner or later. We should get out of here—they're waiting for us up by the border."

"Five *years*, Talia. Five years I've been waiting for this moment. Cut me some fuckin' slack, okay?"

"Whatever," she said, pouting. "Want a beer?"

"No," he said, turning back to Painter. "I want to cut his face off."

I clutched the gun tighter. Should I try to shoot him? But there were two of them, and Deanna—no, *Talia*—had a gun, too. Would I cause more harm than good?

Talia started toward the fridge and I saw something move on the floor near her foot.

Duck.

His eyes were open, and he was tracking her. Catching my breath, I watched as the old man struck faster than a snake, catching her ankle and jerking her down to the ground. The gun went flying and he dove for it, raising it smoothly. It went off with a roar and Marsh was down.

Like, *down*—as in the top half of his skull was just missing.

Talia screamed, rushing toward Duck. She started kicking him as she fought for the weapon, and as I watched in shocked horror, the stain on his pants started to grow.

Rapidly.

Blood was pouring down his leg, running across the floor. A flood of it—bright red arterial blood. He didn't even seem to notice he was bleeding out, he just kept fighting until his body sagged to the floor, a sinking ship in a sea of red. Talia wrenched the gun out of his hands, raising it triumphantly as she shot him in the chest. Then she whirled around to Painter, raising it for another shot.

I raised my gun faster.

My first bullet caught her in the shoulder, shattering the window between us in an explosion of glass. The second went wide, and the third hit her leg. The fourth punched through the floor about six inches from Painter's foot, and I nearly dropped the gun, shocked by how easy it would be to accidentally kill him.

Talia was screaming and moaning, rolling around on the floor. Darting around the back of the house, I reached for the door, praying it wasn't locked. It wasn't, thank God—about time we had some good luck. Running into the kitchen, I launched myself at Talia, slamming her head into the floor as hard as Todger had slammed mine.

She went quiet.

I stood warily, looking for the gun she'd dropped—it'd skittered across the floor, stopping next to the stove. Grabbing it, I threw it out the shattered window, into the mud. Then I stumbled over to Painter, pulling the gag out of his mouth.

"Are you okay?" I gasped, running my eyes over his knife wound. Didn't look serious, thank God.

"Yeah, it's just one cut," he said. "That was amazing, Mel."

"I've got to get you free—do you know where the handcuff keys are?"

"Tie her up first," he said. "For all we know she's got another gun. Then check on Duck."

Duck was deader than a doornail—I knew that without checking. The old man was toast the minute his artery blew, I thought with professional detachment. I'd freak out later, but right now I had work to do.

"Duck's gone," I declared flatly. "He bled out—nobody survives that. What should I tie her with?"

"There's probably some rope under the sink," he said. "Duck keeps shit like that down there."

Crossing the kitchen, I had to wade through Duck's blood to reach the sink. As I passed, I knelt down for an instant, checking his pulse out of habit even though I knew it was pointless.

Nothing.

Not a surprise. Taking a deep breath, I pushed away the emotion, pretending he was just another patient in the ER. We lost them every day—if I shut down every time it happened I'd never make it through a shift.

Under the sink was a tarp, some rope, a big box of black garbage bags, duct tape, and a hacksaw. I blinked. *Don't think about it right now. Don't think at all. Just take the rope and tie her up.* I grabbed what I needed, moving back toward Talia's still body. I tied her hands first and then her legs before checking for a pulse.

It was there—faint, but definitely present.

Ripping open her shirt, I examined the bullet wound on her shoulder, then looked around for something to apply pressure. A towel, a cushion. Anything.

"She can survive this," I said tightly. "But we'll have to get her to a hospital fast. It'll be hard to get the ambulance back here, but—"

"No," Painter said. I stilled, turning to him. Blood still ran down his face, and his eyes were cold—like some monster out of a horror movie. "Look at what she did to Duck."

Following his gaze, I stared at the old man lying dead on the floor.

"Think about it—killing him wasn't enough for her," he continued. "First she fucked him, used him to lure me out here. You saw them—they planned to torture me, and they already admitted doing it to Gage. If we call an ambulance, we'll have to explain all this, and I don't know how it'll end."

I looked back down at Talia, watching as more blood oozed out. If I didn't do something very soon, she was going to die.

Could I sit back and watch?

Duck had given his life to save us. She'd wanted to shoot Painter—she'd been *bored* by his suffering. Closing my eyes, I tried to *think*. Tried to figure out what I should do . . .

"If she survives, she'll come after us again," Painter said softly. "What about Izzy?"

No, he was wrong. She wouldn't hurt an innocent little girl, would she?

She might.

I stood slowly, backing away.

"Do you know where the handcuff keys are?" I asked, swallowing. "I should get you loose."

"Probably in Marsh's pocket," he said, wincing. "You'll have to hunt for them."

Stepping over to the big man's body, I reached down and dug my hand into his jeans. He smelled like iron and meat, with a whiff of shit. God, how many times had I smelled that in the ER?

Too many.

I found a set of keys, pulling them out. "These little ones, here?"

"Looks right," Painter grunted. I crawled over to him, and a minute later his hands were out of the cuffs. Looking around, I found Marsh's knife and handed it to him. He sliced through the ropes holding his feet, and then he was free.

"Fucking hell," he muttered, standing slowly. "Come here."

I fell into his arms—covered in blood and mud—as my burst of adrenaline started to fade. What a mess. What a huge, disgusting mess, and I had no idea what we were supposed to do about it. Painter rubbed up and down my back, soothing me.

"You did good. It's okay," he whispered. "We'll figure it out. I need to call the club."

"I already did," I told him. "I mean, I texted them. London and Reese."

"They'll send someone," he said. "Let's go outside and wait. It's going to be okay, I promise."

Moving slowly, we walked back through the house and out onto the porch. Less than five minutes later, a Jeep Wrangler turned off the main road and started down the long driveway toward us.

"That's one of Reese's rigs," Painter said. "It's them."

The Wrangler pulled to a stop in front of the house, and the two Reaper prospects jumped out, both of them carrying guns. Right behind them was London. Not the version of her that I knew, but a woman you wouldn't want to mess with.

"What happened?" she asked, her voice clipped.

"Duck is dead," Painter said, sounding as exhausted as I felt. "So is Marsh—he used to be the president in Hallies Falls and he's the one who attacked Gage. Long fuckin' story. His sister, Talia, is inside. I don't know if she's dead or not. The bitch called herself

Deanna, and the whole thing was a setup. I didn't recognize her with the dark skin and the kinky hair. I mean, she looked like a black chick. Hell of a disguise, but when I met her five years ago she was definitely white. No fuckin' idea how she pulled that off."

"I'll go check on her," one of the prospects said. I tried to remember his name, but drew a blank. Everything seemed blank.

Shock.

"Mellie, are you hurt?" Loni asked, coming up to us. Her voice was softer now, gentler. I shook my head, thankful to have Painter holding me up.

"No, I'm fine," I said. "But I think I'm a murderer now. Or maybe not. Either way I need a shower."

Loni and Painter shared a look, and I was struck again by how hard her face was. Tough. Loni had layers I'd never seen before . . . Looking at her now, I could see her as a badass.

"Boonie is on his way," London said quietly. "Reese and the others, too. We'll handle this. Painter, can you take her down to the road, drive her out to our place? You can get cleaned up there, then go home to Izzy."

"I can stay and help you," he said. She shook her head.

"No, Mellie and Izzy need you more right now. I'll keep Reese posted—I'm sure he'll want to talk as soon as he gets back. Go get cleaned up. It'll be fine, I promise."

God, I hoped she was right.

PAINTER

We buried Duck that night.

Cremated him, actually. Reese and Boonie talked it over, and the verdict was that all the bodies needed to disappear, along with all the evidence. No way we'd be able to get a real death certificate for him, let alone bury him in a cemetery.

We took him and the others out into the forest and burned them, then buried them in two separate places, Talia and Marsh sharing an unmarked grave. We rolled a big rock across Duck's, though, pouring out a bottle of whiskey over it for good measure.

Then we took his colors back to the clubhouse and hung them on the wall in the chapel.

We figured he'd understand.

EPILOGUE

TWO AND A HALF YEARS LATER
MELANIE

I lifted my arms, trying to stretch out my back. I could definitely tell I was older with this pregnancy—things were creaking that hadn't creaked with Isabella. Not only that, I had a fraction of the energy.

Only two more weeks, then you get your body back again.

Well, except for the midnight feedings, lack of sleep, and general volume of poop to clean up. Grabbing my tablet, I walked into the living room, settling down on the couch. Izzy was over at Reese and London's place. Painter was working on a mural in the baby's room. It was a boy. I was pretty sure Painter already had a tiny baby Reapers cut made up for him. He'd bought him a little motorcycle ride-on toy, too. I kept pointing out that we had a good year before the kid would be big enough to use it, but Painter didn't care. He had baby fever. Seriously. I'd even caught him reading *What to Expect When You're Expecting* and taking notes.

We had a little intervention after that.

Sitting down, I flipped through the local headlines online. There was a new pizza place going in on Sherman Avenue. The public safety levy had passed, but the fund-raising campaign for the Fourth of July fireworks show was behind in their goals. A car had been found in the lake, and human remains were inside—they were in the process of identifying the body, but the cops didn't suspect foul play. The Post Falls Police Department had gotten a new police dog, and her name was Peaches.

The baby started to kick, and I set down the tablet, rubbing my belly slowly, admiring my diamond solitaire wedding ring set. I hadn't wanted anything fancy, but Painter insisted I deserved the real deal.

Now that his son was beating the crap out of my kidneys, I sort of had to agree.

"How's it going in there?" I asked the kid. "You about ready to come out and meet us?"

He kicked me again, harder. Persistent little shit. Rolling onto my side, I closed my eyes, drifting.

Might as well enjoy a nap while I still could.

The doorbell woke me up.

I blinked rapidly, hearing Painter's footsteps as he walked over to answer it.

"Can I help you?" he asked, a touch of challenge in his voice. Blinking, I pushed myself up to find a cop at the door. That was enough to wake me up—Duck's still body flashed through my mind, along with an image of Talia bleeding on his kitchen floor.

"I'm Detective Sam Grebil," he said. "I'm looking for Melanie Tucker."

"I'm her husband," Painter challenged. "Why do you want to talk to her?"

"I can really only talk to Ms. Tucker," he said, spotting me. I pushed myself up awkwardly, turtled by my big belly.

"I'm Melanie," I managed to say. "Melanie Brooks, now."

"Can I come in?"

"What's it about?"

He sighed. "Ms. Brooks, I may have news about your mother." That caught my attention in a big way. It'd been nearly nine years since she'd ditched me and my dad, and I hadn't heard a thing from her since. I rolled off the couch sideways, struggling to my feet.

"Excuse me?"

"It's about your mother—I spoke with your father already, but he indicated you aren't in touch with each other."

"He's kind of a bastard," I said bluntly. "We haven't talked in years."

"A car was found in the lake by a recreational diver earlier this week," Grebil said. "A woman's remains were found inside. Her body was badly decomposed, but she had Nicole Tucker's purse and driver's license in the car with her. The windows were closed, and we found the remains of groceries in the back seat—plastic yogurt cartons, that kind of thing. We're still investigating, but it looks like she drove off the road, rolling the car into the lake. The underbrush is thick enough through there that nobody noticed the wreck. Did anyone ever file a missing persons report?"

I shook my head slowly, trying to process his words.

"No, she took off," I said. "I mean, she and my dad, they didn't get along. He used to hit her sometimes. One day she was just gone—we figured she ran away from him."

"We'd like to get a DNA sample," he said, eyeing me with compassion. "So we can positively identify her. Until then we won't know for sure that it's your mother, but it's her car, her ID, and the height is right. I don't think she ran off and left you, Ms. Brooks— I think she died in an accident."

I swayed, and Painter put an arm around me, offering his strength.

"I can't believe that," I whispered. "She . . . she *left*."

Grebil just looked at me, his face tired but compassionate.

"Like I said, we won't know for sure until we get the DNA."

"There's no chance my dad . . . *hurt* her . . . is there?"

"No evidence for it," he told me. "At least not yet. We're still investigating, but there's no sign of trauma. The medical examiner thinks she probably drowned."

"Can I see her?"

He coughed, looking uncomfortable.

"Ms. Brooks, her remains are skeletal. I don't think it's a good idea."

"I'm a nurse. I'm used to seeing bodies."

"Not like this," he said firmly. "Will you allow me to collect a sample?"

Nodding slowly, I stepped aside, letting him into the house. He asked a series of questions about the day my mom left—not that I had much to offer, since it wasn't like she'd said goodbye—and took a cheek swab. Then he gave me his card and left.

That was it.

The whole interview took less than thirty minutes, yet it changed my whole world. She hadn't abandoned me—it'd been an accident. Beyond her control. I felt almost dizzy, torn between sadness and a strange sense of comfort that she hadn't abandoned me.

"How are you?" Painter asked, studying me carefully. We were sitting on the couch and I leaned into him, holding my stomach.

"I don't know," I admitted. "This is probably going to sound wrong, but I think I'm relieved."

"Because she didn't leave you?"

"Yeah," I said. "I'm not happy she's dead, of course. But . . . she didn't ditch me. It was an accident—that changes a lot."

He rubbed my hair, kissing the top of my head.

"It changes everything."

We sat there for a while, him playing with my hair and me thinking over what the detective had told me. Then I glanced at the clock and saw what time it was.

"Shit," I said, sitting up fast. "We're supposed to be out at the Armory right now. I promised Loni I'd be there by four to collect Izzy. She's got all the food to organize for the party."

"I texted her, gave her a heads-up," Painter told me. "We can skip the party—they'll understand."

I considered his words. Did I want to visit with people tonight? Em and Kit were in town . . . and Marie had a car seat she'd offered to lend me. Not only that, I'd promised Dancer I'd give her boys a ride home later so she could stay and party with Bam Bam.

"No," I said, shaking my head. "We should go. I want to see everyone—be around people."

"Are you sure?" he asked. "This is a lot to take in. Nobody would blame you."

"It's not about them blaming me," I replied slowly. "But hearing something like this—it's a lot to process. She was my mom, my family . . . But Loni's kind of my mom, too. And now we have a new family. Not just you and me and Izzy, but the rest of them. I really think I'd rather be around our people tonight."

Leaning over, he kissed me.

"All right," he said. "But if you need some space, let me know."

I smiled.

"I will. I think I'm fine, though. Really. You're my family now. I still miss my mom and I always will, but I'll get through it. And I love you."

"I love you, too."

I would be okay. *We* would be okay.

And we'd live happily ever after.

For real.

AUTHOR'S NOTE: *This bonus epilogue takes place in Hallies Falls, on the day following Painter's confrontation with Marsh in Ellensburg.*

BONUS EPILOGUE

TINKER

"Are you sitting down?" My best friend, Carrie, sounded breathless over the phone. "Do you have wine? I have news. Big news."

My hand halted, wineglass inches from my mouth. Damn, she knew me far too well . . . *You're getting predictable with old age.*

"Yes, I'm sitting on the porch with my wine, just like every Sunday afternoon," I admitted. "Just half a bottle, though. It's been a shitty week—I've earned it. Am I going to need more?"

"Maybe," she said, her voice far too serious. *Uh oh.* "You know your sexy tenant? The one who's been doing all that work around the building, and mowing the lawn without his shirt?"

"I'm aware," I replied dryly, taking another sip of wine. "I'm the one who invited you over to watch him with me, remember?"

It wasn't something I was proud of, but I'd developed quite the weakness for my newest tenant, Cooper Romero. He'd been living in the unit directly behind my house, which fronted one side of the C-shaped apartment building my parents had owned my entire life. He was gorgeous, friendly, nice, and had a girlfriend who was not only hotter than hell, she was probably fifteen years younger than me. Seeing as I pegged him at my own age or slightly older, I obviously wasn't his type.

Didn't mean I couldn't enjoy the view.

"Well, something big happened down in Ellensburg yesterday, at the car show. You know he's been hanging out with the motor-cycle club a lot, right?"

"Yes, I'd noticed," I said, my voice turning sour. I wasn't a fan of the club, at least not in recent years. They'd always been a part of the town, but lately they'd gotten out of hand. People were scared of them these days, and with good reason.

"Well, they got in some kind of big fight and tore up a bar. Then the cops arrested all of them. Not just the guys in the club, but any-one with them, and Cooper was right in the thick of it."

"What?" I asked, sitting up. Cooper didn't seem like the violent type. I mean, he was big and tough and all that, but he was always so gentle with me. I'd thought the time he was spending with the Nighthawks was just because of his girlfriend, Talia.

Their president was an asshole and a bully, and his sister—the hated girlfriend, and yes, I'm saying that out of petty jealousy—was flat-out mean. She'd caught me staring at him a while back and threatened me. Like, seriously threatened me. With a knife.

Said she'd cut me if I touched her man.

Despite all that, I'd held out hope for Cooper. I mean, he was definitely a biker, but he'd been fantastic about doing work around the place in exchange for reduced rent. Reliable. Friendly, even. We'd had a few dinners together, watched a movie one evening. I'd have thought he was interested in me if Talia wasn't spending four or five nights a week at his place.

Screwing the skinny little witch was bad enough, but this busi-ness of getting arrested . . . that was a bigger deal.

"Guess I didn't know him as well as I thought," I admitted, stomach churning. "Although anyone can get caught up in a bar fight. Just because they arrested him doesn't mean—"

"There were drugs," she added, and I heard genuine regret in her voice. "Lots of drugs. Meth, apparently. I guess a bunch of the guys were carrying it."

I coughed. "Meth?"

"Yup," she said. "They aren't saying what'll happen to them, but it's not good. This might be the end of the club here in Hallies

Falls. I wonder if he has drugs in his apartment. You should go check—if he's dealing, you need him out of there. You can't trust a guy just because he's hot and mows the lawn without a shirt."

Lifting my glass, I chugged it dry. My nose prickled, and I sniffed. Shit, why was this bothering me so much? It wasn't like I really even knew him.

"Thanks for telling me," I said. "Guess that's one fantasy man I can cross off the list."

"I'm sorry," she replied. "But it's for the best. If he's a bad guy, it's better to find out now so you can evict his ass. That club has gotten worse and worse, everyone knows it."

"I can't evict someone for getting arrested. That's illegal."

"It's a month-to-month lease, right?" she asked. "You don't need a reason. Just give him thirty days' notice and get rid of him. You don't want that kind of trash around your place, Tinker. You've got enough on your plate already."

Carrie was a great friend, but she'd always been bossy, ever since kindergarten. She'd given me the information, which I appreciated, but I also wanted to process it on my own.

"I have to go, Carrie. There's someone coming, one of the other tenants. I'll talk to you later."

Hanging up the phone, I looked across the empty porch toward the equally empty sidewalk, wondering why the news about Cooper bothered me so much.

Had I really been stupid enough to actually fall for him?

Maybe a little bit.

Crap.

Reaching for the wine bottle, I refilled my glass. *Should* I evict him? It seemed like common sense to get rid of a potential trouble-maker, but one of the main reasons I'd left Hallies Falls all of ten minutes after my high school graduation was to get away from the gossips. This town was full of small-minded, judgmental people who wouldn't hesitate to brand someone for life for one stupid mistake.

No, I wouldn't evict him.

Cooper had been arrested, but he hadn't been convicted. Innocent until proven guilty—that's how I'd approach this. I'd give him the same respect that I wished people had given me.

It was just after ten that night. I leaned forward into my mirror, rubbing moisturizer on my face and wondering if the tiny lines at the edges of my eyes were bigger than they were yesterday. Of course not, that was ridiculous . . . but I was definitely getting older, no question.

Thirty-six.

Only four years from forty, which meant I'd be officially middle-aged soon. I wasn't *ready* to be middle-aged—half the time I hardly felt like an adult. It wasn't fair. The roar of a motorcycle outside caught my attention, and I walked over to my bedroom's second-story window to look outside.

There he was—Cooper.

I watched as he backed the bike into the curb, then swung his leg over, glancing toward my house. The outdoor lights he'd installed for me less than a week earlier cast long shadows in the darkness, and I cocked my head. Something was different. I studied him, trying to figure out what it was. He wore his usual leather boots and faded jeans. Dark hair pulled back in a braid, leather vest with . . . Wait. This wasn't the one he'd been wearing every other time I'd seen him. That one had a Harley Davidson patch on the back, but this looked more like what the Nighthawk Raiders MC wore. Not the same as theirs, but the same style.

I waited for him to walk over to his apartment entrance, a small doorway off the ground floor not far from where he'd parked. Instead he started around the side of the building toward my porch. Crap, he was obviously coming to talk to me, and here I was without any makeup, my hair pulled back in a ponytail, and wearing jammies. Not sexy jammies, either, just a pair of boy shorts and an old T-shirt that'd been washed so many times I'd forgotten its original design.

Downstairs, my doorbell rang.

For an instant, I considered pretending I wasn't home. *Brilliant,*

Tinker. Your car is parked outside and your lights are on, but I'm sure he won't notice that you're hiding. Instead, I grabbed a long, flowing satin robe and pulled it on over my jammies before tying the belt around my waist—it'd always reminded me of something a 1940s movie star would wear. Hopefully it would give me confidence as I faced him.

Would he mention the arrest? Should I? God, how awkward. The bell rang again, and I ran down the stairs, opening the door in a rush.

"Sorry," I said breathlessly. "I was upstairs, and . . ."

My voice trailed off as I realized something was wrong. Really wrong. Cooper's face was hard, and his eyes burned with strange intensity. He also seemed bigger somehow, like I was seeing him stand up straight for the first time. This was the man I knew, only different. Still sexy as hell, but with an edge of danger I'd never felt before.

I stared at him, wondering why he was here and hoping to hell he wouldn't notice that my nipples had just gotten hard. I'd had to start investing in a whole new set of padded T-shirt bras since he'd moved in . . . too bad I wasn't wearing one right now.

"Hi, it's a little late—"

"Time to talk, Tinker," he said bluntly, pushing into the house. He caught my arm, jerking me away from the door before he slammed it shut and locked it with a decisive click. Then he walked across my mother's prized front parlor like he owned the place, stopping next to her antique mahogany credenza.

"What's going on?" I asked. He ignored the question, reaching back behind his vest to pull out a handgun, which he set down on one of Grandma Garrett's hand-knitted doilies. Then he caught the end of his belt, unhooking the buckle. Wait. Why was he doing that? Talking doesn't require taking off your belt. Oh, and there was the whole gun thing. That wasn't exactly comforting either.

I thought about what Carrie had told me. This was a mistake, a huge mistake. I should've listened to her, kept my doors locked. So what if he thought I was hiding?

"Cooper, I think—"

"Gage," he said shortly, whipping the belt out of its loops, freeing a big knife I'd never noticed him wearing before today. He dropped it next to his other weapon.

"Gage?" I asked hesitantly, swallowing. My instincts were screaming at me to make a run for it, except that was crazy. Maybe I didn't know him very well, but if Cooper wanted to hurt me, he'd had plenty of opportunities before tonight. The back of his vest caught my attention—there was a patch in the center with a skull on it. Above it was another patch that read "Reapers," and below a third that said "Idaho."

I knew jack shit about motorcycle clubs, but even I'd heard of the Reapers MC. Fucking hell, what was going on here?

"My name is Gage," he said, turning and stalking toward me.

"Your name is Gage?" I parroted weakly, taking a step back. "But I saw your ID, with your rental application."

"Fake," he said bluntly. "All of it was fake. Lot of shit's gone down in the last two days. Things have changed, so it's time for us to talk."

Cooper—no, *Gage*—invaded my space, pinning me against my own front door. One hand came up, cradling my throat for an instant. I felt the strength in his tough, calloused grip and another wave of fear hit me. Unfortunately, a wave of lust hit, too, because our bodies were officially touching more than they ever had before. It felt every bit as good as I'd imagined, too. Then the hand slid upward, and he dug his fingers into my hair, pulling it loose from the hair band. Not completely, just enough for him to cradle the back of my head.

"There's a lot of ground to cover, so I'm gonna give you the short version for now," he said harshly, catching and holding my eyes. I swallowed as one of his thighs pushed between my legs. He surrounded me, using up more than his fair share of oxygen. It left me dizzy. "I haven't been free since I got here. Now I am, which means I'm taking what's mine."

I squeaked, blinking rapidly as I tried to decide if I was scared or turned on. He leaned into me, nose brushing my ear as he took a deep breath.

"What do you mean, you're taking . . . ?" I was so confused that I wasn't even sure what question to ask. None of this made any sense. He'd never treated me like anything but a friend, so what the hell was going on here?

"I'm taking *you*," he said with quiet force. His leg separated mine, and I felt something long and hard against my stomach. My hormones surged, because I knew what that was, and I knew what it wanted, too.

Oh, *wow*.

This couldn't be happening. Could it? I'd had so many dreams about him over the past two months. Maybe I was asleep. Yeah, that had to be it. I'd wake up in a minute, and then I'd be able to laugh at how silly I'd been.

"You're mine now," he continued, rubbing his nose along my cheekbone. Then he pulled back, catching my gaze again. "A lot's gone down, but right now the critical information is that you belong to me. You're my property. You don't understand what that means, and that's okay. I'll teach you. But when you look back at this moment, I want you to remember there was a before I claimed you and an after. Now it's after. You got me?"

I'd never *gotten* anyone less. I swallowed, then bit my own lip. Not to be coy, but to wake myself up, because this dream was getting less sexy and more scary. *Ouch*. Okay, that should do it . . . Staring at him, I realized he was still in front of me. This was *real*.

"What about your girlfriend?"

"First, Talia has never been my girlfriend—that bitch is nothing. My club sent me here to check on the Nighthawks, and she was the easiest way to get inside. Fucking her was like fucking a praying mantis. She's gone, or she will be soon. Either way, I'm done with her."

I frowned, shaking my head because that was a nasty, nasty thing to say. Just hearing it sent a thrill through me, though, because apparently I'm a terrible person. Still, this was all too much, so I pushed against his chest, trying to get some space. In an instant, he caught both my wrists and raised them over my head. Then he was holding them with one hand while the other slid into my hair again, this time holding it just tight enough to hurt, twisting my head up toward his. He leaned forward, lips hovering over mine, and spoke.

"I've been watching you twitch that ass of yours for too long," he whispered, licking his lips. "You sit on that pretty little porch of yours with your friends. You pretend you aren't scoping me out, but you are. You've wanted it bad for a long time, and now you're gonna get it."

Then his mouth took mine, tongue shoving inside. *You belong to me now,* he'd said. *Remember this moment.*

Holy. Crap.

What'd I gotten myself into?

AUTHOR'S NOTE: *This is a prequel short story about Melanie and Painter's first meeting. It takes place one year before the beginning of* Reaper's Fall *(when Painter is released from prison), against the background of action from* Reaper's Stand. *I thought you might enjoy reading it.*

SUGAR AND SPICE

MELANIE

I fell for Levi "Painter" Brooks the first time I saw him, although in all fairness I did have a head injury at the time.

It was a weird start to a relationship, too.

You see, I blew up a house.

It wasn't on purpose, and in my defense I'd had a really shitty day. My mom had taken off earlier in the week. Just up and left while I was at work on Monday, and she never came back. Neither me or my dad heard a thing from her, and while she'd always been sort of flaky, she'd never done anything like this before. By Wednesday night, I broke down and asked him if we should report her missing to the police.

He'd thrown his beer bottle at me, shouting about how "the whore" must've gotten herself a new man. She'd left me because I was nothing, just like she was nothing.

Then he'd told me to go buy him more beer.

I decided to call Loni instead.

Not long afterward, I blew up her house.

• • •

London Armstrong was my best friend's aunt. Jessica and I had been tight for years, and as my own mother drifted further and further from reality, they'd become my second family. She'd told me to head on over to her place and let myself in, that she'd see me later that night. I went over there and made myself some macaroni and cheese on her gas stove.

A couple hours later the house exploded.

Gas leak.

Nobody said it was my fault, but I knew it had to be. I'd been the last one to use the stove, so there you have it. Anyway, fate has a weird sense of humor, because that's how I met Painter. The next day, I mean. At the hospital.

He gave me a lift on his motorcycle, and I fell in love.

God I was young. Young and stupid.

"I sort of thought you meant a car when you said you'd give me a ride home," I whispered, staring at the tall, beautiful, terrifyingly perfect man standing in front of a shiny black Harley with custom gold trim. He'd been introduced to me as Painter, and apparently he was part of the same motorcycle club as Loni's new boyfriend, Reese.

"She did have a head injury," London pointed out, her voice tart. She held my arm protectively, staring between me and Painter with worry written all over her face.

"Sort of thought the car was implied," said Reese, sighing.

"You didn't say and it's not like she's really hurt or anything," Painter replied with a shrug. He glanced at me. "You got a headache?"

I did, but he was so pretty and perfect and I didn't want to jinx this. Blond, spiky hair. Strong, straight cheekbones and muscular arms that I just knew would be strong enough to pick up a girl like me and carry me wherever I needed to go.

"No, I don't actually," I said, feeling nervous but excited, too. I shot another look at the bike, imagining what it would feel like to sit behind him, holding him as we flew down the highway. "Although they said no sudden movements."

"So you'll hold on tight," Painter said, eyes playing with mine. He licked his lip and I felt my insides twitch.

Ohmygodhe'ssohotandhe'slookingrightatme!

"Oh, for fuck's sake," Reese said, reaching into his pocket for his phone. "I'll call someone else."

"No, it's okay," I said quickly, hoping Mr. Hot Bod wouldn't change his mind about giving me a ride. "I'll try riding the bike."

I'll try riding you, sexy . . .

Wow. Those kind of pervy thoughts weren't like me at all. Painter winked and I would've fainted on the spot if I wasn't so damned healthy and not the fainting type. Shame, too, because he'd totally catch me with those muscular arms of his. I could sense it. I gave him a little smile, hoping I wasn't coming off as dorky.

"You watch yourself with her," London snapped, crossing her arms and jutting out a hip. I stared at her, shocked—that wasn't like Loni at all. Had she just ruined it for me?

Painter raised a brow.

"Fuckin' priceless, prez," he said, then smiled at me again, a smile so beautiful that it made me dizzy. *You're dizzy because you have a concussion,* my common sense pointed out.

I gave it a mental finger, because fuck common sense.

"You comin' or not?" he asked, swaggering over to his bike and climbing on. Deliberately avoiding London's gaze, I followed him, hopping up behind before he had a chance to change his mind.

"Hold on, babe," he told me, his voice low and smooth. Like whiskey. Not that I drank much whiskey, but I'd had some at our high school graduation party, at the beginning of the summer. Putting my hands up, I touched the sides of his hips hesitantly. He caught them, pulling them tight around his stomach. I could feel his hard abs through the thin fabric of his shirt, and smell the leather of his motorcycle vest thingie. My entire front was leaning against his entire back, and I felt dizzy again. Then he reached down and touched my knee, giving it a quick squeeze.

Oh. My. God.

• • •

The ride took about ten minutes. Ten glorious minutes that included a short stretch of highway as we left Coeur d'Alene behind, which meant we got to go *fast*. Then he was pulling off and parking in front of an old farmstead that had a well-lived in, well-loved kind of wear around the edges. He turned off the bike, and the sudden absence of noise and vibration left my ears ringing. We sat there for a minute as I collected my thoughts. He touched my knee again.

"Gotta let go if you want off the bike, babe," he said softly.

I jerked my hands back instantly, wondering how big of an ass I'd made of myself. Then I was scrambling to get off, looking everywhere but his face because I couldn't bear to see him looking disgusted, or worse yet, sorry for me.

"Come on," he said, touching the small of my back gently, guiding me toward the porch. "I've got the code to get you inside. You can go crash for a while, get some rest."

"Thanks," I said, daring to look up at him. His eyes were everywhere, scanning the yard for what, I had no idea. Five minutes later we were upstairs, looking at what had to be a girl's bedroom.

"You can stay in here, Em won't mind," he told me. "I'll be downstairs if you need anything."

"Who's Em?" I asked.

"President's daughter," he answered, and his voice held a hint of something. Not sadness, but . . . *something*. "She's a little older than you, about my age. Get some rest."

I waited until I heard his footsteps going down the stairs before I pulled off my jeans and climbed into the bed. My head really was hurting now, and while they'd given me pain meds at the hospital, I wouldn't be able to take another dose for a while longer. Lying there, I stared at the ceiling, wondering what Painter was doing downstairs.

Did he have a girlfriend?

Right, like it even mattered. He'd been sweet to me, but he was probably sweet to little old ladies, too. Guys like that didn't go for girls like me.

Girls who were nothing.

The thought hurt, but eventually I drifted off. When I woke it was nearly five. Wandering downstairs, I found Loni and Reese sitting in the living room, her perched on his lap as they talked quietly.

"Sorry, I didn't mean to interrupt you," I said, feeling like an intruder.

"Don't worry about it," Reese replied, sounding resigned. Loni pushed off him, then came over to study me carefully. She was shorter than I was, and I felt awkward and gawky next to her.

"How are you feeling?" she asked, her eyes sharp.

"Good, my head hardly hurts at all," I said, and this time it was the truth. "Although I'm starving."

Then I snapped my mouth shut, because it sounded like I was begging for food, which I guess I was. I mean, I was sort of trapped here, out in the country at a strange house owned by a man I didn't even know, and whose only tie to me was that he was sleeping with my best friend's aunt.

That's pretty damned tenuous.

Loni smiled. "If you're hungry, that means you're healthy. I picked up some new clothes for you earlier. They're in the bag."

She pointed to a Target bag sitting on the floor next to the stairwell. I'd just leaned over to grab it when Painter walked into the room from the back of the house.

"How you doin'?" he asked.

"Better," I managed to reply, feeling shy.

"Get changed and we'll go out to dinner," Reese announced. "It's been a long day."

"Okay," I said gratefully, then ran upstairs to put on my new clothes. Hopefully Loni had gotten me something cute.

Painter invited himself along with us, which pissed Loni off for reasons I couldn't quite understand. I knew she was protective, but it wasn't like he was doing anything.

Sure, he'd insisted that I ride with him to the restaurant (which kicked ass, I might add). And he was sitting next to me in the booth, his thick, male thigh pressed up against the side of mine, which gave me little flutters and chills. A couple times he leaned over to ask if my food was all right, and when we finished he draped his arm across the back of the booth, right behind my head.

I'd sat there, wanting him so bad it took everything I had not to shiver. I'd have given anything to kiss him. At one point he even reached down and gave my knee another of those little squeezes, nearly giving me a heart attack.

Loni glared at him throughout.

Reese rolled his eyes and ordered another beer.

Afterward, Painter gave me a ride back to Reese's house, and I swear if he'd asked me, I would've done anything for him. *To* him. But he didn't . . . Nope, he just dropped me off.

But as I got off his bike, he tucked a strand of my hair back behind my ear and skimmed his fingers across my cheekbone. I really did shiver then, because how could I not?

Two days later I was bored out of my mind.

I'd found myself in a weird limbo out at the Hayes house, because I had no transportation or way to get to work. There wasn't anyone to talk to, either—Reese and Loni were gone most of the time, her working and him doing club stuff. There had been some big party the night before, but yours truly wasn't invited.

Instead I just sat around, waiting for something to happen. Reese still made me nervous, but I trusted London and it wasn't like I had any other options. Even the money I'd managed to hide from my dad was gone, burned up in the explosion. Now all I had were the clothes Loni had given me.

Two pairs of panties. One bra. A pair of shorts and a pair of jeans, two tank tops and a sweatshirt.

That was it—the sum total of all my worldly possessions.

I needed to take action, figure things out . . . But when I tried to talk to Loni and Reese about the next step, neither of them had time for me. Loni had work stuff, Reese had club stuff, and they both just kept telling me to rest up and let my head heal.

A girl can only rest so much, though.

That's why I was just sitting on the porch Saturday afternoon, trying to read when I heard the bikes coming. Now, if I'd learned anything over the past two days, I'd learned that there were always bikes coming and going from Reese Hayes's house, so I didn't think too much of it when I saw the motorcycles turn into the driveway. Then I recognized one of the riders as Painter, and my heart clenched. (Okay, so it wasn't my heart that clenched, it was something centered a lot lower in my body, but don't judge me. Painter was the kind of hot that no sane woman can resist. It never occurred to me to try.)

"Hi," I managed to say as he swaggered toward the porch—and yeah, he had the swagger down cold, trust me.

"Hey," he replied, giving me that same slow grin that'd first melted me at the hospital. (And the house. And the restaurant . . .) "This is Puck. Me and him are gonna hang out here tonight."

I shot a look at his friend, who was a tall, solidly built guy with darkish skin, darker hair, and a nasty scar across his face. He didn't look much older than me, but the flatness of his eyes sort of freaked me out.

"Reese didn't say anything about someone coming over," I replied, torn. I wanted Painter around, but his friend? Not so much. "I should probably check with Loni."

"Feel free," Puck said. "But we got orders. President says we're watching the house and keeping an eye on you, so that's what we're doing."

Painter scowled at him. "Way to scare her, fuckwad."

Puck didn't say anything, just crossed his arms over his chest, making it clear he was here to stay. Okay. This was getting weird fast.

"You know, why don't you just come in?" I said quickly. I hated it when people fought. Mom and Dad fought all the time, at least until she stopped giving a shit and started smoking pot constantly. "I think there's some pork chops in the fridge. I'll make them for dinner, does that sound good?"

Painter smiled at me again, and this time there was something strained about the expression. "Sounds perfect, babe. Can't wait."

• • •

Dinner was weird. For one thing, we didn't talk. None of us. We just sat and ate in the same room together, the clicking of our knives and forks almost painfully loud. Painter was nothing like he'd been before . . . He was still nice to me, but distant. No little knee touches, no lingering glances.

Nothing whispered in my ear.

The situation with Puck was strange, too. I'd assumed they were friends, but soon realized they hardly knew each other. Not that it mattered—they'd been sent to the house with orders to watch over me, and that's what they planned to do. This burst my bubble in a big way, because I'd been secretly hoping that Painter had wanted to see me again. In reality, I was an assignment. I didn't know why Reese thought I needed a babysitter, but he obviously did.

I'd just finished my pork chop when Painter suggested we watch a movie.

"It'll help pass the time," Puck agreed, anything but friendly. "I'll see what's available. Good food—thanks."

He stood and carried his plate into the kitchen, then passed by us again on his way to the living room. Painter leaned back in his own seat, looking me over.

"How are you doing?" he asked, and it sounded like he was actually interested in the answer. I shrugged.

"Good," I said. "Although it's a little weird . . . I don't feel safe going home. Loni's place is gone. I'm not quite sure what I'm still doing out here, but I don't have anywhere else to go, either. I can't even get to my job, because I don't have a car. Loni and Reese are never here. It's hard to wrap my head around what comes next, you know?"

Huh. That was a *lot* more than I'd planned on sharing. I stared down at my plate, wondering if I sounded like a whiny little girl. Painter didn't respond, so I shot him a look under my lashes. He was studying me intently, although I couldn't read his expression.

"Wish I had an answer for you," he finally said. "It's a fucked up situation and I got no idea what happens next."

That caught me off guard, because it was so honest. Whenever I managed to corner Loni, she'd just tell me that everything would be okay, and that she'd take care of me. Reese said to calm down, that it would all work out.

Hearing the truth was scary, but refreshing, too.

"Thanks," I blurted out.

"For what?" he asked.

"For being honest. Everyone is telling me that things are fine, but they aren't. I've got no home, no family to help me, no transportation and if I don't find a way to get to work soon, I'll lose my job. Not that I'd even *know* if I got fired, because my phone blew up with the rest of the house. And I've probably got a bazillion dollars in medical bills, too. It *is* a fucked up situation, so why is everyone pretending it's not?"

He seemed startled by my sudden burst of speech, which I could understand. I'd startled me, too.

"You know, the house probably wasn't your fault," he said slowly. I shook my head, wishing it were true.

"I think I left the gas burner turned on after I made my macaroni and cheese," I admitted. "What else could've caused it?"

"Melanie, leaving on a burner for a couple hours doesn't blow up a house," he told me, the words gentle. "I mean, it's not something you want to go around doing, but whatever happened, it was because of something bigger than you cooking macaroni. It's not your fault. And Loni's insurance will probably cover your medical bills, too."

"I really hope that's true about the house," I said, although I knew in my gut it wasn't. I'd caught a whiff of gas earlier that evening and had meant to investigate. Instead I'd gotten distracted thinking about my mom. "And I guess the medical bills don't really matter anyway. Not like they can collect."

He nodded, reaching for the beer he'd grabbed from the fridge earlier. Taking a long drink, he glanced toward the living room, where I could hear Puck rummaging around.

"You don't have to watch a movie with us if you don't want to," he said quietly. "You can go upstairs and rest."

"I'll watch it," I insisted, and not just because I wanted to spend more time with him. I'd had my fill of rest over the past two days. Just having another human being around to talk to was a relief— the fact that he was a super sexy human made it that much better. "Here, let me get your plate."

"No, that's all right, I'll take it," he said, so we carried the dishes into the kitchen together. He stood and watched while I loaded the dishwasher. Every time I passed him, I caught his scent. Leather and something strange . . . like paint thinner.

"Is Painter your real name?" I asked, avoiding his eyes.

"Nope, my real name is Levi Brooks," he said. "But I like to paint, and most guys in the club use a road name, so there you have it."

"Like, paint houses?"

He laughed. "No, pictures. I'm into art."

That surprised me. I must've shown it on my face, because he gave another low chuckle. "Let me guess, you assumed bikers aren't sophisticated enough to appreciate art?"

I coughed, looking away. I'd be damned if I'd answer.

"You're cute when you blush," he said, reaching over to catch a lock of my hair, tugging on it gently. *He called me cute!* My heart stopped for an instant, and it was hard to follow the rest of his words. "And yeah, I like art. I do a lot of the custom work down at the body shop. All the gold on my Harley is my own, too. Sometimes I do bigger projects. Usually painting on boards for customers who want portraits of their bikes, believe it or not."

"Wow," I said. God, he was so out of my league—hot *and* talented.

"What about you?" he asked. "What do you do?"

"Well, right now I'm waiting tables," I told him, wishing I had a more interesting job. "But I'm starting school in the fall, at North Idaho College. And once I get all my prerequisites done, I'm going to study nursing. I like taking care of people."

"Yeah, I can see that. You're friends with Jessica, right? London's niece?"

I nodded.

"You take care of her a lot?" I shrugged, because I took care of her all the time, but he didn't need to know that. At least, I'd taken care of her until she'd run off to California to live with her mom. She'd been super pissed at London for dragging her out of a party at the Reapers clubhouse, which was my fault in a way.

I was the one who ratted her out.

I'd heard a lot of rumors about those parties, about how wild they were. How a girl could get into trouble. Looking at Painter, I believed those rumors, too—if he crooked his finger at me, I'd come running like a shot.

The thought caught me off guard, and I frowned. Since when did I come running for a guy?

"You okay?" Painter asked.

"Sure," I said, although I was feeling more than a little off-balance. Not physically, but mentally, because in the past two days I'd gone from being afraid of bikers to really, really liking this particular one.

How many girls did he have waiting for him, back at that club-house of his?

I looked up to find him staring at me, his face thoughtful.

"Let's go see what Puck found for movies," he said. "And Mel?"

"Yeah?"

"Things aren't okay, but they will be. You can get through this."

"Thanks," I whispered, and to my disgust I felt hot tears filling my eyes. I hated crying, hated the kind of girls who cried. Hated looking and feeling weak, but Painter just pulled me into his arms, holding me tight as sobs started shaking my body.

I missed my mom really bad, and I was scared.

He rubbed my back, whispering softly into my ear, although I had no idea what he was saying. All I knew was that for the first time in forever—maybe years—I felt safe.

An hour later, that whole "safe" thing had passed.

I was sitting in the living room, huddled in a blanket on the couch as I watched a scarred and twisted man carrying a chainsaw creep up behind an innocent young woman.

He was going to kill her.

I knew this because I'd already watched him kill at least ten other people with his horrible weapon, and the movie wasn't even halfway over yet.

Why the hell hadn't I gone upstairs when I had a chance?

Now I couldn't, of course. Not alone in the darkness of the stairwell—not even if I turned on every light in the damned place. My mind could tell me there wasn't anyone lying in wait to kill me all it wanted, but my gut knew better—the instant I stuck my feet outside the blanket, they'd get cut off.

This sucked, because I really had to pee.

"You okay?" Painter murmured, leaning down close to me. I jumped, startled, and then he was wrapping his arm around my shoulders, pulling me closer to him. The saw roared through the sound system, and I closed my eyes tight as the girl started screaming and screaming. Painter's hand rubbed my shoulder, and he gave me a squeeze. "You want us to turn it off?"

Shaking my head, I burrowed into the warmth of his body.

The saw roared again and I moaned.

"Seriously, we can turn it off," he whispered, close enough to the side of my face that I could feel the heat of his breath, and smell the faintest hint of beer.

"I'm fine," I insisted, wondering if I'd ever sleep again. I hated horror movies. *Hated* them. Jessica made fun of me for it all the time, but I'd be damned if I'd admit how scared I was. Not to Painter.

"Okay, then," he said, and I felt something brush my hair. His hand?

"Good news," Puck announced, sounding almost cheerful. He was sitting in a chair across the room, watching us with something like humor in his eyes. "This is a whole series. We can do a marathon."

I moaned again, wondering if I could just roll up into a ball and die, right here.

It would be better than spending the night watching blood spurt.

Would it ever end?

• • •

I woke up in bed, fully clothed under the bedding.

Staring at the ceiling, I blinked, trying to figure out how I'd got-ten here. There had been the never-ending, hateful movie marathon. Painter holding me, which was significantly less hateful. London coming home, talking to him in the kitchen and then locking herself in the bedroom.

Had I fallen asleep next to Painter on the couch?

Maybe he carried me upstairs, tucked me in. God, how sexy was that?

Not as sexy as him crawling into bed next to you . . .

A wave of heat spread through me. What would it feel like to sleep with him? Or maybe we wouldn't sleep at all, just spend the night—

Stop it, I told myself firmly. *Stop it right now. If he wanted to make a move, he could've. He didn't. Get over yourself, already.*

"Mel, how much longer until I can put you on the schedule again?" asked Kirstie, sounding impatient. She was my manager at the restau-rant and I was talking to her on my new phone. She'd been horrified to hear about the explosion and so far hadn't complained about all the time off, but that wouldn't last forever. Either I needed to move somewhere I could walk to work, or I needed a car.

At least I could make calls again.

The phone was a gift from Reese. He'd tossed it casually across the table at me over breakfast on Sunday morning, not long after I'd dragged my chainsaw-traumatized ass downstairs. Puck was sitting at the breakfast table, and I looked around, hoping to see Painter.

No such luck.

After we finished eating, I tried to pin Loni down again, but she didn't want to talk. Neither did Reese. Everyone just seemed to think I should sit quietly in the corner and stay out of their way— but how was I supposed to rebuild my life stuck in a corner?

There was a reality disconnect here, and it felt like I was the only person who could see it.

I spent Sunday sulking, and by Monday—yet another day alone in the house—I was on the edge of losing it. London came home in the late afternoon and started fixing dinner, even more distracted and out of focus than she'd been before. I tried to help her, but I just kept getting in her way so eventually I went upstairs.

By myself.

Again.

I was lying on the bed, reading an old science fiction book I'd found in the closet. It wasn't really my thing, but seeing as this was my fourth straight day of doing jack shit, I'd decided to expand my horizons.

A crisp knock came at the door.

"It's open," I called, and looked up, expecting to see Loni. Instead I found Painter. He gave me that super sexy smile of his, walking toward the bed with long, loose strides. Then he sat down next to me, and I swear to God, my heartbeat doubled.

"Hey, Mel," he said, reaching over to slowly pull the book out of my hands. "You want to go out for a while tonight?"

"Like, on a date?" I gasped, then could've smacked myself, because how desperate was that? Painter didn't seem bothered, though.

"Yeah, a date," he said, sounding bemused. "I thought we'd get dinner, maybe go see a movie."

That sounded amazing, unreal . . . except for the movie part. I couldn't do it again, I realized. Not even with his arms around me.

"No horror," I said, hoping it wasn't a deal breaker. Painter grinned.

"How about this, I'll let you pick," he replied. "I want you to have fun. You ready?"

I thought about my hair, which hadn't been combed all day. Maybe my clothes weren't great and I didn't have any makeup, but I still wanted to primp a little before we left. Hell, what I really needed was a moment alone to catch my breath.

Levi "Painter" Brooks was taking me on a date!

"Give me five minutes," I told him. "Then I'll be ready to go."

"Sounds great," he said, standing up again. He reached down, offering me his hand. I took it, and he pulled me up and into him. We stood there—touching—for an instant, before he stepped back.

"Sorry about that," he said, but he didn't really sound sorry. I tried to keep it casual as he turned away, leaving me alone to get ready. It was almost impossible. I wanted to jump and dance and scream like a little girl. That's how excited I was.

Instead I splashed some cold water on my face and brushed my hair, wishing I could do more to pretty myself up. Unfortunately, the options were limited.

It would have to be good enough.

He took me to a bar and grill in midtown, and to my surprise they didn't bother carding me when he ordered a beer for each of us. I guess when your date is a six-foot-plus biker who's simultaneously badass and beautiful, the average waitress isn't paying attention to anyone's age.

The first sip was bitter, nothing like the Bud Light kegs at our high school parties. I sucked it down, though, and by the time our pizza arrived I had a nice buzz going. Obviously it was a lot stronger than Bud Light, too.

"I really need to find a place in town, so I can walk to work," I told him, trying not to gross him out while I ate. The pizza here was good. Really good. They'd brought it hot from the oven, and there was melted cheese running all over the place. It tasted amazing, but it didn't lend itself to delicate eating.

"Either that or a car," he said, nodding his head. "I'll talk to the prez—maybe he has something you can borrow."

"Do you have any idea what their plan is?" I asked him. "Loni and Reese, I mean. They're still not talking to me, but I'm done sitting around like a potted plant. Tomorrow I'm going to work even if I have to walk."

A strange look crossed Painter's face, and he sighed. "You can borrow my car."

I sat back, stunned.

"I wasn't trying to beg," I told him, suddenly uncomfortable.

"Look, I'm not using it much anyway," he replied. "It's summer—I'd rather ride my bike. I'm heading out of town for a couple days, but I'll have one of the prospects bring it over, drop it off for you. That way you can start working again, get back on your feet."

I didn't know what to say.

"That might be the nicest thing anyone's ever done for me," I whispered. Painter's smile grew strained, and something dark flickered through his eyes.

"Don't thank me too much," he said. He looked away, waving toward the waitress. She hustled her ass right over, and I couldn't blame her. I'd be hustling too, if he was sitting at one of my tables. "Can I get the check?"

"Sure," she cooed at him. I watched as she leaned over, flashing her cleavage. He wasn't looking at her, though.

He was looking at me.

"I'm sorry," he said quietly.

"Sorry for what?"

The waitress came back, handing over our check. Painter pulled out his wallet and grabbed several bills, stuffing them in the little black folder. Then he was on his feet and it was time to go.

He never told me what he was sorry for.

I picked an action movie.

There was a romantic comedy that looked good, but after he offered to loan me his car that just seemed cruel. He bought the tickets and we started toward the theater. We were almost inside when he paused to check his phone. Then his face turned grim.

"What's up?" I asked.

"Nothing," he said shortly. That was a lie if I'd ever heard one.

"No, something's wrong. Do you need to go?"

He hesitated, and I knew he did.

"We should go," I said firmly. "You can take me home, and then deal with whatever that was." I nodded toward the phone.

"Yeah, we might want to do that," he admitted. "I'm sorry—I didn't mean to cut things short."

"It's fine. I've had a great time. I'm just sorry the tickets are wasted."

"No worries," he replied. "C'mon."

The ride back was different. I'd lost the sense of breathless expectation that'd filled me earlier in the evening. Painter's body was tense. Whatever message he'd gotten, it wasn't good. We pulled up to Reese's house to find it dark. I stepped off the bike and looked around, startled to see that Reese's motorcycle was gone, along with London's van.

"Where is everyone?"

"Let's go inside," Painter said, dodging my question. I followed him in, then turned, looking at him expectantly for an explanation. Something was up, this was obvious. He knew what it was, too.

"Well?" I asked when he didn't answer my question.

"Reese and Loni are leaving town," he said. "Most of the club is going with them. We've got some business to deal with in Portland. You can just stay here for now, okay? I'll have the prospects bring my car over for you in the morning."

He reached down and pulled out his wallet, opening it and counting out a stack of cash. "You can use this to get a place if . . . Well, if things don't work out here."

I stared at the money blankly—those were hundred dollar bills.

"I can't take that."

He reached for his phone, checked it again. "I don't have time to argue with you. Take the fucking money."

With that, he grabbed my hand, wrapping it around the bills. Then he started toward the door, something almost angry about the way he moved.

"Painter," I called after him, confused. He turned back to me.

"You can do it, Mel."

"What?"

"You can make it through this. Whatever happens, don't forget that."

"Painter, what the hell is going on?" I demanded. There was a seriously bad feeling in the pit of my stomach. He shook his head, taking a step toward me. Suddenly his hands were in my hair, jerking me into his body as his lips touched mine.

It wasn't a movie kiss.

He didn't stick his tongue in, and it hurt more than anything. Just a mashing of our lips together like he couldn't help himself, until he shoved me away.

"Go to bed," he growled, wiping off his mouth with the back of his hand, like I disgusted him. Something painful twisted inside.

"Why?"

"Just go to fucking bed, Melanie. Tomorrow you can take the car and you can start looking for a place."

Then he turned away and walked out the door.

The next morning I woke up to find a dark blue Toyota SUV in the driveway and a set of keys on the dining room table. I drove it to work, and after my shift I went to the library so I could use the Internet.

I needed to find an apartment.

That was Tuesday.

On Wednesday I sat alone on the porch, wondering if anyone would ever come back. By Thursday I'd given up on them. Loni was gone, just like my mom, and she'd taken Painter with her. I worked a double shift, and talked to one of my fellow waitresses about a bedroom in the house she rented with friends.

She thought one of them might be moving out in a couple weeks.

Friday morning, I woke to the sound of a big diesel truck in the driveway. Rushing downstairs, I opened the front door to see London climbing down from the vehicle, looking exhausted. Reese was already out, and then another person slid out of the crew cab. My best friend, Jessica—the same girl who'd thrown a tantrum and run off to California not long ago. Her hand was bandaged and strapped to her body in a sling. Bruises covered her face.

There was no sign of Painter.

Reese walked over to me slowly, glancing at the SUV parked in the driveway.

"He said you can borrow it as long as you want," he said bluntly.

"Why isn't he with you?" I asked, but I could already see the answer written across his face. Something had happened. Something bad.

"He's in jail," Reese said. "And I think he'll be there for a while longer. He said to tell you he's sorry."

"For what?"

"I don't know. Maybe you should write and ask him."

31901056714787